WHITE ROOK

by the same author
THE MURDER OF FRAU SCHÜTZ

WHITE ROOK

A Novel

J. Madison Davis

Walker and Company
New York

First published in the United States of America in 1989
by Walker Publishing Company, Inc.

Published simultaneously in Canada by Thomas Allen & Son
Canada, Limited, Markham, Ontario

Library of Congress Cataloging-in-Publication Data

Davis, J. Madison.
White Rook : a novel / J. Madison Davis.

ISBN 0-8027-1096-4 :
I. Title.
PS3554.A934636W5   1989
813'.54—dc20   89-16606

Printed in the United States of America

2   4   6   8   10   9   7   5   3   1

FOR MAMA BLUE

ONE

"How's your southern?"

Dub blinked, sat up, and blinked again. The digital radio showed what looked like a red four twenty-seven, but it must have been nine twenty-seven. The top bar of the nine only worked when it wanted to.

Dub closed his eyes and rested against the receiver as if it were a pillow. "How's my southern what?"

"How's your southern accent, yur'all?"

"It's 'y'all,' Calabrese." Dub glanced over his shoulder at a gaunt, bleary-eyed woman with a faint mustache. He tried to smile. "Phone," he said. She squinted as if she were trying to remember him, then sank back into the pillow with a moan.

"Whatever," said Calabrese.

"What's up?" Dub fumbled for cigarettes in the end table and then recalled that Brenda—Was that it? That's right, Brenda something Polish—had said she was allergic to cigarette smoke.

"I've been trying to get you since yesterday. We've got a real good job, but it needs somebody who can do southern."

"Southern?" Dub cleared his throat. "Who's banging who?"

"This isn't a divorce. How about it? This is a maybe murder."

"A maybe murder?"

"Undercover job. How about that?" He asked the question like a deli owner who has just poked a shaving of something exotic into a customer's mouth.

Undercover. A lump caught in Dub's throat like a mis-

[1]

swallowed ice cube. He inhaled. He wanted to open a window. "Yeah," he said, coughing. "What's the deal?"

"Unlimited budget. You get a third more than usual and you stick at it until the client gives up."

Dub picked at a toenail that needed cutting. He could use the extra third. "The problem, Calabrese. What's the case?"

"It's a subcontract. The Devraix Agency wants an operative with Pennsy papers. You're it. Devraix himself will be coming with the client at eleven-thirty. Or sometime thereafter depending on 'Agony Airlines.' Pick him up. Flight four fifty-seven. They'll explain. Something other than a cheesy divorce. How about that? That twang finally did you some good."

Calabrese hung up. "John?" Dub asked the dial tone. What did he mean by "twang," Dub thought. My accent isn't that strong, except when I want it to be, is it? No divorce. How about that?

He rested his elbows on his thighs. Sore from the back of his knees to his neck, he thought about how hard his body had once been, about how his belly was once flat, and about how tiredness once evaporated at the whiff of sex. He didn't want to be nineteen again, he knew, but it would be nice not to feel mugged in the morning.

He unsteadily bent to pick up the condom wrapper by the bed, then stumbled into the shower and adjusted the water very hot. It was soothing until it began its usual fluctuations between ice water and ice. When he came out, Brenda was sitting against the headboard, smoking. He avoided her eyes and crossed his hands over his groin.

"I thought you were allergic to tobacco smoke," he said.

"I was trying to give them up. Smoke makes me nuts." She exhaled a plume toward the ceiling. Her breasts showed her to be at least as old as Dub, and her cesarean scar was the old-fashioned vertical cut. Ah, romance, he thought.

He turned his back and pulled on his shorts. "My boss called. I've got to meet somebody. Can I drop you?"

"I can call a cab."

"No trouble.

"I'd like to rest here a bit. Is that okay? I won't nose around."

"It's all right." He zipped his trousers "I keep my art collection in a vault. There's some instant in the kitchen. I think."

"Decaf?"

"Uh-unh. Maybe in the back of the cabinet."

She stared thoughtfully as he slipped on his socks. Each morning he bent over, his toes seemed further away.

"Do you do this often?" she asked.

"He likes to call at three a.m."

"No. Do you sleep with clients?"

"No," he said, but he remembered two faces. One brought a twinge. "I mean I don't like to because, you know, some women are, well, vulnerable when they get the proof. I don't want to take advantage."

"And me?"

"It didn't seem that way." He was lying to himself again. She had said she needed a drink. Bourbons became dinner. Dinner became nightcaps. Somewhere along the line he had lost a dozen years and she had turned into the belle of the prom. Now they had changed back into pumpkins.

"Maybe I just wanted to get even."

He remembered how bitterly she had once called her soon-to-be ex-husband a "Hungarian tail-hound." He shrugged and buttoned his shirt. "That's your business, I guess."

"I was just using you." She threw her head back defiantly and hungrily swallowed the cigarette smoke.

"I don't get so well-used that often."

"Any prick would have done." She was spoiling for a fight.

He moved toward her for a kiss. She raised her cigarette between them. "Don't," she said.

"I just—"

"Don't. Harry kissed me good-bye every morning for twenty-three years. Religiously. It didn't mean a goddamn thing. Not a goddamn thing."

"Harry's a jerk." He hoped it didn't sound too contrived. She seemed to accept it, though, smiling awkwardly. He patted her on the thigh and lifted the flat picture on the end table. His little girls: Elizabeth and Carrie. He had put it down last night, as if the picture could see. Their innocent faces still embarrassed him. He left his apartment with the feeling he should say more to Brenda. He didn't know what. Sex always left him with the feeling he had forgotten something.

The plane was two hours late, something you get used to in Pittsburgh, so he waited in one of the restaurants whose pancakes you could never get used to. Honoré St. Jean Devraix turned out to be a tiny man, odd, delicate as a filigreed brooch. He was neither black nor white nor mulatto, but with skin the incredible golden olive of the oldest Creole families. He extended a tiny hand.

"Mr. Delbert Greenert?"

Behind him was Clementine O'Dell, wearing huge black sunglasses and a broad hat concealing her face. She offered her hand and said, "How do you do?" in a tone that indicated she was a lady. She seemed a little stunned to find herself in Pittsburgh, but determined to see it through. "Is there some place where we could get started?" she asked. "Some place we could talk?" She tilted her head toward one of the restaurants.

"You don't want to eat here," Dub said. "I know an Italian place. Is that okay? And call me Dub. I hate Delbert." Clementine rode in the back seat, clutching her purse. Dub glanced at her in the rearview mirror, but could tell nothing much about her, except that, without any reason for it that he could explain, he didn't like her behind him. A couple of stabs at chitchat went nowhere. Devraix didn't say much, either, but gave the impression he was absorbing everything. When he did speak, he had the whispering feminine sound of a tenor in an old Motown group.

It wasn't until they had settled into a booth in the restaurant that anyone brought up the case. Devraix shoved a file across the table, and Dub flipped a few pages. "You're the client, aren't you?" he asked Mrs. O'Dell.

She nodded.

"Why don't you just tell me about it, in your own words."

"Is that necessary?"

"That's what I'd like."

She turned toward Devraix. "Are you trying to gauge me in some way?"

Dub couldn't be sure of her attitude to this. She stayed hidden behind her glasses, and all he saw was the reflection of his own white forehead shining back at him. He decided it was the southern belle about her that made him twitchy. He'd just have to deal with it. If you only worked for people you liked and trusted, you wouldn't work very often. "I like to get a feeling for the client," he said. "I like to know who I'm working for."

She turned slightly toward Devraix, sighed, and began. Devraix studiously began eating as if he didn't care what she said. He reminded Dub of a furnace. You shovel in coal and it's gone. Dub had the thought the antipasto was the whole lunch, but Devraix was just starting. He ate like a Pittsburgh Steeler but didn't seem hyped enough to burn off one-third of what he consumed.

The story was long, but not particularly complicated, and Clementine O'Dell told it carefully, as if she were dictating. Her husband Michael O'Dell had been very successful in discovering chefs in a town where the only thing more important than sex is food. O'Dell was old money from New Orleans, but he was able to look beyond accents, clothing, race, and criminal backgrounds to recognize culinary talent. He'd "audition" promising cooks in his Garden District mansion, and those who measured up found themselves in kitchens paid for and leased by O'Dell. The deal was, usually, that it was up to the chef to make the place go, and he had five years to buy out O'Dell. In the five years, O'Dell absorbed most of the profits in order to recoup his investment. If, at the end of five years, the place was well established, the chef would have no trouble finding financing. If it had failed, which very rarely happened with O'Dell's instinct for food, O'Dell usually recovered most of his investment and the chef was out nothing but five years. The chef got a golden chance at O'Dell's expense. O'Dell hadn't turned the family millions into billions this way, but it wasn't likely his children would ever run short of pressed duck.

Almost three years back, however, he had been approached by a restaurateur named Eddie Viek. Viek ran tourist traps in Florida, Mobile, and Savannah: microwaved prime ribs and B.F. Goodrich lobster tails. He had picked up on the Cajun thing from Florida tourists out of New York. He charged off to New Orleans and, since he didn't know jambalaya from blackened redfish, sought out O'Dell. He proposed a coast-to-coast franchise: *"Gumbolaya!"*

O'Dell wasn't crazy about the idea at first. He didn't like franchises. He didn't like Viek. He particularly didn't like the exclamation point, but "*Gumbolaya!*" seemed a pretty good idea after a few days, and despite the fact that Eddie talked about tanker-truck wines like they were Chateauneuf-du-Pape, he seemed good enough at the business end. O'Dell found out that Viek had only lost money on one venture, a patch of Georgia swamp that was supposed to be a place for grown men to play capture the flag with paint-pellet guns. O'Dell cut a deal. He was getting old. He wanted to sit back and let a good investment carry him. Normally suspicious of the "sure thing," he must have let Viek's quick talk jam his radar. He rarely made mistakes, but this was the biggest one of Michael O'Dell's soon-to-be-ended life.

O'Dell put up half the money, and selected one Louis Vollard, a parolee who had spent the last six years cooking for inmates in the state prison system, to devise the recipes. Viek was to arrange supplies, advertising, and locations. Eighteen months later, Viek was still scouting locations, and had yet to sell a franchise. It was loss-cutting time for O'Dell. For a man who could smell the age of a red snapper, it was eventually no problem to smell a rat. He flew to Tampa with his accountant and argued bitterly with Viek, who kept his books locked away God knows where. O'Dell flew home and contacted his lawyer. Vollard was under a personal contract to O'Dell, so it was easy to close up that end of things. O'Dell promised Vollard his own restaurant in a hotel that was losing its chef. He also prepared to file suit. He didn't really expect to get much back, Clementine said, but he thought the threat might coerce some settlement.

Viek bothered them at home several times and shouted he had friends who might make O'Dell more cooperative. The O'Dell family, however, had their acquaintances too, ever since Prohibition, and Michael told Clementine he had made some inquiries. Not only was Viek un-connected, he was distinctly the kind of guy that big-shot mobsters avoid, a penny-ante schemer who could get you into trouble. O'Dell's "friends" were kind of surprised O'Dell hadn't seen this. It made him feel stupid. The loss wouldn't impoverish him, but it bruised his self-respect badly. He was obviously depressed. Michael,

Clementine O'Dell said, shook his head and muttered about getting old and losing his instinct.

Two days later, according to the Louisiana state police, he left his house at noon. No one saw him alive again.

His white convertible Mercedes was reported as having broken down on a pull-over on the Lake Pontchartrain bridge. When Officer Swazy got there, it was abandoned, with ten miles of bridge and water to the nearest dirt. Swazy assumed the owner had hitched a ride. The keys were in the ignition and the car started like the dream it was. That was a little strange, but new cars with all their computers and fuel injection and such can be temperamental, Swazy theorized. He impounded it. When O'Dell didn't come home, there was an all-out search until two boys found what was left of him stuck among the reeds of their favorite fishing spot.

The coroner, of course, ruled it a probable suicide.

At the funeral, it was impossible to ignore the huge and tasteless chrysanthemum horseshoe Viek sent. Clementine was shattered, however, and passed it off as another example of Viek's crudeness. She didn't want to think about it, and she didn't, not until Michael's clothes were selling down at the Salvation Army, Michael himself moldering in his tomb in the Lafayette Cemetery, and their children returned to their jobs around the country. One morning, she accepted a call from a hopeful young Greek immigrant, who had been promised an audition. She had difficulty making him understand that her husband could no longer be interested in aioli sauce. When she hung up, however, it was, she said, like she had taken off a pair of dirty glasses. The grief had confused her. Michael O'Dell would never commit suicide. He was too clear-headed. She had seen him in adversity and he was even more sharp when challenged; under fire he was as cool as a great general. The police humored her, so she went to the FBI. The supervisor said it wasn't their jurisdiction, then sympathetically escorted her home. Her daughter said she'd think about it. Her youngest son suggested an analyst. The lawyer said she needed to put the tragedy behind her and think about how to handle Michael's legacy. The insurance company figured she was angling for the five hundred thousand dollars that wasn't payable because of suicide. Clementine's world blurred. She believed someone had forced himself into Michael's car—a drug addict, maybe—and that they had been infuriated by Michael's rarely carrying cash. She juggled other theories. She suspected Viek, then Vollard. Had Michael been closer to the old family "friends" than she had known? She suspected chefs, brokers, food suppliers, anybody. Finally, she suspected her own mind was slipping. Why should she think it was murder? The answer was always the same, always clear. Michael O'Dell would never kill himself. Never. Why not? *He just wouldn't.*

It didn't take long for Viek to move on Clementine. He sent a letter with three short sentences of condolence. He hated to bring up business, he wrote, but he was hoping that they could come to some arrangement about *"Gumbolaya!"* There was a fortune to be made. He would call her in a couple of days. Not sure whether her sorrow and imagination were getting the best of her, she decided to talk to Viek face-to-face. Could Michael have been more despondent than she knew? Long marriages often made spouses miss the obvious. She didn't wait for Viek's call. She flew to Florida and straight to his house in Boca Raton.

It took some begging, but the maid looked at her black clothes, sat her in the study, and turned on the wide-screen television. She even brought Mrs. O'Dell a sandwich when the afternoon faded. They called four of Viek's restaurants and left messages. Clementine waited. Anxiously. Not certain she wanted to hear what Viek might say.

The huge screen enlarged television's boredom, but she managed to bear it for three hours. There was nothing in the magazine rack but girlie stuff, *Soldier of Fortune,* and a tabloid-shaped imitation of it called *Mercenary.* That fit in with the crossed M-16s hanging over the fireplace and the Uzi cigarette lighter. She scanned the books behind Viek's desk and discovered that the upper shelves were covered with simulated leather spines with no books behind them, despite the impressive gold-leaf titles. The lower shelves were filled with videotape cases also designed to look like books. She opened six or seven, found titles like *Lydia's Love for Leather* and *Jumping Bunny's Bones,* and gave up on those too.

She wasn't certain why she opened his desk drawer. She didn't even do it furtively. She just reached out and tugged the brass handle without thinking about whether it was proper, or whether the maid would see her. Inside, there was a chrome-plated revolver, a roll of stamps, and a tray of paper clips, the gaudy kind coated with bright plastic. Under the revolver there was a scrap of torn newsprint.

It was the want-ad page from the back of *Mercenary*. In among advertisements for survival knives, camouflage makeup, and freeze-dried food was a column entitled Personal Services. The third ad was circled:

> PROBLEMS? I know what you mean. I can get what's in your way, out of your way. Medal-winning vet ready to serve. Location no problem. Satisfaction guaranteed. Call Castle. I am your Man.

Centered under it, in boldface, was a phone number with an 814 area code: northwest Pennsylvania. The ads above and below it said similar things, but this was the one that was circled. She thought about it for several seconds. It didn't make any rational sense, but she felt a chill, she said, "like a ghost touched me." She turned over the sheet, found what she wanted in the corner, and wrote it down: "*Mercenary*, March, p. 38, Castle."

She immediately flew back to New Orleans. It took most of the night and three connections, but when she finally landed, she was beginning to think again that maybe she *should* get an analyst. She had always known she needed Michael, but she had not known how much. She almost threw the note away. She had to pull herself together. She was turning her life into some kind of bad dream. She told herself to calm down, to face up to reality, and to go on. She tried not to think about Michael, and did not think about Viek except when refusing his calls.

Viek wouldn't be put off, however, He pushed his way past Clementine's gardener and housekeeper one day when the dogs were being groomed. She was in the library trying to arrange Michael's tax papers. Viek's eyes bulged. The veins stood out on his shiny forehead.

"Why won't you talk to me?" he demanded.

"We have nothing to talk about," she said unsteadily. The

gardener appeared in the doorway with pruning shears raised as a weapon. She told him to go back to his hedges, everything was under control.

Viek looked at the gardener. The gardener asked if Mrs. O'Dell was sure. She nodded. Viek eyed her for several seconds. He mopped his head.

"There's no reason not to talk to Eddie," Viek said of himself. "Eddie was Michael's partner."

"Yes, well," she said, "*Eddie's* partner was very unhappy with him."

"Michael was making a big mistake," said Viek. "He made a big mistake."

She hesitated. "What do you mean?"

"I mean there's a fortune to be made in this Creole stuff."

"Louis Vollard is a Cajun chef."

"Whatever," said Viek. "One year it's soul-brothuh shit, the next year it's tofu." He inhaled and stuffed his damp handkerchief in his jacket pocket. "Listen, Mrs. O'Dell, I don't know what was bugging Michael. These things take time. I mean, the way it all went down, you know, maybe—and I don't want to hurt anyone's feelings—but maybe he was sliding off the deep end."

"Michael O'Dell was the most sane man on this planet."

"I'm not saying he wasn't, understand, but things happen. It's like biology. Maybe it was a disease, like Alzheimer's disease."

Clementine turned her head in disgust. Viek reached out to touch her arm. She nearly jumped to avoid it.

"Look," he said. "Look. It takes time. Your husband was too impatient. He just had to wait a little longer—"

"Michael always had a brilliant sense of timing, Mr. Viek. He also knew when someone was looting *Gumbolaya!* for his own businesses. That someone was you, Mr. Viek. It's only a matter of time before my lawyers will be into your books, Mr. Viek, and then we'll see who has timing."

Viek looked at his two-tone oxfords, then took a deep breath. He forced himself to be calm and tried to be charming, but his forehead veins were writhing like hot snakes. "Look, Clementine, can I call you Clementine?"

"You may not."

He touched his chest with all of his fingers. "Look, nobody's sorrier about Michael than Eddie is. Believe me. But I stand to lose a lot of money—you stand to lose a lot of money—if we don't go on with *Gumbolaya!* Those are the facts, Mrs. O'Dell. Simple facts. I'll be your partner—same terms. I guarantee I'll double your investment—Michael's investment—before two years. Two years! Chain restaurants are the thing, Mrs. O'Dell. Look at your Burger Kings and your Popeyes and your Shoney's. It's the way, Mrs. O'Dell. Think how much of a legacy you'll be able to leave your children."

"I'm sure you'd like that," she said sharply.

"Huh?"

"You'd like me to be leaving a legacy too."

Viek squinted. "I don't get you."

"I think you do. I think you know more about Michael's death than you've said."

"Mrs. O'Dell—"

"Michael would never commit suicide. *Never.* Especially over a thief. Oh, yes, he was unhappy about being tricked, but it's only a matter of time until our accountants find out how you've shuffled the money away. Michael would have staked you to an anthill before he was done, and so will I."

Viek stood and leaned over her. His breath reeked of cheap fish. "Don't fuck with me, rich bitch. One blue blood is no bigger than another."

"You're threatening me."

He straightened up and looked around as if he were suddenly aware that she might have someone listening in. "No," he said. "I'm just saying that it's bad luck to back out of a deal with Eddie. It's always bad luck to back out on Eddie. It's like ignoring a chain letter to back out on me. Sooner or later something happens."

She was scared. She knew what he meant, or at least thought so. She pushed out the words: "Something like Castle?"

Viek was rocked. He reached for a cigar in his coat pocket. "I don't know what you mean."

"I think you do."

He took three strikes to light a match. It finally flared.

"Please don't smoke in here. Mr. O'Dell hated tobacco. It dulls the palate."

He puffed it defiantly. "I don't know any Castle. You understand? And you'd better not think I do." He pivoted and marched to the library door. He paused. "I'll call you in a few days. About *Gumbolaya!*—you think about it. You think about it real good." He pointed to the group of photos on an end table. "Those are nice-looking kids you have. Real nice."

She stared at the pictures in horror. When she turned back, Viek was gone. The confrontation had left her dizzy. She lurched through the French doors and vomited into the rose bed. Later she called her lawyer. She was in Devraix's office by nine a.m. the next morning.

Dub gave up eating and sipped a Galliano to soothe his strained innards. Usually southern belles had souls of iron and only pretended to be delicate. Mrs. O'Dell was sane enough, but she had been under a lot of stress. He wished he could see her eyes, not so much because he could tell much from them, but they might hint at her state of mind.

"Well?" she asked.

"I don't know," Dub mused. "It might be worth looking into."

She leaned forward. "It is. That's why we're here."

Yes, an iron soul, he thought. But could she be trusted? He asked Devraix what he thought. Devraix was skeptical. "It seems ludicrous that anyone wishing to take up the profession of murder should place a want ad, as it were, or that someone else using this type of service would leave the clipping in his drawer. It enlarges one's sense of human stupidity. I have told Mrs. O'Dell this. Especially after the business in Arkansas a few years ago. You know about that, Mr. Greenert? Several murders were supposedly arranged through notices in *Soldier of Fortune*. There was a lawsuit."

"This Castle could have gotten the idea from the news, but it's a stretch." Mrs. O'Dell lifted her chin as if angered. "Anyhow," Dub continued, "what links Viek and this Castle?"

"I have a feeling," said Mrs. O'Dell. "I am willing to spend nearly anything to prove Eddie Viek was behind Michael's murder."

Dub turned to Devraix. "Do you think it's murder?"

Devraix stretched his hand toward his Chianti. He flipped the other hand over limply. "I cannot speculate. We are hired to gather what facts we can. It seems unlikely that Mr. Viek would hire a killer through an advertisement, and if he did engineer Mr. O'Dell's death in Lake Pontchartrain it also seems unlikely he would hire someone he does not know. On the other hand, unlikely things happen every day. What supporting facts we have ascertained are on that blue summary."

Devraix ordered cannoli while Dub scanned a numbered list entitled "Verifiable Facts." Devraix was certainly organized, much more than Calabrese and the Keyhole Agency had ever been.

"Well, he called the ad number in Erie, or so say the phone records."

Devraix nodded.

"And he flew to Buffalo a week later, rented a car, and drove far enough to have gone to Erie." Dub mulled it over. "He used his own name for this?"

"Yes."

"That doesn't make sense."

Mrs. O'Dell fidgeted with her napkin as if she had heard this opinion before and it angered her.

"He used his own Visa card as well," added Devraix.

"That's another stretch. It says here he tried to use his American Express card, but hadn't been making his payments."

"That's likely normal for Eddie Viek," said Mrs. O'Dell.

Devraix touched her wrist to calm her. "The airport clerk remembered how indifferently he watched her cut the card in half."

"With all respect, isn't that pretty stupid? I mean, if I were planning a murder . . ."

Devraix raised an eyebrow and squeezed Mrs. O'Dell's arm.

"You got to be barking up the wrong tree."

Devraix looked for the waiter. "It seems likely, but there are many stupid people in the world. If there weren't, you and I would likely have no business."

"Perhaps Mr. Greenert isn't interested in our business."

Her voice was frosty. Dub scratched at a sauce spot on the tablecloth.

Devraix asked the waiter for espresso to go with his cannoli. The waiter wasn't sure the machine was working. He would check.

Dub turned the blue page. Another item was listed. "And then, after Mrs. O'Dell confronts him, he calls that number again, from a phone booth."

Devraix nodded. "Mr. Calabrese was good enough to check the long-distance records for this Castle's number."

"And that isn't enough for you?" asked Mrs. O'Dell.

"Well, it's interesting, I'll admit," Dub said, suppressing a belch, "but you'd never get Viek to jail on this. It's tissue-thin."

Devraix spread his hands. "If it were anything but, there might be police interest."

"Exactly. Now I'm in your plans?"

"Precisely, Mr. Greenert."

"Perhaps," said Clementine.

Oh, well, Dub thought, back to divorces.

The waiter interrupted. No espresso. "*Dommage,*" muttered Devraix. He took one nibble of his cannoli, made a face, and put it down.

"Just to explore the possibilities," said Devraix, "we should like someone to contact this Mr. Castle and discover whether he is amenable to certain activities."

"That's the undercover part. But why me?"

"You're highly recommended, I have worked with Keyhole Agency before, and I trust Mr. Calabrese." He faced Mrs. O'Dell. "Mr. Greenert received a Silver Star for his undercover work for the military police in Vietnam."

Dub's chest tightened. Damned indigestion again, and the restaurant was too warm. "That's, ah, a long time ago. How did you know about that? Did Calabrese tell you my real name was Delbert?"

"I have a very good agency," said Devraix, mildly amused.

Dub blinked. "But why me? He said something about a southerner."

"You have the right accent." Devraix faced Mrs. O'Dell. "Don't you think?" She nodded.

[14]

"Charleston. I graduated the Citadel. But you probably already know that."

Devraix puckered his lips, rolled over his cannoli with a fork, and studied it like a biologist classifying a jellyfish. "Your father was a full colonel, your grandfather a general, your great-great grandfather served with Joseph E. Johnston at Vicksburg and Atlanta. You gave up on the military after the defeat, or 'peace with honor,' if you prefer; you worked here and there, then you got your license."

"Do you have all the dates?"

Devraix peered straight at Dub. He had pupils like twin onyxes. "There is nothing to be ashamed of."

Dub thought of the long line of soldiers on his family tree and how he had let them down. "Maybe not," he said. "But that's not the point. Why don't you use your own guys?"

"It is my procedure. I once had two operatives jailed in Canada for treading on local toes. I want a local license on the case, with local connections. But I also want someone to lure this Castle to New Orleans. Michael O'Dell might, shall we say, not be as important to Pennsylvania officials as he is to us."

Dub studied Mrs. O'Dell for a moment, then Devraix. Undercover, he thought. He inhaled deeply, held the air as if precious, then pushed it out. "All right. Give me your plan. I'm your boy."

By supper time Dub was on a plane to New Orleans. By twelve-thirty of the next day he had become Vernon Krider, with gaudy business cards that dubbed him "the King of the Deal Royale!" The setup was better than anything Dub had seen in the military. From what he could tell, Devraix took no chances. The real Krider owed a big favor to Devraix and was sent to the Bahamas for a month, though none of his employees knew it. A collection of notes Krider had left and a number of telephone inquiries gave the illusion he was either at home or at another of his dealerships. As "tax auditors," Dub and Vonna Saucier, a plump, walnut-brown Devraix operative, had free access to Krider's offices. They met there.

Dub settled back in Krider's comfy desk chair and watched Vonna bend over the tape recorder across the room. Her butt swayed as she plugged in the wires. Too much carry-out, he thought. Like me. She *must* be a detective.

"Ready," she said.

Dub took a deep breath and dialed the number in *Mercenary*. There was ringing, clicking, more clicking, then a pause. Dub thought either the local phones were lousy or Vonna's machine had messed up something. Then a tape came on: "Hello, this is George Castle, veteran and soldier of fortune. Whatever the problem I can handle it. What obstacle's in your way, I can remove it. Leave your name and number at the tone and I'll get right back to you." The beep was long and loud.

"Ah, this is Krider, Vern Krider," Dub said. "I don't know if you—never mind." He hung up.

Vonna stuck out her lip. "What'd you do that for?"

"It felt right." Dub winked. Vonna wasn't pleased.

"You're supposed to connect with this guy."

"*How* is important too. I follow my instinct."

She gave him an "Oh, great!" look. "Now what?"

"We wait, say, fifteen minutes. More than enough time for three good belts, then the desperate Vern calls again."

She nodded.

"So," Dub said, "tell me about yourself."

"Nothing to tell."

"I mean, what's a nice girl like you doing in a racket like this?"

She wasn't amused. Her dark eyes glared. "I'm not a nice girl. That's why I'm in a racket like this. Nice girls don't do shit like this."

She wasn't joking. She was probably right too. Dub stared her straight in the eye and thickened his accent. "Honey, you're just putting on an act. I'll bet you're a marshmallow inside."

Her gaze fixed for a few seconds, then the corners of her mouth turned up slightly and she stood. "You got that wrong," she said, slapping her hip. "I'm marshmallow on the outside, honeychile, but my heart's Carborundum." She had said it before. You could tell. She let it sink in, then added, "I'm going to the john."

Dub fooled with Krider's Duesenberg transistor radio until

Vonna came back sipping a diet soda and chewing a Pay-Day. Dub dialed.

This time, after all the clicking, he said he wanted to speak to Castle. He said he wasn't sure Castle could help but he'd pay anything to the right man. He also said he could only wait half an hour for his call.

The minutes crept by. Dub fidgeted with the radio. Looking bored, Vonna scanned a brochure about conversion vans, but when the ultramodern phone tootled, she jerked and slopped soda on her thighs.

"Hello?"

"Mr. Krider?"

"Yes. Who is this?"

"You called me."

"Castle? Are you the guy with the ad?"

"No, it's King Tut. You got a problem?"

"Yes."

"I take it it's a serious problem?"

"Yes."

"Something that takes more than halfway measures?"

"Yes." There was a pause. "Look," Dub sighed, "I'm not sure I—are we talking about the same thing? I'm not sure about this."

The man on the other end sounded sarcastic. "I don't know, Vern. What are *you* talking about?"

"I'm not sure," Dub stalled. "Listen, I just—could you tell me about yourself?"

"I know weapons, I know men. What else do you need to know?"

"I mean, you could be anybody."

"I could, but I'm not. You need a Rambo, I'm your Rambo. No movie stuff, I'm the real thing." Vonna, listening on the earphones, made a face. "That's the deal. No questions asked except the necessary ones. No obligations, no money-back guarantees, just satisfaction and you never see me again."

"This is hard to buy, buddy."

"Maybe. But that's the way it works. Look, I don't need to waste time, mister. When you know what you want, you call me."

"Wait," Dub said. "I need a drink." Vonna looked exasperated while he paused several seconds, then cleared his throat loudly.

"You got to stay away from that stuff, Vern," Castle said. "Makes you talkative. Bad for your health."

"I don't know who the hell you are," Dub said. "I don't know why I called."

"I think you do, Vern. I've helped a lot of people like you. I can clear the way. It's just up to you." His voice was as soothing as a cool breeze.

Dub loudly took a deep breath. "Okay. Okay. I—you see, there's this—"

"No," said Castle. "In person. You want to talk to me, it'll cost you a hundred up front."

"You don't know what I want."

"I've got a pretty good idea. A hundred bucks."

"Suppose you—"

"The hundred is mine, regardless. You pay to talk to a lawyer, don't you, or a doctor? I'm the doctor of your life, Vern. I'm going to fix you up. Where are you at, Vern?"

"New Orleans."

"Thursday, you meet me. You fly to Pittsburgh. You rent a car. You get on Interstate seventy-nine and drive north, straight into Erie, Pennsylvania. Once there you find Parade Street."

"Why don't you meet me here? I got a business to run."

"Wrong. You find the intersection of Thirtieth and Parade. There's a bar there. Huey's. Come straight to the back booth. Don't talk to anybody else. Meet me Thursday at two-thirty."

"I've got to check my calendar, I—"

"Huey's. Thursday. Two-thirty. Either it's important to you or it isn't."

"Thirtieth and Parade."

"Have a nice day, Vern." There was a click, then half a dozen clicks followed. Finally the dial tone hummed.

Dub looked at Vonna, she at him. He was suddenly aware that he didn't usually look into a woman's eyes unless he was trying to figure her out.

"What do you think?" she mumbled.

"He sounds like he takes himself seriously."

"He's an asshole. What do you mean?"

"He's too much. He sounds like he's got a blowhard

bumper sticker that says, 'I'll register my gun when you pry it from my dead fingers.' If he believes this Rambo stuff about himself, I don't know. Smells like a con, a cheap one. What do you think?"

"He didn't say anything definite."

"He could be trying to sign me up to be born again for all he said. You'd better check the tape."

"It'll be fine."

"It's always better to check."

She looked resentful, but she ran the tape back slightly and held out the tiny earphone. *I'm the doctor of your life, Vern. I'm going to fix you up.* Good enough?"

"Too good," Dub said. "Nobody's this stupid, are they?"

She grunted, and he knew what she meant. Nobody who's ever done private investigating has ever touched the bottom of human stupidity. He felt a little better about working with her. She'd been around the block.

"I know this," she said.

"What?"

"All that clicking: The phone call's being relayed. Bookies do it."

"He's gone to a lot of trouble, you're saying."

"I'm saying he might have a few surprises."

"I hate surprises," Dub said. "You think this Krider's got any Alka-Seltzer around here?"

TWO

Loitering in front of Huey's, Dub wanted to look nervous. It was easy. He was.

You're always afraid your inside will show, Dub thought. Lots of people like to tell you they can see inside. They say they can see past the shape of your nose or the color of your skin and read your eyes or tell what you're thinking from your voice. Private eyes like to say that, and maybe some believe it, but it doesn't make any sense. Inside and outside are just ideas. A person isn't a "true self" in a skull and nobody can do anything about a guy because they think they see adultery or murder behind his eyes.

Dub knew, logically, that when you went undercover it was all a matter of playing a part. There wasn't anybody out there with X-ray eyes. All the same, it was like ghosts: Believe in them or not, everyone was skittish in a haunted house.

In Saigon, the woman hadn't suspected him until he'd told her; and he wouldn't have trusted her if he hadn't read her wrong. Her eyes, her lips, even the way she pushed her hips against him had told him what was in her heart. But it had been a lie.

Against his will he recalled the betrayal, the amused curl of her lip as they shoved him across the hangar. No!

He spun sharply, twisting his heel so that the shock to his ankle would break the thought. He couldn't allow himself to think of that. Not now. Stay in the present, he ordered himself.

He meticulously went over his appearance, thinking about the way he'd looked in the mirror back at the Holiday Inn, thinking about car dealers and if there was anything that would give him away.

The sun was bright. He glowed like he was radioactive: white patent leather shoes, lime-green jacket and slacks, white shirt, a turquoise and silver buckle on the white patent belt and a matching lanyard around his neck. He paced. He lit a cigarette. He tried to look like a man trying to be calm, like an edgy man afraid of being seen. Across the street was an abandoned theater. A rusty grid sealed the doors, and obscenities had replaced the movie posters. The marquee was shattered in one corner and the ends of three blackened fluorescent tubes showed. The buildings on either side were also abandoned, and high up in a stone semicircle near one roof line were the words "Proctor Building, 1892." Nothing in the whole block seemed occupied except Huey's and the second floor of the old store on the corner.

A curtain fluttered out of a window. Someone was playing salsa. Dub threw his cigarette in the gutter and lit another. A man walked by carrying a sleeping kid and Dub thought of Elizabeth and Carrie. With the extra money from this gig maybe he could buy them something special, something impractical for a change. Something their mother Beth and their "new daddy," as they called him, would never use the support payments for. He crossed his arms high on his chest and dug his fingers into his shoulders. Quit stalling, he thought. Get your butt in gear.

Glancing toward the dirty red van parked halfway to the corner, he saw Vonna silhouetted behind the hazy windshield. A crummy van for a crummy neighborhood. She moved, either reaching for one of the Mars bars she had squirreled away under the seat or throwing the switch on the tape recorder. Dub flicked away the cigarette and went inside. The old door clunked behind him and he stopped, blinking to adjust to the dimness.

Inside were a bartender and two customers. One was a weary-eyed man in denim with white hair combed up and back like it was 1959, like he'd been mourning on that stool since Elvis died. He studied Dub's shoes. At a table, a man in stained mechanic's overalls and a faded "Bucyrus-Erie" hat held his cigarette between gnarled fingers, oblivious to the ash dropping into his beer. "How do?" he said.

Dub quickly, awkwardly smiled. "Fine." He cleared his throat. "Fine." He eased to the bar. "Excuse me?"

The massive bartender did not turn. The back of his sleeveless jacket was embroidered with a death's head and the words: "PLEIKU. I'VE SERVED MY TIME IN HELL!" He was bending over something and the hairy crack of his ass showed above his belt. He squinted in the part of the mirror not covered by a huge Confederate flag and continued twisting a black whatzit onto one of his kegs. "Yep?"

"I'm—I'm looking for Castle."

The bartender gestured with his head toward the last booth.

"You Castle?" A shadow nodded. Dub edged around an empty table toward the shadows in the back.

"Hey!" said the bartender, over his shoulder.

"Yes?"

"You drinkin'?"

"Drinking?"

"This *is* a fucking bar."

The old mechanic laughed ethereally.

"Beer," Dub said. "A draft."

"Draft ain't workin'. It'll take a few minutes."

"Bourbon, then."

The bartender didn't move.

"Any brand. Jim Beam, anything." Dub looked around as if the distractions were confusing him, then paid and moved into the last booth. He leaned toward the dark face. "You're George Castle?"

When the man lifted himself out of the corner Dub saw he was square-jawed, with a red mustache and skin leathered from too much sun. The twist of the mouth implied disgust. "Give me some quarters," he said hoarsely.

"Huh?"

"Quarters! You got any?"

"Sure. Sure. I couldn't hear, I've had a cold. . . ." The coins rattled on the table.

"Got to keep the music going. Meet me in the john."

"Huh?"

"The john. Meet me in the shitter."

"Why?"

"Just do it," Castle growled.

The stench in the washroom was suffocating. Above the urinal, someone had scribbled "Flush hard, MacD's is five blocks away." No one had taken the advice. Cigarette butts drifted on yellow swill. Dub pushed the handle. Nothing happened. The picture on the condom machine was of a blonde with an open red mouth and her head tossed back. Above the coin slot it promised that for fifty cents your woman would "squeal with *ECSTASY!!!*" Dub stared into the mirror at his pale face, and gently prodded the puffy skin under his eyes. His sweat felt oily and the room was tight as a coffin. The door swung back sharply and glanced off his shoulder.

Castle looked him over. "Don't move."

"Huh?"

"Don't move."

Castle flicked his cigarette into the urinal. Dub stepped back and bumped his head against the condom machine. "I don't understand."

"Take it easy." Castle's hands reached out and unbuttoned Dub's jacket. His hands went under as if he were going to embrace him.

"Hey!"

"Relax." The voice was like ice. The hands pressed Dub's chest and under his arms. Castle dropped to one knee and patted his legs, then spun him and carefully felt his back. Dub was glad he'd talked Vonna out of the body wire, but he had to get Castle back into the booth. Castle spun him around again. "What's your name?"

"Krider. Vernon Krider. What's all this? You know that from the telephone." Dub widened his eyes. "Are you a cop? Aw shit, I knew I—"

"Would I be here if I was?"

"I never done this. How would I know? Maybe you just got me in here to feel me up."

Castle's eyes narrowed. "You watch your mouth or you're fish food. It's a big lake out there."

Dub licked his lips. "Hey, I'm sorry, bud. How do I know

what's going on? Maybe your ad was like, like I didn't understand. It was like a code."

"I've got to check you for a wire, right? Anybody can read the ad. Anybody."

"But that's what the ad's for, ain't it?"

"I shouldn't even talk to you. Christ, I told you to come straight to the last booth. But no, you got to make a big point of asking the barkeep."

"I'm sorry. I couldn't sleep last night."

"Sorry doesn't slice bread."

"Couldn't we still talk? Let's go and have a drink. Ain't no harm done, is it? I come a long way. I'll give you a hundred just to talk. I promised that on the phone."

"Up front."

Dub fished the bill out of his wallet. "Here. Just like I promised." He spread the billfold. "See, it's all I'm carrying."

"If you don't trust me not to rob you, how're you going to trust me to take care of business?"

"I don't know." Dub glanced up at the barred window near the ceiling. "I—I just know I've got to do something. Look, can't we go sit down? This smell is making me sick."

"Sure," said Castle. "Beer's getting warm."

The daylight from the open front door blinded them. A black woman in sneakers, looking heavier because of a GMC windbreaker and polyester stretch slacks, walked toward the bar. Vonna. Shit, Dub thought. She hesitated when she saw Castle and him leaving the rest room, then turned to the bartender. "Yes, ma'am?" he asked.

"Do you have a pay phone?"

"Busted." The bartender wouldn't meet her eyes.

"I've got to call my boyfriend. It's personal."

"Two blocks over. There's a Country Fair store."

She turned to leave. Dub and Castle stood still, watching her.

"You live near here?" asked the bartender. "Weren't you in here earlier?"

"Just visiting. I had a sandwich here around lunchtime." She started for the door, but the bartender spoke again.

"Right," he said, "salami. You aren't from around here, that's for sure. More of *your* type lives up in the lower numbers:

[25]

East Second through Tenth, or so. You get what I'm saying. Nuthin' personal."

Dub thought her eyes flashed. She said, "My boyfriend works for GE. We ain't settled yet."

The bartender nodded, then sniffed. Vonna bought a long bag of honey-roasted cashews as if to prove he couldn't chase her off, thanked the bartender, and left. Castle did not sit until the door clunked shut. Dub remained standing.

"Laying off half of GE, but importing niggers!" the bartender announced.

"Ain't it the truth!" said the mechanic.

Dub looked disturbed. "This place is too busy," he said. "Strangers walking in—I'm getting out of here."

Castle grabbed his arm. "Come on, Vernon. We're just two guys in a bar on a Thursday afternoon. You paid your hundred. Say your piece."

He licked his upper lip and bolted his whiskey. He drummed his fingers for several seconds. "Okay. This ain't easy. It's just I can't take it no more. I just—well, I saw your ad." Dub took a scrap of paper from his pocket and laid it on the table. It was part of the want ad section from *Mercenary*. "This *is* your ad?"

"Put that away."

"You said on the phone you could take care of any problem. *Any*."

Castle nodded.

"Is—well, I saw a story on the news, about advertisements in *Soldier of Fortune* magazine—is this like that?"

"Better."

"They got caught."

"It's why we're better. They screwed up. We don't. It's all a question of logistics."

" 'We'?" Dub didn't expect an answer. Castle was stone-faced. Dub fidgeted with his shot glass. "Well, you see—"

"Let's stop the fan dance, Vernon. My guess is you'd like somebody out of your way."

Dub stared.

"I'm right, then." Castle smiled. "That can be done. People die every day. Can you afford it?"

"That's no problem."

"No?"

"You ever been to New Orleans?"

"Maybe."

"I've got six dealerships. Used cars. Two in Gretna. One out near the airport. One in Slidell—"

"Business is good, eh?"

"Too good. I can't trust nobody who works for me. I've got to go from place to place a lot and my wife . . ."

"Your wife's busier than you are."

"It ain't funny."

"Old story. You caught her?"

"I hired a detective."

"Don't you think if she turns up dead that this detective might suspect something?"

"Not if you can make it look like the nigger done it."

"Nigger?"

Dub ground his teeth until his jaw muscles stung, then hissed between his teeth, "She's screwing a nigger."

Dub's little twist on the story yanked the brass ring. Castle shifted slightly. His eyes tightened. He turned his back to the wall and put his feet up on the bench seat. "Now this is something. Gone after licorice. That's a sick bitch, Vernon. Can I call you Vernon?"

Dub stared into his glass. "My friends call me Vern."

"Okay, Vern, let's say I know somebody who could take care of this problem for you. We're talking a lot of cash, Vern. Wouldn't it be cheaper to get divorced? You've already got the dope on her. A lawyer, a Louisiana judge—hell, you'd be rid of her for good. We'd do the spook for a discount."

Dub leaned forward until his breath was in Castle's eyes. "You think I want to be known for this? You think I want everybody to know? That cunt has got to die. I'll pay anything. She's got to die!"

Castle was silent. He drained his beer.

Dub squinted over his shoulder at the bartender. The other barflies were hidden by the booth wall. "Well?"

"Hold your horses. I'm thinking."

"Look, are you going to do this? I didn't fly all the way up here and drive three hours just to tell some stranger about this. I thought we were here to do business. Can you do it or not?"

"I can have it done," said Castle calmly. "I know the right people. It's tricky, though. I'm just figuring whether we want to do it."

"Who is we? I want you to take care of this personally. That's why I'm talking to you. Name your price."

"Fifty thousand before. Fifty thousand afterward. But I don't work alone."

"Then who works with you? How do I know you haven't been infiltrated by the cops or something?"

"You watch too much TV, Vern. Most cops might like what we do. Others can be bought. It's better you don't know everything. Then you don't have to worry about these people I'm going to fix you up with."

Dub wiped his finger around the inside of his shot glass and licked it. "A hundred's a lot."

"Hey, we're not haggling over some old Chevy here. It's a big job and you can afford it. Have a Fourth of July sale."

"What if I give you the money and you don't—"

Castle leaned forward, the texture of his face stony in the light. "This isn't K-Mart. No returns, Vern. We keep at it till the job's done." He poked with his finger. "I've trusted *you* enough to hear *you* out. Now you've got to trust me. Do you, Vern?"

Dub crossed his arms. His fingers worked at his shoulders. "I've got to think—it's not easy. I don't know you. You'll kill her?"

"Look, Vern, I'll help you out. It's just money to me. You've got a problem, I've got the solution, eh? It's up to you whether you want to make up with Mrs. Krider, divorce her, play sloppy seconds to a coon. . . ."

"Shut up!" Dub wiped his face on his sleeve. Castle's teeth shone. He had Vern Krider right where he wanted him. "I want another drink."

Castle gestured at the barkeeper. The toe of his boot was visible above the table edge. It kept rhythm with the Johnny Paycheck record. It was like he didn't care Dub was there. They were silent until Dub tossed back his drink.

He slammed the glass down so hard the napkin holder jumped. "All right. Do it. Her name is Allison. We live at—"

"No, no," said Castle. "Money first, details later."

"I haven't got it with me."

"That's okay. We meet in New Orleans on July fifth. I'll call you and tell you where. What's your number?"

He fumbled in his pockets. "I've got a list, here, on my card. The six dealerships. You call and leave a message. I never know where I'll be. Say Castle's in town, and you're an old army buddy."

"No. I'll say Mario's in town."

"Who?"

"Mario," Castle laughed. "He's a local politician."

"Mario, Mario. Like Mario Lanza. All right."

Castle's face instantly hardened. He clamped his hand on Dub's arm. The movement was so swift Dub jumped.

"Remember this, Vern. What we can do to your old lady, we can do to you."

Dub looked at the big-knuckled hand crumpling his sleeve. "You're hurting me."

"There's no hiding. The police, nobody, can protect you. There's backup, even if you get me. And there's no turning back. It's decided. When I spend that first penny on heading south, it's done."

Dub nodded. "I want this done. I want it done. I'm sure."

"Fifty thousand. Nothing bigger than fifties. Old bills. July fifth."

"Mario."

"Right." Castle smiled. "It's going to be a pleasure doing business. See ya." The door clunked as he left.

Dub rubbed his arm. Castle had a grip like a car crusher. He peeked over his shoulder at the bartender and began working his index finger into the napkin holder. He felt the bug, pulled out a wad of napkins with it and stuck them in his jacket.

"Hey!" said the bartender. "Put those back!"

"I got a cold," Dub said timidly. "I thought—"

"They cost me good money. Too cheap for Kleenex?"

"I just—look, I'll put them back." He held them up.

"Nah, you probably got dirt on them. I don't want everybody catching cold off my napkins. You want another drink?"

"I'm sorry. I wasn't thinking." He said it to the death's

head on the man's jacket. The bartender had already turned to rattle something beside the cash register.

Dub waited a few minutes, then left. He peered up and down the street, taking what would seem like a particular interest in a tanker-truck that rumbled past. He headed south. He was nearly at the end of the block when Vonna started the van, swung into the street, and followed. She wasn't supposed to do that. He walked slowly, hoping she would pass him and get out of there, but, despite his dawdling, with the help of a red light she stayed behind him for three blocks. He took a quick left on a narrow street of cheap-looking houses. He was sweating as if Vonna were an enemy and Erie had turned into Saigon, 1970.

The van turned, passed him, and pulled over. Vonna gestured with her thick arm. "Get in."

"What the—" Dub turned. The street was empty.

"Come on in, Vern," she said. "You want somebody to see you?"

THREE

Dub's first reaction was to hiss through his teeth; his second was to think, "That's what I get." Behind him a Chevy with more Bondo than body roared down Parade, startling a woman on the porch two houses down. He climbed into the van.

"What the hell are you doing?"

Expressionless, Vonna spoke into the rearview mirror. "No reason for you to walk."

"What do you think this is, woman? Some cheap Cajun divorce?"

She pursed her lips and rolled her jaws like she was tasting the anger. "Hey, man," she said. "No harm."

"Maybe. Maybe not." Dub climbed into the back by the taping equipment. "Go on. Go on out of here." He tried to say it with disgust, but it came out more like resignation. He wiped his face with his hand. "Christ!"

Vonna ground the gears and half turned her head. "You work for us, remember?"

"Wrong. The Devraix Agency hired me, and it goes my way or it don't go. Devraix wanted me. I'm the one with the Pennsylvania license. When I tell you we're not seen together, I mean, goddamn it, we're not seen together!"

"Give me some credit, I can spot a tail."

"So you say." Dub took the bug out of his pocket. "Here." He tossed it onto the passenger seat. "Saved you a trip. You don't want to go back in that place."

"They don't shake me," she said.

"You were in there once too much, already. I could've shit when I saw you."

"I didn't know what was going on," she said dryly. "I had the weird idea to help you. I waited ten minutes. What'd you want me to do? Wait'll he flushed you down the toilet in little pieces?"

She was right, maybe. Dub didn't know. He didn't care. The hour with Castle had drained him. In the investigations business you don't get many chances to work on murder, or even a maybe murder. Murder is police business. Dub normally got to tell husbands their wives were banging the manager of the bowling alley. He got to tell wives their husbands' nights out with the boys were a bit more recreational than poker and beer. The work got boring mighty fast—the dramatic plopping of the photos in front of the client was the worst part. You find out how pathetically predictable people are, and then it's just one job after another, after another. Murder, though, a murder the police weren't interested in—that had kept him pacing and smoking until sunup. Or was it the chance to face up to one last undercover, to put Janet and the Saigon nightmares behind him?

About three a.m. he'd started practicing his southern accent. Like he could get it wrong. Like the Devraix Agency had hired the wrong guy. When you put on a mask you can forget your own face.

"Look," he said to Vonna, "don't take me back to the Holiday Inn just yet. You don't go anywhere near it. Just cruise around. Maybe take the loop around the beach. I'll dictate everything that happened away from the bug. You got his picture?"

"As he was going in," said Vonna.

"What about a car?"

She shrugged. "He came from the alley. I scoped out that direction while I waited for you, but there were like half a dozen on the next street and a supermarket store a block on. I took down the closest plates, but if I was him I'd have parked at the grocery."

"Did any of those cars have Confederate flag stickers? Maybe gun control things?"

"Why so?"

"He was some kind of Yankee redneck. He meets me in a

redneck bar. He likes hardcore country music and cowboy boots. All he needed was a Dixie twang and—"

"I didn't notice anything. And I didn't appreciate that 'killing niggers' stuff, by the way."

"Sorry." Dub's ears flushed. "Everybody's a sucker for a good story. Juicy adultery, a complicated killing—it gives Castle something to think about besides whether I'm genuine. It's the role."

"If you say so," she said.

"I'm not that way, Vonna. Really."

"A regular Rainbow Coalition type, are you, Delbert?"

Dub didn't answer. What was there to say? I got nothing against you Nee-groes? It would sound feeble and patronizing, like his father talking to a waiter. "Don't call me Delbert," he barked.

She glanced at him, seemed sorry to have said it, and changed the subject. "You get the details on tape," she said. "Where's the beach you mentioned?"

He told her to stop in a gas station. Late at night on Pittsburgh TV he'd seen advertisements for Presque Isle, a peninsula sticking out into Lake Erie. The ads made it look like Hilton Head. Dub had once tailed a man who was supposed to be going duck hunting there. The guy got up at three-thirty, loaded all his gear in the station wagon, kissed his wife, but only went across Pittsburgh to Sewickley and the bungalow that held wife number two. Introducing the two women to each other had been like pitching acid in a fuse box. They ended up hating each other more than they hated their husband. Vonna found out that Presque Isle was on the other side of Erie, but that wasn't far. Dub had finished dictating before Vonna parked. They were surprised by the number of cars. It was too damn cold to swim, but the Erie-ites were all dizzy with the sunshine.

"Let's walk by the water," said Vonna.

"In these clothes? I might be seen. The world's full of weird coincidences." She sat back and Dub felt like he'd refused a peace pipe. She didn't think, did she, that he didn't want to be seen in public with a black woman? "Good tape," he offered.

Vonna faced him. "There's nobody better," she said harshly.

Dub ignored it. "This guy's a killer. I feel it. Maybe I'm wrong, but I'm sure. He's too cool. He'd kill his mother for a buck. He's got eyes—Christ!—you should see what they're like in low light."

"What have we got, though? You might get me in jail with all this, but, hell, he's white. He's got rights."

"I called Calabrese this morning," said Dub. "The phone is registered to a George Castle."

"No shit," mocked Vonna. "Huh! You don't think he's stupid enough to use his real name?"

"No way," Dub said. "I've seen those eyes before." That got her attention. "LBJ. When I was an MP." He had said it without thinking. "Long Binh Jail. Vietnam." He looked away. "Killer's eyes."

"Oh. How about we check out the address? It's an office on State Street."

"You shouldn't," Dub said. "You've put in too many appearances already."

"Well, *you* can't do it. Maybe there's enough there to shut the man down. Or at least get him to talk."

"All right," Dub said. "Then we go to the state cops."

"Devraix wants him nailed in Louisiana," Vonna reminded him. She watched the brown waves shatter against a breakwater. "You think this Castle does the killing himself?"

"If I had to guess?"

"Uh-huh."

"He's got the eyes. But who knows? It looks like a one-man thing. How many could be involved? A mob guy would be more professional, don't you think? Not that I've known mob guys."

"The mob's different these days—new players, silk ties," said Vonna. "So maybe we get him picked up on conspiracy and then he talks and then we get Eddie Viek."

"Maybe. Suppose—I mean it's still possible—that Castle conned Viek out of fifty thou and then did nothing. Am I right it's really Viek we want?"

"*If* he killed Michael O'Dell," said Vonna. "If he didn't, I don't know."

They considered all this for several seconds. Dub fumbled in his jacket for cigarettes, but he had left them somewhere.

"We need more on this Castle," said Vonna.

Dub sighed. "The further we go the more dangerous it gets."

"The further we go the more likely we'll tip our hand and it's scot-free time."

Dub wiped his face with his hand and peeled off the lime jacket. It wasn't the heat, he thought, it was the humidity. Out through the windshield half a dozen families were scattered on the sand. Kids were digging and wading, but most of them wore windbreakers or sweatshirts. It looked safe enough, but he shook his head. He pressed the heel of his hand against a gas bubble in his chest and tried to burp. "Open the window. Let's run through this thing again."

Vonna recited the facts. Dub nodded and occasionally said "That's right," or filled in a detail. They checked a few items in the file. No matter how they squeezed them, only a few drops came out:

1) Castle was, at the least, posing as a gun for hire.
2) Viek had telephoned him.
3) Viek had flown to Buffalo and possibly met Castle.

In the end they decided there was really nothing left to do but draw Castle in further. How many moths might come to the flame? mused Dub. How many and how big?

FOUR

Dub climbed out of the van in an alley and walked back to the Holiday Inn. It was sunny but awfully cold for three weeks into June and he wondered what it was like in New Orleans. His nose was running by the time he checked out. He remembered what torture it was to take the parade ground with a cold on those humid Fridays back at the Citadel. He also remembered the black housekeeper, Opal, gently spreading a pea-sized blob of Vicks under his nose and rocking him to sleep in the hot kitchen. He bought some green tablets from a machine in the Pittsburgh airport. They nearly knocked him out but he tried to look like an agitated man while he ate a long dinner and lingered over a double Jim Beam. As soon as he plopped into his seat on the 727, he dozed. He didn't even notice the takeoff.

While Dub played easy to follow, Vonna strolled into the office building on State Street in Erie, looking for the phone registered to George Castle. Most of the building was empty, and there was no Castle listed on the mailboxes. Vonna pretended to be a confused job-seeker sent by Unemployment. By elimination she decided that, of the six tenants, only two were prospects: small offices on the fourth floor whose occupants had never been seen by the secretaries for the mail-order business on the first floor and the independent accountant on the third. Light came through the pebbled glass at 412, so she knocked. No response. "Manager!" she called out. Silence. She studied the door for a security system, then picked the lock. The room was filled with cardboard boxes of Nature's Lanolin Soap: somebody's get-rich pyramid scheme had turned to dust and stained the walls. No telephone.

Room 431 had a similar glass door: Czypanski & Loomis, Attorneys-at-Law. The gold paint had chipped. "Law" was nearly gone. There was white dust on the doorknob. No one had been there for a long time. Again she picked the lock, but this time found what she was looking for.

Against one wall was a desk. On it was a cheap variety of home computer—the kind usually used by kids—hooked to a couple of other electronic gizmos. The phone line went straight into a black metal box. She delicately traced each wire with her finger. It was exactly what the clicking on Dub's call had told her. With enough time she could hack out the number the calls were being relayed to, but she'd heard of bookies rigging charges to their setups. The best thing to do was to sketch it out on a scrap of paper and write down the registration numbers. The dust was heavy on everything so she was careful not to touch it. She jumped when the black box started clicking. The drives in the computer came to life. Then everything was silent again. A murder being arranged? She locked the door and left.

Forty-eight hours later Dub and Vonna were in Devraix's office with Clementine O'Dell. Without her sunglasses she looked less the southern lady than Dub had imagined in Pittsburgh. Her gray hair was cropped short, her face was solid and square. She was tall; her body looked powerful, not particularly athletic, but robust. Her delicate white skirt and satin blouse hung oddly on her. In her eyes he could see how deeply she had been wounded. She settled into the wicker chair next to the window and clutched her purse as she had in Pittsburgh, eyeing the P.I.'s as if they were muggers. That's all right, lady, thought Dub. I don't trust you either.

Devraix introduced her to Vonna, then offered coffee and tea with his fluid gestures. No one took any. He asked Vonna to summarize what they knew. It didn't take long. Mrs. O'Dell's eyes twitched from side to side at each hint of Viek's guilt. They dropped to her lap when the long list of what the detectives didn't know was recited.

"Finally," said Vonna, "there is no record of any long-distance calls made from the computer, so it is relaying to somewhere in the Erie area. There is no record of a George Castle on the tax rolls, marriage licenses, driver's licenses, and none on the phone records—except for the one in the office. The lease for the office says George Castle's address is in Girard, outside of Erie, but the place is an abandoned tool and die factory. There seems to be no match in the military records either. All the George Castles are the wrong age or something.

Mrs. O'Dell glared at Dub. "But you were face to face with the man."

"Yes, ma'am," he said, "but he could just be a con artist."

"Or," said Devraix, "he could claim that, should he ever be pressed."

"What about his fingerprints?" she said sharply. "You could have gotten his fingerprints."

"Well, there wasn't—"

"Mrs. O'Dell," said Devraix, "Mr. Greenert did as much as possible, I assure you. We are confident that our Mr. Castle shall contact Mr. Krider, if only to steal the first fifty thousand dollars. If you like, I will hire the Keyhole Agency to watch the bar where Mr. Greenert met Mr. Castle, but I consider that to be a wasted effort."

"Expense is no object," she said.

"There is little object in wasting money."

"Very well." She lowered her eyes and sighed. "I'll never be the same. I know that. With Michael gone, I'll never be the same. But I must have some peace, and the only way to get it is to punish Eddie Viek."

Vonna bit her lower lip. Dub thought she felt guilty.

"What I fail to understand, Mr. Devraix," Mrs. O'Dell continued, "is why you haven't gone directly after Eddie Viek. If this Castle is a confidence man, we'll have risked a great deal chasing a phantom."

"This could be," he said, "but at the least, he may be able to attest that Viek was *looking* for a killer, and that would give us something."

"But why haven't you gone after Viek?"

Dub shifted forward on his seat. Devraix deferred to Dub with his clean, thin hand.

"Viek doesn't have any handles, if you know what I mean," said Dub. "Mr. Devraix thinks, and I agree, that all we'd find out is that he's cheating on his taxes or substituting whitefish for crab or something trivial. Nothing, anyway, to prove he had anything to do with Mr. O'Dell's death."

"In any case," said Devraix, "you have sent your auditors after him and this will alert him."

"I shouldn't have done it?"

"There is no question you should have, Mrs. O'Dell, and we believe it helps. The auditors will distract him. That gives us time."

Mrs. O'Dell nodded, then scanned the three of them. The strain of her doubts showed in wrinkles around her lips and eyes. A lesser person might have broken down. She rose. "Is that all you can tell me? If so, I'll be on my way. I'll expect another report on July seventh."

Devraix stood. "Certainly. Let me escort you to the door."

"Excuse me," Dub said, stepping in front of them. "You haven't told anyone about this, Mrs. O'Dell?"

She tilted back her head as if offended. "No. Just as I agreed with Mr. Devraix."

"You can't tell anyone. Not your children, not your maid, not your chauffeur, not your priest."

She peered into his face as if trying to remember something. "I told you I have not."

"It could kill me if you do. It's not that any of these people are involved, understand, it's just that they too might trust someone who can't keep their mouth shut. You understand?"

"It's quite clear."

Devraix and Mrs. O'Dell left. "I wouldn't have told her anything yet," Dub said to Vonna.

"Why not? It's expensive," she said. "Devraix wants to give her every chance to get out if she's not, you know, committed."

"She doesn't look good."

"Who's to say? Tomorrow's the fourth. We wait. Maybe we get something, maybe we don't."

"Ain't it the truth," said Dub. But they sat silent for a while, knowing this was a bigger deal than whether some middle-aged man was popping his secretary.

On the fourth, Dub squeezed his way into the crowds in the French Quarter. He bought a pastry in a sweet shop, scanned a toy shop for something for his daughters, and gradually pushed past the street musicians and artists with their "instant" portraits hanging on the Jackson Square fence. He strolled Decatur toward the French Market and glanced in the windows of Tujaque's, Mr. Gyro's, Greer's Fish Market, Sbisa's Cafe, and the French Market Café, where a pot boiled in the window, visible from the sidewalk. Next to the market itself were wholesalers: Tony's Produce; Dixie Produce; Frank Fouchi and Son, Trucking. At the very end was an iron fence enclosing the Old U.S. Mint and the streetcar named Desire. It all reminded him of Charleston, only bigger, rougher, and less genteel.

He wandered back between the trinket peddlers and the vendors of enormous apples and ropes of garlic, then settled onto the bench on the Moon Walk and watched the couples below buying rides on the surreys until dark.

Fireworks were launched from a barge in the Mississippi and afterward Dub's wallet was somehow lifted as he pushed back toward the St. Louis Cathedral. The thief was a bad judge of marks: Dub had spent most of the day's expenses on an overpriced, but famous, brunch in a hotel. If the dip keeps snatching from guys like me, thought Dub, he won't make minimum wage. Dub didn't notice the wallet was gone until he tried to pay for a beer and a bowl of gumbo at the Café Pontalba. He used the Visa card in his vest pocket, and because the amount was so small, the cashier didn't check if it was over the limit.

Dub thought about pushing his luck by taking the card up to Bourbon Street, but as he strolled up one block, the smiling prostitutes and the shoving crowds made him queasy. It was too much like the whoring district of Saigon in 1970. A death-pale, wispy blonde asked him if he was "sportin' " and kissed his ear. He shoved her away and she called him a fag. The holiday feeling evaporated. He was simultaneously aroused and frightened, and the air grew thin.

He hurried back to his hotel, his shirt wet with sweat. He turned out the lights and stared out his window at the people shouting and carrying on down on Canal Street. He saw someone trying to escape the ocean of human bodies and Dub became him, swimming away from the sharks, swimming and swimming. . . . He was panting, couldn't stop sweating. His chest burned. He turned up the air conditioner though he knew it had nothing to do with that.

Body bag . . . something about that blonde hooker. Why? She hadn't looked anything like Janet. The panic was back like an attack of malaria. After seventeen years it had weakened enough in the last few to let him hope he was free. He wasn't.

His wrists and mouth itched as if the adhesive tape were on them again. The murmur of voices in the hotel corridor startled him.

He checked the door locks. He smoked his last cigarette. He tried to telephone Calabrese, but got no answer. He tried to telephone the girls, but Beth and their "new daddy" would have taken them to the fireworks in Charleston. He turned on the lamp and opened the telephone directory before he realized he'd forgotten Vonna's last name. And why her? Maybe because she didn't seem to like him very much. It was safer that way. He didn't know what he would say to her if he did call. He couldn't picture asking her out, let alone anything more. Not because she was black, he thought. She might be married. Is there anything wrong with asking a woman you work with to go out for a drink? Or *is* it because she's black? If you're born in the South and you hate the prejudice you grew up with, you're always watching yourself for signs of it. You watch too much, he told himself. It's just her. She isn't friendly. She's a cipher. Never mind. The feeling will pass. It has to. It always passes. This is just some combination of the tropical climate, the chaos in the streets, and the undercover.

He hadn't really been undercover since Saigon. He had pretended to be repairmen or health inspectors or whatever was needed, but not with killers. Even if he wasn't sure Castle was in the murder business, Dub was sure he would kill.

The woman at the Devraix Agency's answering service sounded as if he had waked her. She wouldn't give him Vonna's number, of course, but she took his. The phone rang a long twenty minutes later.

Vonna didn't sound annoyed. She didn't sound friendly either. "What's up?" There was a rumble as she turned away from the phone and coughed.

"Did I wake you? Am I bothering you?"

"Huh? No. I was watching TV."

"Anything good?"

"Are you kidding? What's up?"

Dub fiddled with the Gideon Bible on the end table. "I had an idea. It, ah, came to me as I started to fall asleep."

"Yeah?"

"Did anybody check *Mercenary?* Like who put the ad. They've got to have a record of it."

He could hear her breathing.

"Maybe a cancelled check."

"Is that all?"

"Hey?" he said, "you said you were just watching TV."

"No, no," she exhaled. "I meant of course we tried it. One of the first things."

"I didn't see it in the file."

"It ought to be in there. Devraix'll be pissed."

"He doesn't seem like the kind of guy to get pissed."

She laughed. Or he thought she did. She'd always been hard to figure. Her accent turned saccharine. "He's more of a slow burner, if you know what I mean, honeychile."

"Uh-huh."

"He wants that paperwork straight."

"Well that's a good thing." He heard her breathing. She seemed to be listening. "And?"

"And *Mercenary* wouldn't tell us a thing. The man who checked it for us in Tampa said he had the impression they would like a murder hung on their want ads. They think they're going to put *Soldier of Fortune* out of business someday. *Soldier of Fortune* had murders linked to their want ads; *Mercenary* wants it too. *Playboy* gets LaToya Jackson; *Penthouse* wants her too. You up for increasing *Mercenary's* circulation?"

"If I can get a commission."

"Amen."

"Eventually they said a guy paid cash and gave the name Steve Jones."

"Right." Dub flipped a few pages in the Bible, then closed it. "Whoa!" he said. "Viek's in Tampa."

"So?"

"A good coincidence."

"So he put in a want ad for this Castle, so he'll have somebody to hire?"

"Doesn't make sense, does it?"

"It might make sense in Pittsburgh, but it sure stinks in New Orleans."

"Maybe the rag is commoner in Tampa if it's published there."

"You think so, Sherlock?"

"All right, all right," he said. It didn't fit in with the way she had always treated him, but he had the impression she was glad he called. It was not like she was trying to keep him on the phone. It was more like she didn't mind it if he stayed on. "Listen," he said, "I'm having a hell of a time waiting here. Is there someplace in this town we could go and get some coffee and doughnuts?"

"Now?"

"Well I'm told the Big Easy never closes."

"The question is, when *can't* you get food in this town. That's my problem."

"Where do you live? I'll get a cab and pick you up."

"Jesus, it's past one."

"Well, all right." He scratched at his armpit. "I'll let you get back to your movie."

"I'll pick you up," she said wearily. "Thirty minutes. Out front."

"No, that's all right. I—"

"The movie stinks and you've got me thinking about beignets. I won't sleep now, anyhow. Thirty minutes." She hung up before he could say anything else. He blinked. Light from the street glided across the wall. He was cooler, breathing easier. He knew he could sleep now, but she was on the way. He splashed his face and poked a deodorant stick between two buttons on his shirt and into his armpits. He wasn't up for sleeping with her, and that made him feel old. At the Citadel a couple of the boys had always bragged about "dark meat," and tried to get Dub to go along with them. He'd avoided it, had never had a black woman, and if he ever did, he hoped she'd be friendlier than Vonna. He also hoped she wasn't planning on it, but you never knew what a woman was thinking. He'd feel like hell in the morning if he did it, and he didn't want that when

Castle called. Did she think he was treating? You never knew whether a woman expected that any more, either. He cashed a check in the lobby just in case.

What they talked about until dawn Dub didn't much remember afterward. They got a corner table at the Café du Monde and put away six beignets—a kind of doughnut with powdered sugar—and as many cups of chicoried coffee. He joked that he thought a "beignet" had something to do with French plumbing and feminine hygiene. She just rolled her eyes.

He told her about the guy from Uniontown who had hired the Keyhole Agency to find out who his wife was cheating with. When they'd finally gotten close enough to get a good look, the wife turned out to be the client in drag. The client turned out to be one of the most split personalities anyone had ever heard of and couldn't be convinced that he was she. He had accused Calabrese of sleeping with his "wife" and plotting against him.

As the dawn approached, Vonna lost some of her aloofness. She told him about a runaway twelve-year-old she had found turning tricks in an alley near Preservation Hall. The girl's father beat her to death and shot himself in the mouth shortly after the police had returned her to Texas. When Vonna noticed how closely Dub was listening, she became embarrassed, like a woman who discovers her bikini top has slipped and shown too much. "It's just something that happened," she said, and she was more careful afterward.

He didn't learn much about her otherwise, nor she about him. She'd learned electronics in the Army between 1975 and 1978, but got tired of the men hitting on her. She asked if he was married and he told her about the girls and the divorce. She told him she had never been "really married," then changed the subject. That was the way the night went: a couple of lone wolves needing company, but circling each other instead.

As the last bleary-eyed drunks staggered home, Vonna handed him a set of keys. "You might as well get some sleep, Vern," she said. "Castle might show any time tomorrow." She wrote Krider's address on a napkin.

"I just hope the 'King of the Deal Royale' has a nice soft bed," he said.

She patted at the powdered sugar spilled on the table and licked it off her fingertips.

"I'll get a cab," he said, and she was gone.

Dub picked up his Vernon Krider clothes and headed for the home, a low, wide suburban ranch off Williams Boulevard in Kenner. There were odd, expensive-looking plants in the flower beds and an odder bronze reproduction of Michelangelo's *David* by the arch leading to the double doors. There was enough oak in them to build a complete dining set. Dub had seen smaller garage doors. The right door swung back smoothly and he squinted for the burglar alarm shut-off in the front closet. He was half inside, the key lifted to the gray steel box, when the cold barrel of a pistol lightly, almost caressingly, touched his ear.

"It's off," said Castle. "If you weren't such a dumb motherfucker, you'd know."

FIVE

A .357 is huge. Five times bigger than any handgun needs to be. Dub stammered, "What are you doing here? My wife could come home any minute."

"Cut the shit," said Castle. His knee came up before Dub could think. The world flashed white. Dub crumpled into the closet, curled up like a fetus, gasping as windbreakers and umbrellas tumbled on him.

"Get up, motherfucker," said Castle, "or I'll kill you there." Dub squirmed, but he wasn't quick enough. Castle grabbed him by the hair and jerked him forward. Dub rolled once across the mile-deep carpet and raised himself on one arm.

"What—" he gasped, "what are you doing? I—"

The gun barrel clipped him hard across the forehead. He rolled back again. Castle's boot thudded into his upper arm. He flopped dazed against a chair and Castle squatted over him. He shoved the gun barrel into Dub's mouth. The metal ripped his palate. Castle's breath burned his eyes.

"Now, listen, motherfucker," Castle said. "I can kill you hard, or I can kill you easy. Either way, you're one dead son of a bitch. Did you think you could fool us with that bullshit impersonation? You're so fucking stupid. You don't know who the fuck you're dealing with."

Dub blinked. His groin throbbed and his stomach juggled wads of beignet. He wanted to fade, to pass out. It might be the only way to keep from moving, the only way to keep from throwing up. Castle stared into his eyes for what seemed like a year, then jerked the barrel out. The taste of metal and blood spread over Dub's tongue. Castle jerked him up by the collar and shoved him toward the living room. Dub collapsed against the white sofa arm for support.

"Sit," Castle said. "I think we understand each other."

Dub nodded.

Castle settled onto the thick glass coffee table. "Don't be fooled," he said with pleasure. "You're a dead man. But first, you're going to give me all the details, right? You do that and maybe I'll make it a little easier on you."

Body bag. Saigon again. But how had Janet betrayed him this time? How? Don't lose it, thought Dub. Don't lose it. "You—you don't think I'm alone, do you?"

"That so?"

"The house is being watched."

Castle jerked suddenly. Dub's knees came together and he twisted sideways. Castle smiled, loving the fear.

"You can do better than that."

Dub's nose was running. He touched it and saw blood on his fingers. "Probably not," he said.

Castle touched the .357 to Dub's forehead. "Nasty cut," he said. "Don't worry. It won't hurt long."

Dub had been taken so much by surprise he was still unable to think. He knew he had to stall. Something—anything—might interrupt. Time was everything: a minute, a few seconds. "How did you find out?"

"You talk to me, then somebody goes into my relay room that afternoon."

"How did you know?"

"Oldest fucking trick in the book, troop. Powder."

The dust Vonna had noticed on the doorknob. "How do you know I knocked the dust off? Anybody might have done it. What about mice?"

"Let's just say I have a nose for these things. Then, bingo, I find out that Vern Krider gave his key to the pool man."

"That doesn't mean I'm not Vern Krider."

"No? What do you take me for?" He cuffed Dub with the flat of his hand. "All those nice family pictures and not a single one of you. Strange, wouldn't you say?"

"All right. I fucked up. You got me."

"You're damn right." He was calm, satisfied. Dub could

tell it wasn't the killing he enjoyed so much as the domination of someone he was going to kill. Dub wondered how much he had tormented Michael O'Dell. Maybe that wasn't convenient in the middle of the Pontchartrain Causeway, and Castle was going to make up the difference on Dub. As far as Dub was concerned, he could take years if he wanted. A good hit man would never waste time like this, Dub thought. My brains would be drying on Vern Krider's raincoats by now and Castle would be halfway to Ouagadougou.

"Viek thought you'd be easier to trap," Dub said.

Castle blinked.

"I guess he underestimated you."

Castle's eyes drifted upward and slightly to the left. "What do you mean?"

"I thought you had it all figured out."

"Don't get smart with me."

"Viek figured you were pretty dumb—"

Castle raised the gun.

"Hey, I'm just telling you what he said." Dub blinked and wiped blood on his sleeve. "All I had to do was sucker you out of Erie and then make you disappear."

The look on Castle's face was odd, as if it had just occurred to him that someone might do to him what he had done to others. "Who's Viek?" he asked.

Dub stared him straight in the eye and chuckled. "Everybody's a comedian."

Castle grabbed him by the collar. "Who the fuck is Viek?"

"The guy who wants you dead. Remember Michael O'Dell? Lake Pontchartrain? You gonna try the same on me?"

He shoved Dub back with a snap of his wrist. He was strong, very strong, but he was trying to think and the strain was showing. That was good. It kept him preoccupied. What wasn't so good was the way he had reacted to Viek, O'Dell, and Pontchartrain. That was bad. If he knew about it, he was awfully good at covering, something Dub didn't really believe. "So you're a hit man?" Castle asked incredulously.

"Bingo. You win the washer/dryer."

He pressed the gun against Dub's nose and rummaged through Dub's jacket pockets. He found the brunch receipt and crumpled it. "Where's your wallet?"

"Got no wallet."

"What do you mean?"

"I mean I don't carry anything to ID me."

"You got to have a driver's license."

"Got six or seven, but I keep them someplace safe."

This lie seemed to interest Castle, as if it was something that would be useful in the future. "This Viek sent you?"

"Have I got to spell it out, Castle? Viek wants the loose ends tied. He wants you disposed of. He hired me to dispose of you. Seventy-five thousand dollars."

"That much?"

"I'm the best, but I gave him a cut rate on you."

"Cut rate?"

"I always give a cut rate to mob guys."

"This Viek's in the mob? Like in Mafia?"

"Can we stop playing twenty questions? You know."

Now Castle really looked muddled. He had thought he was clever finding out Dub wasn't Krider, but all of this new stuff was flying by like hailstones. Everything told Dub that Castle didn't know Viek.

Castle suddenly turned his head from side to side, shoved Dub back, and headed for the phone in the foyer. Dub touched his thumb against the raw roof of his mouth and assessed his chances. The fireplace tools might have made good weapons if they weren't six feet away, if Castle weren't only twenty feet away, and if he didn't have a gun. Castle dialed. If Dub had been all there, he would have tried to catch the number. Castle waited as it rang, lifting the gun, aiming it at Dub and mouthing "Bang." Finally someone answered. He turned three-quarters away. He was speaking so Dub would not hear, but out of the mumbling Dub heard, "Viek. Yeah. Viek," then, "No, sir. The Mafia. Why the fuck would I make it up?"

Turn away, Dub thought. Turn. Just a little further. Instead Castle looked straight at him. "No, sir," he said clearly. "How should I know?" He raised his arms in exasperation and turned his back.

Dub spun himself over the sofa arm and charged the arch to the dining room. An end table clipped his side and crashed to the floor. "Hey!" Castle yelled. He fired and plaster sprayed the doorway. Dub flipped chairs behind him as he ran for the door opposite, his legs heavy as beer kegs, praying it wasn't locked. It popped open with a screech of its spring, then a four-finger hole exploded in it as it closed. The splinters peppered the kitchen and stung Dub's neck. The force of the shot, or the slickness of the floor, or the jelly in his knees made him stumble into the work island. He heard Castle crashing through the chairs.

Dub stood and snatched up the only thing in reach, an iron cooking ring on the stove. He turned as Castle kicked back the door, and flung it. Castle ducked, but the ring caught him hard on the cheek. He thudded against the door frame and fired again. Plaster rained from a gritty cloud, and Dub charged, catching Castle's gun arm between the swinging door and its frame, crushing the door against Castle's arm. He then grabbed the arm and pulled like he wanted to rip it out. Dub punched out, once, twice, three times. Somehow, the gun fired a third time, but the bullet smashed into a cupboard. Castle's free hand caught Dub on the ear, then he grunted and with a twitch of his entire body flung Dub against the cooking island. He lifted his bruised arm, still holding the gun, and lurched forward. He smiled with a bloody mouth and began to aim the Magnum, exhaling in pain. He had just brought up his other hand to steady his aim when Dub flung another cooking ring, which totally missed. Dub threw his shoulder into Castle's midsection and they careened backward. They scrambled, pushed, and fought for the gun, rolling along the counter, bouncing against the refrigerator. Dub couldn't get the gun out of Castle's hand. When they tumbled back into the cooking island, their heads ringing the copper pans dangling above, Castle got the gun over his head and brought it down on Dub's shoulder. Dub fell back against the opposite counter, and dropped to his knees. He reached up to stand, but it was too late. Castle was holding the gun in Dub's face with his left hand. The killer's face was like an amazed child's for a second, then his nostrils flared. "You broke my arm, you motherfucker! Get up," he hissed. "Get up! I've got questions for you and then you're dying hard."

Dub clawed at the counter edge and leaned over it toward the sink window. Strangely, he could hear someone squawking on the telephone in the foyer. The ceramic tiles felt cool. There wasn't enough air. His chest hurt. Dub wanted a drink of water before he died. Just one sip. This would be easier than Saigon, even if Castle beat him. One shot. No body bag. So much easier.

"Hello! What's going on? Hello!"

A strange, timid voice. Castle turned just slightly. In one movement, Dub plucked a self-sharpening knife from its holder on the side of a cabinet and brought it back and down in a large arc across Castle's face. Castle screamed, lifting both hands up to his split eye. Dub jammed the knife up hard into Castle's belly, throwing himself against Castle, pressing him against the butcher block, and ripping the knife through his midsection. His last, wet gasp of breath sprayed Dub's face, then he crumpled to the floor in a sitting position, his head settling into the gore between his knees. He died still holding the huge revolver.

Dub slumped against the sink. He reached to turn on the water, but his hands were shaking. He had turned into some kind of fevered, blood-mad animal. When a hand touched his shoulder, he thrashed out as if struck by an electric spark. The policeman jumped back and his partner yelled, "Cool it! Cool it! Hands high! HIGH!" The neighbor who had bumbled in was as pale as porcelain, with eyes like teacups. Dub looked back at Castle, face down in his own guts, and passed out.

SIX

The homicide detective's name was Ben Hawkins. He was a black bulldog with an old-fashioned pencil mustache and a jowly head with jaws that looked like they were made for chomping criminal throats. The only psychology he understood was hanging on until the suspect weakened and collapsed; a man born too late for his time, Dub thought, who would have been a rubber hose artist, but now spent his career assigned to two-dollar killings.

He sat Dub on a stool within six feet of the dead Castle and mirandized him as if he was too busy for legal malarkey. "Tell me about it," he barked.

Dub spoke in a daze. "I want to see Honoré St. Jean Devraix."

"Whadda you want to see him for?"

"I work for him."

"I know who works for him. You don't work for him."

Dub shook his head and cradled it in his hands.

"You're just stalling."

"I want to talk to Devraix."

"What's your name?"

"Devraix can explain."

Hawkins jerked Dub's chin up. "Look at me. You got a right to a lawyer and he ain't no lawyer. Now are you goin' to talk to me? What're you doing in this house?"

Dub twisted his head, but Hawkins's vise grip held. "Devraix!" Dub snarled.

Hawkins said "Aaa!" in disgust and raised a heavy hand as if he were going to slap Dub. It was a gesture perfected for

[53]

suspects who weren't sure Hawkins didn't have a rubber hose somewhere. "Look over there," he said. "That's a human being you killed. Maybe a family man. Maybe even a decent guy."

Dub turned toward the corpse, but closed his eyes. Even six feet away was too close. He felt like his bones had jellied. There was no silence like that of the dead.

"You got a minute to think about it," said Hawkins, "then you're gonna be a sorry bastard if you don't talk." Hawkins went into the dining room. Dub now expected the white lieutenant who was Hawkins's partner to play "good cop," but he merely stood with Hawkins in the dining room and whispered.

A crew showed up for fingerprints and photos. They dusted all around Dub. They examined Castle's body. He had no identification. The coroner's face as he straightened out the body had an impassiveness born of years of seeing gruesome things done to the human body. He sniffed as if the smell were mildly annoying. He unrolled rubber gloves to his elbows.

Hawkins gave another shot at intimidating Dub, telling him he knew that this was about drugs. It was probably just a ruse to get Dub to say something. Hawkins seemed resigned when it failed, and Devraix arrived ten minutes later. He talked with the detectives in the living room for twenty minutes. All Dub heard was Hawkins shouting, "You gonna tell me that was ordinary force?!" Dub's ears were filled with a low buzzing, as if he were going deaf. He held his head, both hands over his face, as if it might roll off. He was thirsty. He had never gotten the drink he wanted when he thought he was going to die. When Hawkins gestured that Dub should be brought into the living room, a patrolman had to help him walk.

"Dub, I've been explaining to the gentleman how we've been doing a security check for Mr. Krider," said Devraix.

"I want to hear it from you," said Hawkins to Dub.

"We'll totally cooperate," said Devraix.

"Quiet! Okay, now, Devraix is here. Talk."

Dub looked up. "It's like he said. Krider's on vacation." He sucked in a deep breath to blunt the sharp twinges in his chest. "He's—he's worried his alarm system isn't good enough. I came in to check and this guy was here with the gun. He was going to kill me. We struggled. I—I somehow got into the kitchen and there was the knife."

"Perhaps," interrupted Devraix, "we could come down tomorrow and give a statement, Detective Hawkins. Mr. Greenert hardly expected to kill anyone today."

Hawkins glared at Devraix. The dislike in his look was more than the usual disdain of regular cops for private ones. There was something about Devraix's refinement that really burned Hawkins. Maybe it was Devraix's superior Creole attitude, or perhaps Hawkins's visceral distaste for a half-breed more white than the whites. Whatever it was, it was plain Hawkins had now turned his anger toward Devraix and the anger was compounded by the knowledge that the case was going to be easily wrapped up by Devraix's explanation, though there must be more to it. The white lieutenant already looked bored, though he obviously didn't like the Creole any more than Hawkins did.

"Look, man," said Hawkins to Dub, "I don't see why a guy like you wasn't satisfied with a couple of stabs. You cut his face in half, then you gut the guy. You cut all the way through a three-inch cowhide belt, for Pete's sake. Why'd you do all that?"

"I don't know," Dub swallowed. "It happened fast. I didn't know what I was doing. The guy was going to kill me and—" He thought of his little girls. "He was going to kill me."

"You better fucking hope I don't find a connection between you two."

The white detective looked up from his notepad. "You're working for Devraix for two days and bingo, a guy tries to shoot you. Welcome to New Orleans. Try not to make our lives so tough, eh?"

"Don't worry. Pittsburgh looks better by the second."

"One other thing," said Hawkins. Dub tilted his head to signal he was only pretending interest. "Lots of blood in here. Maybe you ought to think about an AIDS test." He paused to let it sink in, then lifted one lip as if amused. "Have a nice day, Greenert."

There were reporters out front, so they slipped Dub out the back while Devraix and Hawkins distracted them. Vonna waited in an old Ford. They were silent for some time after they pulled away, then Vonna tapped the dash. "There's gin in the glove compartment."

"I'll mess your seat," said Dub.

"I'll find you a toilet."

He nodded. They stopped at a Popeyes fried chicken. He felt steadier when he came out, but the concern on her usually passive face made him try a weak joke. "Crimestoppers' tip, Vonna: Never kill anybody on a stomach full of beignets."

She lifted one eyebrow and drove on. "R.I.P. Castle," she sighed.

Dub traded his ticket to Pittsburgh for one to Charleston. He called Calabrese and said he needed a week off. His ex-wife and her new husband greeted him coolly—they didn't like him showing up unannounced—but Beth was obviously going to be having a third child in a couple of months and after a cold beer they gradually gave in to their general good feelings. They didn't, he noticed, give in to their natural curiosity about the Band-Aids on his forehead and cheek.

Dub always felt odd visiting his girls. The job made it impossible to predict when he would be free, and he envied divorced fathers who could specify two weeks in December, weekends in the summer, and so forth. Although there was a decree somewhere outlining the amount of time to which he was entitled, neither he nor Beth had ever paid much attention to it. He called, usually, and arrived like a good uncle, bearing gifts, sloppy kisses, and trips for soft ice cream.

When Beth and he had divorced ten years previous, there wasn't that much enmity. High school sweethearts, they had married during one of his leaves just before he was sent to Vietnam, and by the time he got back, both of them were different: He was desperately trying to refind what he had lost in the two years; she had found much more of who she was. They hung on for several years, then ended with more whimper than explosion. The sex had lost its spark. It was never really good with anyone after Janet in Saigon, but they tried it enough that Elizabeth, the eldest daughter, was born two years after he left Vietnam and Carrie eighteen months after that. Both were perhaps the result of trying to recover all he and Beth had felt in the prewar past as golden as legend, but most of the girls' life had been spent with their "new daddy."

Neither why they were conceived nor their life with their stepfather mattered. Dub loved them like he had never loved anybody, including Beth. Maybe even more than Janet. Like he could never love anybody again. Whenever the mood was upon him, late at night in a lonely car on an empty street, when he thought of his own death or when he noticed another story in the *Pittsburgh Post-Gazette* about a kid's accidental death, he would think how any time he saw them could be the last time, and all he wanted to do was squeeze his girls tight against him, smell their hair, and tell them how much he loved them.

This mood was on him during his visit. Elizabeth, who was going to be gawky tall, found him embarrassing a few times and said so. She was already at the age at which she was proving to everyone she wasn't a child. If Dub hugged her in public, she said seriously, it might look like some ancient sugar daddy with his bimbo. Dub laughed and hugged her again. She was just over twelve and looked it, even if she did sneak a little mascara on her eyelashes. He might be taken for a child molester, but never an old guy with his bimbo.

Carrie, on the other hand, was still both old enough and young enough to enjoy her childhood. When he took them to the open market in Charleston and they bumped among the tourists, Elizabeth fretted about being seen eating a Nutty Buddy and chattered about how much better Häagen-Dazs was. Carrie simply ate. Dub watched Elizabeth trying to pick out the most adult scarves while her eyes wandered to the stuffed animals. Carrie read risqué T-shirts out loud, saying, "Look! Look! Not that one. The *really* gross one!" and forced Dub to play father by making him refuse to buy something she could get any time she wanted. Like a concerned parent, Elizabeth told him, "Momma says she wishes you'd settle down and stop catting around." Carrie recited the entire plot and most of the jokes of *The Princess Bride*. It was a happy three days. He took them to Fort Sumter, which they had seen dozens of times, but they enjoyed the boat ride and scrambling over the rocks. He took them on a tour of a Navy destroyer. He took them on a tour of an antebellum mansion, though the cab cost them over twenty dollars each way. He even, because Elizabeth said she might like to go there, took them to the Citadel on Friday to watch the trooping of the colors. It made him fidgety, though he tried not to show it, and he sensed he should go back to Pittsburgh before he got used to being with them.

It was another week before anyone decided to call him from New Orleans and tell him that everything had been covered. Vonna explained that with Vernon Krider's corroboration (Krider must have owed Devraix an enormous favor) the police accepted that Dub had stumbled in on a robbery and had killed to save his life. The police had found out nothing remarkable about George Castle. His real name was Lamont George. He'd been born in Willow Grove, Pennsylvania, and educated in Parris Island and Hue. Gone bad after that, he hadn't worked for a long time, and had no known residence in Louisiana. The police assumed these things were explained by his having taken up crime. They turned up a license for his .357 in Philadelphia. The gun was first registered in 1978.

"The police didn't get on to the Erie stuff?" asked Dub.

"They never knew he was there, about the ad, nothing."

"Shouldn't they know?"

"You must like trouble."

"What would happen if they ever turned up the people that saw me in that bar with him?"

Vonna chuckled. "You'd have a hard row with that. Forget it. No relatives. Nothing. Nobody knew Lamont George or Castle or whatever the hell. Nobody claimed the body."

Dub drummed his fingers on the desk. "You really think that? Christ, Vonna, I don't know. The guy was in the murder business. He called somebody. He said 'we' this and 'we' that."

"I say the man was in it for the con. He just went after you because he'd been stung. The dude stripped a few gears. You don't set up Murder Incorporated with a registered gun you've been hauling around for ten years."

Dub could still taste the gun. His tongue touched the scar on the roof of his mouth. He remembered what it felt like to drive the knife into Castle's belly.

"Yo! You there?"

"Yeah. Yeah. I guess you're right. Still . . ."

"So maybe he had some friends. We got no way of knowing that."

"He called somebody, Vonna."

"He could've had a girlfriend."

"Come on! You don't believe that?"

"There's just nowhere to go with it. It was a local call or there'd be a record of it. Maybe there was somebody with him at a hotel. Who knows? The trail's cold. Unless something else turns up. . . ."

"What about Eddie Viek?"

"Well, that's gone to nothing too. Mrs. O'Dell's accountants, slow as they are, aren't finding much. One of them thinks he's dealing with a false set of books, but hasn't come up with anything that proves it. We'll stick with it as long as the old woman wants, but I don't know. I think Viek's either too slick, or just didn't off O'Dell. The last time Mrs. O'Dell came in, she didn't look too good. I got the idea she was thinking about putting the whole business behind her. She got real shook about what happened to you."

"What does Devraix think?"

"He never says."

"And you?"

"I think we ought to try to follow the relays and find out where the calls were going. I expect we'd just find an answering machine in another empty office, but you never know."

"I'll do that," said Dub.

"If you say so. I guess you can send the bill to Devraix."

"No, I want to do it. I hate loose ends. You get enough of the damn things in this business."

"Send the bill anyway. And, say, if you ever get down here again maybe I'll show you some places not in the tour guide."

"Thanks," said Dub. That was nice of her. He hung up wondering if she'd meant to imply more than she said. He remembered their all-nighter at the Café du Monde. He had the feeling that too much had been left unsaid.

Dub's trip to Erie wasted a whole day and cost $150 for Calabrese to come up with a kid from Carnegie-Mellon who could find out what number the computer was relaying calls to. The office Vonna had checked was no different, that Dub could tell, from her original description. The doorknob hadn't been redusted. The whiz kid found the relay number in twenty minutes. They called Calabrese, who found out the location. It was a vacant apartment four blocks away. No computer, no furniture. No one had ever seen the tenant move in or out. At first Dub got excited, thinking that this proved Castle had an accomplice. Somewhere on I-79, however, while the college boy studied a fat math book, it seemed just as plausible that Castle had pulled out the equipment when he discovered the first location had been compromised. Dead ends. Loose ends in dead ends. Who had Castle called from Krider's house?

Life went back to normal. Long cold nights with a thermos of cheap coffee and a loaded camera waiting for another adulterer. The flash and run. The plopping of the photos in front of the wronged spouse. The endless fencing with coy clerks who imagine that every detective has a pocket full of sawbucks that they give away to anyone who can identify a photo. The runaway teenagers who don't want to be found. The store managers who have things disappearing from the loading docks. It gets to be a way of life and "normal life"—the life you see on TV—begins to seem a fantasy. One night, one very lonely night, he telephoned Brenda. She called him a son of a bitch and hung up. He felt almost relieved by it. He got drunk instead and lost $100 shooting pool. When he got back to his apartment, it was three a.m. He couldn't call Elizabeth and Carrie, so he started writing them a letter that would make them laugh. He fell asleep on it and when he was late to an appointment the next morning Calabrese told him he ought to get his shit together, stop paying child support to a woman who didn't need it, and buy himself some clothes. Along with saying Dub must be the only moron in the nation still making his support payments, it was Calabrese's standard advice, and he knew Dub would never take it. Those payments were the most material thing connecting him to his daughters. Relying on love was too chancy. Or maybe it was some kind of expiation to Beth for having lost himself. Whatever it was, Dub kept mailing the money orders, implying to Beth it was merely pocket change, and plodding from paycheck to paycheck. If you're getting by, don't ask too many questions, he told himself. Just relax.

It was a rainy Labor Day when Vonna called him at home. He was in his underwear, eating Fritos and bean dip, and watching a preseason comedy of errors between the Steelers and the Falcons. She didn't identify herself or ease into the conversation. "I think this might interest you," she said. "Clementine O'Dell blew away Eddie Viek yesterday. Her lawyer wants to see you."

SEVEN

The ticket was waiting when he got to the airport Tuesday morning. Dub hesitated at the door of the plane and smiled at the stewardess while thinking once again that it wasn't such a good idea to go back to Louisiana. Mrs. O'Dell's shooting Viek might bring out enough to make Hawkins pissed enough to come up with an obstruction charge on the Castle killing. Making him extradite Dub from Pennsylvania might slow him down just enough to keep him from doing it.

"Can I help you with something, sir?" said the stewardess.

"No," said Dub. "No." He shrugged. "I was distracted."

"Why, thank you," said the stewardess, blushing.

Dub stepped forward and a man in a blue jacket clunked the door shut behind him. The sound was solid, permanent, and final.

By late afternoon he was in one of the large offices of Diehl, Everman, and Pallette. Devraix said, "How do you do?" Vonna nodded.

"Take a seat, Mr. Greenert," said the man behind the desk. They all waited for the attorney to begin. Everman, with carefully styled white hair, looked like a television evangelist, despite his red bow tie and peach suit. He fiddled constantly with a ballpoint pen, often chewing at it. He'd probably just given up smoking, Dub guessed.

"Now I tell you what, I don't really trust private investigators," Everman said. "I tell you that up front, Mr. Devraix, just so's we understand this ain't got nothing to do with you being colored. But I been protecting the O'Dell money a good while and my daddy before me, and I mean to protect Clementine, and that means, I think, I got to trust you three. She was a beautiful young woman once, and she's still beautiful to me, and I'm not about to see her stuck in some jail or treated like she deserves it."

"None of us would like to see that," said Devraix.

"I'm glad to hear it. Now everything I'm telling you in this room stays in this room. It's all going to come out in discovery this Thursday anyhow, but I'll be pretty teed off if I find it in the *Times-Picayune* tomorrow morning."

"You can count on our discretion," said Devraix.

"Glad to hear it." Everman opened a brown folder. "Okay, now, this is what we're gonna explain happened when we go to court. Unless something happens, we're gonna plead self-defense. Now maybe I can get the state to drop the charges that way—who knows? If they don't want to deal we'll lay it out for the judge and fight it every inch of the way with every delaying tactic I know."

Detective Hawkins's angry face flashed across Dub's eyes.

"August fifteenth, the accounting firm of Johnson and Courtland called Mrs. O'Dell and told her they had proof that the *Gumbolaya!* books they'd been auditing were false. Viek had made them up somehow." Everman looked up. "He was a shifty guy, but damn good at this. If it wasn't for this one accountant, a Vincent Puzzoli, who used to work for IRS, well, who knows? Puzzoli spotted fake deliveries to building sites; most trucking companies don't work on Sundays. He noticed the dates were Sundays."

"It's the simple stuff that gets you," said Dub.

"You bet," said Everman. "All right, then. Clementine hears, gets all excited, calls me. I tell her to hold her cards to her—ah—self, but she can't resist calling Viek. She tells him she knows. The next day he shoves the gardener into a birdbath, breaking the poor fella's collarbone. He knocks the maid down when she tries to slam the door in his face. He finds Mrs. O'Dell in her library and she puts six bullets through him. Does this sound like self-defense to you? Sounds awful good to me. The state won't want this in front of a jury."

"Sounds clean to me," said Vonna.

"Sure does. The only things working against it are the fact that she bought the gun only two weeks before and that she emptied it into him. Two weeks could look like premeditation."

"But Viek came to her," said Dub.

"Absolutely. She shot him in the shoulder, grazed his ear, then scattered four in his torso. It's not the shooting of someone who's cool and collected. More, I think, like somebody fearing for her life. Am I right? So, what's the problem, you're thinking." He closed the folder. "Killing this crook Viek ain't the problem. The problem is this possibility that Viek might have killed Michael. You people, me, and Clementine are the only ones who know about this Castle business."

"I'm afraid you need to enlighten us simple colored folks, Mr. Everman," said Devraix, gesturing in a way that made Dub realize he was being included in the "simple colored folks." "In what sense does this harm her case?"

"She'd be even more afraid of the dude," said Vonna.

"Yes," said Everman. "*If* you people had come up with anything tying Viek and Castle together. But you didn't. It's mighty easy to make the whole thing into a fantasy."

"So?" said Vonna.

"Right," said Dub. "She killed him because she was afraid or she killed him because she thought he killed her husband. Either way—"

"Naw, naw, naw," said Everman, "you miss the point. There's big money involved here. I don't want that woman branded unstable, damn it. She isn't. We all know that. I don't know what you know about her children, but two of them, well, let's just say I wouldn't put it past them to, ah, exploit the situation. This isn't entirely a question of shooting Eddie Viek, you see. I don't want all that dragged in. Some discretion here is what is needed. If the police do a little poking in Clementine's checkbook and find out she hired the Devraix Agency—"

"Mrs. O'Dell hired us to look into Mr. Viek and his associates," said Devraix.

"That isn't a lie," said Vonna.

"No," said Everman. "For all we know this Lamont George/ George Castle character did kill Michael, but he's dead now and so is Viek."

"I don't particularly want anybody finding out about Castle either," said Dub.

"Good," said Everman. "I think we understand each other. Understand, there's no need to lie. As an officer of the court I would never counsel you to lie." He opened his drawer. "Now, I believe it would be appropriate to settle a bonus upon each of you for such fine work. Does five thousand seem appropriate?"

"No," said Dub.

"Seventy-five hundred, then?" Everman looked irritated, but not surprised. There was a lot of money in keeping Mrs. O'Dell's business out of her children's hands.

"I mean I don't want to be paid off," said Dub.

"I'm not bribing you," said Everman. "How about you two?"

Vonna looked disgusted. "No. He's right. We've been paid. The job's finished." She popped out a puff of air as if she hated herself, but wasn't going to give Everman the satisfaction of proving "coloreds" would go for the money when Dub wouldn't.

"Are you sure? It's all—"

"And how is Mrs. O'Dell?" asked Devraix.

"She's at home. Sedatives. I don't think they'd have hauled her in at all if they weren't afraid somebody'd say they're soft on the rich. People say it anyway, regardless."

"Maybe because they are," said Vonna.

"The rich have nice clothes," said Everman indifferently.

On the street, Vonna punched Dub in the arm. "Next time speak for yourself, won't you? Damn! Five thousand."

Dub winked at her. "You wouldn't have taken it."

She squinted angrily. "Maybe. Maybe the bastard would have talked me into it. What's wrong with a tip? A b-i-i-i-g tip."

"It makes us look lily-white if everything falls apart," said Devraix, climbing into the back seat.

"Okay, boss," said Vonna. "O-kay."

"One other thing," said Devraix seriously. "I want you to report to my office tomorrow. I'm going to have to put a disciplinary note in your file."

"What?" She had just begun to turn the car away from the curb. The car lurched when she slammed the brake.

"Again and again I've told you to be careful with case files, and now I discover the Michael O'Dell file is missing."

"Missing? What do you mean 'missing'? I—ohhhh."

"I am totally shocked," said Devraix. "Imagine if someone wished to subpoena it, for instance."

Vonna had a twinkle in her eye. "I put it right on your desk last week, boss. I'll write you a memo about it."

"You have got to learn to be more careful. I'll check with the cleaning woman."

"Yes, indeed," said Vonna. "Yes, indeed."

Vonna dropped Devraix at the office. She squinted through the glaring windshield for several seconds, then said, "You ever been to Gator's? Let's go to Gator's."

"What's Gator's?" asked Dub.

"Best red beans and rice in the world," said Vonna. "Hot enough to make your nose run."

"Hey, I just want to get the next plane out," said Dub. "This town makes me jumpy."

"You don't come to New Orleans without eating, mister," said Vonna. "They'll stop you from leaving. It's the law."

"That so?"

"Sure, when you go through the X-ray, they make sure you got some food in you."

"Well," said Dub, "as long as I leave tonight."

"I'll even treat. I'll walk in on your arm like I'm your brown sugar."

"Christ," he said, "you do know how to persuade a guy. Drive on, woman. Put the pedal to the floor."

Gator's was a black hangout in a very black neighborhood. The sign was hand-painted, and the whole place was peeling in the humidity. In Pittsburgh or Philly the street would have been one of those out-of-sight, out-of-mind places that make politicians start pitching the word "bootstraps," and cabbies avoid. But there were a dozen cars in the seedy parking lot, and two gangly adolescents near the front door tap-dancing for tips. Inside there were only a few empty tables. The air was fragrant with thyme and frying sausage, and each of the twenty or so rickety tables had a worn vinyl tablecloth and a bottle of hot sauce. Vonna gestured toward the only two white faces in the place and said, "See? Crackers come in here all the time. The food's so good it makes you color-blind." All the same, the appearance of a mixed couple made several people look up, then go back to their dinners.

The portions of red beans and rice were enormous and all sorts of marvelous smells rose from each forkful: onions, garlic, different types of sausage and meat, fat kidney beans, and fingers of chili pepper that swelled the tongue. Vonna and Dub drank long-necked Jax and told each other more wild stories from the business. Vonna let out that Devraix had opened his detective agency because of a weakness for Nero Wolfe novels. She also confessed that after the Army, when she had worked for the post office and the carrier's bag was heavy, she had thrown away some of the junk mail. They ate and laughed until it hurt. She was a different person, not as controlled, comfortable to be with. It hardly felt like being with a woman at all. Dub almost forgot about flying home.

About nine, the food and beer started making him sluggish. Dub yawned. "Excuse me. Maybe I'd better get out to the airport before I fall asleep on the table."

"Don't go," she said. She bit her lower lip as if embarrassed for having blurted it out and picked at the Jax label. She was being shy in a way he didn't think she could be. It was cute, Dub thought. She was a nice woman under her toughness.

"Well, really," he said, "I ought to get out of this burg."

She looked up from the beer. "Charge a room to Everman. He won't care."

"Hotels charge too much for a lousy sleep. Anyhow, I keep thinking that if I don't get out of here I'm going to get into something deep."

"Come home with me."

They were both startled. It was instantly clear that this had nothing to do with simply staying or with the price of a hotel, and Dub simultaneously realized how difficult it was for her to say it. He started to explain that he hadn't meant that he was afraid of getting in deep with her. He hadn't really thought of her as someone to sleep with. He'd really been thinking of Hawkins. "It's the climate," he said. "It throws me." He didn't know why he said that. Maybe it was the beer.

She stared down at her peelings of label and avoided his

eyes. "I'm sorry," she said. "I won't complicate your life. It's just one night. Every now and then I need it, so I get it."

"It ain't you. I had a bad time in Saigon," he said. "The heat, the humidity, it sort of takes me back." He paused and thought of Janet—her golden body, her legs around him, the look on her face as the body bag closed. He shook it out of his head. "It was tough on the fourth, you know, when I called you. When we talked it was—well, it carried me through the spell. I really appreciated that. Lately the spells even hurt." He tapped his chest. "Like a real bad heartburn. Sometimes I have the same problem when I visit my daughters in Charleston and it's warm there. It takes all the energy in me to fight it, but I've got to see my daughters. Sometimes it comes over me in Pittsburgh, but that isn't too often and I just wait it out. There isn't much I can do about it other than move to Alaska or someplace that's always cold. Am I making sense?"

"What happened over there?"

He twitched his shoulder. "Bad stuff."

"When I was in, I met some dudes who told me about some pretty bad times."

"If they could talk about it, it wasn't that bad."

She nodded. Her aloofness had returned. For a woman who had gone way out on a limb and sawed it off by propositioning him, she was pretty game. "You could tell me about it. You want another beer?"

"I'll bust a gut."

She nodded and finished her stripped bottle. "I guess we'd better get you a plane," she said.

"No," he said touching her arm. "I'll stay. If you want me to, I'll stay." He didn't know why he was saying it, exactly. It seemed like he had opened himself up to her, though he really hadn't, and that meant there should be more intimacy between them.

"Hey, I don't need charity."

"It's for me," he said. He knew that's what she needed to hear. He was sure he wasn't saying it because she seemed lonely, though maybe it was because he was feeling sorry for himself. She took his hand and laced his fingers through hers. He continued, "I can't promise anything. I—"

She tossed her shoulder, trying to make a joke of it. "I've

been hurt too. Hey, it's just a night." Then she squeezed his hand. She was strong, he realized, but only faked being hard.

On the drive to her apartment the whole thing took on the quality of an illogical dream; he was being led who knows where for unknown reasons. He thought they ought to go to a drugstore but he didn't know how to ask her. He thought, I've never been to bed with a woman this heavy, and tried to imagine her body, but he only came up with naked Aunt Jemimas and felt guilty for it. He got anxious that all the beer would make him unable to carry it off. On the other hand, it had been a long time since the night with Brenda. When he was younger there hadn't been such gaps in his love life and maybe that meant he was losing it. The red beans and rice also seemed to be swelling in his belly, making him dopey. Was he intimidated by a black woman? He tried to rev himself up with the fantasy that all black women were passionate, experienced wildcats, but was put off by the parallel myth that they were always disappointed by white men. Was he big enough? You could rationally know all this was nonsense but still have it ticking in your head. I don't know about this, he sighed to himself. I don't know. If I wasn't so packed with food. . . . If I wasn't so tired. . . .

Her apartment was 1960s suburban: two-floor boxes with balconies facing the swimming pool and parking lot. Monster air-conditioning units roared at the end of each building. It started to rain. Big, tropical drops the size of bottle caps exploded on the car windows. They hurried into the corridor and looked back at the downpour and he realized that he was really going to go through with this. "It's like a monsoon," he said. Still holding her keys, she put her arms around his neck and kissed him for so long and so intensely he thought she might try to have him there on the linoleum. Their lips parted, they hugged tightly, and listened to each other's breath.

"Hell of a rain," she said.

"Yes. Listen," he said, "I feel a little stupid about this but I think maybe we should have stopped at a drugstore."

"Are you afraid I'm dirty?" she asked quietly.

What was in her voice? Offense? Did she think he would assume a black woman was more dangerous than a white? "No," he said. "But babies, well, you know."

"Are you trying to chicken out?" she purred. "I have some in my apartment."

"Some?" He grinned. "Are you sure there are enough?"

"I hope so, but then, maybe, I hope not." She leaned back, a hand on each of his cheeks, the car keys tinkling in his left ear. "They were giving them away in Jackson Square one day. It's not like I do this often. I don't. You look so serious."

He didn't know what to say. Just after the kiss he had begun to feel detached again. Maybe it wouldn't be any better with a black woman. Maybe the shields would always be up.

"I put them in my medicine cabinet. I didn't know I was saving them for a cracker."

"Ain't love wonderful?" he said.

Their laughter echoed in the empty corridor. He quickly pressed his lips against hers and once again the old hurts faded. He felt comfortable for the first time in weeks.

EIGHT

Dub woke. The twilight before dawn glowed under the hem of the heavy curtains. It took him a few seconds to see he was not in his own room, though his pants were dumped in a heap near the closet door, his white underwear beside them, and his jacket on a chair. An iconlike portrait of Martin Luther King Jr. hung on the opposite wall with a sprig of artifical lavender on top of it. King's face phosphoresced in a bar of light and his eyes seemed to be watching the swirling motes. Dub rolled onto his back, saw Vonna snoring softly, her lips parted and swollen, then lay back on his pillow blinking at the ceiling. You shouldn't feel guilty, he told himself, it was a need for you and a need for her. You didn't pretend. You didn't say you loved her.

She inhaled a tiny moan and pushed her face against his shoulder, making him feel guilty for not telling her he loved her. He could have told her he loved her for that one night, just for that night. She was a woman, up-to-date or not, black or not, and probably liked to hear it, true or not, but he had withheld it as if it made him a bit more moral. In the heat of the act he had wanted to, but he held back. She was a woman, he reminded himself. For once he had not thought of Janet's breasts when kissing a woman's breasts. He had felt able to give himself over to her without seeing Janet's cold stare, without feeling the air getting tight. For once, he had slept an entire night with a woman without once waking up and imagining that her elbow was the elbow of the poor bastard in pieces he had thrashed around on top of. Maybe this was the solution. Janet had been so white. Maybe all he needed was a woman with chocolate skin and nipples of dusty violet. "Brown sugar," he mumbled. His mouth was cottony and he wanted to get to the airport. He closed his eyes, however, and went back to sleep.

Sometime later the phone rang. Vonna jumped into a sitting position, her fragrant shoulders filling most of Dub's view. She plopped back when she understood it was the phone. "Shit!" she said, eyes closed and arms crossed to cradle her heavy bosom. "Go away." It must have rung half a dozen times before Dub asked, "You want me to get it?"

She exhaled. "Shit!" She rolled over and lifted the receiver off the floor. "Huh? Give me a break! It's—it's"—she picked up her clock radio, also on the floor—"six-thirty. What the hell for? Huh?" She was suddenly wide awake. She shifted around, breasts swinging, exposing her entire body as if she had forgotten she was naked. She covered the mouthpiece. "It's Devraix," she whispered. "Ho-ly shit." She touched her forehead like someone trying to recover from a dizzy spell. "No. Dub is here. I meant in town. No, I'll call him. Well, really, he's on the sofa." She rolled her eyes in exasperation. "Right. I'll get him." She put her hand over the mouthpiece again.

"You ain't gonna believe this, baby. I guarantee you." She nodded her head as if counting the time it would take to get Dub from the sofa. He lifted himself on one elbow, leaned, and impulsively kissed the light coffee of her inner thigh. She quickly planted a kiss on his receding widow's peak and handed him the phone.

"Hello?"

"You certainly took your time."

"I was in the living room."

"That is between you two. Listen to this: 'PROBLEMS? I know what you mean. I can get what's in your way, out of your way. Medal-winning vet ready to serve. Location no problem. Satisfaction guaranteed. Call Castle. I am your Man.' "

"So?" said Dub, wiping his face with his hand. "Castle's ad."

"But this is the *Mercenary* that was delivered to the newsstands *last night*."

"So? Lamont George expected to be in business a while. He bought six months' worth."

"The telephone number is different."

Dub blinked.

"The number in the advertisement has changed. Do you understand me? The area code is for Maryland this time."

"Where in Maryland?"

"I don't know. I haven't called. Somewhere in Maryland. It isn't that large a state, is it?"

"Hold on. Let me think."

Dub put his hand over the mouthpiece. His eyes moved from side to side as if the answer might be written on the carpet or curtains. "Okay," he said quickly. "It was intentional. Maybe Castle moved regularly. Like every so many months. State to state." He turned to Vonna, his face twisted. "Do you believe that?" She rolled her eyes and shrugged. "I don't either. But it's possible, isn't it?" He thought some more. "Okay, wait. I've got it. I've got it. Sure."

"Well?" asked Devraix.

"When Castle saw that his relay in Erie had been compromised, he called in a change on the ad. Alternate location. Bingo."

"Possible," mused Devraix. "But possible only. Write down this number, then dial it. *Don't*, however, say anything to the machine." He dictated the number, Dub recited it, and Vonna wrote it on the pad she kept on the nightstand. "I think you'll find it illuminating. I'll meet you at Junior's in forty-five minutes." He hung up.

"He said he'll meet us at Junior's."

Vonna nodded. "What does this mean?"

He dialed the number. There was ringing and clicking as one relay transferred the call to another. Vonna pressed her ear against the outside of the receiver and they listened to it between them. "Hello, this is Castle, veteran and soldier of fortune. Whatever the problem I can handle it. If there's an obstacle in your way, I can remove it. Leave your name and number at the tone and I'll get right back. Thank you."

" 'We'!" said Dub. "George kept saying 'we'!"

She took the phone from him and slammed it in its cradle. They stared at each other. It hadn't been Lamont George's voice.

Dub and Vonna dressed and reached Junior's ten minutes early. Antique fans rotated slowly above the mahogany bar. Dub drank three cups of coffee to jump-start his brain. Vonna ate a raspberry-filled donut. She looked at her watch and said, "Shit! I should've taken a shower." Neither mentioned the previous night. Dub felt like something had been lifted off him. Vonna, however, avoided his eyes. The post-sex blues, he thought.

Devraix flopped the *Mercenary* next to Dub, almost flung a chair from another table against theirs and sat on it backward, arms crossed on top. It was odd to see a man so nattily dressed sitting like that. "Well?" he asked.

"We call up the new guy and set up another killing," said Vonna. "How else we flush 'em out?"

"You have read my mind," said Devraix. He touched her arm. "Who do I say I want killed?"

"Hold on," said Dub. "Are you forgetting what happened to me?" He rubbed his forehead where there was still a small white scar from being struck. "We can't go into this easy. Anyhow, Lamont George wasn't too fond of people your shade. Maybe they won't work for you."

"I sound whiter than you on the telephone, God forgive me," said Devraix.

Vonna shook her head. "He'd have to see you sometime. Dub's right. You can't bleach God's paint job, Honoré."

Devraix gave her a look. He didn't like being called Honoré, but he was more disappointed because he knew she was right. He studied Dub.

Dub shook his head. "I stuck my head in the lion's mouth once already."

"That's right," said Vonna. "I'll call them. A woman might be a good cover: cry a lot, shit like that."

"No, no," said Dub. "Wrong color again."

"You don't think I can do it. You sure as shit can't do it. They might know you."

"That might be good," said Dub, "for drawing them out, but, look, how much did we find out from locating Lamont George? Dead ends. Zip."

"So whatever can we do? Trace the telephone lines?" said

Devraix. "We would have to do it extremely rapidly, or they would simply cut the chain ahead of us."

"You're right," said Dub. "Maybe we should step aside and let the FBI go with this. It's across state lines. I think it's time for the Federales."

"Dub's right," sighed Vonna, "and setting up the thing will cost big money. It's federal to use the phones for criminal purposes, isn't it? Let the FBI do it."

"You know you don't mean that. This is the hunt! We try a phone call. A meeting's set. You and Dub pretend to be cops, perhaps the man panics and can't stop talking."

"Maybe he says, 'Where's my lawyer?' " said Vonna.

Devraix pursed his lips. He knew confessions only came out of witnesses on "Perry Mason." Dub contemplated the grounds at the bottom of his coffee cup. He tapped the *Mercenary*. "How about another approach? Somebody placed the ad. Somebody paid for it. There's got to be a record."

"We tried that. We didn't get anywhere," said Vonna.

"But you were trying to get them to cooperate, to give it to you. I say we try to get somebody on the inside."

"We tried to bribe a clerk. They're real loyal, or at least that's the way it came out," said Vonna.

"I say call the number," said Devraix.

"The *Mercenary* angle first," said Dub.

"I think Dub's right," said Vonna.

"You're hardly impartial this morning," said Devraix pleasantly. Vonna looked away.

They talked it over several times but got no further. Devraix gradually calmed down, turned around, and assumed his usual expression, that of a lama placidly spinning his prayer wheel. He began to hint that they should, if they were sensible, abandon any case that lacked a paying client behind it, but he began tapping the tips of his fingers together, which Vonna knew meant his early excitement was still working on him. A conspiracy of murderers was exactly the kind of thing that gave publicity and could help business immensely, as long as it didn't irritate the police. By lunchtime he had decided. "A compromise," he stated. "We shall pursue it in a limited fashion, but as a hobby, as it were. We shall not neglect other business for it. Account for your expenditures the ordinary way."

"And what about Dub?" asked Vonna.

Devraix thought. "Very well. I shall allot four days at usual rates for his seeing what he can uncover in Tampa. If nothing comes of it, I'm afraid you'll have to go back to Keyhole."

"That's fair," said Dub.

"And what about me?" asked Vonna.

"I need you," said Devraix. She hissed with disappointment. She had ways, she said, "brother" ways to find out things, but Devraix said flatly that Dub was very good, according to Calabrese, and that there was a very profitable electronic surveillance waiting for Vonna. She complained again, but Devraix repeated that Dub could do it alone, as long as he contacted the agency Devraix had ties with in Tampa. "If there is anything to get," said Devraix, "Dub shall get it. Am I right?"

"You bet," said Dub.

After three days in Tampa, however, he was beginning to wonder if he'd left all his skills in Pittsburgh. *Mercenary* was on the top two floors in a five-floor glass box with security at the front door. He watched the normal routine for one day and night, learning very little. Supplies were delivered into a garage in the back, through a very well-lit steel door. On the second day, Dub dressed up in a hunting vest and a Cat hat, filled his mouth with chewing tobacco, and went inside to place a classified. The front-door guard said he should call it in. Dub did a kind of "Shucks, I was just driving on by" number and the guard checked upstairs. "Sign in," said the guard. "Fourth floor. Ask for Lex Tyrone."

"Thank ye," said Dub. He crossed the black marble floor and pressed the elevator button. He scanned the directory. The second floor had the Central American Freedom League and a law firm with Spanish surnames. The third floor held Comex, Liberty Books, and the All-American Industry Group. Each of these had to be pretty large, he thought, if so few were on each floor. The elevator door opened and three Hispanics in sunglasses and expensive suits emerged. He had just stepped inside when he noticed a man in camouflage fatigues walking quickly by the guard. He was followed by two lean, bodyguard types, wearing suits and aviator sunglasses. The guard nodded at them and none of them stopped to sign in. Dub held the elevator. The bodyguards stepped in front of the man they were guarding and looked Dub over.

"Goin' up?" he asked.

"Get in," said the man.

They moved in. One of the bodyguards pulled out what appeared to be a gold watch chain and stretched a key out to the lock beside the number five. Dub noticed that the guards wore identical fat rings. They would do a lot of damage on a face. "All the way up, eh boys?" said Dub, grinning idiotically. "Why you must be the owner! Are you the owner?"

The bodyguards looked threatening, but the man said, "Yes, I am. Robert Belgrade. Do you work with the printing staff? I don't believe I've met you."

"You do your own printing? Right in this byootiful building? Doggone. I'm on my way up to put in a classified. I got some guns I got to sell."

"We thank you for your interest," said Belgrade. "Are you a vet?"

"Yessir. During the Tet. I call myself a Tet vet." He grinned like an idiot again.

"I appreciate it," said Belgrade, shaking Dub's hand warmly.

"I 'preciate your magazine," said Dub, "an' all ye do for us." The doors opened on the fourth floor.

There was security by the elevator also—a uniformed guard with a sign-in sheet and an Alsatian lying on the floor behind him. "I was tol' to ask for Lex Tyrone?"

"Sign here. End of the corridor to the left, when that splits, turn right." He scrutinized the signature. "Third office on the right, Mr. Taylor."

"Thank ye." Dub spat sloppily into a wastebasket.

This wasn't going to be easy, thought Dub. And why does a magazine need all this security? Afraid of a raid by *Soldier of Fortune*? Afraid the Red Army will assault the building? And Belgrade! Wearing fatigues to the office to maintain his image. How to become a millionaire. If he'd ever spent any real time in fatigues, with mud up to his ass, he sure wouldn't wear them in his limo. Did the world ever make sense any more?

Dub deliberately turned right at the end of the corridor in an attempt to get lost, but that only led to the huge double doors of the print shop, briefly open as a woman pushed a hand cart through them. He went back the other way and found the glass door marked Classified. There were three desks. Two women were typing. A third was on the telephone. Both side walls were lined with file cabinets. The back wall was smoked glass through which he could barely see an inner office.

"I was told to see Lex Tyrone," said Dub.

"He's in a meeting."

"Oh," said Dub. He blinked stupidly and sucked at a tooth.

"Well?"

"Well I had these guns I wanted to sell. . . ." He gave her the "aw shucks" business again and spat into another wastebasket. She took a sheet from another desk. She wrote out the false ad after explaining they'd prefer him to call in. He pretended to want to pay in cash, but she said they could bill him. There was a discount for being a Vietnam vet, if he wrote that on his bill. It would come in a couple of days and he would have to pay before the ad would run, deadline in two weeks. "No problem there," said Dub. "You sure got a lot of files in here. Is them all advertisements?"

"Not all. Can I do anything else for you, Mr. Taylor?"

He was getting a little nauseated from the chewing tobacco and decided to take a chance. "You know, I met a guy once who said he got great results with your ads. Castle was his name. George Castle."

He thought maybe one of the other secretaries moved, but he wasn't sure. This woman just placed the order sheet beside her blotter and said, "That's nice to hear."

Back in the motel the red light on his phone was blinking. Vonna had called three times, Devraix once. What was he going to say? The building was like Fort Knox. The office with the records had a glass wall. The Alsatian might mean that at night the offices were patrolled by dogs. There might be some way of wheedling the records out of one of the three secretaries, but that would take more time than he had. He didn't call New Orleans. He took the phone off the hook and thought about the problem until he fell asleep. The next morning, with a different guard at the front, he faked a delivery to the Central American Freedom League, which turned out to be some kind of Contra lobbying organization. He watched them X-ray the padded envelope before they split it open with a paper knife and revealed a Spanish to English dictionary. This didn't calm their paranoia. To all their quesions, he said, "Hey, I just deliver them," and they finally let him go.

He called Vonna. "I give up," he said. "The place is paranoia central."

"I had an idea," said Vonna. "How about a fake court order? You come in like the police and—"

"It's no good," said Dub. "This is a waste. We'll talk when I get back on Thursday. Maybe we're just blowing smoke."

"What about letting Devraix call the number?"

"Tell him to wait until I get back."

"Well," said Vonna, "I guess if you can't get the records, can't nobody."

"Guaranteed. Anyhow, we wouldn't find out anything. I mean I bought a classified with a totally fake address. That's probably what Castle did."

"Okay," she said. "Will you be staying in New Orleans long?"

"No. I've got to make a living. I guess I might spend the night."

She didn't react. There was a slight pause, then, "See you Thursday."

"Right."

What he didn't say was what he had planned. It was illegal and risky as hell, and it was better nobody knew. That way, in the worst case, they couldn't be called accessories.

NINE

The way in, he decided, was the delivery garage. It might have been possible to bribe a deliveryman into letting Dub ride in among the cargo, but there was no guarantee that he could stay hidden or even get out of the truck without being spotted. You can't take trucks into a building without ventilating them, however. Especially when they were so careful about sliding down the steel door behind every vehicle.

He dozed in front of the motel TV until two a.m. He put on navy slacks, a black turtleneck, and black sneakers. He lifted the liner out of his battered suitcase and pulled out an Army belt dyed black and heavy with the tools in each pocket: string saws, dental tools modified into lock picks, tiny flashlights with red lenses, extra batteries, waterproof matches, wire cutters, glass cutters, a cylinder of mace, and various other vials and bundles of things that might come in handy.

"The problem is," Dub remembered his Army Intelligence instructor saying, "that there's always something you don't expect, don't know is there, and aren't prepared for." Dub looked at himself in the mirror and thought of all the balding men who try to recover their youth by dressing up in their old uniforms on the weekend, drinking beer, and making fools out of themselves by telling war stories. "You're too old for this," he thought. He put on his sports coat to cover the belt and look less like a burglar and drove to a dark street two blocks from the building.

The ventilator shaft he had noticed ended about fifty feet from the garage entrance. A steel grid was mounted on a lip inside a decorative wall four bricks high off the ground. The wall was the only cover. Eight bolts held down the grid, but they felt rough and the flashlight showed the rust. He sat behind the wall and squirted WD-40 on the bolt. He took out a folding crescent wrench that was barely big enough and tried it. He strained until he was afraid the wrench might crack. He gave the bolt a sharp rap and tried again. It creaked. The noise was sharp and seemed loud. He saw and heard no reaction to it, however. The building was dark except for the second floor, where a light someone had left on illuminated an empty desk.

The deserted street carried the distant noise of a siren, then a car with a broken muffler. He tried the bolt again. It never really weakened and each turn took an enormous effort, but it finally came out.

He checked his watch. It was two-thirty. The one bolt had taken almost fifteen minutes. He quickly squirted WD-40 on all the remaining bolts, hoping it would soak in. Bolt two wouldn't budge. He cussed it, tapped it, squirted it again. He took out his butane lighter and heated it until the oil smoke stung his eyes. No go. He cussed, assembled a daggerlike hacksaw and slowly cut away the bolt head. Another twenty minutes had been lost. He moved on to the third, then the fourth, his knuckles bleeding from being scraped against the brick and the grid. His back was killing him from the positions he had to take to do all this, and when the skies opened up like a fire hose, he was miserable, though it was now taking less and less time as he found the best ways to lever the wrench or cut. With three bolts to go, he tried lifting the grid to get enough space to squeeze under it. It wouldn't yield enough. Only the fifth bolt came out easily, and he almost gave up on the sixth. It was four twenty-four when the grid came free. His arms felt like rubber. He propped it open with the wrench and leaned in. Rain splattered on a concrete floor about seven feet down. There was a dark opening in the side of the wall toward the garage. He tied a string to the wrench, propped up the grid with it, and awkwardly dropped down. He jerked the string and the grid dropped into place. It would be hell to climb out. He was standing in water up to his ankles. The drain at the bottom was plugged. The rain kept pouring.

The opening was three feet square. He was soaked already, so it didn't seem particularly irksome to belly-crawl through the water, though he was beginning to shiver. As soon as he was in the tunnel, however, it began to slant slightly upward and the water level gradually decreased until he was crawling along on an algaelike slime. Body bag memories. "Just keep going," he told himself, fighting claustrophobia. "Just keep going."

He shone the light ahead of him and saw fat water bugs clinging to the sides and roof. Undisturbed by the red light, they rustled above and beside him, fluttering down onto his wet hair and arms. His elbow crunched some as he crawled. "Goddamned fucking Florida," he muttered. "Goddamned lousy fucking place." The wet clothes made him itchy and the itchiness felt like the roaches were scrambling through his clothes. "I'm gonna kill somebody for this, Goddamnit. Goddamnit."

A faint light seeped into the tunnel. The concrete grew drier and the bugs fewer. The tunnel dropped a bit and he could see the silhouette of four fan blades. He couldn't squeeze under or through them. The fan was mounted on a rack that was bolted to the floor and ceiling. The nuts felt rusty, of course, but they came loose fairly easily. With a little wrestling, he moved the whole fan assembly to the side. It would be easy to put back. There was only a louvered aluminum grill between him and the garage. He delicately lifted one louver and saw a set of fluorescent lights, concrete columns, and a loading platform. There wasn't enough light, he was sure, for television surveillance. When he leaned far to his left, he could just make out the booth in which a guard sat all day. Nobody was home.

He pushed at the grill with his hands, but couldn't knock it loose and couldn't turn around to kick it out. The louvers, however, hung on wires the thickness of a coat hanger. He took one more look at the empty garage, then carefully pulled them out of their holes. He heard his shoes squish as he dropped to the floor. He listened to the silence and smelled the acrid residue of diesel exhaust. Now for the hard part, he thought.

He checked his watch. Five-ten. Fifty minutes before the day security arrived. He quickly unscrewed the grill from the wall and reassembled the louvers. He used a dolly in the garage as a ladder and put the fan back in place. He replaced the grill. No one would know anything had been disturbed.

He was soaked, chilled, and exhausted, but also revved with adrenaline, alert as a cat, all five senses working overtime. The stairwell was locked from the inside. He quickly picked it, gritted his teeth at the *clack* when it opened, listened at the empty stairwell, then climbed to the third floor. He flattened himself against the wall and quickly peeked through the wired glass. He pressed against it and saw nothing that looked like either a motion detector or TV surveillance. He went in. He was directly opposite the plate-glass door of Liberty Books. Large posters flanked it. "*Underground: Managua*," said one. "The True Story of Sandinista Oppression. By The Man Who Saw It. Go Beyond The Whitewash." The other portrayed an evil-looking professor pointing to a hammer and sickle on his blackboard and hailed a book called *Parasites: The Infestation of Communism in the American School System.* "The SHOCKING Truth of the Threat to Our Moral Fiber!" it shouted. Dub imagined the landlord's lease: "No pets, no loud parties, no liberals."

He slipped down the corridor to the All-American Industry Group. The layout was much the same. Glassed-in offices, a few plants, a coffee station in a foyer between rest rooms. The whole floor, except for the arrangement of the glass walls and the lack of a security station next to the elevator, was nearly identical to the *Mercenary* offices one floor up. There was no sign any dogs had been there, either.

The coffee station offered the only possibility. He used the rest room without turning on the light and without flushing, then he stood on the coffee table, pushed the ceiling tile aside, and with much puffing pulled himself into the space above. He rolled onto one of the suspension beams, carefully avoiding the ceiling tiles, and slid the open one back into place. A rubber strap held his ankles and neck against the support beam, the belt secured his waist. He hung like an awning curled up over the front of a store. He crossed his sore arms over the steel "V" in front of him, and peered across the huge open space above the offices. He thought so. The partitions between offices, corridors, and companies only extended to the false ceiling. That would make it a lot easier upstairs.

Halftime, he thought. He closed his eyes and slept.

"No. I mean, look, he either wants it or he doesn't. Why should we go sucking up to him?"

"It's not that simple."

"Why the hell not?"

"Because it's not."

"Look at that, the sugar's all wet. Cripe. I'll see if Marge has any."

Dub blinked. What time was it? His clothes were still damp but he was sweating. It was warm in the rafters, even with the air-conditioning duct behind him. He listened carefully. When the air conditioner started up, he would shift to keep the tightness in his muscles from getting too strong a grip. He checked his watch about three times that day and by three p.m. he didn't know which was worse, his hunger (he should have thought about that) or the certain knowledge that whatever muscle decided to seize up next, it would be worse than the last (he was definitely too old for this). He remembered the flight across the Pacific in the belly of a cargo carrier. He had sprawled and twisted his body into a thousand shapes to get through the ride and he even slept—you learn to sleep anywhere in the Army, on or in anything—but that was a long time ago. The blood didn't move so good anymore. Why the hell was he up here? What the hell could he find out that was worth it? Christ!

Finally he heard people heading for the elevators, the frequent ringing of its bell, and then, silence. Or so he thought. About five-thirty someone went into each bathroom. They came out, met, talked softly, affectionately. "Not again," he heard the woman say. "I've got to go." The man growled a bit, then they headed for the elevators. Even right-wingers did it in their offices, despite the threat to their moral fiber. Dub couldn't get away from these situations, even when he wasn't working a divorce. After ten minutes of silence he felt pretty safe. He unstrapped his neck and tried to whirl the pain out of it. He unhooked his ankles and moved his hardened legs. About seven, he cautiously lifted the ceiling tile and saw that all the lights were out. He lowered himself to the floor.

From watching the building, he knew the cleaning people came in about eight-thirty. That gave him plenty of time unless there was an all-night guard upstairs. Then what? He didn't know. He paused to eat two stale but otherwise untouched doughnuts he had found in the rubbish bin next to the coffee island. He then slipped into the stairwell and moved up to the fourth floor. No one was visible through the wired glass, but he couldn't get a good view. He thought he was off the corridor leading to the print shop, but couldn't see enough to tell. He squeezed the button and tugged the door. What sort of paranoia led a magazine to be almost as tight as a bank? He picked the lock and froze when the *clack* resonated in the stairwell.

He counted to ten and stuck his head into the corridor. The print shop was to his left; the advertising office to the right. He heard the faint sound of a television and noticed mirrors mounted where one corridor met the next. If he could see the guard watching his two-inch screen, the guard could see him. He moved carefully into the men's room, eased the door shut, then quickly climbed onto the sink counter. He popped up a ceiling tile, took a deep breath, and hefted himself into the space. A lot of dusty crawling and one wide detour around an air duct finally brought him to where he thought he ought to be. When the ceiling tile was lifted, he was over the hallway, however. He tried again and found himself over an office, but not the right one. He lay on a board that was the top of the corridor wall and tried to estimate where he was and how to get where he wanted to be. Everything looked the same up here. Shit!

He crept back to where he started, carefully lifting a ceiling tile in each fifth row with his index finger, peeking through the narrow space. When he reached the concrete wall, he recognized it as the one enclosing the staircase. He was soon lowering himself onto Lex Tyrone's desk, crushing the pen set with his feet. He saw no one, heard nothing. He put the broken pieces on the floor and walked into the outer office.

He read the little cards on the fronts of the file cabinets. All those on the left wall were labeled "Classified," and they were arranged by date. Okay, Dub, he asked himself, when was that ad running? "March. Right? That's when Mrs. O'Dell—" He was talking to himself, he thought; he was cracking up.

The cabinets were locked, but that was a minor obstacle. Inside were hanging folders for each biweekly issue. The March

8 folder was thick. He sat behind a desk and leafed through it, scanning with the red flashlight. The orders were printed out on sheets that resembled telegraph forms with the billing address in the upper right and printer's instructions on the left. If the ad was a new one, it was stamped "NEW" in red. If it was a continuing one, the billing address was usually absent and a small clipping of the ad was glued where the text was normally printed out. That's how the Castle ad was set up. In the area of the billing address was the black outline of a castle tower with the letters "LT" in the center. A few of the other ads had this stamp too, but otherwise they had nothing in common. "LT"? Lex Tyrone?

Dub checked Tyrone's desk. In the locked center drawer he found the LT stamp and an ink pad. He looked over the other things in the drawer, found a few travel brochures, a Polaroid of a woman in black lace underwear, and two memos from Robert Belgrade. He went back to the files. The March 22 slip was the same. "Okay," he mumbled, "you can either go all the way back to when the ad first showed or"—he wiped his face with his hand—"get lucky on when they changed the phone number." He checked his watch. Quarter to eight. The cleaners entered the building in about forty-five minutes. Say, half an hour. He looked for September 19, the issue in which Devraix had noticed a different phone number. The file wasn't there. "Jee-sus Maria!" Dub muttered. It was too new to be filed. He twisted toward the secretaries' desks.

A noise. A shadow moved in the hall. He got ready to back into Lex Tyrone's office, then dropped behind one of the desks. On the smoked glass of Tyrone's office he could see the outline of a cleaning woman working a squeegee over the outer wall. Dub's stomach twisted tight and hot sweat flushed out of him. He had to keep himself together. Together. Concentrate. This isn't Saigon. They don't have body bags. There is some way out. He heard the woman joking with the guard, then the clinking of keys and the opening of the door. Run for it? Break for the stairwell? It was just as much a trap as the elevator. Go up, hide in the ceiling? He looked at his bloodied knuckles and wondered if he still had the arm strength to knock out the woman with one punch. One for the poor cleaning lady; one for the guard. Fat chance, he thought. Fat chance.

He waited. The woman squeegeed the inside for a while and then turned on a vacuum. She didn't seem to be moving it, though. She was dusting, or something, along the cabinets, and had gotten far away enough from the corridor that her reflection became even more obscure. Dub heard her brush against the front of the desk he was behind. He crouched. Waiting. Waiting. When her back came fully into view, he jumped. In a single motion one hand clopped hard across her mouth and a leg clipped her behind the knees, collapsing her to the floor. The other hand reared back for the knockout across the chin, but somehow she rolled. Dub tumbled sideways against the next desk, which boomed from the impact. "You motherfucker!" the cleaning woman hissed. She threw herself on Dub and slammed the desk again. She had grabbed Dub's hair and he had clutched her uniform pockets when they both stopped.

"Vonna?!" said Dub.

"You dumb motherfucker!" she whispered.

There was noise in the corridor. Vonna stood, kicking Dub toward the leg hole under the desk.

"What's going on here?" asked the guard.

"Would you believe," said Vonna, "I fell down?"

"Huh?"

Vonna walked forward and cut off the vacuum. "I went over there to turn on some lights and plop, I goes down like Raggedy Ann." She laughed. The guard laughed.

"You got to be more careful."

"You betcha, boss."

"What's your name again?"

"Maybelle."

"You got to watch those big feet of yours, Maybelle."

"Yassuh, I shorely doo." They laughed some more. The door closed. Dub heard Vonna say, "I'll big-foot your ass, turkey-shit."

"What are you doing here?" whispered Dub.

"Getting what you can't."

"Can't? What the hell am I doing here, then?"

"Nothing that I can see. You know anything?"

"Not yet."

"Well, you better get cracking. I figure the woman I'm

supposed to be replacing will be showing up in about twenty minutes."

"Maybe less. You watch for the guard. I've got the files figured."

Dub went back in time through the files. Each time he found the slip, there was no address. The initials on the castle tower disappeared in 1984, and someone else wrote them in ballpoint. Vonna turned the vacuum on and off. She hummed and slowly emptied each wastebasket into a can on her cleaning cart. She stuck her head into the hall and complained about people who stick gum under their desks. "Have you got it? Have you got it?" she whispered.

"It's the same damned thing," said Dub.

"How much more to go?"

"Three years left."

Vonna tapped her watch. "Try from the start. We got to go."

Dub pulled out the slip in the folder he was searching. He thought he had it, but the castle tower was merely replaced by initials, and the text of the ad showed only a change of phone number. "Shit," he hissed. He went to the first file, unlocked it, and pulled out the folder for the first issue. They weren't as organized. They hadn't used the slips. Dub couldn't find anything like Castle's ad, so he quicky moved to the next file. Nothing. The next file. Nothing. The next file. Nothing. He began to look at every second file. The slip system came in two years after the magazine was founded, but Castle's ad wasn't there. In mid-1984, it suddenly appeared, but with no address. Dub went back one file. No slip.

"We got to go," said Vonna.

"There's got to be bills," said Dub. "They had to bill somebody." He moved across the room and saw a file marked "Incoming." He didn't know whether that meant checks or what, but he started to unlock it. Vonna grabbed his arm.

"We're out of here," she whispered. "Out."

Dub's watch said eight thirty-five. They heard the guard's telephone ring. They looked at each other. "How you getting out?" asked Vonna.

"The ceiling," said Dub.

"No good."

"Huh?"

Vonna pointed to Lex Tyrone's office. The desk lamp was lit. "Call the fire department." She held out a box of wooden matches.

"Huh? We can't—"

"You like to go to jail?"

"Maybelle! Say, Maybelle!"

Dub quickly slipped into Tyrone's office and behind the desk. In the leg hole Vonna had piled a mound of crumpled papers covered with greasy rags.

"Consuela is downstairs," said the guard.

"What?" said Vonna. "Can't be no Consuela. She's flat on her back sick."

"John says it's her and she don't know you."

"Naw, the company said—can I talk to them?"

"I got them on the phone."

"Consuela got the flu. Now I don't know Consuela but . . ."

The outer office door closed. Tyrone had one of those modern telephones with automatic dialing buttons and a digital readout. Dub dialed the fire department. The call wouldn't go through. Why did everyone want to complicate their own lives? He looked up at the ceiling, then dialed 9, hoping it would give an outside line. It did. "Emergency," said an astringent female voice.

"I was just drivin' down Tarpon. There's an office building. I seen fire in it. It's burning."

"The address please."

"The only big office down there. The glass one. About twenty-five hundred."

"Your name, sir?"

"No way, José! I'm just passing by!" He hung up. He struck the match on the desk edge and lit the paper. It caught and moved under the rags. The smoke rolled over the desk edge and billowed toward the sprinkler head above. Dub wanted quicker results. He threw some papers off the desk on it. He picked up the desk blotter and waved the heavy smoke toward the detector mounted on the side wall. There were photos under it. With the desk lamp on, he could see the photo that he had originally taken for an old Army group shot because of the helmets and other equipment. The men were carrying AK-

47s: Kalashnikov rifles. He kept waving with one hand and pulled the picture off the wall. George Castle/Lamont George had his foot propped on a log. Dub pitched the blotter on the fire—the smoke was filling the room—and in a moment of inspiration swept up Tyrone's telephone, yanking the wire out of the wall.

The alarm went off. The details of Tyrone's office were swallowed in the churning cloud behind the smoked glass. Dub ducked into the leg hole of a desk just as the guard came running in with an extinguisher. The sprinkler system opened but the guard charged through the cold artificial rain and opened Tyrone's glass door. The smoke staggered him and he turned to see Dub bolt for the outer door.

"Hey!"

Vonna was just outside the offices in the dry corridor. Dub shoved her aside and turned toward the stairwell.

"I'll get him!" said Vonna to the guard.

They heard the guard crashing down the steps behind them until they passed the firemen surging up on the second floor, then they simply walked through the chaos in the lobby, saying "Fourth! Fourth floor! Fire on the fourth floor!"

TEN

They scrambled into Dub's car. "Do you think anyone recognized you?" Dub asked Vonna.

"Hey, baby," she puffed, "all blacks are cats in the dark."

"What the hell does that mean?"

"A nigger's just a cleaning lady; a cleaning lady's just a nigger. The guy at the front door saw me for a little while; the guy upstairs quite a bit. But we all look alike, don't you know."

"We shouldn't have set the fire."

"And how was I supposed to get you out of there?"

"I was going to walk out."

"I'm sure. And what'd you steal this telephone for?"

"Don't touch it. It's one of those fancy phones with all the numbers keyed into the buttons. That way you don't need to dial. It's like Lex Tyrone's little black book. Can you get the numbers out of it?"

"If it's got wires I can figure it out."

"I hope so."

They pulled into Dub's motel. "You duck down," said Dub. "They may have your description out. We'll drive back to New Orleans."

"Drive?"

"They could be watching the airport."

"I hate long drives," said Vonna.

"Maybe *you* want to try jail?" Dub shut the car door and spoke through the window. "Get down," he said. Vonna glared at him, but put her head on the seat. "Say," added Dub, "you didn't leave any fingerprints?"

[95]

"I clean two damn offices, my eyes're still watering from the ammonia, and the man asks me if I left any prints. Shit."

"Okay, okay." He winked.

Her lips curled into a slight smile, but then she turned away. He knew for certain now that she was resisting; she wasn't permitting herself to like him. That made them a pair, he thought. It was exactly what he had done with every woman, including his own wife, ever since Janet.

They said little and stopped for nothing but gas until they were north of Pascagoula. They had a greasy breakfast of eggs and sausage in a truck stop. Although they had traded the driving each time the tank ran low, Dub hurt from his toes, which never stopped with pins and needles, to his ears, which rang like a doorbell with a wad of gum on it. They scrutinized the photo Dub had taken from Lex Tyrone's office. A diagonal of mountain slashed the sky behind the four men: a severe mountain. "The Rockies?" asked Dub.

"That really narrows it down."

Dub sipped his coffee. "One of these must be Lex Tyrone, right?"

"Likely."

"This guy has a Big Red One patch. Or it looks kind of like it."

"Maybe it came with the shirt. They buy their outfits from a surplus store, go hunting. Maybe it don't mean nothing."

"You don't hunt with assault rifles. Not four-legged animals, anyhow."

Vonna lifted a flap of egg with her fork. "I guess you white people always eat this shit."

"Yep. That's how I got this fifty-pound gut."

"That much? It don't show. Well, not too much. Not like me."

"What's wrong, Vonna? Jesus. Come on."

"Nothin'," she said, studying her reflection in the window.

"All right. All right. Help me think here. Pure business. I'm so beat up I can't uncross my eyes."

Vonna shoved her plate aside. "My man, we still don't know who placed the ad. We know Lex Tyrone puts it in for three years, putting his little chess piece in the corner. Lex is our man. This guy is Castle, Lamont George. One of these is

Tyrone. The other two, old army buddies. They like hunting. They take up a sideline eliminating problem people." She made a gun with her hand. "Bang."

"So maybe when Castle was trying to kill me, he called one of these guys."

"Maybe."

"So what if we go to the owner—"

"Of what?"

"*Mercenary*. We go to Belgrade. We tell him what Tyrone is doing—no! Remember? Someone else approved those ads back in the beginning. A different advertising manager. Used initials."

"But you couldn't read them."

"No."

"One of these guys."

"Maybe." Dub twisted uncomfortably. "We don't even know these four guys are close. Maybe they're not friends."

"We could still tell Belgrade," said Vonna. "Maybe he'll ID them. Of course, I don't think we'd be too popular if he figured out we set fire to his building."

Dub wiped his face with his hand. "We've still got the phone, but Christ, it's like those damn relays, this thing. You get a lead, you follow it to a dead end. Another lead, another dead end. Castle is George, a vet from Philly. Maybe. He's Tyrone's friend. Maybe. They're accomplices. Maybe. He uses his rubber stamp and nobody bothers with an address." Dub stopped short. He blinked and stared at his soft toast. "Whoa," he said, "you said it was a chess piece."

"The castle," said Vonna. "It's a chess piece."

"Like the game? What's the significance?"

"What significance?"

"That's what I mean. Does it imply anything? Something to do with *Mercenary*, mercenaries, anything like that?"

"Each side has two. They sit in the corners, they move straight and sideways. They don't do much in the beginning, but they are the big guns after the queens are killed and you got to protect the kings."

"And? You know this game good?"

"I've played it. In the Army. There wasn't much else to do. When you weren't ducking horny officers."

Dub thought for a few seconds and crushed out his cigarette in his plate. "Damnit, there's something I'm missing. Tyrone. Chess. Castle. Belgrade. There's something here." But he came up with nothing. It was maddening, like trying to remember the name of a movie you were crazy about five years ago. He looked at Vonna, whose mind was elsewhere. "You told me you were married once?" he asked, knowing as he asked it that he wouldn't have blurted it out if he hadn't been so tired.

"The question startled her. "Not exactly. Not legal." She looked away. "I was real young."

"How young?"

"Too young," she said sharply. "Not old enough to have good sense. Are we gonna sit here all night?"

"We can wait a minute or two."

"Then I'm hitting the john," she said, standing. "Get a receipt. Devraix ought to pay. I don't pay for garbage like this."

"Right," said Dub as she walked away. I was married too young too, he thought. The first time you're always too young.

Back in New Orleans they went straight to her apartment. They tried calling a few electronics shops to find out how the phone worked, but none of them stocked that model and no one knew where an instruction manual could be found. One guy thought the company, "Ohiophone," was bought out by Ikita and no longer made phones. He wasn't sure. Dub was for trying to figure the phone out by trying a few buttons, but Vonna told him to be patient, something could be lost that way. She'd sort it out. Dub left a message with Devraix's answering service and went to the airport to exchange the rental car for his own. The woman at the counter didn't like it, the car was supposed to be dropped back in Tampa, but in the end she just called in and found a hefty fee to tack on.

He got back to Vonna's about six. Fatigue bristled all over him like a gray fuzz. When she opened the door he saw Devraix eating Chinese food in the dinette. There were six steaming cartons spread around his plate.

"Well?" Dub asked.

Devraix stuffed strings of meat into his mouth, then gestured with the chopsticks for Dub to sit down.

Dub lifted the phone. "You know how this thing works?"

"I think so," said Vonna.

"Well?"

"He's impatient," said Vonna to Devraix. "He spent one night in a ceiling and the next night in a car."

"Please," he swallowed. "I do not wish to know. I authorize nothing illegal. That's on your back."

"Thanks," she said dryly.

"Does anyone care about the phone?" said Dub.

She squinted, then explained it had only taken a few minutes to figure out how it worked. They were lucky it had a battery backup because the memory portion ran on the regular phone current. She had put in a new wire, then hooked it into her own phone circuit, and pushed a button marked "Auto-dial." A green "#?" appeared in the narrow window. She pushed "01" and the name "BELGRADE" appeared. At number 15, "LAMONT." Various other names came up, none of which seemed to mean anything, but Vonna carefully listed them. Some were companies, presumably regular advertisers, or maybe people Tyrone regularly bought from: "SURVIVAL CO," "BUCK KNIFE," "IRON BOOT," "COMPASS." At 80, the window read, "ENTER NEW NAME," and Vonna handed the list to Devraix.

"And this is it," said Devraix triumphantly.

Dub's lips moved as he skimmed the list. "Can you get the numbers out of that thing?"

"I know somebody who's got a computer that can read it. It works on tones. You just need to get the pitch of each tone. We'd want to know what the number is by 'LAMONT.'"

"Right," said Dub. He swung his legs in the air and stood. His feet were going to sleep again. He rammed both heels against the floor and said, "Probably another dead end."

"Don't be so cynical," said Devraix.

"You weren't paying attention," said Vonna. "Looky here." She lifted the telephone and punched 21. The bright green letters said "WHITE ROOK."

ELEVEN

When Devraix had noticed "WHITE ROOK" on the list Vonna had made, he had not only put together "castle" and "rook," but after the tones had been converted to numbers, the Montana area code confirmed Tyrone had been in touch with the American Values Conservatory Nation. Neither Dub nor Vonna had ever heard of the AVCN, Marshall Wescott, or his enclave in the mountains on the Canadian border. "I have done a considerable amount of reading in my life," said Devraix, probably referring to his genteel days before he decided to found a detective agency. "And when you learn of a particularly ugly tiger in the jungle, you tend to recall it. Particularly when that tiger refers to your distinguished ancestors", he growled the words, "as an 'immorally mongrelized mix.'"

The next day, the three of them went to the Tulane library to look up whatever had been written on Wescott's group and found mostly speculation. Some journalists thought the AVCN was merely another ultraconservative survivalist group. Other reporters had tried to make the White Rook into a kind of Jonestown. A *Chicago Tribune* reporter had compared the White Rook to Heritage U.S.A., and called Wescott a "handsome, nonlibidinous Jim Bakker," and hinted the whole thing was a confidence game. The reporter got a death threat for his remarks, but nothing came of it. People who had been to the Rook—women and children included—didn't talk about it except to say they had a good time and learned a lot about America. Some refused to talk about it at all, as if afraid. In public Wescott seemed no more dangerous than Pat Robertson or any other right-winger, except that his ideas were more extreme. Wescott touched on a lot of the frustrations of lower-middle-class blue-collar and rural whites, it seemed. He had also had some success, it was said, with audiences in Canada when he had come to the support of a history teacher named Keegstra who had been telling his students that Auschwitz, Treblinka, and Dachau were all Zionist fabrications.

What this all meant in relation to Michael O'Dell, neither Devraix, Dub, or Vonna was sure. Either the AVCN itself sponsored murder (for the moment that seemed too bizarre, even for the super-race), or certain members of the group—Lex Tyrone, Lamont George, and others—were renegades.

Later in his office, Devraix refused to theorize. It seemed to be his method to systematically eliminate all elements that could not be verified in order to clarify. He listened to hunch, conjecture, and theory, but he would dissect each with terse questions that revealed just how speculative these lines of reasoning were. It made Dub wonder if Devraix was capable of making the kind of intuitive leap that he had always thought was what separated a genius from an ordinary gumshoe. On the other hand, Devraix would never be misled by preconceptions. Faced with the old riddle about the surgeon, he would never automatically assume—as most would—that a surgeon was a man, so the riddle couldn't snare him.

Dub was having a hard time keeping his mind on the discussion. He couldn't figure why Vonna had become so animated. Normally unexpressive, she had been particularly distant since last night. Exhausted by their long trip, Dub and she had tottered into her bedroom as casually as an old married couple. He heard her gently snoring almost immediately, but his legs had hummed with tiredness and he couldn't drop off. He had rolled over and nestled against her back. She moved and clipped his chin with her shoulder. The smell of the truck-stop grill where they had eaten breakfast was still in her hair, mixed with whatever she normally sprayed on, or combed in. He pressed his face into it and her hair was coarse, but comfortable, like the warm roughness of a Ragg sweater as you pull it over your head. Her hair was nothing like the silk of a blonde, you could feel that. And if it were dyed, it would be obviously false, a betrayal of what it was in texture and truth. Tired as he was, it somehow aroused him. He slid his hand under the loose T-shirt she had worn to bed and along her skin soft as thousand-dollar leather. He cupped her breast, then slid his hand down into the moistness between her legs.

She didn't respond at first, but she soon stirred, murmured, and pressed her hips back against his. He felt like a seducer, someone who had crept into her bed, an incubus. She had been dreaming perhaps and now he had become part of the world of shadows. She became more intense, much more intense than when they had first made love. That time she had kept a certain reserve. She had not held back on giving or receiving pleasure, but she had seemed matter-of-fact enough that it had relaxed him, made him enjoy it more. They had been just a couple of consenting adults scratching their respective itches with no particular expectations or commitment. This time, her passion startled him but he too, burying his face deep into her hair and tasting the dark warmth of her shoulder, was swept along by it. They had performed the last time, but this time they simply were and did. She had talked the last time, but not in the same way. This time the words tumbled out, as if they were not calculated to please him, and they had no meaning to him other than as an expression of hunger.

"White man," she groaned, "do me, white man, do me, do me—" and she flicked on her bedside light and pressed his shoulders up so that he rested on his stiff arms and she could watch him enter her and withdraw and she could run her hands over his white, white chest and claw at his nipples and hiss words through her gritted teeth as if she were furious.

At the end, he collapsed on top of her, tasting her hard purple nipples, then burying his face in her hair. "It's never been like this with any woman," he moaned, then tried to remember whether it was true, or whether it was just words. It was certainly true since Saigon, and before that he had been just a boy, even when he had married. He also tried to figure out it if it was because she was black, if it was the novelty of looking down at her café au lait skin as he moved inside her. He realized he had never really thought of black women as beautiful. Beauty was thin, blonde, and fair-skinned. His wife Beth had been like that, though she liked to tan. And Janet, in Saigon, had been like that. The perfect image of that. But since he had come home, when he saw that type in movies, on television, in centerfolds, they produced no erotic response in him. Daryl Hannah, Brigitte Nielsen, Susan Anton: They were as cold as perfect diamonds. Vonna was the physical opposite of the ideal, and he wondered if sleeping with her had been a way of punishing himself—some Southern Baptist thing had stuck to him when he was a boy, and it was making this sex so intense because it was degrading. He hadn't slept with anyone's ideal of a woman for a long time. Maybe he was so screwed up that this was the way his taste now ran. Maybe it had been so good because, in the foggy back alleys of his mind, Vonna was as low as he could crawl. He didn't want to think that kind of bias was in him, he wouldn't allow it, but when he tried to say something to get away from thinking about it, all that tumbled out was, "I guess what they say about black women is true. That was something!" He felt like a fool.

She pushed him off her. "Shit," she said. "I'm all wet."

"I got carried away," he said. "I forgot the rubber."

"Yeah. Sure." She sat up and mopped between her legs with her undershirt. He looked up at her broad back and trailed his middle finger over her buttocks, across the stretch marks that looked like striations in burled walnut. She squirmed away and stared blankly. He felt ridiculous with his belly and saggy chest.

He touched the four parallel scratches over his heart and said, "You really got me." Her silence made him feel more awkward.

She turned off the light and said, "Go to sleep."

"Is something wrong?"

She did not answer.

Her mood, snit, whatever it was, continued the next morning at Devraix's office, in the Tulane library, at lunch, and in the car. That was why, when they returned to Devraix's, her sudden gushing forth of one hypothesis after another astounded Dub. At first he thought maybe she had gotten over her mood or had just needed the oyster po'boy she'd wolfed down at lunch, but when she went on, leaning almost halfway between her chair and Devraix's desk, Dub began to think it was forced, a desperate throwing of herself into the case to avoid something else. Dub then noticed how she would ignore his remarks until Devraix reiterated them and would only look directly at Devraix. The notion flashed into his mind that Devraix and Vonna had once had a "thing" and that's what made her nervous, but he rejected it.

Shortly after one, Devraix shifted his shoulders, stretched his arms forward, and splayed his delicate hands flat upon the blotter. Something about the gesture signaled the discussion had ended and Vonna stopped almost in midsentence. There was a long pause during which Devraix seemed distracted by one of his cuticles and raised his finger to study it.

"Well?" said Vonna. "Are we going to get after these shits or not?"

"First, I will discuss it with Mr. Campbell."

"Who?" asked Dub.

"Agent Lawrence Campbell," said Devraix, "of the FBI."

"We're giving it away?" said Vonna loudly.

"Very likely," said Devraix. "We have a business here and, objectively speaking, very little to continue with."

"Maybe you should talk with Mrs. O'Dell," Dub volunteered.

"Yeah," said Vonna. "What will she say about giving up?"

"At this point, I would advise her to abandon the inquiry and to assume that Lamont George killed Michael O'Dell. We can't prove it, but if this is a conspiracy of the scale we imagine, then we haven't sufficient resources to take it on ourselves."

"Aw, shit!" said Vonna. "I don't believe this."

"Excuse me?" said Devraix.

"We just get somebody to sign up," she said.

"And they will give this infiltrator all the records of their assassinations? No. We've discussed this too long. I mean to give it to the Bureau. I am certain they would be interested in this, perhaps they even know about it. They are always watching these groups."

"You know damn well they go after 'uppity niggers' more than white-power types."

"That isn't true," said Dub. "They went after the Klan, didn't they?"

"How many Black Panthers you seen lately?" Vonna stood and walked to the window. She sighed, then slapped the windowsill.

Devraix glanced at Dub and coyly raised an eyebrow, as if to ask, "Well, well, have you lovebirds been squabbling?"

Dub gave him a sharp look. Devraix studied his cuticle one more time and said, "The decision is made. I shall call Mr. Campbell immediately."

"I must have some work to do," said Vonna. She left the room without looking at either of them.

Devraix perused Dub again with the question, "What's with her?" in his eyes. Dub shrugged. Devraix opened his Rolodex and dialed.

Campbell didn't want to hear about it on the phone, and by two-thirty, Dub and Devraix were being led down a long corridor to Campbell's office in the New Orleans branch of the FBI. Campbell turned out to be like the secretary, the carpeting, the desks, even his handshake and words: standard government issue.

"How are you, Honoré? It has been a while, hasn't it? The disappearance of the Fucello girl, wasn't it?"

"Until she bobbed up," said Devraix wickedly. "In Takula Bayou."

"Yes . . . ," said Campbell. "And you're Mr. Greenert." They shook hands. "Take a chair. Make yourself at home."

Campbell sat behind his desk, took a file from his drawer, then laced his fingers on top of it. "Okay. Fill me in. I've talked to Washington. What about the White Rook?"

Devraix opened his calfskin valise and laid his notes on his lap. He explained how they had become involved, but did not use Mrs. O'Dell's name. Campbell did not seem to have heard of Michael O'Dell and began taking notes. When Lamont George came up, Campbell opened his file and used the tip of his finger to scan a long list. He stopped on the second page, then closed his file. His eyes grew wider when Devraix tersely explained that "one of his operatives" had killed George in self-defense.

"And the parish police know about this?" Campbell took another note. His expression was getting more serious.

"Only that there was a killing in self-defense," said Devraix. "It was linked to a security problem for Mr. Krider."

"Who was your operative?"

"You assured me this conference would not constitute a formal inquiry," said Devraix.

"Honoré," said Campbell, "you're talking about a possible homicide, a definite homicide, concealment of evidence from the proper authorities—though, don't get me wrong, we don't want the locals to get into this. I'd say you've been pretty busy for rent-a-cops." Campbell was nearly sneering when he said it.

Devraix's dark eyes flashed. "I beg your pardon?"

"You're amateurs. You don't belong in this kind of thing."

Devraix stiffened like a grandee about to demand satisfaction in a duel.

"It was me," said Dub. "I killed George." Campbell studied him for a second. Dub felt childishly sheepish, as if he'd been caught smoking in a high school lavatory.

Campbell nodded. "And who is your client? You said someone hired you who suspected Eddie Viek?"

"You have no need of that information," said Devraix.

"I'll be the judge of that."

"Then I'm afraid this interview is concluded."

"Like hell it is," said Campbell. "We've been sniffing around David Duke—the Grand Wizard who got elected to the state legislature—for damn near a month, and getting nowhere. I'd like to know if he's hooked up with the AVCN or anybody like that. You told me you had information connecting Marshall Wescott and *Mercenary*. If you know anything, you'd better talk."

Devraix began putting his notes back into his valise. "We have no interest in Mr. Duke, the voters of Metairie, or the problems of the Republican party. Our information would seem to be of no consequence." The refusal was now just a matter of Devraix's pride. It wouldn't take much for the FBI to find out Mrs. O'Dell had hired them.

"Look, Mr. Campbell," said Dub. "Humor us. We're not supposed to reveal our clients without their permission. It's maybe not a big deal, but it's our code."

"Right," said Campbell sarcastically. He turned to Devraix. "Don't shuck and jive me. Just remember who you are. Your ethics, as you call them, don't make you cops. They don't even make you meter maids. If you don't cooperate you won't even have a license to drive. Now what about *Mercenary?*"

Campbell peered straight at Devraix and raised his pen. Devraix's expression was stony, though his eyes glowed. Campbell turned to Dub, who glanced back at Devraix. Ultimately, without ever averting his angry stare from the FBI man, he inserted his delicate fingers into the valise and brought out his notes. "We proposed," he said in clipped tones, "to ascertain who it was who had placed the advertisement. We used an agent in Tampa to get information from *Mercenary*'s files. We were only able to get Lex Tyrone's phone list. The number of the White Rook was prominent among them."

"That's it?"

"Yes."

"Who was your informant in Tampa?"

"We didn't use an informant."

"We could use that person. Who is it?"

"We didn't use an informant."

"I got into the offices," said Dub. Devraix glared at him to warn him to shut up.

Campbell nodded. He flipped through his papers.

"I assume," said Devraix, "that if you can use an informant you are investigating either Robert Belgrade or his magazine."

"We investigate many things," said Campbell, "that are strictly out of your league. Gentlemen, the Bureau appreciates your information. It isn't much, but who knows, it might help a bit."

"You mean to tell us nothing?" asked Devraix.

"Not at liberty. And I never said anything to you guys about Duke. Is that clear?"

"We came in good faith."

"I made no deal. You'll be lucky if we don't seize your records."

"Very well," said Devraix. He stuffed his notes into the valise, stood, and spun on his heels.

"One other thing," said Campbell loudly. "You're off the case. You go to your client and tell him you've got no more leads. You don't get anywhere near Belgrade or Wescott or anybody who's been within a hundred miles of the White Rook. You got that?"

"What is the issue?" Devraix said without facing him. "Are you afraid we might uncover something? Perhaps these members of the white race fill a government need." He snapped open the door and was gone.

Campbell stood. "You make that little twerp understand, Greenert. If he fucks around in this, he's finished. He'll be tap-dancing on Bourbon Street before we're through with him."

"And he's too old to compete with the pickaninnies, don't you think?" said Dub, smiling nastily.

"You've been warned," said Campbell. "You'd better get your ass back to Pittsburgh."

Dub caught Devraix at the elevator. The door slid shut behind them. Devraix was silent, but Dub could feel the heat coming off him. "I thought that boy was your friend," said Dub.

"I gave him the Fucello case on a platter. He wouldn't be in charge here if it wasn't for that. Now I am just a chocolate 'rent-a-cop.' "

"Well, we've been warned off."

"They do not want these scum exposed. It's the conserva-tive trend."

"Maybe they just think we'll interfere."

" 'Shuck and jive,' he said! I will not be treated like some common burrhead."

The elevator opened. Devraix crossed the lobby at a speed Dub had never seen from him. In the car he seethed in silence until they were almost at the office. A truck stopped in front of them and began to unload old floor lamps. Dub leaned out of the window to see if he could go around.

"Would you be willing to go under?" said Devraix quietly.

"Huh?" said Dub.

"You have experience undercover. Would you go under to get more on Wescott's group?"

Dub blinked. Somebody behind them blew his horn. "I don't know. Let me—" The horn blew again. "Shut up, god-damnit!" The truck's driver waved them around.

"Well?" said Devraix.

Dub pulled into the parking lot of a Popeyes fried chicken place. "You heard what your buddy Campbell said. And he means it. They'll get your license. You'll be out of business."

"Campbell treated me as if I were an inferior. I will never submit to such bullying."

"Look," said Dub, "he's an asshole, okay? He shakes your hand because he learned it in school. He's everybody's pal until they want something."

"*And* he is a bigot and does not admit it to himself."

"All right. And there's some bigot in me, in you, in everybody. He was just more unzipped than the rest of us and showed more than he should have. But you got to go after O'Dell's murderer because you want O'Dell's murderer. Not because you want to get even with the whiteys at the FBI. It ain't easy to get even with the FBI."

"Your point is taken. Does it mean you decline?"

Dub sat back and watched two gawky black teenagers playing push and shove. One thumped against the side of a van, then laughed as he beaned the other with a biscuit. "Let me put it this way. I killed a guy in this business. I'd sure like to know why I had to do it. But getting in deeper don't seem the logical thing to do."

"Do you not consider me a rational man? I am determined. It will be you or it will be someone else. I would rather it be you."

A thin blonde wearing a red and yellow uniform came out of the side door of the Popeyes with two dark plastic bags. They were the color of body bags, Dub thought, and when she reached up over the side of the dumpster, her cap blew off and her hair looked like Janet's. Dub's heart began to race and a slight twinge made him bring his hand up to his chest pocket. A message from the gods, thought Dub. Don't do it. Not again. He swallowed hard. "I don't know. Could we do it right?"

"What are your requirements?"

"Well, I can't go for nothing."

"You'll be paid handsomely. Fifty percent more than your wage in Pittsburgh."

Dub moved his head to one side.

"Then double," said Devraix.

"Mrs. O'Dell?"

"I'll pay it myself, if necessary."

"And expenses."

"Of course."

"And you increase my insurance policy for my daughters. Say by two hundred thousand dollars."

"Certainly. How do we begin?"

"Wait. I haven't said I'd do it yet."

"But you will."

Dub shrugged. "We would need a way to get in. And a legend."

"We shall be entirely under your direction."

Oh shit, thought Dub.

Vonna wasn't at the office when they got there. Her note said she was tired of paperwork and had gone to the French Quarter to help look for a runaway boy from Shreveport. Devraix left Dub alone in the office and he sat at Vonna's desk. He tried to call his girls in Charleston, but got no answer and remembered they took ballet lessons after school. No one answered at Vonna's apartment either. The windows darkened as clouds moved in off the Gulf of Mexico. He smoked several cigarettes and tried his daughters again. Ring, ring, ring, ring. Nothing. Goddamnit! He flicked a pencil across the room. Undercover. Again. The idea was tightening the muscles in his chest, making it tough to breathe. Janet, you bitch! he thought. You and your body bag. After all these years you're still trying to spook me. But you're dead and I'm not. You can't beat me unless I let you.

Almost desperately he dialed his daughters again. No answer. He dialed Vonna. He recognized that Elizabeth and Carrie might be pacifiers for him. When fear got into him, he always thought of them. But why tonight did Vonna seem an equal alternative? It couldn't be sex. Horniness had nothing to do with his daughters. Usually, after he had found a woman, any woman, to take care of his body, the sadness afterward made him think of Elizabeth and Carrie even more. He tried to remember, and, yes, it was true—that sadness hadn't come over him after sleeping with Vonna. Why? Maybe it was just the distraction of the case or the fact that he'd never slept with a black woman. Whatever it was, it couldn't be love. He was too old for that. Love, blonde and thin and trust-inspiring, had nearly killed him.

He cruised around the French Quarter for an hour, ate a

soft-shelled crab sandwich, then called Vonna's from a pay phone. It was busy. He had some trouble finding her apartment, but when he got there he could see the light on and her sliding balcony door open. He climbed the stairs and knocked. No answer. He could hear gospel music—not loud, but there. At first he wasn't certain it was coming from her apartment. He knocked again and when he got no answer thought about leaving. Maybe he was interrupting something.

He climbed back down the stairs, but when he got to the sidewalk and peered up, he saw her shadow move across the rippling drapes.

"Vonna!" he shouted. "Vonna! It's me. Dub." A man walking his rat terrier eyed Dub from the end of the parking lot. "Vonna!"

The drapes parted. Vonna looked out. Her face was in the shadows, but her head was bright with a towel wrapped like a turban on her head. She didn't say anything.

"I wanted to tell you about the meeting. Can I come up?"

She went back in silently. The drapes stirred in a rush of wind. He hesitated a moment and went upstairs. Her door was unlocked. He pushed it timidly, half expecting a guy with a baseball bat to jump him. On the radio, a woman with a resonant voice was singing "Just a Closer Walk With Thee." Vonna was on her sofa, her bare legs under her. She was wearing a shiny pink robe that clung in damp spots to her nipples. Unbuttoned, it revealed her cleavage, the bulge of her belly, and the sparse top of her pubic hair. She indifferently tipped back a fifth of red-pepper vodka, took three good swallows, and shuddered as it burned its way into her veins.

"Having a party?" asked Dub.

"What are you doing here?"

"We're going after them. The FBI won't, so we are. Devraix's really pissed."

"So am I," she said somberly. "Ain't that what you white folks say, 'I'm really pissed'?"

Dub wiped his face with his hands. It was gruesomely humid with the balcony door open. "The Brits say it. I guess I heard some Americans say it too. That ain't the way Devraix is pissed, though. He's mad. So, is that stuff good? Why are you 'pissed'?"

Her skin was shiny with sweat. "I don't know."

"You're gonna feel lousy tomorrow, baby."

"Don't you 'baby' me, white man."

"What's bugging you? You've been cold to me all day. Did I do something to you? Did I say something? We got to work together, don't we? Look, maybe you didn't like going to bed with me, I don't know, but let's at least be friends."

She did not look at him. "Ain't you gonna tell me how good I am? Ain't you gonna tell me I really know how to move my butt?"

He sighed and sat in the easy chair. "Hey, last night was really good, it's true. Wasn't I affectionate enough afterward? Is that it? I didn't know you wanted me to be that way. I thought—"

"You thought we were just taking care of business."

"No." He protested too quickly and knew he was lying, or at least he knew he had gone to bed with her for the first time just because he needed it once in a while. "Maybe. But it was better than it was supposed to be. Okay?"

"So you come back for more, white man?"

"I came back to tell you about going after Lex Tyrone's boyfriends. And, Christ, what's this 'white man' shit?"

"Don't you feel bad about turning on your own kind?"

"You're a mean drunk, woman. I'll just drift on down to the closest motel and we can talk tomorrow. Or not. Shit, Vonna, you know those people aren't 'my kind.' Shit!" He headed for the door.

"No!" she said, looking at him directly for the first time since he had come. "I—stay here. On the sofa. You don't want to go to a motel."

"It'd be better, don't you think?"

She covered her eyes with her hand and nearly dropped the vodka trying to set it on the table. "Please . . . it ain't you, Dub. It's—shit. I—it ain't you. I don't know why—" She pulled the turban off her head and wiped her face.

Lord, how I love a weepy drunk, sighed Dub to himself. He sat on the sofa and touched her damp calf. "Hey, it's okay. I won't take it personal."

"But it *is* personal. I just used you for my sick little

purposes like I done a hundred times, and, just like I always do, I hate myself afterward and I—"

"Hey, come on, hey. It's okay. I got no illusions. I think we hit it off better last night than most people ever do, but, hey, I been hit upside the head so many times I'm as punch-drunk as any old fighter. It don't have to be true love and you don't have to feel bad about it. Why would you?" He touched her shoulder and she twisted and threw her arms around his neck, sobbing into his shoulder. He kissed her ear and tasted the salt in her sweat. "It's okay. It's okay," he repeated. She couldn't be in love with him, could she? He didn't want that. He couldn't give that back. He couldn't feel that, hadn't felt that. What kind of life could two private eyes, one black, one white, have? She just needed to sober up. Christ! he thought.

Her sobbing slowed and she blew her nose into her towel.

"Come on," he said. "You're drunk. You need to sleep it off. I'll tuck you in and then I'll take the sofa. Okay?"

"No," she said. "You got to know. I never told nobody, especially no—well, I want to tell you, 'cause if I get straight I'll never be able to tell and you won't know." She looked into his eyes, bit her lower lip, and turned away. She took a quick sip and turned out the light, as if she couldn't bear to be seen. She pulled away from him.

"I was a real skinny little kid," she said. "Ain't that funny? I was all bones. You'd never believe it now, would you?"

"I was a lot lighter myself once."

"Don't talk," she said sharply. "Just listen." He sat back against the sofa. The drapes moved on a breeze again. "I was real skinny. Had my cornrows and my yellow dresses for church and Sunday school, and my momma she was a real good woman. She was a teacher, and some people said she had the power to heal. That's what they said. She never said it. She said God heals. But she got sick and God didn't heal her."

She hesitated for long enough that Dub thought she had passed out, but she took another quick sip and continued. "Anyhow, I was twelve and the minister, he worked it out to get me into a real nice place for orphans. I just didn't have nowhere to go. My momma's sister was dead. My daddy was— nobody knew, in Detroit, maybe. Dead. Out west, maybe. Anyhow I went to this place and the white man who run it was thought to be like a saint. It was up north, closer to Arkansas than here, and he had kids of all races, and some of them went to college afterward and everything. Reverend Fisher was his name. Called himself the Fisher of Souls and they thought he was a saint." She laughed abruptly, then became silent again.

"You see, my momma didn't talk about sex. She was real straight, you know. I suppose she might've told me eventually. I was already getting curious about it. I'd already heard some things, but, you know, I didn't know nothing really. Well, the Reverend, the Reverend Fisher, he—" Her voice choked out.

Dub suddenly understood. He pressed his face with both hands, wiping it as if he were trying to rub the skin off. "Jee-sus Christ," he muttered. "Jee-sus H. Christ!"

"He didn't do it right away," said Vonna. "He was real nice to me, and I'd just had my fourteenth birthday when we finally—"

"Oh, Vonna," said Dub.

"He was careful, you know. He kept saying he didn't want to hurt me and he didn't just force me, he kind of talked me into it, I guess. It did hurt, but he stopped and cried and I felt bad for letting him down."

Dub was so agitated he stood and paced. Elizabeth and Carrie flashed into his mind. What sort of luck puts one girl in the hands of a Reverend Fisher and keeps another safe? "The bastard raped you! Jesus!"

"He didn't make me do it when I didn't want to."

"Aw, shit, don't say that."

"No. He didn't. But he made you feel guilty if you didn't, you know, and then you'd want to do anything he'd want when he was preaching because everybody said he was a saint and you were something special to him."

"So he fucked your mind too. How long did this go on?"

"I was seventeen when they arrested him. They didn't catch him 'cause of me. Something about a boy in the toilet of the train station. I didn't say nothing. Nothing. I never said a thing."

He knelt and laid his hands on both her knees. "You can't feel guilty about that. They got him, Vonna. You were just a kid. He was the bad one."

She sobbed again, pressing her forehead against the top of his head. "I know," she murmured. "I know. And at first it hurt, but later it felt good, and I know it shouldn't have felt good and I shouldn't have wanted his wrinkled white hands in my pants but I couldn't help it, you know. He was the only sex I knew anything about, I just didn't know how bad it was, and when I figured it out I hated myself but I didn't stop."

"Ssssh! Sssssh! It's okay. That's the past. Let it die. That's—what?—twenty years ago? Dead and gone."

"Dead like a highway cat. Stinks up my life. All of my life. I should be able to stop, but I can't. After all these years, I still can't. I talked about it with a psychiatrist in the Army. He just laughed at me. Then about five years ago I was really down so I went to a women's clinic and talked to a psychologist there. She wasn't much help. I mean she wanted to put it all on men. Period. What it done, though, was made me see myself."

"Well they say understanding's the first step to the cure."

"*They* know everything, don't they? But I don't. I even married a good man, a black man, and all I did was make him feel like a failure. I can't get it without a white man, and every time I do it, I hate myself." She inhaled deeply. "I—I just was using you, it's true. It's sick, but I need to once in a while. Like I needed those white officers in the Army and told myself I would get bad ratings if I turned them down. And then, afterward, I'm supposed to hate you, you know, blame you, like I did them. I do it so I can hate your white man's fingers and your pale ass. But if I hate it, why do I do it in the first place, you know? I know what's wrong with me and I can't do a fucking thing about it."

Dub fumbled in the dark until he found her hands.

"I wanted you to be like all the others, you see. Bing, bang, thank you ma'am. You could go off and brag you'd done a nigger, a real hot-blooded coon, and I—"

"Jesus, I wouldn't do that." He thought about how, just as they had first climbed the stairs into the apartment, he had thought about how passionate black women were supposed to be: the darker the skin, the hotter the pot.

"—and I took advantage of it."

"Look, lady, you didn't take any more advantage of me than I did of you. Everybody feels guilty afterward, don't they?"

"I'll bet," she said. "I sure hope not or it's a depress-depressing world."

"You mean it ain't?" he said.

"Oh God!" she sighed.

"We've all been burned, haven't we? Right? We got to go on after that, though. Right?" He smelled the liquor on her breath and thought of Saigon. What he was saying, he should have been saying to himself. "I've got my scars too." He felt like there was something more he needed to tell her, but he couldn't. "Everybody does."

She squeezed his hands hard. "I shouldn't get loaded. I'm a real shit when I'm loaded."

"Aaaa, you're not so bad."

She pulled his head against her neck. "You don't need a mess like me."

"Would it be easier if I go?"

"Maybe. But don't." She lay flat on the sofa and pulled him up. There wasn't much room for him, but he hung on the edge, arms around her waist, his head against her damp breastbone. There was a moment when he inhaled and was going to tell her about Saigon. Why? Because she had been stripped naked and, as in a nudist camp, it was impolite not to strip also. She had offered, and it was time for him to reciprocate, but he hesitated. He wasn't sure he could tell her, and before he could gather up the strength to do it, she began to snore.

He eased out from under her arm and felt his way to the balcony door. It was raining: a regular Vietnamese monsoon. Great torrents rushed across the parking lot. The rain gutters on the building were all overwhelmed and water poured over the sides in sheets. He lit a cigarette and watched it come down. Funny he hadn't heard it raining. It was one hell of a rain, he thought.

A hell of a rain.

TWELVE

"It's still not too late to back out," said Vonna, touching Dub on the thigh.

The hand startled him. He had been staring at the gray Doric columns of the county courthouse, watching the flags stir in an indifferent breeze that occasionally revealed the full stars and bars of the Georgia state flag. "I want to do this," he said, a bit too forcefully.

"You won't take any real chances, will you?"

He studied her face. They had shared her apartment, but they hadn't had sex at all during the ten days it had taken to set up the infiltration. Dub had wanted to; it contributed to his sleeplessness to lie on her sofa and hear her turning in her bed. But she wouldn't have been comfortable. She would have been doing him a favor and he wouldn't have been able to enjoy that. She had told him too much. There are things in a person's mind that clamor to get out like blue crabs in a hot kettle. They click, click—the desperate Morse code of panic—but you press the lid down tighter. You know what it's like inside, but you wait, hoping the endless sad tapping will fade. It is hard enough to face up to yourself, but when you have let someone else see, you can't forgive them for knowing. In the pauses in the work of planning Dub's undercover, he had often glanced at Vonna and she had averted her eyes and talked rapidly about anything, just anything. She knew he knew, and he understood that it made her feel naked. To look at him was a reminder of what she wished no one knew, what she wished even she didn't know.

Last night, they had been walking after dinner back to

their motel rooms just outside of Atlanta when, all at once, Vonna had stopped, grabbed him by the shoulders, and hugged him. He had been startled. He watched the traffic on the interstate behind her and squeezed her waist. She pulled away and went to her room silently. He continued watching the traffic and wondered if her impulse had come from some premonition, or intention, that she would never see him again after he had weaseled himself into the AVCN. He considered going to her room to spend a final night forgetting himself in her body, but he smoked three cigarettes instead, then watched an old episode of *"The Honeymooners"* on TV.

A truck full of chickens raised a cloud of dust and Dub remembered where they were and why they were parked there. "I won't take unnecessary chances. Doing it at all is taking a chance," he said. "But so's crossing the road." He wished she would take her hand off his thigh. Like last night's hug, he didn't know what to make of it. Did she care about him? Could she? He didn't need more to think about.

"You don't have to do it, Dub. Maybe there's some other way. It isn't really our business."

"You don't believe that. They kill people," said Dub. "And that isn't the worst of it. They're just like the pricks I went after in Saigon and I want to hurt them." He closed his eyes. It had slipped out. He had to keep Saigon out of his mind. His breathing deepened.

"What happened in Saigon?" she asked.

He shook his head. It was nearly time for the march. The courthouse square of Breckenridge, Georgia, was filling, not just with lines of state police, but with clusters of blacks, some wearing Muslim amulets or dreadlocks or pseudo-African clothes. Men with bullhorns were trying to stir up their groups with chants, and thin, gentle men in church robes raised their hands in the ancient attitude of prayer and led their followers in "We Shall Overcome." Six whites and one black emerged from a VW van as if out of a time machine launched from the late sixties and unfurled a long banner with a hammer and sickle sloppily painted between the slogans "STOP RACISM!" and "END BOURGEOIS EXPLOITATION!" Cameramen from television stations were scurrying for position on picnic tables and on the courthouse steps. Other than teenagers, there didn't appear to be too many locals gathering, except in front of the barbershop and stores safely opposite the courthouse. Their dull little town, thought Dub, wasn't theirs any more. It was just a place to scratch the nation's scabs.

"I better get over there," said Dub. "My boys'll be along in fifteen or twenty minutes." He opened the car door.

"You all set?" she asked.

He wiped his face with his hand and nodded.

"Take care," she said. He stuck one leg out of the car, then leaned back and kissed her. She hadn't expected it and made a quick noise like she'd had a chill.

He pulled away quickly. Her eyes were closed. "Bye," he said.

She bit her upper lip. "You shouldn't have done that." She looked away. "Somebody could've seen us."

The crowd was now pushing closer to the line of policemen, who had donned helmets with plastic face guards. The carnival mood of some of the spectators contrasted sharply with the policemen's stony faces. They didn't like being there, they didn't want to be there, they didn't understand why a court had ordered that the march could take place. They didn't understand why they had to stand between the two sets of troublemakers. Let the bastards kill each other and let God sort them out. "Where are the marchers?" Dub asked one of the cops. The cop lowered his eyes to Dub's face, then raised them to continue scanning the crowd.

"I said 'Where are the marchers?' It's okay. I'm with them."

The cop pursed his mouth. "The lot behind the Mobil, edge of town." He twitched his head to one side.

"Thanks."

"Yeah. Thanks a whole hell of a lot."

A balding white man in a flannel shirt grabbed Dub's arm. "You're with them? Racist pig!"

Okay, thought Dub, now's as good a time as any. "Go back to Russia." He turned his back and the man yelled.

"Fascist! Here's one of them over here! Racist!"

Dub faced him. "I tell you what, I'll go join the Americans and you go back to your queer friends up north."

"What do you mean 'queer'?"

"Oh, I'm *so* sorry. I'm supposed to say 'gay,' ain't I?"

The man leaped forward, but an older man caught him around the chest like a ballet dancer catching his partner. "You racist bastard! I'll knock your teeth down—" The older man managed to hold him, people closed in to see what was happening, and one of the cops stepped between them.

"Hey, hey, *hey!*" he said. "Knock it off! We don't want any trouble here!"

"Let him go," said Dub. "I'll shut his trash mouth."

"You go about your business," said the cop sharply, "or I'll shut both your mouths."

Dub pushed two people aside and edged through the crowd. "Damn nigger lovers!" he heard someone say. A woman immediately shushed the speaker. By the time Dub had moved to the end of the block he was just another anonymous spectator. He bumped into a gray-haired black woman with spectacles. When she looked at him over the glass, she seemed to be probing his true nature. It was exactly the kind of look Opal had given when she was trying to gauge whether "young Mr. Delbert" was lying to her.

"I'm sorry," he said. "Lots of pushing."

She said nothing.

The crowd thinned out. He saw the Mobil station and a smaller assembly of people with placards surrounded by half a dozen police cars. Ku Klux Klan uniforms gleamed. Six brown-shirted men and women wearing riding boots, jodhpurs, and red armbands stood with their thumbs through their Sam Browne belts. Slouching around them were pimply teenagers in motorcycle boots: skinheads. Most of them, despite the heat, wore leather jackets decorated with Nazi regalia, though some had sleeveless T-shirts. Their heads were enflamed by swatches of razor burn and the toughest of them seemed to be a girl with rooster-comb hair and a death's-head tattoo on her cheek. All of the marchers were clustered in a huge circle, as if getting instructions. Those to the outside of the group bobbed on their toes to hear or see better. Two policemen noticed Dub and intercepted him.

"Sir?" said one. "Your business here?"

"My business? I'm with them."

"You're a member of these"—he jerked his thumb—"ah, groups."

"I'm marching with them."

"You're a member?"

"I'm with them. I heard about the march on TV and I—"

"Which group do you belong to?"

"All of them."

The policemen looked at each other. "Listen, fella," said one, "there's a lot of people would like to see something bad happen today. I'm not saying you shouldn't believe what you believe, just that it's a good idea to stay away from real flash points."

Dub raised his voice. "Are you telling me to go home? You got no right to say that. This is America and I can stand up for America."

The other cop inflated his cheeks and whooshed out a sigh. "Yeah, and you'll get the American Civil Liberties Union to screw up my life, right? Let me see your identification."

"What is this, a police state?" Dub held out his wallet. The cop scrutinized it. "You're harassing me."

"You're not carrying any weapons. No weapons, right?"

"This is a peaceful demonstration," said Dub, "unless somebody makes trouble."

"And you wouldn't do that, would you, Mr. Clements?"

"Naw."

The second cop told him to lift his arms and patted him for a concealed weapon. All of this had drawn the attention of one of the Nazis, who strolled over with his hands cocked on his hips. His crewcut made his round face look even more pubescent. "What seems to be the trouble, officers?" he asked. One cop looked at him, sniffed, and scratched his chin.

"I'm here to march with you," said Dub.

"It might be dangerous," said the Nazi with delight.

"The white man's got to stand up for what's right."

"We will get you a membership application. You are the kind of man America, the world, needs." He lifted his chin.

"Satisfied?" Dub asked the cops.

"It's your nuts in the grinder," said one. The other crossed his arms.

"Come with me," said the Nazi.

"What's up?"

"Ssssh!"

They pushed past the skinheads (who didn't seem interested in talk) until they reached the parley at the center. In a circle stood the Nazis' leader, John Arthur Ford; two silk-robed Klan dragons; and, looking out-of-place in an expensive gray suit, Marshall Allan Wescott, president of the American Values Conservatory Nation. He was more striking in person than in the photographs Dub had seen. Except for the styled silver hair and wire glasses, he reminded Dub of General Mark Clark when he was in charge of the Citadel.

A short man in overalls, a red shirt, and a fedora-shaped panama gestured with a cigar. "Now I know you all got a right to march where you want, or at least that's what the court tol' us. But why here? Breckenridge is just a small town. We're jus' ol' folks and farmers. We ain't got no quarrel with nobody. We dint ask nobody to march up here last month. They made their speeches and they went away. It won't our idea. People could git hurt. There's been calls all day and all night and all the last week. Do it as a favor to Breckenridge? How 'bout it, boys?"

John Arthur Ford raised a fist. It didn't seem angry or threatening, more like a habitual gesture. "You didn't try to stop the niggers from their march, Mayor. Why are you trying to stop loyal Americans? Would it have anything to do with nigger votes?"

"Right!" yelled Dub. He caught the eye of one of the suited toughs flanking Wescott. The protestors murmured.

"Fuck him!" yelled a skinhead. A Klansman looked back in disapproval.

"He's stalling," said someone else. "Let's go!"

"I'm gonna make sure all the good white voters of this county know about this," said the Grand Dragon or Wizard or whatever he was.

"Don't tell me about my town," said the mayor. "All I know is suddenly half the country wants to make speeches here. It was a fair trial, the boy was convicted. What the hell else we s'posed to do?" He poked his cigar back toward the town. "Ah don't know what scuz is worst: them Commonists back in the town or these here punks."

"Hey, fuck you, old man," said the tough girl. "Scuz this!"

[124]

She hefted one of her breasts. The sheriff moved in her direction.

"Come on," she said. "Come on! I'll take yuh!"

"Don't let them provoke us," shouted Ford. "It is a ploy to stop us before we start!"

There was pushing and more yelling until Marshall Wescott raised his hand like a preacher. He wore an enormous ring with a white rook inlaid on an onyx oval. "We are here," he said, "neither to impugn your role as mayor, nor to question the decision of the Breckenridge County jury. They did their duty. We are here to support them. We are here to demonstrate that support. We are here to ensure that the color of that criminal's skin does not guarantee his freedom. The coloreds marched to say that the legally appointed jury had done a miscarriage of justice. We are here to say that he deserved everything he got. Why do you question our motives?"

"Oh Lord," muttered the mayor to the sheriff behind him, "it's like talking to a post. Go on. Go on ahead with it. Do what you want. Jus' remember how much Breckenridge folks appreciate all the turmoil you people bring on us. Take me back to the town hall, Erwin. It's up to the state police now."

There was some clapping and a momentary disagreement about who should lead the march into Breckenridge: the eleven Nazis or the Klan. They drew straws and the Nazis, plainly disappointed, then wanted to line up in the rear. Wescott said that it had already been decided the AVCN should follow, because they had no official uniform and would look like a ground swell of popular support. Wescott spoke plainly, but intelligently. He was patient and very persuasive. He didn't go in for the world-conqueror posturing of John Arthur Ford or the oaflike directness of the Grand Wizard. It might be possible to laugh at the others as silly devils, gargoyles of the American mind. Wescott was more dangerous. Except for the line of argument, he might be a presidential candidate hanging around outside a New Hampshire factory.

Dub drifted toward the people without uniforms. He spotted a man with an American flag on one lapel, a white rook on the other. His blue suit hung loosely on his wiry frame. "How do?" said Dub. "I'm Carl Clements." It was like shaking hands with vise-grip pliers.

"Danny Devlin."

"Hey, we have rhyming names."

Danny looked puzzled.

"Carl Clements; Danny Devlin. All we need is twenty-four others and we'd have the alphabet."

"Oh."

"Say, Danny, is Lamont here?"

Several heads turned.

"Lamont George. We were kind of buddies. I knew him in Nam, then we ran into each other in Erie. Pennsylvania. North of Pittsburgh."

"Lamont isn't around."

"Too bad. He said he was doing important work for Mr. Wescott and he might give me an intro, you know." Dub sighed. "It ain't been good since Nam. What the hell were we fighting for? So some spook could take our jobs? So some Jap could get rich?"

A bullhorn barked. "Ever'body five across!"

Another man with a white rook ring rushed up like he wanted to stand next to Devlin. "Hi. Carl Clements," said Dub. "You know Danny?" The man hurried off to the next row. "Did you serve?" Dub asked Devlin.

"No. Underweight." It obviously stuck in his craw.

Carl nodded. "You look fit, though. A lot of you guys look fit. That's one thing Lamont said. He said you guys could whip me into better shape than I was in in Nam."

"Lamont said this?"

"I saved his life once. I guess he saw what a wreck I was and—"

"Ever'body remember!" said the bullhorn man. "Hold your place! All the cameras are on us. They'll do whatever they can to make us look violent."

"Awesome!" said a skinhead.

"No matter what they call you, hold your place!"

Dub pointed at the white rook. "Say, does that stand for the AVCN? How can I get one of those?"

Danny scrutinized him. "You came all the way down here from Pennsylvania?"

Dub gestured with his thumb. "Atlanta," he said. "Like

the job in Erie. One after another after another. You could fill a plantation with the niggers I worked with over the past year."

Devlin seemed to be thinking. The march began. The state police led with one car, followed with another. Breckenridgers watched from their porches or shooed their children inside. One block before the corridor formed by the police began, the marchers were signaled by the Grand Wizard, raised their flags and placards, and began singing "America the Beautiful." Even the skinheads seemed to enjoy that. Almost simultaneously chaotic noise rose from the town square. Loud booing was orchestrated by one group. There was spontaneous clapping here and there. Someone shouted, "Hang all niggers!" and two policemen broke from the line to pull the fighters apart. Cameramen scurried like roaches.

There was too much disorder, too much good stuff for the evening news. Dub scanned faces twisted in rage, shouting, gesturing. He saw Vonna staring, placid, the only expressionless face in the crowd. He thought of the despicable things he had been saying for his role and avoided her eyes. He then saw a black man in dreadlocks placing a Soviet flag in the rein hands of the equestrian statue in the town square. A circle of black men and women were holding hands and singing "We Shall Overcome" at the top of their lungs, but the Muslims were shouting through portable loudspeakers and playing a speech at earsplitting volume. Anywhere in the crowd could be a man with a knife, a woman with a pistol, a child with a hand grenade. Dub's sweat was stinging his eyes, the sunlight shining through the bare trees blurred. He wanted to see Elizabeth and Carrie and hold them close to him.

The Klan mounted the courthouse steps. The Nazis followed and lined up along the bottom as if protecting the building. The AVCN was forced to push between them, but the skinheads seemed to relish lingering as close as they could to the crowd by scattering along the police line. There was a momentary lessening of the noise as the leaders huddled. John Arthur Ford wanted to change the order of the speeches. He had a feeling that if he spoke third, after the Grand Wizard and Wescott softened up the crowd, he could have them in the palm of his hand. He closed his fingers as if crushing the angry crowd in his fist. "Oh, fer Chrissake," shouted the Grand

Wizard, "yer worse than the mayor. We decided this all two hours ago." Wescott placed a hand on each leader's shoulder and pulled them into a huddle. Dub wryly remembered his mother intoning "Blessed are the peacemakers" every time he scrapped with the neighbor kid. The banners behind the police cordon drooped slightly as if the crowd were marshaling its strength. Dub felt as if everyone were watching him. As bad as Saigon had been, his role had never required him to be on display like this. Nobody had ever looked at him with the hate he saw across the street. He began to think it was possible to be hated to death. He scanned the nineteenth-century tops of the stores opposite and tried to read the carved names and dates despite the dazzling sun.

The Grand Wizard took the microphone held out by another Klansman, who then lifted the small P.A. system off the steps. "We come here today to show our support for the United States of America and to the republic for which it stands." Hoods bobbed as the Klansmen agreed. Feedback screeched. The Wizard tried to position himself away from the loudspeaker. "It took us a court order to be able to say that. We ain't allowed no real platform to talk from. We ain't even allowed to set up real speakers, even though the demonstration two weeks ago had those things, and every Breckenridge politician for the last hunnert years done spoke from this spot without being told he couldn't have those things. I think it's a sad day in America when politicians get together with northern liberals to try and stop a man from speaking his piece.

"But we ain't here to criticize the United States or the flaws in its court system. Them things will be righted sooner than most people think." There was some hooting and shouting. "That's right. I don't care what nobody says. We're here to say that the court system done right by the people of Breckenridge County when they convicted Lemuel Turner." Booing and shouting rose louder and didn't subside, so the Wizard shouted, "And we don't want no federal judge telling us that the life of Annamae Kiefer is less important than a killer's!"

"Free Turner! Free Turner!" a bullhorn barked. The crowd took up the chant.

"Shut up and let the man speak!"

"Free Turner! Free Turner!"

"Free all political prisoners!"

A fight had broken out by the equestrian statue. Three skinheads were trying to pull down the Red flag. When the dreadlocked owner of it tried to stop them, one of the toughs clubbed at him with a sixteen-ounce RC bottle. Four policemen soon had all of them spread-eagled against the statue's base. The Communist tried to protest; the cop jabbed him with his club. Several people shouted at the cops and they, more threatened from behind than by the fighters, prodded the crowd to hold it back. One of the skinheads broke away and disappeared into the crowd. The cops raised their sticks as a threat when some people mocked them. In the midst of all this chaos, a black minister had regathered his flock, formed a huge circle, and begun singing "We Shall Overcome" again.

Dub looked at his new companions. The Nazis held their backs ramrod stiff, though a couple of them licked their lips as if nervous. The tough girl taunted the crowd, curling her fingers to egg them on, though if they had broken the police line they would have swept over the marchers like a tidal wave over a sand castle. The skinheads smirked, however: they fed on all this. The Klansmen by contrast looked either frightened outright or bewildered. They didn't know what all the fuss was about. They were just ordinary folks, they thought, who felt ordinary things. Later they might decide that all those hostiles in the square were outside agitators sent in to abuse decent folks, but for the moment their eyes were big with all the chaos they had released.

The White Rook boys were like none of the others. They stood with their hands over their groins, legs slightly spread: soldiers at ease. Each face was emotionless, though alert, eyes shifting from side to side like those of a quarterback checking the defense. Devlin, in particular, gave off a feeling of power, as if he had sealed in a tremendous force. A tap and the nitro would explode. They reminded Dub of elite troops, particularly of Army Rangers or the even more fearsome Navy Seals. He doubted there was enough fat in all of them put together to grease a waffle iron. They were ready. They didn't particularly look forward to trouble or avoid it. They were just ready.

John Arthur Ford began his harangue. The booing was loud, even from some rednecks on the north end of the square, who seemed to be having a tailgate party on the hay bales in a pickup truck. It took Ford only a few sentences to warm up to a sputtering rage. He gesticulated with his free arm raised in a fist, regularly driving the P.A. system into a muddy shriek, several times gesturing with both hands so that the microphone was waving at arm's length and nothing of his speech reached the crowd. He spoke so rapidly at times that strings of words became single words like "Communist Jewish industrialmatrixconspiracy" with "Communist" sounding like "commonest" and "Jewish" like "juice". "Zionist" rhymed with "finest" and "Soviet" with "forfeit". As he went on, however, nobody seemed to know what he was talking about except his followers, who, every time he reached the end of what was supposed to be an irrefutable point, gave the stiff-arm salute, or shouted "Yes!" or "No!" to whatever rhetorical question he had closed with. They had been coached or had heard the speech several times, thought Dub.

As the tirade stretched past fifteen minutes, the opposing banners began to droop. People struck up conversations with each other and no one bothered to drown him out. Dub's sleepless night caught up with him and Ford's speech was like a hot rum punch on top of it. Dub checked his watch and settled onto the courthouse steps, resting his arms on his knees. Devlin's thigh bumped his elbow. "Show some respect," he said out of the side of his mouth. Dub looked up. Devlin was suppressing a smile. Dub rolled his head from side to side and remained sitting. He was going to like Devlin, he thought. That would make it harder at the end. You had to keep a cold, hard knot inside, so that you could be indifferent to your own feelings.

Ford had come to what his followers thought a stirring conclusion. They were chanting, "America! America! America!" The skinheads joined in, but the Klan merely watched. Some applauded politely. Wescott moved to take the microphone from Ford, but Ford's followers continued chanting while he basked in their adulation. Wescott stood politely behind him until Ford finally handed him the microphone and raised his arm in the Nazi salute. Dub stood. He saw the crowd stirring in anticipation of Wescott. The Muslims were getting ready to drown him out. The circle of singers was beginning to form up again. The banners were being spread high and straight. The anger and hate was coming back into the people's eyes and Dub looked away at the store tops. People had climbed onto the roofs for a better view. There were about a dozen over the barbershop, some with lawn chairs. There were two silhouettes walking hunched behind the raised brick top of the Western Auto.

"Friends," said Wescott, "we are not here to criticize any race. We of the American Values Conservatory Nation have no interest in punishing any person because of his race, religion, color, or creed. . . . "

Hooting, hissing, and various obscenities rose from the crowd. The bullhorn chanted, "Li-ar! Li-ar!" and the skinheads flung back obscenities.

"But we," said Wescott, "are a nation of laws, and law without justice is no law at all. What doubt is there that Lemuel Turner committed the crime of which he is accused? A jury of Breckenridge County citizens found him guilty. Guilty. And—"The shouting grew so loud Wescott stopped. He didn't look perturbed or angry. He simply lowered the microphone and waited. This incited the crowd momentarily while Klansmen shouted, "Let him talk! Let the man talk!" John Arthur Ford stepped up beside Wescott and shrieked, "Listen to the *enemy!* These are the swine who have destroyed our country!" The crowd couldn't have heard him, but they must have seen his gestures and the volume increased. Their faces were distorted, reddened with fury, shining with sweat. They were nightmare people, and Dub felt dizzy with trying to remember that they were right, that he stood with evil on those stairs and, no matter how threatened, couldn't allow himself to forget it.

It was when he looked at the roofs opposite that he saw one of the dozen over the barbershop jump up and point to a figure over the Western Auto. There was a glint or a shape or a movement that Dub instinctively knew was the aiming of a rifle.

"Gun!" he shouted. "Gun!" He swept Devlin aside with the back of his arm and dived toward Wescott as the first shot was fired. People were stunned. Two of Wescott's men reached at Dub as he flew at Wescott. Stone exploded as the second shot cracked between Ford's boots. He cried out. Dub came down on top of Wescott. Wescott's men crouched. The Klansmen stumbled and fell down the stairs. The tough girl spun around as if she couldn't believe that what she really wanted, a rumble, had come to pass. One of the Nazis produced a pistol and started firing wildly. A policeman brought him down with one blow of his club. Dub was covering Wescott and could hear him crying, "I'm hit! I'm dead! Sweet Jesus!" Another bullet struck the stairs and Dub felt a sting in his ear and forehead. The panicked crowd had knocked down and trampled the police cordon, and the police, confused and battered, were scattered about the street shoving and clubbing and pivoting with drawn guns, looking desperately for the source of the gunfire.

Dub had just noticed the blood in his eye when two of the White Rook boys scooped him up by the arms and dragged him behind one of the courthouse columns. Two others put Wescott behind another column. Dub peeked out and saw John Arthur Ford rolling down the stairs as if dead, but at the bottom he crawled behind a nearly full trash can. There were maybe two dozen people lying prone or crouching behind benches and trees in the park. Others lay flat in the open. One wriggled and held her knee and screamed. There was a volley of shots from the direction of the Western Auto, then a long unearthly silence as if the universe had stopped to take a breath, then sirens, police boots on pavement, and the crackle of walkie-talkies.

Dub turned his back to the column, leaned against it, and slid down to a sitting position. He touched his ear and felt blood. His eyebrow was also hot and sticky with it. He peered over at Wescott. Devlin and another White Rook were bent over, trying to get a good look at his wound. Wescott waved them off. "Get away from me! I'm all right. Get away!"

Well, thought Dub, didn't I get lucky! "Are you all right, Mr. Wescott?"

"Take care of that man," said Wescott. "If it weren't for him . . . "

"I'm okay," said Dub. He stood and walked slowly. Devlin reached up to hold his arm.

"You're bleeding," said Wescott. "Sit down. Sweet Jesus!"

"It just grazed me."

"It's more than that," said the other White Rook.

Dub sat on the cool stone. "It looks like fragments got you," said Devlin. "Bullet fragments. Maybe stone."

"I always knew I had rocks in my head," said Dub. No one laughed. He turned to Wescott. "Where are you hit?"

Wescott touched his forehead. It was bloody and deeply scraped. His nose was swollen. "I think you banged my head on the stairs. You might have broken my shin too." Devlin squatted and lifted Wescott's pants leg. There was a blue knot half the size of a softball.

"I'm sorry," said Dub.

"Better beat up than dead. Who are you?"

"Carl Clements. I come down from Atlanta to stand with you all on this march."

"I'm very happy you did."

"Well, it doesn't look like he was a very good shot. You might've been safer if I'd left you alone."

"I don't believe it, Carl. You saved my life." He had a sudden thought and pointed at his guards. "Which is what *you* were supposed to do."

"It happened so quick," said Devlin.

"People are quick or people are dead. Are you a vet, Carl?"

"Yessir. In country four years."

"It shows. You'd really be sharp if you lost a little weight, started working out—"

The other White Rook stepped over Wescott and intercepted a television cameraman. Two others were charging up the stairs after an unsteady John Arthur Ford. His jodhpurs were torn, either by the shattering bullets or by his scramble over the pavement. They were also wet. "He pissed himself," said Devlin, sneering.

"This is our opportunity," said Ford. "This is the incident that will vault us to power."

"It was probably a screwball," said Dub.

"No, Commandant Ford might have a point—" Then the cameramen were upon them and an overly perfumed blonde poked a microphone in people's faces and battered them with questions. Wescott was very calm. Ford gesticulated. Dub just waved her off and said he was a bystander. Ambulance men brought stretchers. Dub said he could walk and Ford said loudly that it would take more than some nigger Communist to kill him. By the time they reached the ambulance there was a small crowd gathered. They were told there were only seven victims. A Klansman wounded in the thigh was the only person actually hit by a bullet. There was an unconscious Nazi under arrest for concealing a weapon. Three skinheads were hand-cuffed facedown in the flower bed and one was moaning from the thrashing someone had given him. Others had been hurt in the stampede. Wescott made the ambulance attendants wait as he sat up on his gurney and answered the questions of two new reporters. He was calm and very precise in his words. "I'm more hurt spiritually," he said at one point, "that someone could actually shoot up a rally in support of American justice."

The impromptu press conference was interrupted by the sheriff's car screeching to a halt across the street. The mayor, still in his overalls and panama, huffed over, the sheriff chasing. His anger seemed to melt people out of his way.

"Look what you cocksuckers done to my town! I tol' you not to hol' your lousy march. I tol' you, gawdam, I *begged* you. You know there's a seven-year-old boy was trampled? He's got six broke ribs. There's a seventy-year-old nigra woman that wet-nursed half the men in this town. Her hip's so busted she won't ever walk right. And it's your gawdam fault."

"Mayor, I resent that. Americans have a right to—"

"Is the identity of the sniper established?" interrupted the reporter.

"Charles Leggett," said the sheriff. "He thought he was taking revenge for Greensboro."

"Greensboro?"

"Some Nazis killed some Communists; I don't know much else about—"

"He was after me," said Ford nodding.

"Well, I wish ta hell he won't such a lousy shot. And a twenty-two, yet. He must've been going for yore brain!"

Ford raised his fist. "Your attitude will be remembered!"

"I whupped you bastards in forty-five and I'm not too old to—" The sheriff grabbed the strap of the mayor's overalls, but Ford leaned breath-close to the mayor.

"You, old man, will—"

What he intended to say he'd never remember—the mayor's round fist landed on his face like a fifty-pound country ham. The ambulance attendants looked at the unconscious would-be dictator of the Fourth Reich, shrugged, and unloaded another gurney.

THIRTEEN

In the waiting room of the tiny hospital that served Breckenridge, Dub was told to sit on a chair borrowed from an office
while a young Filipino doctor rushed from patient to patient
in the first multiple emergency he'd likely ever encountered
there. When Dr. Carletto saw the uniforms and arm bands of
the two unconscious Nazis, he looked at his black nurse, who
shook her head with amusement, then lifted Ford's eyelid to
shine a penlight into it. The state police kept the other Nazis
outside, so the doctor wouldn't be pestered. Ford moaned. The
doctor moved off to check a skinhead who couldn't see out of
his swollen eyelids.

"Shit," muttered the kid. "Shit. Louis? Is Louis here? Am
I gonna see again, doctor? Am I gonna see?"

"No problem," said Carletto.

"Why do the police want the fucking foreigners to take
our country, doctor? Shit."

"I don't know," said Carletto.

Wescott watched the doctor with resentment, but said
nothing except whatever would answer Carletto's questions.
Two policemen were speculating what the sheriff would charge
Ford with in order to help out the mayor.

"Carl," said Wescott from his gurney. "Sit with me."

"Feel a little naked without your thugs?" said a man to
Wescott's left.

"Leave Mr. Wescott alone," said Dub.

"Don't you think that's enough for today?" said a cop,
staring.

Dub rolled his chair to Wescott's right.

"Quite a picnic," said Dub. "Can I get you something, Mr. Wescott?"

"Thank you no. Carl, right?"

Dub nodded. "Carl Clements."

"My people didn't do me a lot of good today," said Wescott, leaning against the rail. "I owe you a great deal."

"It was just an accident. I mean, I saw the guy, I jumped."

"How can I repay you?"

"Repay? Naw. It was just automatic. In Nam you had to have an instinct or you were dead. You don't owe me nothing."

"You're from Atlanta?"

"Well, no. I got—I had a temporary job there. Wiring. All I could find. I'm not an electrician. I just did the dirty work: running cable, drilling holes, and so on."

Wescott gestured toward the doctor. "Your bill here will be taken care of."

"Aw, you don't have to—" He smiled. "All right. I guess I could use it."

"And what else? If I can't do it for you, I'll tell you. Speak up. Maybe you need work."

Dub raised his hands as if unable to come up with anything. "I take care of myself. Say. There is something."

"Yes."

"I'd like one of those rings." He pointed at Wescott's hand.

"The White Rook?"

"Yes."

"Why?"

"Because I like them. Because you're speaking up for the right things. As a kind of souvenir for marching with you."

Wescott smiled. "Well, I tell you, Carl, these aren't just symbolic. They're special. They're bronze and cloisonné. You have to earn them."

"Oh," said Dub. "Well, that's all right, I—"

"Is there a Mrs. Clements, Carl?"

"Besides my mother? Too many. Three."

"Three?"

"Don't get along too well with women since the war." The legend fit the truth; that was always good. He leaned close to Wescott. "I mean I ain't queer or nothing, but, well, that's how it goes."

Wescott grinned and whispered, "I heard that sideways stuff spoils you for American tail. Is that right?"

It always threw Dub when guys who looked like Wescott said something dirty. "Well, hell," he said, "you may have something there."

Wescott laughed and leaned back. "I'll tell you what, I can do this for you, Carl. I can set it up so that you can earn one of these rings someday. How would you like to go to the White Rook?"

Bingo, thought Dub. We have a bingo right here. "The White Rook?" he asked. "I heard of that, but, hell, I'd want to pay my own way."

"You will be my guest, Carl. We can't let a little thing like money hold back a patriot like you."

Dub blinked like he couldn't believe it. "Well, I'll be damned. This is my lucky day."

"I believe so," said Wescott, "and we're lucky to have you."

And ain't that white of you, thought Dub. Yessir. Real white.

The two difficult parts of setting up the undercover had been the legend and the entry. He had to have a legend that would seem to go along with the backgrounds of Lamont George, Lex Tyrone, and the White Rook boys who had come to the attention of the press and police. Combat vets who had trouble readjusting, they had turned to survivalism or fringe right-wing groups rather than drugs, psychiatry, or crime. Tyrone had been arrested as a member of the Posse Comitatus in South Dakota, but the charges had been dropped. Lamont George had subscribed to Nazi magazines and gone to a couple of meetings, but had officially joined only the John Birch Society in Philadelphia. At some point, however, all these affiliations were cut, presumably when they fell under the spell of Wescott and joined the AVCN.

Dub had said he wouldn't go inside unless he could get an airtight story. Devraix had asked, like Vonna had, why not simply use his own name? A lie has to have a flaw in it somewhere. The closer you were to the truth, the safer, but Dub simply said it was better all around, for everybody, if he could get a legend from the pros. Just making up a name and some I.D. wasn't enough. It was too easy to check. Everybody had a computer. *Everybody* checked.

Dub tracked down the captain who had sent him into Saigon. He was now a lieutenant-colonel. He hadn't talked to Dub since 1974, but Dub didn't remind him how much he owed his rise in the ranks to the Saigon undercover. There was a shade of awkwardness in his voice as if he didn't want to be reminded of how close he had come to sending Dub to his death. The greetings were as superficial as those between strangers on a bus.

Then, during a silence, Dub asked. The lieutenant-colonel hemmed a bit. He said that the legend file was only for military use. Dub explained that the false identity wouldn't be compromised and could be used again. The lieutenant-colonel said, "Please don't ask me. How do you know it won't be compromised? These things cost up to twenty-five thousand bucks to set up. I can't give one to a civilian. I don't even know what you're going to use it for."

Dub said, "We're after some killers, some smart killers. They may have wasted a hundred people for all I know. We need to know who these guys are, and this is our only way to find out."

"I believe you if you say so, but you must have your usual ways."

"Usual ain't good enough this time."

"Aw, Dub . . . "

"I need this, Captain," said Dub. "The nightmares don't go away."

There was silence. As a ploy, calling him captain to remind him of the old days was clever. As a ploy, referring to the nightmares was brilliant. But the ploy was as much confession as manipulation. It flashed memory across Dub's mind again and broke him out in a ferocious sweat.

"I'd think," said the officer, "that you'd want to avoid the situation."

Dub cleared his throat. "Hair of the dog," he said. "Maybe it'll put it to rest once and for all."

"Therapy's less dangerous." The man was silent for a while.

"Well?"

"All right. But stay away from the women. I won't be there to save your ass at the last minute this time. I'll give you a name and facts, that's all. You provide the papers. I can't get the Army in on that. You never heard of me. We never talked. Give me your number."

The entry turned out to be too easy. Normally it would take weeks of hanging around guys on the periphery of an organization, gradually winning their trust. It had taken nearly six months in Saigon before he had infiltrated the lowest levels of the heroin ring, and then he had only gotten to the grunt level: the guys who were cruel enough to stuff the baggies of uncut heroin into the chest cavities of dead soldiers. It was maybe the loneliness of playing one of the creeps and his eagerness to end it and go back to being clean that had made him start working on Janet, perfect Janet with her silky hair and wiry body. And then came the sex, and then the love, and then his knowing she could be trusted. And then, of course, the ultimate, inevitable betrayal.

This time would be easier. In Breckenridge, a protest march about the first-degree murder conviction of Lemuel Turner had led to the Klan's announcement that they would countermarch They were denied a permit because of the possibility of trouble. The sheriff would not be able to guarantee the safety of such a demonstration. A day later the AVCN, with its own lawyers and a "friend of the court" brief by the ACLU, had used the Skokie case to persuade a federal judge that he had to order the permit for two weeks hence. Everyone said there would be trouble, and that's what Dub had been hoping for—a chance to get noticed, a chance to let the White Rook boys know he was one of them. It would cut the long process of buddying up to an insider.

The day he and Vonna drove out of New Orleans Dub had found the hardest thing about becoming Carl Clements was taking Elizabeth's and Carrie's pictures out of his wallet. He even pressed the tiny photos against his cheeks, closed his eyes, and tried to imagine the girls hanging on his neck, kissing his ears and eyes. He had planned to see them before going under, but the entry had come up too suddenly and was too good to pass up. At the last moment he couldn't bring himself to call them. He wasn't going to say good-bye. He was going away for a while, maybe a long while, but he had to believe he was coming back and there was no reason for good-byes.

He packed his wallet with all sorts of scraps, receipts, etc., including a dog-eared photo of a naked Asian girl. The Breckenridge entry had come out even better than Dub had anticipated, if getting a few people trampled, beaten, and wounded was "better." The flap about the march had been lucky, and then the shooting had been lucky. He just hoped that wasn't the end of it. Luck was better than brains or skill, but it doesn't stay with anyone all that long.

Each time he changed from one plane to another, it was smaller. The final one had only six passenger seats, smelled like deer, and landed in a meadow. The next one would be a two-seater biplane, he thought, but an old-fashioned jeep rumbled out of the trees, with Danny Devlin at the wheel and beside him a tall woman with a long braid. The plane barely waited for him to unload his suitcase before it revved to take off.

"Christ!" said Dub. "How'd you get here so quick?" He shook Danny's hand.

"Straight from Breckenridge to the airport," said Devlin. "Carl, this is my wife Joan." Her hair was dirty blonde. She had high cheekbones and big hands. Her parka was unzipped and he could see the outlines of her brassiere under her olive T-shirt.

"How do," said Dub.

"Welcome," she said.

"I didn't know you were married," said Dub. "It's nice your wife goes for this kind of thing."

"She's a natural," he said proudly. "She teaches martial arts."

"No shit? Hell, my wife didn't do anything but eat." He patted his belly. "I'm still wearing some of that marriage." His little girls popped into his mind. "I didn't realize it'd be so cold. Christ!"

"Fatter men than you have come. You're not really bad," said Joan. "We'll get that gut off you in no time."

"I'll shiver it off." He watched his breath puff out in clouds. Joan suddenly touched his shoulder and turned him around. "Look," she said, pointing to the mountains. "Isn't it incredible?" The sharp gray crags scattered with snow patches loomed like gods.

"You can't get that into a picture," Dub said. "But does it ever get warm here?"

"Sometimes there's a Chinook," said Danny, "but it can snow through May."

Dub whistled. "You take my coat," said Joan. She was already taking it off.

"Naw, I'll be all right, I—"

"You just give me your sport coat. I'm acclimated. I could go swimming today."

He demurred again, but she insisted. Her parka was a good fit on him, but his jacket was tight across her powerful shoulders. He even raised the furry hood. She also insisted on his taking the passenger seat while she hunched crosswise in the back.

The road was rocky and the drive bone-shattering. Danny was adept at the gears and took breathtaking turns as if he were on the Pennsylvania Turnpike, not a one-lane road stuck uncertainly over what looked like 89.9-degree slopes. Dub clung to the dashboard and tried to bounce with the jeep as it ground and rumbled like a maddened lion. A pine branch flicked the top of his head and after they hit the bottom of a slope and crashed up the beginning of a roller-coaster incline, Dub turned to see if Joan had been flung out. She seemed more concerned with keeping the dust out of her eyes with a cupped hand. The ride was nothing to her.

They crested the hill and dropped down a lengthy series of switchbacks until they bottomed out in a narrow river valley. The mountains seemed so close it was like looking up from the bottom of an envelope. They followed the riverbed for a while, scaring a moose, which disappeared into the pines, then took a dirt road into an opening valley. It was at least another forty minutes before they entered another narrow ravine, met a slightly better gravel road, and drove another twenty minutes to a gate, which was like a rustic picture frame wrapped in barbed wire. Two telephone poles supported it. American flags jutted from them and a consummately white rook on a rectangular plaque hung from a rough-cut crossbeam.

A man in camouflage and shiny black boots shifted the strap of his Kalashnikov and shouted, "Hey, Danny."

"The password's, ah, 'buttress,' " shouted Joan.

"No, it isn't," said Danny. "It's 'parapet.' "

"Today's Wednesday," said Joan wearily.

"Oh, you're right," he grinned at Dub and gestured with his thumb. "You can't live with 'em and you can't live with 'em."

"You need passwords? Out here?" asked Dub.

"Two a day," said Danny, and the jeep lurched past the guard, who was talking on his radio.

The road was straight as a telephone line until it crossed a log bridge over a heavy stream and veered right. The jeep passed a squad of women in T-shirts and shorts doing frantic calisthenics. They were different sizes and shapes. One was having a hard time keeping up, but all the others were lean, some muscular, some wiry, some skinny. All of them were flushed on their faces, arms, and thighs with the cold and exertion. Dub saw a shooting range, and the entry to an obstacle course, each marked by a white sign with stencilled lettering. There were cabins of various sizes, one with a church steeple, a covered swimming pool, a picnic pavilion, and a playground circled by a picket fence. They continued, however, into a grove that suddenly ended in a huge open space dotted with boulders and some stubborn patches of snow.

Flat in front of them was the sheer face of a mountain. It rose out of the level ground like the side of a quarry. Up to a quarter of the face, however, appeared to be sheathed in concrete. At the bottom, a tunnel poked out with steel doors large enough to drive a semi through. A white rook was painted on each door. The jeep screeched to a halt.

"So," said Danny, "what do you think?"

"Christ! The Guns of Navarone. What is it?"

"The White Rook!"

Joan leaned over Dub's shoulder. "It could take a direct hit from a Soviet missile and the people inside wouldn't feel a thing."

"There's enough food preserved in there to keep three hundred people alive for eighteen months," added Danny.

"Twenty," said Joan. "They just upped it."

"There's enough ammo to take over South America and half of Africa."

Dub blinked. "There are three hundred people here?"

"Well, no," Danny said, "not yet."

"But we're close to a hundred and fifty. Only the CRs live here year-round."

"The Castled Rooks. It'll be explained," said Danny. "I'm one."

"I want to be the first woman one."

"She's really pushing for it." He wasn't all that pleased, from the sound of it.

"Back there looks like Boy Scout camp," said Dub, "but this! How the hell was this built out here? Did you all hollow out the whole mountain?"

"Not exactly. It goes in at a slant. You'll find out. Wescott calls this the Valley Forge of our time, Carl, and you're going to be part of it. Get your suitcase. You'll want to get cleaned up for dinner."

Inside, the tunnel sloped like the passenger ramp to a 747. As it leveled out it opened into a room with a domed ceiling, indirectly lit. A brightly lit mural arched on the wall over what looked like the reception desk at a Holiday Inn. Washington standing beside a desk, a Bible in his right hand. Sam Houston on horseback ordering the cannon fire at San Jacinto. Robert E. Lee pointing to a battle map. A Cobra spitting fire at the Vietcong below it. The two battle scenes had enemies toppling like bowling pins, and whether in Mexican uniforms or black pajamas, the enemy died in the same way—arms flung in the air, mouths gaping. Their brown faces were nearly identical.

"This is my good friend Carl Clements," said Devlin, patting Dub on the back.

"Carl Clements!" said the man behind the desk, thrusting out a beefy hand. "Quick thinking!" Dub shook and nodded. "In Breckenridge," explained the man.

"It was just an accident," said Dub.

A second clerk, also muscle-bound, heard the name and left some mail he was sorting. "I'd like to shake yore hand!"

"They ought to put you up there," said the first, pointing toward the mural. "You saved Colonel Wescott and that's almost as important as, I don't know, Bull Run."

"We were lucky," said Dub.

They looked at him with a smile. "You're gonna be something with training," said the second. He prodded his companion. "Ain't that right?"

"You bet. He's got the instinct."

"I'm just kind of visiting," said Dub. "Mr.—Colonel Wescott asked me. . . . "

"You're gonna love it, I can tell you. Yore nose gets clear of nigger and the whole world changes."

Devlin interrupted. "Carl'll be around. But right now there's only forty-five minutes to dinner, guys."

"Yes, sir, Captain," said the first clerk. Instead of a room key, he handed Dub a yellow octagonal plate the diameter of a silver dollar. It was thicker in the middle and had a nylon string on it. A turret was pressed into the front; a number in the back. "You wear this all the time around your neck. "Don't go anywhere without it."

"We have a lot of enemies," said the other.

"You can take it off when you sleep," said Joan, "but don't go anywhere without it." She lifted it over his head. He noticed that her T-shirt held the outline of her disk just above the rise of her breasts. "Your jacket." She took it off.

"Oh," he said. "Your parka."

"I'll see you later." She smiled and went down a corridor to the right.

He watched her recede. "That's quite a wife you got there."

"Yeah. All mine," said Danny, but Dub had noticed that they hadn't said anything to each other on parting.

Besides the amulet, they gave him a large packet of papers, which they said he could fill out later, and Danny led him into the corridor on the left, running deeper into the mountain. The concrete walls were painted a flat white with the monotony only relieved by stark lights in wire cages. A set of glossy black steel doors ended the corridor as another set had begun it. There was a circular room with half a dozen metal doors all painted different colors. Dub tried to glance through the portholes but the wired glass was also pebbled. Danny led him through the door directly opposite and into a short corridor that opened into a vaulted living room, complete with pit group, soda machine, and rustic fireplace. Numbered rooms adjoined the area.

"Your room's four fifteen," Danny said. "At seventeen hundred we have dinner, so don't be late. I'm going to wash up too, so I'll just leave directions. He pointed. "Corridor to blue, corridor to red, then red again, you'll hear all the people. Gotta run. We'll talk after dinner." He backed up two steps, then left.

"Sure," said Dub. "Great!" Footsteps echoed. Dub peered at the domed ceiling above him. It was as seamless as the outside of a robin's egg and just as blue. The living room was pleasant. A painting of a New England village hung over the fireplace. The soda machine had four selections of fruit drinks and a mineral water, but no sodas. When he found his room, he suddenly remembered that the "clerks" hadn't given him a room key, but there was only a tiny slot in the doorknob, like on a bathroom door. It only locked on the inside and a nail file could click it open from outside.

His room had the universal appearance of a chain motel. The king-sized bed held a spread decorated with historical scenes. On the early American bureau a small tray with plastic-covered glasses and ice bucket stood beside a booklet describing the whole enclave with pictures of happy families swimming, playing baseball, and shooting targets. Next to the bureau was a television and video player. The movies in the rack included *Flying Leathernecks*, *Green Berets*, *Fort Apache*, and several Randolph Scotts. There was also an anthology of "G.I. Joe" cartoons, a Tarzan (with Johnny Weissmuller, Dub affectionately noticed), and four documentaries: about Wescott, Central America, Afghanistan, and the Hungarian Uprising. Just as in a motel, the back wall was covered with a curtain over a heater/air conditioner. Behind the curtain was not a window, however, but a huge, slidelike, 3-D image of rolling hills and a serene farmhouse. When he drew back the curtain, bright light poured through the scene, but it didn't make the illusion more convincing. Home sweet home, Dub thought, deep in the guts of the earth.

The bathroom, was no bigger than a closet: a stainless steel sink opposite a curious toilet. There was no water in the bowl and it reminded him of a train or bus toilet. A sticker on the lid warned the user not to throw anything in it that would not burn and listed glass, paper clips, broken cups and saucers, wire, razor blades, light bulbs, bottle tops, and a dozen other things. Dub pictured some poor bastard wondering whether the kidney stone he was trying to pass would ruin his toilet. He laughed. It was out of silliness, or weariness, or the claustrophobic tension he had been suppressing since he had entered the tubelike outer tunnel, but he laughed hard and loud until the echo of it seemed to buzz the steel counter. He looked at himself in the mirror.

His eyes were teary. He wiped his face with his hand and sniffed. He touched the Band-Aid on his head, studied the Mercurochromed scab on his ear, and stared into his own eyes. He was crawling on the belly of the beast, he thought, and if the beast ever noticed, he'd be squashed like a maggot.

FOURTEEN

Dub entered the dining hall five minutes early and was led toward the head table. The room was set up as if for a testimonial, with a lectern and seven rows of picnic tables lined up below. Women sat to the right with small children (some in child seats) scattered among them. Men took the tables to the left, with older boys gathered at the ends farthest from the podium, while six men wearing the heavy White Rook rings, Danny Devlin among them, sat directly beneath the speaker.

Every generation seemed to be represented, including one glassy-eyed man in a wheelchair. There was even a handful of skinheads, though several of them seemed to be growing their hair back, and had more of an air of teenage rebellion than threat.

The room was big, considering it was in a mountain, but it wasn't all that big and the closeness made the number of people seem enormous. Their voices echoed off the barrel-vaulted ceiling, and when a child banged his spoon against his plate it stung the ear like the bell at a prizefight. The people were pressing, pressing, against Dub as he moved to the front and he began to breathe rapidly. He concentrated on keeping control, on keeping Saigon caged, but he couldn't keep it from lunging against the bars. Only when he reached the relative openness behind the podium tables did the claustrophobia subside. He wiped his face with his embroidered cloth napkin and sagged into his seat.

By precisely four fifty-nine, everyone was seated, only to rise in silence a moment later when a door unlatched at Dub's left. Dub glanced around and rose also, just as three men in

[149]

blue suits strolled single file into the room with Wescott limping on a cane behind them. The third man stopped at the lectern and adjusted the microphone while the others lined up behind their chairs and lowered their heads. A baby squealed and the mother picked it up, but that was the only movement in the audience except for the palsied trembling of an old man's arm.

The speaker raised his hands palms out over his head, closed his eyes, and lowered his chin to his tie. Almost everyone copied him. "Lord," he said over the sea of hands, "bless this house and all who come to it. Make them strong and righteous. Give them steel in their arms and fire in their hearts, and succor them in the hours of temptation and need. Bless, oh Lord, the children as Jesus did and lead them into the paths of righteousness for thy name's sake. Bless and help us to preserve the American way of life against the godless few who would allow criminals to run rampant in the streets and who would foist foreign corruptions upon thy servants. And bless, oh Lord, the righteous arm of Colonel Marshall Wescott, who with thou as his shield and thy anger as his sword will mow down the enemies from without and within. Amen."

Take it easy on those within, thought Dub. When the audience loudly said "Amen," he silently moved his lips and lowered his tiring hands. The preacher, however, rolled straight into the Lord's Prayer and the audience chimed in. With the echo it was deafening, noise enough for a cave-in, Dub thought, peeking with one eye at the ceiling. When the prayer had ended, he had to flex his fingers to get the blood circulating again. Carts were rolled in with large bowls of stew and heaps of biscuits on them. Steaming plates began circulating and the steady roar of conversation filled the room. A young man in an apron filled Dub's plate and placed two biscuits next to it with silver tongs. Small wheels of carrot, cubes of potato, and marble-sized onions swam in a dark gravy with shredded meat.

"This looks mighty good," said Dub to the man next to him. "I'm Carl Clements."

"I know," said the man. "You're the honored guest."

"Well, I'm a guest, anyway." He tore off a chunk of biscuit and tasted it. "Umm! I don't think I knew how hungry I was. Great. Just great. Who does the cooking?"

"There's a rotation among the women, but they're all supervised by Leon Parish. He was a Marine cook."

"Umm. We never ate this good in the Army."

"Nothing fancy," the man said casually, "but exactly what we'll be eating when the big war starts and everybody else is dying."

Dub had a chunk of meat on his fork but it hung suspended while the comment sunk in. "How do these people all end up here? I mean this place is a big mystery to the press and all. Somebody said there's three hundred people here." He scanned the room. "It doesn't really look like three hundred."

"Not everyone's here at one time. Many go on with their ordinary lives. When international tensions look bad, Colonel Wescott calls them in. It's happened three times so far. Then it's really crowded. Eating's in shifts. It takes real genius to organize something like this. When the war comes, we can protect a thousand men, women, and children, all together."

"Amazing," said Dub. "All under this mountain!" He shook his head. He let the man eat for a while, putting away quite a bit himself. He belched as quietly as possible and tried to get an idea of how many were really in the room. He figured no less than sixty, no more than seventy-five. "I'm really amazed," said Dub. "When they said Montana, I thought there'd be a couple of shacks on a snowbank. How long has this been here?"

"Opened eighteen months ago."

"Huh."

"Cost twenty million."

"Naw! For real? That much? Who paid for all that?"

"Wescott, others"—he gestured his fork at the people eating—"everybody."

"But all those people, how much each?"

"According to their ability. Some deeded their houses and farms. Some paid by sweat alone. But all are carefully screened Christians and patriots. People will give up anything to have a future."

"And they don't have a future?"

"If we don't stop all this stuff out there, we'll be swallowed like goldfish."

"You bet!" Dub didn't ask him what "all this stuff" was,

but thought that if these people had ever had a future, they'd signed it over to Wescott.

After the stew, small bowls of vanilla pudding were passed. The woman serving paused to tell an Ethiopian joke. It took a few seconds for the man to get it, then he laughed until he coughed. He told her to tell the joke to Wescott, but she blushed and said she couldn't. The pudding tasted like it was made with powdered milk.

"I didn't know Mr. Wescott was a colonel," said Dub. "What branch was he in?"

"The American Values Conservatory Nation."

"Excuse me?"

"He's the commander of the White Rook."

"So it's like an honorary title, like a southern politician?" The man cocked one of his heavy eyebrows and glared at Dub. His face was familiar. Good Lord, thought Dub.

"He's *our* colonel," said the man sharply.

"I—I didn't mean nothing. I just thought he'd be general."

"He's our colonel. There may be other colonels soon. Other rooks."

"Is there a general?"

"Of course."

"Well? Who? The preacher?"

"He isn't here," said the man. Dub saw one of the men near Wescott rise as the pudding was being cleared away.

"Say," said Dub, "didn't catch your name."

"Captain Lex Tyrone."

"Captain," said Dub, nodding. "You must be important."

"All of us are important," said Tyrone. "You can't lead without followers. Colonel Wescott always reminds us."

"You know," said Dub, "your name sounds familiar. Did we ever meet?" I'm your friendly office torch, thought Dub.

"I don't recognize you, Carl. Ever been to Tampa?"

"Naw. It's like I know your name, not your face."

"Your name has that sound too. It's just the sound. Lex Tyrone/Lex Luther. It's just the sound."

Lex Luther's a few seats up, thought Dub. Too bad Superman isn't here.

Tyrone turned his back to listen to the man at the lectern. "As you're finishing your dessert—don't rush it, there's plenty of time—we'll just get a few announcements out of the way." He squinted at an index card. "The Wilsons, Lewis and Janice— where are you Lewis? Janice? Stand up, will you?" Janice covered her mouth with her hands like she was a contestant on a quiz show. Lewis peered sheepishly across the heads toward his wife and rocked on the heels of his cowboy boots. "Well, a quite reliable source informs me that the Wilsons have been up to their old tricks—" There was scattered laughter. "Yes, yes. And their fifth child is due in four more months. Isn't that wonderful? And they say the Chinese breed like rats!" The applause was loud and enthusiastic. Men stood and slapped Lewis on the back. "It's—it's amazing what this rest and exercise will do for you, isn't it? Of course, I'm not saying they get much rest. . . . " Janice flushed red. "Oops! Sorry! That sort of slipped out." The speaker beamed. "Anyhow there's going to be a little party next Tuesday after dinner and every-body's invited. Join me in congratulating the Wilsons."

He shuffled his cards. "There will be a foul-shooting con-test, basketball, for teens tomorrow afternoon starting at two. Is this for boys or girls?" He leaned toward someone to his right. "Both? For both. The winners get ribbons. So come on down and try your hand." Another card. "Also, there will be a guest speaker on Saturday. Mr. Jan Grootewerk—did I say that right?—Grootewerk will tell us the truth about South Africa. This should be real interesting. He'll have slides. Mr. Groote-werk has served as a mercenary in countries I can't even pronounce and is a sixth-generation Afrikaner. He's now an elected member of South Africa's democratic legislature.

"Finally, the general staff had a meeting last night, and there's some very good news. Good indeed. On the promotions: seven men and four women have been commissioned lieuten-ants of the American Values Conservatory Nation." There was wild applause. He read their names and each stood, several of them shaking both fists as if showing their biceps. "The induc-tion will be held next Wednesday in this hall, at four. Every-one's invited, of course. Also, the board has chosen a new captain." Some oohing rose from the audience. "Yes, that's right. Another rook has been castled. That restores the ranks to six, filling the spot vacated by the tragic car accident that took Captain Lamont George, so there won't be any more castlings for at least six months. I don't think when you hear the name there will be any particular surprise. This individual has stood out almost from when he arrived. Matt Klinghofer!"

A barrel-chested blond shot off his seat and gave a little rain dance like a football player in the end zone. Simultaneously, a woman abruptly rose near a distant exit and left. There was no mistaking the tall, muscular figure: Joan Devlin. Danny saw her go. His eyes turned icy, but he casually picked up his glass and sipped. After Klinghofer settled down and the congratulations had ended, the speaker raised his hands for quiet. "And I've got something else that will make everyone very happy. We're going outside! Spring's on the way!" More oohing. Spontaneous clapping. "The general staff has decided that we are going to get out into the cabins in two weeks and enjoy God's country and live like people were meant to live in this beautiful land of ours. Isn't that wonderful? Wonderful! I thought it'd never get here. Wasn't December incredible?" The man then quickly introduced Wescott.

The chattiness that had simmered throughout the announcements died totally. Wescott held both sides of the lectern, braced his injured leg against it, then lowered his head slightly as if praying or reflecting. All faces, even those of the teenagers, turned calm. The old man in the wheelchair lifted his eyes and his palsy slowed. The babies grew quiet as if they knew the room was washed in some supernatural radiance. Dub could see in all of their eyes the soothed enchantment of the believer, and a hunger, an intense and burning hunger, for Wescott's magic. Dub felt as out of place as if he had been invited to a dinner in one of the secret monasteries of Tibet.

Dub couldn't understand why they all didn't immediately recognize him as a spy. He had to be different, didn't he? He had always been careful not to permit himself to feel biased toward blacks, so far as he knew. When two other cadets at the Citadel planned the hazing of a black in their squad, Dub had left the room. True, he didn't report it. And, true, he didn't tell them it was wrong. The boys didn't do it, after all their planning, but should Dub have done more? Should he have spoken up and ruined two big-mouthed, foolish boys' college careers when they were just saying what many of the other students, teachers, and administrators believed? Or was it just that he knew, deep down, he was tempted to join them? Could anyone born in the South, or the United States, or anywhere, ever escape a deep, instinctive fear of a different race? And were those nights in Vonna's bed, those sweet nights reeling toward dawn, fueled by some hidden repulsion? What would it take for him to join the AVCN? To join a lynch mob? He remembered the rage that had conquered him when he rammed the knife into Lamont George's bowels. That monster, that other self was still inside. Was he really different from the people in this room? And if he was the aberration, why didn't it show?

Lost in his thoughts, he didn't notice Wescott quietly introducing him. The standing ovation made Dub look up from the spoon he was toying with, glance around, and nod nervously. The adulation was like a shot of bourbon, sharp and hot. Tyrone cupped Dub's elbow and urged him to rise. The applause turned to cheers as Wescott crossed the podium and embraced him, then leaned back, still holding his shoulders. If he had been French, he would have kissed each of Dub's cheeks. Instead, they looked into each other's faces. Maybe I saved your life, Dub thought, staring into the cool blue eyes. Maybe I should have been on the roof with my own rifle.

Wescott was not a fire-and-brimstone speaker. His manipulations were subtler. His gentle voice got people on the edge of their seats, trying to hear better, and yet nothing was muddied. Each word and phrase was clear and crisp. He had the great orator's ability to make everyone in the room feel as if he or she were in a private conversation with him, and the speech was free of the emphatic rhetorical flourishes that Dub had grown up on in the churches and from the politicians of Charleston. Wescott gave the impression of being a deep and profound thinker as he spoke, and yet none of his ideas were inaccessible. He gave the impression of having come up with a new way of looking at things and yet his new ways were really all-too-familiar notions arrived at from fairly odd angles.

The speech that night was about thirty minutes long, and although Wescott never used a note, many in the audience took notes, and Wescott was as precise as a mathematician. His subject was the rapproachement between the Soviet Union and the United States. The media—he said the word with a sneering intonation on the first syllable—were portraying it as a new realism on the part of the superpowers, a putting aside of their differences for the sake of survival. Not true. He weaved in a number of statistics (spurious or not, Dub didn't know) without bogging down his argument at all. They proved that Russia was getting stronger while the United States was declining, along with getting too timid to police its own hemisphere. He quoted from Lenin, Che Guevara, and Angela Davis on the need for Communism to undermine the West, and how an essential element was the destruction of American family values by means of unnatural and promiscuous sex, drugs, race-mixing, the degradation of the English language with foreign ones, the invasion of illegal aliens, fatty foods that sapped the body, television that sapped the mind, and secular humanism. He didn't have to explain each of these. People nodded in agreement. *Glasnost* was just another way of making America complacent and unable to react when the Communists finally felt strong enough to march. He told his people, however, that they were alert, strong, and intelligent: able to stand like the three hundred Spartans against the greed of an Asiatic tyranny, when most Americans would be crushed. The missile treaty was a sign war was likely to come soon, perhaps by the mid-nineties, and God would have only a few—a happy, happy few—who could stand beside him and rebuild the world after the final victory.

Could Dub accept any of this? Yes. Dub was overweight, had seen too closely how drug money corrupted ordinary, even good men—and women, lithe and beautiful women. Dub had no particular love for the mindlessness of television, though he watched plenty of it. He didn't want his daughters to become slam-dancers, hookers, or junkies, and he knew how often those things had happened to others. Maybe—he wasn't sure—the United States was too timid in handling Nicaragua and Panama. Maybe there was too much silly optimism over the Russians. Maybe, just maybe, a nuclear war was inevitable. But none of these points, he decided, and none of the more ludicrous ones, like the one about interbreeding, was the real reason Wescott was so successful. It was as simple as this: In Wescott's presence people were elected. They became the chosen. All their frustrations about being ignored by those who should care were satisfied by putting the politicians, liberals, and protesters into the category of misled idiots who would learn too late what the people they'd dismissed already knew. Wescott had tapped the great American Puritan reservoir and its liquid bubbled out of people who felt pushed aside. He told them they were shoved aside exactly because they were special, and on the Day of Judgment that would all be revealed. Dub wondered how low he would have to fall before he might need this illusion. How long unemployed, how long lonely, how long locked in an apartment with the feeling of being under siege, how long knowing your family was no longer an emotional whole. How long feeling nothing more specific than a nagging itch, a suspicion that something had gone wrong, that there were termites in the wainscoting, nibbling, nibbling. These people were hungry for what Wescott told them. No wonder they found it so easy to latch onto a devil, any devil, red or black, Mex or Jew.

There was a benediction, and dinner, as banal as one at a Rotary, was over. It was less a Nuremberg rally than a church social. Dub shook hands with dozens of people. Wescott told him they were going to make a videotape of the whole Breckenridge incident and they wanted him to be interviewed for it. Dub caught himself feeling flattered, his mind pulling two ways. No matter how benign these people seemed, he had to remember that what they believed was not merely quaint, it was dangerous. He had to remember that there were murderers among them. During the pudding, something he had learned at the Citadel had flashed into his mind, and it was now obvious who at least one of the "generals" was, maybe who was in charge of the whole thing. What he didn't know was who had murdered Michael O'Dell, and from how high up the command chain the orders had originated.

FIFTEEN

Dub didn't get away from all his well-wishers until past eight o'clock. He felt he was suffocating in the filtered air of the White Rook; maybe he just needed a cigarette.

He wandered back to his room, deliberately losing the way several times, and found several doors with naval wheels on them. Each was marked "NO ADMITTANCE EXCEPT A-1 CLEARANCE." Other than that, the White Rook was exactly what was portrayed in the pamphlet he scanned in his room: a resort hotel in a mountain. He used the funny incinerator toilet, which was silent and nearly odorless, then lay on his bed. The thought of all that stone over him made him even more claustrophobic. He asked two women sitting in front of the fireplace if it was all right to go outside at night. They cheerfully said yes, but that it would be very cold. One called her husband and insisted Dub borrow a wool overcoat reeking of Old Spice. What are nice people like you doing in a place like this? he thought.

The dank tunnel grew cooler as he climbed out. The night air was filled with pine and earth, and its sharp sting was as satisfying as a cold beer. The stars were like splinters of ice on a black marble table. He watched his breath fog, and fumbled in his sport coat for his last pack of cigarettes. The smoke filling his lungs relaxed him. He had better enjoy it. He had only six cigarettes left and the AVCN—he looked back at the Rook—would force him to quit, anyway. He blew smoke in the direction of the mountain like a defiant teenager, then began to walk. He cut through a cluster of the cabins and found permanent charcoal grills, a sandbox, and a jungle gym. There were few lights but puddles of sodium-vapor orange were scattered every hundred yards or so and he made his way from one to the other until the uppermost parts of the White Rook were only jagged shadows against the sky. He walked under a picnic pavilion and sat on a stone hearth briefly. He looked back where he had been and decided to go on a little further, even though he saw only one more light barely visible through a grove of trees. The road wound around it out toward the distant gate, but he decided to cut through.

The fallen pine needles were soft to walk on but made him unsteady. He heard an odd noise and thought of wolves, grizzlies, Castled Rooks. The wind stirred the trees. Something was brushing against them. No. It was just branches. He continued toward the light, pushing branches aside. He listened, then took two steps backward. Something prodded his shoulder. He spun, flailed, and smacked his hand on a huge boulder. "Christ!" he said. His cold hand rung like a bell as he squeezed it under his armpit and did a silly dance, branches flapping in his face.

"Are you all right?"

"Christ! Damn! You scared me!"

"Are you hurt?"

"I hit my hand!"

"What are you doing here?"

Dub shook his hand, then thrust it in his pocket. "I went for a walk. What are you doing here?"

The shadowy head disappeared behind the rock. Dub bent over and looked for his dropped cigarette. He lit a match and the gleam of the white paper showed. The cigarette had been smashed into the pine needles by his own feet. He shook out the match and felt his way around the rock. He thought of a woman he'd once trailed who always picked up strangers, lured them into the woods, then went home to her husband with leaves in her hair and underwear, as nonchalantly as if they had stuck to her in the K mart.

"Do you need help?" the woman said wearily.

"I didn't mean to disturb anyone," he said. "I'll just go on." On the other side of the rock, however, he could see just enough to recognize the tallness of the woman. He leaned toward her. Joan Devlin was sitting in a small semioval in the rock. Her chin rested on her knees.

"Aren't you cold?" he asked.

She sniffed. "I'm a warrior. I put cold out of my mind." He realized why he hadn't recognized her voice. She was stuffed up.

"You ought to get somewhere warm."

"I'm fine."

He sat on the rock next to her. "You didn't like Klinghofer getting castled."

"So what?" she said calmly. "So I've been crying. That just proves what they say."

"What's that?"

"That a woman isn't suited."

Dub crossed his arms. It seemed like an odd issue to come up after what he had seen inside. The AVCN wasn't exactly gaga for women's rights and she had to have known that they expected her to be a helpmeet when she signed up.

"I've blown it for good now," she added. "Walking out like that. They'll never forgive that."

"They'll punish you?"

"No," she said, as if he were a dolt.

"So is it all that important? What is being 'castled,' anyway? You get a raise for it or something?"

"No!" He heard her parka rustle as if she were disgusted, but he couldn't see anything except the tops of her raised knees. The coldness of the stone had penetrated the coat and his trousers. "It's recognition," she finally said. "I deserve it. You'd think Danny would be behind me. He is. With a knife. He's afraid I'm better than him."

"At martial arts? Is that what castling is about?"

"No. Well, everything with Danny is physical," she sighed. "No matter what they say, weight and leverage helps in tae kwon do, judo, all of that. He may be pound for pound stronger, but so is an ant. He made me mad the last time we took the mat, and I threw him two out of three. He knows how to exploit his opponent's weight but I know how he does it." She gave a little laugh. "He wouldn't talk to me for a week." She shifted. "I don't want to talk about it."

"You don't sound like you don't." She sniffed. Dub

drummed his fingers on his knees. "So the CRs, the Castled Rooks, they're like a crack squad for special duty, and they get the ring." She said nothing, which he took for assent. "But what do they do? I mean it isn't like the Foreign Legion, like there are Bedouins out there to hold off, or something."

"Who knows?" she moaned. "Danny acts all mysterious and goes off. They act like a bunch of Masons going off to chant boogah-boogah. For all I know they're out chasing tail and that's why they won't let me in."

"What does the 'castled' part mean?"

"It's something from checkers."

"Chess, you mean."

"Whatever. 'Pieces linked in unison are stronger than all on their own.' "

"I don't know the game." He sniffed and shifted his rear. It didn't help him get warmer. "So if they're out chasing tail or chanting boogah-boogah, as you say, and so forth, what do you care about being one?"

She leaned so close to him he could feel the warmth of her breath. "Because I've worked hard, harder than anyone in this place. Do you know what it was like to drop fifty pounds? Damn it, Carl, until I met Danny I hadn't sweated in my life. I just sort of flopped around with my big feet and hands and legs all over the place. Now my percentage of body fat is as good as a marathoner's. I've taught almost every man in this place and every woman. There are only five, maybe six men who I couldn't take in a competition match. I've been with this place for *five years* and they treat me like the same ugly teenager who graduated from Lamar High."

"You're sure not ugly now," said Dub.

"Oh yeah," she said, settling back into her niche. "They won't give me what I'd deserve as a man and they won't think of me as a woman, either."

"Then they're stupid," said Dub. The words hung in the air and he realized they weren't right for his role. She, however, didn't seem to notice. She was caught up in her own unhappiness.

He listened to the wind stir the trees. Not much of it got into Joan's rock shelter. "I don't know why I've said all this to you. When you tell them what I've said they'll just say, 'Yes, yes, exactly what we thought.' "

"Why would I tell them?"

"Why shouldn't you?"

"I don't know. There are things I could tell you I wouldn't want anyone to know." There were always these moments undercover, he remembered, moments when you want so desperately to pull down the wall between your role and the other person. He hadn't been in the White Rook a whole day yet and he was already feeling the urge. But you can't. Trust kills. The thought brought Janet to mind. Joan's voice was a lot like Janet's. He began lying to her to distract himself. "I guess it's nothing that matters much to anyone else, but I wouldn't—" He could hear her listening. "All right. I was one of the guys who, well, I'd get information out of Charlie or some of the villagers. . . . We'd take them up in helicopters . . ."

"No," she said. Her hand brushed his hair and jabbed his eye. "Oh! I'm sorry. I was trying to cover your mouth. You don't have to drag up those things." Her hand rested on his cheek. It was very warm. He felt guilty the lie had been so convincing. He took his hand from his pocket to take hers off his cheek, but when he felt the back of it he pressed it harder against his face. Her knee had touched his knee. He closed his hand around her fingers, meaning to pull them away, but he turned his head and kissed the strong base of her thumb. There was a metallic, salty, maybe soapy taste to it, but the shiver that went through him wasn't from the cold. The knuckles were big and the fingers were strong. They were hands like Janet's. He pulled back, startled. What the hell are you doing? This is a bad idea, some remote part of his mind signalled frantically, but another part of him was saying, "You don't feel anything: use her like Janet used you. What are you afraid of?"

The sensation that Janet was with him was so strong that he closed his eyes in terror that he might actually see her materialize out of the moving shadows. Joan, however, took his reaction to be some sort of passion. Her free hand clasped the nape of his neck and pulled him into her cove. He kneeled, quaking, in the pine needles. Her nose bumped his chin, then their mouths found each other's. Their heads turned frantically from one side to the other, their tongues never losing contact, breathing one another's breath, whirling down from the sky with only one parachute. And he was letting himself fall, forgetting the ground rising up, touching Joan's shoulders and feeling Janet's, flipping in time from Montana to Saigon and back again. He managed somehow to pull his lips away, but she scattered kisses over his eyelids, nose, forehead, and chin. He felt her long thighs pressing against his hips, and he saw the light from the louvered windows ripple over Janet's golden skin. Their mouths met again and each nerve in his skin was desperately alive. Though two inches of goose down made it impossible, he thought he could feel each detail of her nipples through both parka and coat as he pressed her breasts with his chest, stroking his palms over her back.

He suddenly pushed her to arm's length again. There wasn't enough air. He was sweating as if it were ninety degrees and he wanted to run, but his legs were too rubbery. She pushed his arms aside and bit at the top of his ear, just over the cut from the bullet fragment. With a moan he gave in and pressed his mouth into her throat. She quickly pushed him backward, patting the ground for rocks. She rolled onto her back and unzipped her parka. She fumbled for his wrists, then trailed his hands down her neck, across the thin T-shirt that covered her breasts, over her hard belly, past her sharp hipbones, and onto her thighs as dense as unworked clay. The fear now only intensified his desire. He was young again and if she was Janet, if she was Death, he was her lover and did not care. When he slipped his hand under the khaki covering her groin she lifted her hips to meet it, and the moisture was like a steam in which he lost himself.

It was over quickly. Dub lay atop Joan, brushing his lips across her chin and juggling thoughts that made no particular sense. When the fire subsides, the memory of it is always unreal. Who were those people doing those things? Was that me or someone I imagined? He was shaking, but he knew that his fear had only to do with ghosts, not the White Rook. Oh, sure, there might be real chaos if Joan felt guilty enough to confess or angry enough to throw it into Danny's face, but he tried to tell himself that this might be a way to find out more, that this was just part of his job. He knew, though, that he hadn't seduced her, so that couldn't have been why it happened. It could be useful if Joan fell in love with him. Real love. Confiding love. Like he had felt in Saigon. Janet had made a monkey out of him; now he could pay her back.

That didn't make sense. Joan wasn't Janet. He didn't love her. And he wasn't Janet, was he? He could never betray Joan to someone who could kill her, could he? The sex had been so powerful it had hurt, but he knew that sex, even great sex, had little to do with love. "You are wonderful," she whispered, kissing his eyes, but she too seemed to be withdrawing, embarrassed to let him know her.

His pants were around his calves, his rear end in the air. Pine needles prickled his knees. Her T-shirt and brassiere had been pushed up over her breasts into a twisted rope running from armpit to armpit. Her nipples poked hard through his shirt. Her legs were still bent, the knees above him, but her feet came together under his shins, bound by a tangle of trousers and cotton panties. He wanted to see her face, and yet was glad it was dark. He wanted to look on her nakedness, to remind himself of who she was, and yet he didn't want her to see his own.

He raised himself and glanced from side to side. A fog now obscured the orange lights. A small animal hurried through the underbrush. He settled back down on her and felt his amulet slide against his collarbone. "Shouldn't we go? Won't these things tell them we've been together a long time?" He pressed her amulet, then stroked the goose bumps on her breast with the back of his hand.

"That isn't how they work," she said.

"It feels like it's got a transmitter in it."

"It does," she sighed and pulled his head down.

"We should do this in a bed sometime," he whispered.

"This is my secret place," she said. "I liked you in my secret place."

Almost dozing, he listened to her breathing and thought of Vonna for the first time since Joan and he had started. He felt cheap. Joan, Joan, he thought, I'm just a fraud. Why do I have to be a fraud?

SIXTEEN

Back in his room by ten forty-five, he washed his sticky genitals in the tiny bathroom and after several thoughtful seconds peering into his own eyes turned up the thermostat. He climbed into bed rubbing his feet against each other to warm them. He fell asleep rapidly, but didn't sleep well, waking at least four times. The silence of the White Rook after the eleven p.m. "lights out" seemed to conceal too much menace. Once he dreamed the mountain was so heavy it was sinking into the earth; another time that World War III had begun and Wescott was forcing Joan and him, at gunpoint, to copulate on the speaker's table as the entire AVCN stared in that same worshipful daze with which they had watched the speech. About five a.m. the Band-Aid on Dub's head began to itch. He peeled it off, turned on the reading light, and took the pamphlets from the bureau.

The first was glossy, and claimed the Rook had cost twenty million and was still growing. It claimed that there was easy access in case of a global emergency, but didn't say anything about how the gravel road, let alone the pasture "airport," could get anyone in during winter. There were no surprises except that the Rook was flat against the Canadian border. It would have seemed they would have wanted the thing more in the heart of the United States.

A second sheet was a map of the interior on one side, the outer cabins and so forth on the back. He mused over the latter trying to pinpoint Joan's "secret place," then turned it over. The map resembled a model of some molecule or a Tinkertoy assembly. Rods (tunnels) were connected to disks (chambers) that were given numbers and colors. The dining hall/auditorium looked like a tracing of a corn dog on a stick. Another chamber was labeled "GYM," but if scale was any indication, it wasn't big enough to hold a basketball court. A number of tunnels and chambers were drawn with dotted lines that indicated future building, some of it over or under existing rooms. Dub got the impression, though, that the map wasn't big enough. With his finger he traced his own movements and saw fewer exits from some of the junctions than he remembered. Either the map was out of date, or the "off limits" doors led to another whole set of chambers. All in all, unless the drilling, blasting, or whatever they had done to get into the mountain had been terrifically expensive, he didn't see how it could have cost twenty million. They certainly hadn't gone bankrupt on the motel-type furniture and saggy mattress. It wouldn't be the first time some slick operator had used people's emotions to get rich.

Another leaflet was entitled "FACTS." It listed how many tons of concrete were in the facing of the Rook. How many total board feet of lumber were in the cabins. How many miles of steel reinforcing had been stretched through the concrete. How much potable water was stored inside. How much canned beef, frozen chicken, and corn. How many pounds of pressure the steel doors could withstand. How many megatons it would take to crack the facade (an asterisk pointed out that this was double the power of Russia's biggest warhead).

It also bragged about the high IQs of White Rook applicants, claimed five "doctor's degrees" for Marshall Wescott, and two physicians in permanent residence. It claimed a permanent collection of over 1,011 videotapes and 2,371 cassette tapes, the former screened for "correctly representing American values" and the latter consisting of a variety of styles, "with the total exclusion of non-Christian rock and roll." On the back of the leaflet was a pitch for contributions with a brief explanation of the kind of accommodations each would buy. There was a payment plan, of course, but anyone without a hundred thousand to spend was going to end up in a dormitory. The kind of room Dub had been placed in went for double that.

A chart explained the hierarchy of the White Rook. People

over eighteen were called "guests" until they completed "Survival Bootcamp" and were commissioned lieutenants. Seniority determined which lieutenants were more equal than others. Above them were six captains, a.k.a the "Castled Rooks"; four majors; the colonel; and the general staff. Colonel Wescott was also a member of the general staff, which was otherwise anonymous. There was also a child's group called the "Dawn Patrol" and a youth group called the "Cadets." All of this was tidy, the kind of tidy organization that pays no attention to the people being shoved into slots. As in the Army, a lot of square pegs would end up in round holes. No wonder Joan resented being stuck with the Lieutenants.

One of the Cadets politely rapped on Dub's door at six-thirty and led him to breakfast in the dining hall. Again, many people wanted to meet him. Two asked for autographs. A CR the size of an NFL lineman shooed some of them away, but Dub didn't mind the interruptions. The scrambled eggs were the unvarying yellow that meant they had never been in a shell and the bacon was also some kind of soy product. The "coffee" was the right color, but it too tasted like better living through chemistry. He did not see Joan, Danny, Tyrone, or Wescott. The big CR seemed to be keeping an eye on things. Promptly at seven-thirty the dining hall cleared, as people went off to their scheduled activities. A slightly older female Cadet presented Dub with a sealed envelope. Inside were the application forms for the AVCN, some multiple-choice tests, and two ballpoint pens.

Some of the tests seemed familiar and were probably copies of armed-forces IQ tests: "Cat is to parrot as cow is to . . ." "Choose the word that is closest in meaning to . . ." and "Which of the four shapes below is closest to the underside of the solid depicted on the left?" There was also a vocational test, an aptitude test, and one that tested values. "Which of the following is truest about the U. S. Constitution?" was one question. There were four choices:

A. It guarantees a woman the right to an abortion.
B. It guarantees that policemen cannot do their jobs.

C. It guarantees that all citizens may be armed.
D. It guarantees that all people are, at all points in their lives, equal.

Another test asked questions about hobbies and preferences. Dub was willing to bet that any man who expressed an interest in flower arranging or hairstyling wouldn't get a place in the Rook. He doubted anyone who answered the religious questions too un-Protestantly would ever be a Captain, either. He tried to psych out each of the questions, so as to give the answer that would be most pleasing, without being too obvious. By the time he got to the personal history forms two hours after lunch, he was exhausted.

"Have you ever had any Jewish blood?" No, but then I've never had a transfusion. "Do you have any relatives by blood or marriage with the following names?: Rosenberg, Cohen, Levy, Einstein, Schulberg, Klein, Weinstein, Wein, Tannenbaum . . ." and so on for fifty names. He paused over Einstein, blinked, then checked "No." "Are there, no matter how many times removed, any relatives with Negro, Indian, Mexican, Chinese . . ."—etc., etc.—"blood?" No. "Have you ever knowingly associated with a homosexual?" Certainly not. I'm all aflutter for rough trade, but homosexuals? He warned himself to get serious. He thought about his answers, went back to the question about relatives, and invented a Cherokee great-grandfather. The form couldn't be too clean or they might suspect he was faking.

He turned in his tests and was told to wait in his room for about twenty minutes. He studied more of the pamphlets and got rather interested in one about how the car industry conspired with the Japanese and the Koreans to destroy itself. All of this had something to do with going off the gold standard and the founding of Israel near the Suez Canal. He had seen stuff like this before. An unemployed steelworker had handed him a booklet with this type of grand conspiracy theory in the Monroeville Mall near Pittsburgh, but the pamphlets in the White Rook were relatively restrained. There was a great effort in the writing to appear rational, rather than ranting. You could hear the calm, seemingly sensible voice of Marshall Wescott in every sentence.

After an hour there was a tap on the door and a toothy nurse rolled in a cart. Blood tests. "What are they looking for?" asked Dub as the dark blood filled the empty vacuum tube. "Sickle cells? AIDS?"

"It's just routine, Mr. Clements," she said. She pressed cotton against the puncture and told him to bend his arm. "That's all. Dinner will be ready in an hour," she added. "Have a nice evening."

"Is this it? Any more tests, exams, whatever?"

She appeared concerned. "Did someone else draw blood?"

"No, but I've been filling out questionnaires all day and now this, and I'm just wondering when the doctor with the big fingers is going to tell me to bend over." Her face took on the dopey blankness all nurses master for cranky patients. "I'm sorry," he said. "I just feel a little 'drug through a knothole,' if you know what I mean."

"It sounds to me as if you are nearly through," she said. "They'll probably give you the EKG in the morning."

"What is this? A hospital?"

She quietly left.

Dinner was the same as the night before. Dub was seated at the speakers' table again, this time between the preacher and a lieutenant who had broken the marksmanship record for kill shots at one hundred yards. Lex Tyrone was not there. He didn't see Joan Devlin, either, though Danny gave him a thumbs-up gesture from one of the captains' tables. There was a lecture again from Wescott, chicken á la king on toast, mashed potatoes, and butterscotch pudding. Each was equally bland, though the food was not nearly as dangerous as the speech, he thought, tasting the pudding. Well, maybe not quite as dangerous. He learned nothing new at the dinner from either the preacher or the lieutenant. When he asked about all the tests, they were described as "routine," and everyone reassured him by saying he would soon be "into training."

After dinner he took another walk outside. A silvery mist glazed the pine needles, the swing sets, even the rough wood of the cabins, and he wondered if they were high enough to be inside a cloud. The damp soon penetrated his clothes and he shivered whenever he paused to look at something more closely. The sodium vapor lamps created great fuzzy spheres of orange light. He wanted to find Joan, to get her to talk more. He leaned against a sliding board in the playground and considered how to play it if he saw her out there again. Keep Janet out of mind. Keep Joan in the light. No sex. Pretend to feel guilty, to be vulnerable: I really feel kind of mixed up, I never had sex with a married woman before, especially the wife of somebody I hope will be a friend, and so on. It would seem kind of boyish and naive. She would then feel safe with him and perhaps say more about the Castled Rooks. He ran his fingers along the slick gray steel of a railing. Joan *was* vulnerable, not just playing at it, and the whole game left a bad taste in his mouth. He strolled to the sandbox and spat in it. What did he have against these people anyway? They were just campers with delusions of glory, un-American in their absolute American-ness. Nothing would bring Michael O'Dell back.

He sat on the steps of one of the large cabins, flipped up his jacket collar, and lit one of his last cigarettes. Do the job, he told himself. Do the job. The cigarette burned unevenly because of its dampness. He squinted at the scoop-shaped burn, picked at a strand of tobacco sticking to his tongue, and drew hard to keep the fire burning. Scruples, he thought. Dub, you're too old for scruples. You don't have to believe these people are worse than anyone else, but you have to want to kick them where it hurts. He quickly finished the cigarette and headed for Joan's "secret place."

He bumbled into the pine grove like a fat bear. The branches were thick and wet. Pine sap stuck to his hands. He couldn't find the outcropping of stone. He moved one way, then another, finally deciding he had misjudged how far the "secret place" was from the road. He retraced his steps. The boulders appeared to his left, barely visible ghosts. He stepped over a lichen-covered log, leaned around, and saw the black hole of her chairlike niche. "Joan?" He reached in and felt only the wetness of the air. He squatted down and touched the needles as if there might still be some warmth in them from the previous night. The space was so small he didn't know how they had both fit. He wiped his face with his hand, remembered the tight muscles of her thighs, then stumbled back toward the cabins.

He was walking by one of the dining halls when he first

heard a metallic click. He glanced back toward the swings. They were moving, though there was no breeze, just the swirling orange light. When he slowly turned back toward the White Rook, the silhouette of a man with his legs spread had popped out of the fog. His rifle was leveled at Dub. "Hit the dirt!" he barked.

"Christ!" said Dub. "You startled—"

The rifle flashed three times and Dub dropped, arms over his head. Five pairs of combat boots approached from five directions. He peeked up at gun barrels hovering above his head.

The voice was deep and casual. "You're a dead man, turkey."

SEVENTEEN

They paraded Dub like a captured general into the tunnel entry of the White Rook. His arms were already numb from walking all the way across the grounds with them on his head, so when they got into the light he lowered them slightly. "What's the problem, boys? I was just—"

The CR jabbed a thick finger at Dub's head. "You keep those hands on your head and you don't say a word! You got that?" Lex Tyrone's face was greasy with camouflage paint. What was this? They'd had dinner together. He knew Dub. So had the guys in Saigon. I won't beg this time, he thought. I won't whimper.

"Hey, I'm Carl, Carl Clements. I just—"

"SILENCE! Not a squeak! Not a peep! Not a burp!" He jerked Dub by the sleeve, and two of the rifle barrels prodded Dub in the back. Dub glanced at the man at the entry desk. He avoided Dub's eyes and pretended to be dusting. Uh-oh, thought Dub. They know. How could they? The air was getting thin.

They took him down the corridor to a door marked "NO ADMITTANCE." Tyrone watched one of the other men twist the wheel. The tunnel was narrower and lower than most, and the floor was uneven. It was much more cavelike, and Dub tried not to think of the mountain on top of them. He was breathing too shallowly and might get dizzy. They quickly passed two other steel doors, crossed through a small, round room with a refrigerator and a concrete mixer, then entered a stark room with a single light bulb dangling over a steel folding chair.

"Sit!" barked Tyrone. His voice reverberated off the stone walls.

Dub lowered his arms, flexed them, and licked his lips. Tyrone shoved him on the shoulder and his rear hit the chair hard. "Hey!" Dub said.

"Silence!" The man slowly circled the chair, angrily clicking the magazine of his Kalashnikov on and off. The other four drifted to the sides of the room, leaned against the wall, slung their rifles on their shoulders, and watched impassively.

"What's your name?"

"Say," said Dub, rising, "you know my goddamn name, I saw you at—"

"State your name!"

"I already have, mister, and if you don't—"

Tyrone jerked him off the chair by the lapels. Dub and he were nose to nose. The smell of the camouflage paint was curiously sweet. "Name, turkey," Tyrone said through clenched teeth. Dub's hands were loose at Tyrone's side. One brushed the Kalashnikov hanging from his shoulder. The other was only inches from the combat knife on Tyrone's belt. For a moment Dub thought that going for it would be a better way to die, but then it was suddenly obvious how stupid it was for Tyrone to let him get close to either weapon, even with the other four in the room.

"Name!"

"Carl Clements. Christ! You know that."

Tyrone shoved him back onto the chair. It nearly tipped. "Is that your real name?"

The echo was like a voice out of time, saying the same thing, in the same tone. Dub's guts collapsed into his legs. Did Tyrone also have a body bag? Hang on, Delbert, hang on. He took a deep breath and tried to be casual. His voice quavered. "What's with you guys? I—"

"Silence! You don't ask questions, you answer them. Got it, turkey?"

"Gobble gobble," said Dub dryly.

Tyrone cuffed him on the back of the head. Dub jumped up, but every rifle was turned on him. "Only kidding," said Dub, settling down. "Hit me some more if you like."

"What were you doing outside?"

"Outside? Taking a walk. What'd you think I was doing?"

"You expect us to believe you?"

"I needed a walk. A constitutional. Dinner's a little heavy around here."

"So you don't like our food?" He prodded Dub's belly. "You feel soft, turkey. I think you're crazy for food."

"Me? Never touch the stuff."

Tyrone cuffed his head again. "You got a big mouth, turkey." Tyrone stopped pacing and talked to the person behind Dub and to the left. "You think that's funny, soldier?"

"Nossir. Not at all."

"Empty your pockets!"

"Who, me?"

Tyrone shoved his forehead this time. "Who the fuck you think I mean?"

Dub glared at him and pulled out his wallet.

"Toss it on the floor! Everything! The other pockets!"

He pitched several false receipts and a fried chicken coupon from Atlanta. They fluttered, landing unevenly. He tossed his cigarettes and the box of matches.

"That it, turkey?"

"Yes."

"What?! I didn't hear you!"

"Yes, goddamn it!"

He whacked Dub's head with the side of his hand. "We don't use the Lord's name in vain, turkey. Not here!"

"I didn't mean it in vain. I was serious."

Tyrone's anger flashed in his eyes and he whipped back a fist, only barely restraining himself. The soldier behind him moved forward as if surprised, then settled back against the wall. "You carry a lot of filth," said Tyrone through his teeth. He walked to Dub's cigarettes and crushed them with his boot.

You son of a bitch! thought Dub. If I have to come back from the dead, I'll get you for this.

"You know smoking is forbidden here."

"I never smoked inside."

"You got any more of these?"

"No. Is that what I'm here for? Smell smoke in the boys' room, did you?"

Tyrone's hand flicked to his fatigue pockets. Dub involuntarily flinched, raising his hand. Tyrone smiled with satis-faction. "What's this, turkey?"

The yellow plastic disk that Dub was supposed to wear around his neck. "It's the pass-card thing."

"Real smart. You know whose it is?"

"Let me guess." He patted his chest. "I guess it's mine."

"Well, why have I got it, turkey?"

"I don't know."

"Think."

"Because I don't?"

Tyrone threw it in his face. "Weren't you told to wear it at all times?"

"I took it off to wash up, take a crap, who the hell knows, Lex."

"Call me Captain!"

Dub saluted. "Yessir, Captain Lex! I forgot the thing. Big deal."

"Listen, here, turkey. You don't go anywhere without your tag. Anywhere!"

"Okay, okay. Christ! I forgot it."

Tyrone clutched him by the lapels again. "We could have shot you, turkey. Shot you! All we knew was that you were showing as an intruder. You could be dead, turkey." Tyrone shoved him down again. "I don't like your attitude."

"Okay, okay."

"Take this asshole back to his room!" Tyrone spun to leave.

As he reached the doorway, Dub called out. "Hey, Lex!"

Tyrone glared.

"All right, 'Captain Lex.'" Dub took two steps toward him.

"Captain Tyrone."

"Captain Tyrone, sir. If you ever touch me again, you'll be wearing your nuts for a necklace."

Tyrone sneered and left.

"You hear me, you son of a bitch? You hear me?" Dub's voice echoed down the tunnel. The man nearest the door put a calming hand on Dub's shoulder. He twisted away from it.

The other three shifted awkwardly and picked up their rifles. Because of the low-hanging light they were dark from the waist up. Dub looked at his smashed cigarettes. "Well? You like playing soldier? Huh? Christ!" He kicked over the steel chair, barely missing one man's shin.

The three eased out of the chamber, the last pausing to speak in a tone that implied a peace offering. "Perry'll take you back to your room. You get a good sleep, Mr. Clements."

Dub sighed. The sound echoed. He could see his own breath. "Yeah, yeah, yeah," he said, hanging the yellow disk around his neck.

"He kinda got to you, dint he?" The man offered his hand. "I'm Perry, Perry Wilkins." He stepped into the light: a simple face, freckles, red hair. Dub shook Perry's hand, then wiped his own face.

"Don't take it personal, Mr. Clements. Cap'n Tyrone's gotta make sure nobody's wandering around without I.D."

"Yeah, yeah."

"It's true. Sumboddy could get kilt. There's emotion detectors all aroun' and the disk keeps 'em from goin' off."

"Emotion detectors?"

"Absolutely. They picks up anything biggern a dawg."

Dub suppressed a smile. "Well, I guess I'll have to keep my emotions under wraps."

Perry looked a bit confused, then nodded. "Anybuddy fergits their thing, there, we do this same thing to 'em. Don't take it personal. I seen it three, four times and Cap'n Tyrone still scares me. An' you ought to see Cap'n Devlin do it. I been tol' Cap'n George was the best."

"You knew Lamont George?"

"He did my obstacle course training. We wudden friends or nothin', though. Come on, let's get outta this damp hole." He gestured toward the door.

Dub led him into the tunnel and spoke over his shoulder as he dodged the irregularities in the walls. "What's so special about these Captains?"

"They're the Castled Rooks." Perry said it as if it were obvious.

"So?"

"So they're the best. Elite corps. You know whut I'm sayin'?"

Dub paused. "Sure, but what does that mean? Do they do

something special? Say, I don't know, like other than teaching new recruits?"

"They got special assignments," Perry said reverently. "They take care of gettin' things ready."

"Ready?"

"For when the Russians come."

"Oh." Dub started walking again. "Like what do they get ready?"

"I figgur they puts plastic on bridges and stuff. Under highways and stuff. Then the Russians'll have trouble marching in. Boom!" He laughed.

"You know this for sure?"

"Nope, but I figgured it. I seen Cap'n Tyrone blow up a big ole boulder with plastic once."

"No kidding," said Dub. His pants leg grazed a bag of cement on a wheelbarrow. He stopped to brush it off. "Do you think they ever do anything like get rid of the enemies of America?"

"Whut do you mean?"

"I mean like James Bond, you know. Have they got a license to kill?"

Perry blinked.

"Do they ever assassinate Communist infiltrators?"

"Oh. Buddy, if I knew, I wudint tell ye, even with yur being who ye are. But I tell ye this, they gotta do whut's gotta be done, don't they?"

"Well, that's what we're here for, ain't it, Perry?"

"You bet!"

They were soon out of the incomplete tunnel and into the living areas. Perry stopped near the entry to the small lounge outside Dub's room. "Well, there ye are."

"Come on in, sit a spell," said Dub. "I'll buy you a fruit juice out of the machine."

"Naw. That's real nice of ye, but you gotta rest up. I hear tell yur going right into trainin' soon."

"Yeah? I still got tests they said."

"Don' matter. They kin see like I kin see, cain't they?"

"See what?"

"That yur a tough 'un. Was you a POW?"

"No, I was in country, but Charlie never caught me."

"Well you held up better to Cap'n Tyrone then anybuddy I seen. I seen one guy mess his pants. Yessir. Cap'n Tyrone's scarier than a movie."

"I guess he is," said Dub.

Perry stuck out his hand and shook Dub's ferociously. "It's bin a real pleasure talkin' to Mr. Carl Clements, a real pleasure." He was smiling from ear to ear.

"Hey, it was a pleasure meeting Lieutenant Perry Wilkins."

Perry actually blushed. Embarrassed, he turned quickly and left.

Dub watched him until he disappeared around the bend. He gave a quick laugh and sat on the sofa in front of the fireplace. Poor dope, he thought. Probably the others made him take me back here because they wanted to go to bed. "Ye gotta watch out fur them emotion detectors," he said out loud. "Yessireebob."

EIGHTEEN

By eight-thirty the next morning Dub was lying shirtless on a bed in the infirmary while a nurse squirted dime-sized globs of a beige lotion on him. It looked like carpenter's glue. The flat bottle even had the typical Elmer's shape. "You making a cupboard out of me?" he asked wearily.

"What?" asked the nurse.

"A cupboard. That stuff looks like wood glue."

She explained what the goop was, but he didn't listen. She attached suction cups shaped like miniature bicycle horns: one on each leg, a circle around his left nipple, and one on his right pectoral. He shifted to relieve an itch in his back.

"Don't move," she said. "This thing's been acting up. Just relax."

He yawned and closed his eyes. The EKG machine, about the size of a desk-top copier, beeped. With one eye he watched the curly-haired nurse push buttons. "You from the South?" he asked.

"Don't talk," she said. "Florida. My accent shows, huh?"

She didn't actually have much accent, but she wore too much rouge. "A lot of southerners here."

"Not enough," she said.

"Too many cowboys, though."

"Shush!"

She pushed more buttons, waited for another beep. A chart with heartbeat patterns emerged from the top. She tore it off and scanned it. "No, no," she said to herself. "Can you wait here a while? I'll be back."

"I'm dead, right?"

"It's just the machine. It acts up."

She left him alone. He drummed his fingers on the sheets and closed his swollen eyelids. He hadn't slept, either from the rush of adrenaline he'd worked up in confronting Tyrone or, more worrisome, the waiting for a nicotine craving to start tickling at his hands. He always felt it in his hands. They'd get as cumbersome as zeppelins while developing a hyperactive will of their own. On one cigarette-less stakeout he'd entertained them with an entire box of paper clips. First he straightened each one, then he made spirals of each, then a four-foot chain. Later he took the chain apart and tried to restore each paper clip. By dawn, Dub was twisting his hands around the steering wheel, fantasizing strangling both the Pittsburgh Plate Glass executive he was following and the guy's mistress.

What next? A Roto-Rooter tour up his colon to look for Commies? It wouldn't surprise him. Or a lie detector. That was a real possibility, given all the scrutiny. It wasn't too hard to give one mixed results by twitching the right muscles and concentrating on odd things. Army Intelligence had taught him about that. The Roto-Rooter seemed a worse possibility.

He might have dozed for a minute or two. He wasn't sure. He was overcome by an odd sort of guilt. These people, on the whole, weren't much worse than any others. Were they worse than a bunch of Lions or Elks or Odd Fellows who gathered in their lodge in funny hats and groused about school busing or illegal immigrants or the end of school prayer? People were prejudiced. That was a fact. They could deny it but it was always just below the surface and that wasn't just true of America, he'd seen it in the way the Korean officers had treated their Vietnamese equivalents in Saigon. Dub's father had been no angel. When he retired as a full bird-colonel he claimed it was because the Army was being screwed up by "all the charcoal" they were drafting, though it was more likely because his time limit for promotion had run out. If it hadn't been for Dub's mother, who turned to religion in her husband's long absences and who glorified the spirituality of the black race, perhaps Dub would have ended up like his old man. His mother's notions were a kind of prejudice too, but they counterbalanced the old man's sputtering rages. Dub grimaced as he remembered afternoons ruined by his father's fury over such things as Sidney Poitier winning the Academy Award, or Cassius Clay mowing down another opponent. Their housekeeper, Opal, had never shown the slightest reaction to these explosions as she dusted or fetched another drink for the old man. Christ! Colonel Delbert's rotating in his grave right now over me sleeping with Vonna, thought Dub. Maybe even Opal.

On the other hand, most of those people grousing about the way blacks or Jews or Italians or Cubans were ruining the world had some vague sense that the things they were saying were, at the least, distasteful and would say them in a mock whisper, as if they were secrets. With the encouragement of Marshall Wescott and others, however, these ordinary people in the White Rook had come to believe that their fear of "the enemy" was not only proper, but righteous. Their evil was in wanting to believe that all of the discomfort they felt with the modern world could be soothed.

There might be, and probably were, certain people in the Rook who were pathologically evil in the same way that some of Hitler's gang had been. Somebody connected with the White Rook, after all, Dub reminded himself, had set up a new version of Murder Inc., but most of the others were just nostalgic for an America that had never existed, an America with small towns like you see in Andy Hardy movies or 1950s television.

Wescott's evil was greater, however, than that of these people who thought of themselves as "plain folks," or even that of the pathologicals, if he wasn't actually one of them himself. With his clean fingernails and measured voice, he was egging them on; a pimp telling them their urges were normal. Give in, give in, give in. It would be nice, thought Dub, to prove Wescott had tossed Michael O'Dell off the causeway. That would be a gift to the world.

"Mr. Clements! How are you?"

Think of the devil.

Wescott, followed by Danny Devlin and another of the Castled Rooks, noisily slid a chair beside the bed. His hair was perfectly combed and his fingernails immaculate. Toss O'Dell over a rail? No, guys like this never washed their own dishes. "How's the leg, Colonel? Anything wrong here?"

"Gettin' much better, Carl. Everything's peachy. I just wanted to chat with you myself."

Dub sat up on his elbows. "This is kind of funny. In Breckenridge I was in the chair and you were in the bed."

"And don't think I'll ever forget it, Carl. What do you think of our White Rook?"

"I'm real impressed, Colonel. Real impressed."

"It's especially nice when we move outside. Kids playing on the swings, sing-alongs, barbecues, even an old-fashioned tent revival or two. Good hunting nearby too. But this place"— he swept his hand in an arc indicating the mountain above them—"this place will be our refuge in the coming storm."

"It's hard to believe such a place could be built."

"We had a bit of a head start. There was a mine here once, just started, that didn't produce, then the government started to turn the whole place into a wet-eye arsenal, but had to give up when the Canadian papers made a brouhaha about nerve gas and Congress cut the funds."

"I didn't know that."

"We picked it up on auction."

"A good deal."

"No other bidders. So you like it here?"

"It's really something."

"Well, we've been looking over your tests, Carl, and we like you. Isn't that so, boys?" Devlin and the other CR nodded. Dub searched Danny's face for any sign he knew about Dub's romp with Joan. Nothing. "Bronze Star, Silver Star, three Purple Hearts. You've got quite a record. You've been out of the service now . . . ?"

"Fifteen years. I got sick of drugged-up soldiers and equipment that fell apart. We just sat around while all those shit countries were mocking us."

"I understand. Believe me."

Good, thought Dub. They had checked out the legend and it held, though it sounded as if it would be hard to live up to the combat reputation of the fabricated Carl Clements.

"What I'm getting at is that I'm very interested in getting you into training, Carl. You're a special guy and you deserve better than hopping from job to job." He gestured at Dub's midsection. "You've let yourself go a bit. In a month or two we could have you back to where you were when you were twenty-one."

"That's a while ago."

"You'd be amazed what clean air, good food, and exercise can do for you."

"No cigarettes, I suppose."

Wescott pursed his lips in amusement and shook his head. "No beer, no caffeine. You'll be sharp as a razor."

"You know," said Dub, "this is really great, but how'm I going to pay for my stay while I'm getting trained? I'm down and out as they get."

"You don't need to worry about that. We've got plenty of money behind us. People all over the country. Kids send in their *pennies*, praise the Lord! It makes you proud."

"Lamont used to tell me he did some special jobs for you all. I'd be happy to work off my stay."

Wescott glanced back at Devlin. "Special jobs?"

"He didn't say what they were, but I'm game, Colonel Wescott. Nobody can say I'm not game."

"Well, we'll see. Lamont was a Castled Rook, a Captain, remember. One of the six. You have a way to go before you're ready to be castled. We'll start you on the regular training—that should be nothing for you—and then you'll be eligible for promotion, you see."

Dub shrugged.

Wescott placed his hand on Dub's thigh and leaned forward. "Do you know the game of chess, Carl?"

"Afraid I don't."

"It's a great game. The ultimate for anyone interested in war, or politics. There are two rooks, or castles, on each side, you see. Late in the game, when the going gets tough and the conflict is entering its life or death phase, the best thing you can have is castled rooks. They are united. The one cannot be captured without the other taking immediate revenge. Castled rooks are the most powerful pieces on the board. They can strike a major blow because of their partner and control large sections of the board. They can end the game. We decided it was the perfect symbol for our elite corps. We knew of the need for such an elite corps and then the comparison to chess occurred to us. For each rook we establish we shall select six Castled Rooks."

Dub nodded. He had always thought the term had some

special meaning. It was too cumbersome otherwise. "Then I can get one of those rings, like Lamont's?"

Wescott looked a little concerned. "How much did Lamont tell you about the ring? I'm surprised he was so open."

"We were as close as two men could get. I saved his life once and he saved mine a month later. I'm sorry I didn't listen closer when he wanted to tell me about the AVCN."

"CR's are sworn to secrecy. He could have been expelled for violating his oath."

Dub remembered the sound of Lamont George's last breath. "I guess it doesn't matter now he's dead."

"I suppose not," Wescott said thoughtfully.

"Terrible," sighed Dub. "A car wreck. I always knew him to be a good driver."

"He wasn't at fault."

The nurse came back. A happy-looking bald man was with her. "Colonel Wescott," she said, "I'm sorry to interrupt, but this machine just isn't working right."

The bald man, whom Wescott called Dr. Loomis, held up the first printout and told the nurse to run another. After a few seconds of pushing and beeping, another chart rolled out. Loomis held it up and shook his head. "Can't tell a thing. You could have a heart like a horse or be dead, either way."

"Well," said Wescott, standing, "there's no evidence Mr. Clements has any problem, is there?"

"Not that I can tell, but then, maybe we ought to get a treadmill for a stress test."

"In the future," said Wescott. "You don't know of anything wrong with your heart, do you, Carl?"

"Broke it a few times."

"Let's get this man into training, then. He's healthy. We're just supercautious, Carl, you understand. We only do the EKG because somebody gave us the machine. We're more interested in where your heart belongs than how it beats."

Loomis began fiddling with the EKG machine. Wescott shook Dub's hand, congratulating him. The CR did likewise, then Devlin. Danny's shake was very friendly. He couldn't know about Joan. The nurse pulled off the suction cups. They left blue circles where they had stuck, especially those around his heart.

[188]

Danny Devlin spun the jeep sharply left, skidding the rear end to a dusty stop just in front of the porch of the "Survival Bootcamp" dormitory. The long Quonset hut was tucked up a winding pathway through the pines, maybe half a mile from the White Rook. Behind it was the top of a cliff whose bottom was obscured by the treetops below. The end of the hut had been painted sometime recently, but the roof was spotted with rust, particularly along the seams and at the nail heads. "Why don't you just crash us through the front door?" asked Dub.

Devlin grinned. "I love these old jeeps."

"See what you think of them when you roll one."

"Never happen, Carl. Never." He lifted a duffel bag out of the back and tossed it onto the porch. Dub had strolled toward the cliff to get a view between the trees. "That's Canada out there," said Devlin. "And just beyond that a few million Russian troops."

"Practically next door," said Dub. "This *is* God's country!" He then thought of the irony of applying the expression to the White Rook enclave.

"And we're gonna make sure it stays that way," said Devlin.

"So what now? Where is everybody?"

"Climbing. Marching. The first two weeks are physical training, mostly. This group started two days ago. Instead of waiting for the next, we're putting you in with them."

"Marching, eh?"

"Up one mountain, down another."

Dub looked down the cliff. "Great. It'll be good to get back in shape."

"Nothing like it, I tell you. Your head clears up. Your lungs clear up. You sleep good. You feel like you've got a power pack."

"The Six-Million-Dollar Man."

"He's a wuss compared to us." He lightly whacked Dub on the arm. "Come on. I'll get you your rifle. You can do a little practicing until the others get back."

A month of playing soldier, thought Dub. Real detective work.

"It's terrible at first, but then the juices get flowing."

Devlin pumped his arms. "I'll tell you this, it gets you sexy, too."

"Sexy?"

"You can do it all night, every night. It's like being sixteen."

"Joan must like that."

"Jesus, man," said Devlin, "you don't know much about marriage, do you?"

"I guess not. I'm a three-time loser."

"Well, you should marry for kids. Nothing else matters. Not looks, not cooking, not tail. You can get tail anytime."

"Joan doesn't seem the cooking type."

"Somewhere along the line she forgot she's a woman." Devlin had taken a set of keys out of his pocket. Though his voice was calm, he jammed the key into the padlock like he was trying to hurt it.

Dub knew that Danny didn't want to talk about it, but that was always the best time to press. "She's a real healthy-looking woman, if you don't mind my saying so; she'll give you some terrific kids."

Danny hooked the padlock on the latch and shoved the door open. He turned, squinted up at Dub, and said, "Carl, she's damaged goods. Six months ago she found out about me and, well, this other chick. She's pissed off. It didn't mean a thing but she's pissed off. She gives me a knuckler across the bridge of my nose. I'm out like a light. I didn't see it coming. I wake up looking like a raccoon. I tell the bitch I'm leaving her and she tells me she's missed her period. 'I must be pregnant,' she says, smiling, like she hasn't creamed me with a sucker punch. So I stay with her. I'm nice. I figure it's like women's hormones. But where's the kid? She's not pregnant. She's lying just to keep me. It makes me sick." He peered at Dub, then looked away, as if he'd let too much tumble out. He spun and went inside the hut.

Two rooms flanked the door, each with cots and easy chairs, presumably for the drill instructors. The room beyond was stark, with only lockers and a series of wooden bunks on each side. The gun room was at the other end.

"Did you all go to a doctor?" asked Dub.

"She says that's silly, she's never been healthier."

"You never know." Dub stopped near one of the bunks, frozen by the thought that Joan could be pregnant by him. Danny could have the problem and that would be something the man could never face, even if he suspected it. She could be fine. Dub's kid would be raised in the White Rook. Christ! Danny was preoccupied with his key ring and didn't notice him stop. "She—she ought to go to this guy Loomis. I mean, you got a doctor right here."

"Loomis? Shit. What does he know?"

"Then take her down to Billings or Butte or whatever's near by. Hell, you want kids, don't you?"

"Hey," said Devlin, "it's not your business, right?"

Dub blinked his eyes dopily. "Geez, I'm sorry. I didn't mean nothing."

"It's between me and her."

"Right. Right. I didn't mean nothing."

Devlin opened the closet. Five Kalashnikovs lined the wall with space for many more. Three crates of ammunition were stacked in the rear. "That's a lot of firepower!" said Dub.

"You'll get number fifteen, here," said Devlin. He lifted it off its hook and pitched it to him.

"Never shot one of these," said Dub. "How good are they?"

"The best."

"A Russian gun?" Dub sighted down the long room. "Why can't I get an M-16? Now there's a gun."

"Actually these are Czechoslovakian. The most popular firearm in the world. When the Reds come, they're not going to bring rounds for an M-16."

"So?"

"So when we steal their ammo, we got to be able to use it." It was the most obvious thing in the world to him.

"Oh, I get you. Like when we sneak down out of the mountains here."

"You got it."

"Like the Swamp Fox. Like Charlie."

"You got it."

Dub examined the breech. "But how do you know the Russians will ever get on the mainland? Won't they just fling their rockets?"

"We aren't finished until they're here. And they know it.

[191]

And when we get them here, they're on our turf. Like Afghanistan."

So that was how the White Rook was going to save America. "Well, I'd rather have my M-16. Some guys used to bitch they jammed up, but mine purred like a kitten." Dub lifted the rifle and sighted between the bunks again. "Pow!" he said for Devlin's benefit. "Feels funny. Where'd Wescott get all these guns, anyway?"

Dub looked back. Devlin was in the closet, getting ammo. "It's a free country," he said. "Here, try it out. The shooting range is down the slope to the left. I've got to get back. Got a mission."

"Mission?"

"Don't ask so many questions, Carl. Somebody'll think you're a spy." Devlin winked and left.

NINETEEN

The slope to the left was damp. Dub noticed deer droppings. Birds skittered in the underbrush when the cartridge clips clinked in his jacket pocket. He wondered if the path led out of the enclave. Maybe he could get to a phone and Devraix would pull him out. Dub didn't think he was getting anywhere, really. And it was hard to be patient. He wasn't going to stay under for fourteen months like he had in Saigon. He was going to have to think of something to get the stew cooking here or he'd never get the story. Devlin could be on his way to kill somebody right now, he thought. And what can I do about it? If Devraix knew, he could tail him. Mission, Dub thought. Mission. These guys liked to talk military. Danny was probably just picking up Cheez Whiz. Or more instant pudding. Dub grimaced.

When the clearing opened in front of him he saw the shooting range was more than something recreational. There were five target figures dangling from a wire clothesline. Another five were pop-up figures. Very FBI. Very military. But these were not just silhouettes of anonymous enemies with vital areas marked by white ovals. The targets themselves were freshly painted on pasteboard. There were no bullet holes in them yet. Labels sat halfway to the targets on signs that reminded Dub of the old Burma Shave advertisements. "KIKE," said one. Behind it, a Shylock figure with a Star of David on his chest held an Uzi. Next to him was "NIGGER COP": Little Black Sambo with white triangles for teeth, a raised billy club, and a double-breasted blue uniform. Why cop? To his left was "SPICK": the Frito Bandito with six-guns and a hammer and sickle on his sombrero. Further down the row was "JAP," a toothy, bespectacled Tōjō figure, and "FAGGOT," with a purple scarf and fat red lips. Dub could only make out the title of the first of the pop-up figures: "SECULAR HUMANIST." Whoever had painted it had barely been able to get the letters R and T onto the sign. Secular Humanist? Eat lead, secular humanist! He shook his head and involuntarily grinned. These people were sick, all right, but pathetic too. Pathetic like somebody missing a chunk of brain. He thought of a guy who used to hang out near one of the entrances to Three Rivers Stadium during Bucs games. He would break into wild, lurching dances while banging a gnarled hand against a one-stringed guitar. Some people avoided him; some threw coins. Others, tanked up on Iron City or Rolling Rock, stared and laughed loudly. He couldn't know he was a fool, and that was the saddest part of it all.

Sure could use a cigarette, thought Dub. He sat on a log that was worn on the top and began to fiddle with the Kalashnikov. It smelled of gun oil and was spotless. Ready for the Russians coming across the pole. He loaded it and walked to the firing line. He aimed the rifle at "KIKE," then lowered it. "NIGGER COP"? "JAP"? "SPICK"? He couldn't get into shooting any of them. Maybe "SECULAR HUMANIST." That was meaningless enough. He had bent over and was jerking at the pop-up rope trying to figure out how it raised the figure when he heard heavy boots, huffing, and a man yelling, "Bring up the rear! Bring up the rear! Pussies! Close it up! Close it up!"

The head of a man about twenty showed itself as he struggled up the path to the firing range. He was wearing a huge field pack and carrying his rifle with both hands. He was followed by others, all gasping for air, their olive shirts wet with sweat and clinging to their chests. Red-faced, the first one lurched to the log and dropped down, leaning forward on his rifle. The second stumbled, fell to one knee, and collapsed backward against the log. The others lurched up in various states of exhaustion, until Lex Tyrone, wearing a broad-brimmed jungle hat and fatigues, jogged to the top of the path and yelled down. "Cameron, you pussy! Gooks are on your tail! They're closing up, they're catching you! Move! Move! Move!"

Cameron's face, red and round, appeared. His eyes seemed to be rolling in different directions and his nostrils clawed for air. Neck veins straining, Tyrone leaned at him and shouted as he lumbered along. "Pussy-whip! Men will die because of you! The niggers will get your sister! Pussy-whip! Pussy-whip! You make me puke!" Cameron was too beat to care. He could barely raise his rifle to waist level. He lurched to within a few feet of the log and dropped to both knees. He then twisted and fell back on his pack, his chest heaving.

"Pick up that fucking rifle!" yelled Tyrone. "Pick it up!" Cameron dizzily grabbed it by the barrel and dragged it on top of him. "You make me puke, pussy-whip!" Tyrone kicked the heel of Cameron's boot. The other men were not interested. They were just trying to catch their breath. One of them was trying to throw up behind the log but had nothing to work with. I'm gonna love this, thought Dub.

Tyrone looked at a stopwatch and started into a tirade about these ten being the worst recruits he'd ever seen, he'd trained bitches who were tougher, the Commies had pussies like them for lunch, and so on and so on. After nearly five minutes of this, he wheeled in disgust, crossed his arms, and strode to the edge of the clearing. Dub looked over the muscles on Tyrone's back and noticed a funny curve in his spine between his shoulder blades. Scoliosis, maybe. It was the kind of thing that might keep you out of the military. There was some comfort too in seeing that Tyrone was sweating even though he had no pack or rifle. He was partly human. Maybe.

"Well, look who's here, men," said Tyrone. "The famous Carl Clements." With an open mouth, one of the sweaty recruits looked up at Dub, but just plain didn't care who the hell he was.

"How do," said Dub. One of the men waved weakly.

"Carl here's going to be joining us. Isn't that right?" Dub nodded. "We're talking a big hero. Isn't that right? Carl here got a Bronze and a Silver Star. Quite a man. He ought to show you pussies something about soldiering."

"I don't know," Dub tried to joke. "You boys look a lot tougher than me."

"Experience and deceit will take youth and enthusiasm any day."

"Not every day," said Dub.

"I hope you're not taking us on another march," moaned Cameron.

Tyrone kicked Cameron's heel. "Carl here isn't an instructor. Look at that gut of his. It's not as soft as yours, pussy, but he isn't instructor material yet. He's here for the course. He's here to show you pussies up."

Dub gestured with his thumb. "Don't believe a word he says." Two of the men grinned.

"And I'm glad we ran into you right here," said Tyrone. "You know what else about Carl Clements? Master Sergeant Carl Clements is a hell of a shot. Marksman first class. Took out a gook general at three-quarters of a mile. Clean head shot. Hell of a sniper."

"No such thing as a clean head shot. You guys know everything about my war record?"

Tyrone looked smug. They had checked out everything, but they didn't know he was a fraud yet. The cover was solid. "I figure Carl here can show us how to shoot." He pointed down range.

"Hey," said Dub, "I never handled one of these babies. And it's been years anyway. Now if you got me my old"—he couldn't remember what the sniping rifles were called—"M-16, it'd be like riding a bicycle. You never forget. My old M-16 was better than a wife."

"See what he's saying?" Tyrone paced. "You've got to love your rifle. It's your partner." He kicked at Cameron's heel again. "You don't drop it in the dirt." He turned to Dub. "It can't be too different. Anyhow, you'll get to love this baby."

Dub shrugged. "I'll give it a try." This wasn't going to be worth a damn, he thought. He hadn't been that good a shot even when they had shipped him to Saigon. He hadn't needed to be for his undercover assignment. Squeeze the trigger, he remembered, don't anticipate the report. Calm, calm, calm.

"You get first crack at the nice new targets the Cadets painted up for us." How nice, thought Dub, train the kids early. "How about taking out the spook cop?"

"Why is he a cop? I hate the idea of shooting a cop."

"Because he's a traitor. He's only interested in getting

brothers off. It isn't your place to question orders. You take him out. Clean head shot."

"I'll try." He lifted the rifle and peered down the barrel. He looked at the caricature beyond his sight and remembered Opal again. She had read him *Little Black Sambo* when he was seven and frightened by a hurricane. She had acted out the parts until his stomach hurt with laughing. Often, when he was lonely she streaked butter with chocolate and called it the "tiger butter" that Sambo had made. What did the White Rookers want to kill Sambo for? Dub lowered the rifle and pretended to be looking at something on the barrel. He licked his thumb and wet the sight with it. He held his breath, aimed right between the eyes, and squeezed the trigger. The billy club was punctured.

"You missed," said Tyrone.

"I thought I'd disarm him first."

The recruits laughed. Tyrone was angry. "You obey orders. I said head shot. Between the eyes."

He raised the rifle again. If he held it straight, if he didn't jerk the trigger, the Kalashnikov should have a "slice" (his shooting instructor had always used golf terms). He tried to compensate. This time the shot pierced the cop's shoulder. It hadn't sliced. Splinters of wood from some kind of prop flew up and the pasteboard figure sagged. "Sorry," said Dub. "Takes getting used to."

"Marksman, eh?" Tyrone sneered. He jerked the rifle out of Dub's arm, spun, and fired three quick shots. One took the ear, the next hit the cheek, and the third pinged somewhere off the mountainside. Tyrone slapped the rifle against Dub's chest. "That's what I call a head shot."

"Two out of three," said Dub. "Not bad. And you killed a rock too."

One of the recruits sputtered, suppressing a laugh. Tyrone's eyes tightened. I shouldn't have said that, Dub thought. Nosiree.

The afternoon was spent dismantling and reassembling the Kalashnikovs. Tyrone cursed, timed, and threatened. He particularly picked on poor Cameron, whose pudgy fingers had no agility whatsoever. Dub hadn't changed into his fatigues yet and got grease on his trousers and sport coat. Afterward, they returned to the cabin and the men showed him his locker, the empty bunk, and the outdoor showers. Dub skipped the latter; it was chilly. He scrubbed his hands with the cheap soap, but couldn't get the gun grease smell out. When he lifted his food to his mouth the combination of the soap and grease was even more repulsive than the food: boiled beef jerky, gritty coffee, and potatoes. Cameron ate desperately, then stared at the others eating more slowly. "Take my potato," said Dub. "I ate a big lunch."

"No," said Cameron. "I got to get in shape."

"Potatoes ain't fattening. Take it." He plopped it on Cameron's tin plate. It was gone in two bites. The man's cheeks were stuffed like a chipmunk's.

They were given half an hour to relax before "lights out" at eight, though most of the men had already collapsed on their bunks. The trainees seemed serious, maybe even desperate, types. Except for Cameron they were gaunt, with sharp cheekbones. When they took off their watches, the flesh underneath was almost blue pale and their leathery tans were not the cultivated golden of the suburbs. One, obviously an ex-skinhead, had SS death's-head tattoos on each shoulder and an unhealed hole where his ear had been pierced. Several of them had upper lips and chins that were lighter than the rest of their faces and it was easy to imagine them with beards, mustaches, and greasy billed caps, fixing somebody's roof or sitting in a country bar after fifteen hours in a semi. They were the kind of guys who did the physical labor of the country, whose big dream was to own a mobile home with a La-Z-Boy and a forty-inch TV. They were the kind of guys who got satisfaction out of saying that their last customer at the service station, despite his silk tie and medical degree, didn't know that his BMW didn't have a carburetor. They were the kind of guys who knew they'd been dealt the low cards and figured somebody had to have stacked the deck. For some it would be their wives, for others a conspiracy. The first group would take to their fists, repent, and take to their fists again. The recruits were the second type, only more frustrated than most, soaking up Wescott's preaching and deceiving themselves that they were the salt of the earth who would one day take charge and put things to rights. All that hating the blacks and the Jews and whomever did for them was guarantee that despite their holding the low cards, they could take comfort that somebody else wasn't in the game at all. Two of them were southerners, about half were westerners, but one was from Maine, another from New York, a third from Washington, D.C. There were thousands like them in every state and many thousands more who would cheer them when they set about to right things. The cabin throbbed with their frustrations like the secret heart of white America.

Poor suckers, thought Dub, stretched on his bunk with his hand behind his head. Wescott and his boys didn't organize all this to give it away. When the "American values" were restored, they'd still be the guys who couldn't get their fingernails clean.

The lights went out. Cameron leaned over from the top bunk. "What was the war like, Carl?"

"Like a war," said Dub. "Why do you ask?"

"They really screwed you guys, I know, but we appreciate what you done."

Dub thought for a second. He hadn't actually been in combat. Saigon maybe had been worse in some ways. "Thank you. I didn't really feel screwed, though. Maybe shortchanged. Most of the guys were okay. I knew what I was getting into, or I thought I did."

"You kill many?"

Dub shrugged. Two, and they were ours. "Too many," he said.

"I wish I'd been there with you."

"Why weren't you?" It was a stupid question. It never seemed like he was getting older, only that the world was getting younger.

"It was over. The hippies had lost it for us already. And then Jimmy Carter ruined us for good. Who wants to be in that kind of army?"

"What about President Reagan?"

"Well, he tried, but he's gone now and—"

"Cameron," said somebody, "will you shut the fuck up?"

"We're talking," said Dub.

"You shut up too."

The door to Tyrone's room popped open. He looked out angrily, then closed it.

Two hours before dawn, Lex Tyrone strode up and down the aisle whacking people on the feet with a rolled-up newspaper. They had fifteen minutes to make their beds and be ready for a march. Both Dub and a blond Texan didn't get their blankets tight enough to bounce a quarter, so Tyrone ordered them to do twenty-five push-ups. Dub got to sixteen before his left arm gave way and he flopped onto the floor. Tyrone yelled, prodded Dub with the toe of his boot, and tacked on ten more. Dub managed to get through them by undulating his body and cheating a bit with his knees.

Tyrone was in a hurry to get them on the trail. They stumbled along unable to see the path or where their feet were landing. Dub squinted at the dim outline of the pack in front of him until his forehead hurt. It wasn't long before the man in front was pulling away and the man behind ran into Dub's back. They crumpled into a heap. The man cursed and scrambled to his feet; Dub sat puffing until he realized that if he lost contact with them he might fall off a mountain. He lifted himself to his feet and struggled on, but he, Cameron, and a gray-haired Coloradan were last over the hill and onto the even more treacherous downslope. He helped Cameron up twice and the man from Denver once. They helped Dub up three times and lost sight of the others. When they finally stumbled into the clearing by the target range, the birds had begun to chatter in the early light of dawn and Lex Tyrone was sputtering.

"The Russians got you, pussy-whips! You're dead!" Dub tried to show no emotion, but Cameron was sheepish and the Coloradan's nose was flexing in anger. They were ordered to do calisthenics while the others began shooting. Christ! Dub thought, why would anybody volunteer for this shit? At least I'm getting paid. When the three of them were finally ordered to shoot (prone position, probably just to make them lie in the dirt), Dub did even worse than he had the day before. His head hurt, his eyes were lousy in the light, and the dirt was itchy on his sweaty body. When they set out to do the pop-ups, Dub missed three out of five, only putting bullets into "SECULAR HUMANIST," who was portrayed setting fire to a Bible, and "ATHEIST," who had fangs and reptilian eyes. Some of the recruits applauded when Dub's shot ripped through the groin of "SECULAR HUMANIST." He wasn't living up to Carl Clements' record as a marksman, but he claimed it was because snipers had better weapons and more time. No one cared. They were just delighted they were better than the war hero.

By breakfast at seven-thirty, they were starving. Tyrone gleefully asked if they were hungry. Dub didn't like his tone of voice. Tyrone didn't even force them to run up the hill. In the clearing were about twenty chickens stirring in wire cages and six coffinlike rifle boxes with holes in them. The youngest and most enthusiastic of the recruits, a boy in his mid-twenties from Birmingham, saluted and asked, "Shall I get a firewood detail, Cap'n, sir?"

"Not yet," said Tyrone, and Dub thought, Oh, shit. He knew what was next. He'd heard about this. One of the more notorious parts of Ranger training. You were sure to get the notorious stuff here, rather than the stuff that made you a real soldier.

"You hungry, Cameron?" asked Tyrone.

"Yes, sir!"

Dub wanted to tell Cameron to shut up, but it wouldn't have done any good.

"How about you, Marshall?"

"Yes, sir."

"And you, Clements?"

"I'm still kind of sick from the run, Captain Tyrone, sir."

"Is that so? That's because you're not eating right. Those cigarettes. You need to eat like a man, get healthy. You three stand up there."

Christ! thought Dub. I need this?

"Now let me tell you about parasites," began Tyrone. It was the Ranger thing all right. In the tropics even healthy-looking chickens can harbor parasites in their flesh. As gruesomely as possible he described elephantiasis, trichinosis, and other haircurling diseases, though it wasn't at all clear that you could get these things from a chicken. The point was that in survival situations you often couldn't build a fire, but you could get the high protein, high iron you needed by drinking chickens' blood.

"Oh, man!" said someone, then added, "Sir!" Cameron looked green. Dub sighed.

"Now let me show you how this is done." Tyrone pulled an enormous Bowie knife from his boot. He took a chicken from one of the boxes, sliced its throat, and as the dying bird twitched in his hands, held it over his head and let the blood pulse into his mouth for what seemed like days. The chicken slowed. The blood dripped its last and Tyrone flung the chicken behind him like a magician tossing his last trick over his shoulder. He smiled, his teeth stained red, a shiny line running from the corner of his mouth to his Adam's apple.

Two recruits clapped. "All right!" said the ex-skinhead.

"I've got enough concentrated food in me now to kill niggers for two days!" shouted Tyrone. He struck his chest with his fist like a gorilla. He turned. He looked at the three. The recruits laughed, probably at their expressions. "That's right! You're next. Pick yourself a chicken. Go on!"

Dub expected Cameron to resist, but the man moved zombielike to the cages. Marshall seemed to be trying to psych himself up for it by pumping his arms.

"Well? Get to it, Clements!"

Dub just looked at him.

"What's the matter? Yellow?"

Yellow? Who called anybody yellow? For a moment Dub juggled his options. If he quit he might never get back into the White Rook and he wouldn't have learned anything about the killings. Walking out might be dangerous too. On the other hand, he was fed up with Captain Lex Tyrone, Castled Rook.

Cameron's chicken struggled out of his hands and charged into the brush. Cameron bumbled in after it. Each time he came within a few feet, the hen cocked her head to one side, then fluttered a few more yards away. "Here, chickie! Here, chickie! You damned pissant! Here, chickie!" The recruits were all laughing, some of them rolling backward off the log. Cameron dived face first into a clump of brambles and came out with thorns bristling on his cheeks like acupuncture needles. He was so frustrated and angry he didn't seem to feel them.

"You pussy-whip!" yelled Tyrone. "Catch that chicken!"

Marshall suddenly howled like a beast. He waved his chicken, its head barely hanging on a thread of skin, and danced like a football player who's just scored. Blood was on his nose, his face, his throat. *A-whoo! A-whoo! A-whoooooo!* echoed off the mountains as he danced, spinning. The dust swirled around his ankles.

"Are you getting a bird or are you answering to me?"

Dub flexed his jaws to keep from telling Tyrone to fuck off, and he moved toward the boxes, repeating to himself, "The purpose is to find the murderer, not get into something with this prick. The purpose is to find the murderer and stay alive." He went to the first box, opened it carefully. The speckled hen looked up at him docilely. He lifted it and cradled it in his arms. He could feel its heart beating. Tyrone was staring Dub in the face and smirking. Cameron chased his chicken between them and onto the slope at the other end of the clearing, but Dub's eyes never moved from Tyrone's cold green stare. He seized the hen's neck with one hand and its head with the other. The animal, its neck broken, struggled. Eyes still fixed on Tyrone, Dub took his knife from his belt, opened the hen's throat, and tasted the tinny sweetness, warm and sticky, dribbling into his throat. He wiped the blood from his chin with the back of his hand, then viciously flung the hen at Tyrone's feet.

Tyrone winked, broke their locked stares, and gestured with his hand. The other recruits moved toward the boxes, some of them frenzied with the excitement. Soon they were whooping, jumping, shouting themselves into the killing, sinews taut in their necks. One accidentally sliced his finger. Two got the blood down, then ran vomiting toward the brush. Another was smearing the blood on his face and licking it off his fingers.

Dub stood in the middle of the chaos, squeezing the black handle of his knife, hearing nothing but the throbbing of the veins in his head. If Tyrone had said a word, anything at all, one syllable, one inarticulate noise, he would have cut his throat. He was certain of that. Absolutely.

TWENTY

Dub used his hatred of Tyrone to keep him going. Each day there was more huffing up and down mountain trails, and more shooting. Dub got a little better with the Kalashnikov by mentally blanking out the cardboard figures, which were renewed each day, and imagining that Tyrone was in their place, but he still lagged behind with Cameron and the older man from Colorado on the marches. On the second day Dub was so winded on the afternoon hike, it took all of his under-the-breath cursing to get one foot in front of the other. He began to have chest pains from the exertion and his left arm went numb. He found a tree to lean against and waited until the spell passed, angry that he was falling further and further behind. On the third morning his buttocks, thighs and shoulders were so stiff he couldn't move without a small grunt of pain, and hiking double-time up the trail felt like running on termite-infested stilts. This was a good way to give up smoking: you hurt so much you couldn't lift a match.

By the fourth morning, stinking of horse liniment, and with every muscle in pain including his eyelids, Dub fell so far behind with Cameron that neither of them could hear the others and soon were lost. Dub sagged to a convenient rock. An invisible fist had tightened around his chest again. "The altitude," he gasped. "It's got to be the altitude." Cameron too was beyond caring. Each day had brought more bizarre "training." On the second day they had roasted rattlesnake for breakfast. No one resisted it. Several had been so sick from drinking chicken blood that they had skipped eating meat the previous evening. Yesterday they had dined on some kind of soy protein cereal that would have made Trigger giddy with happiness, and later in the evening Dub had been slumped by a tree when he heard Tyrone telling the guy on the supply jeep that he would need the earthworms on Tuesday. Tomorrow would be Tuesday. Dub didn't figure they would be going fishing. Earthworms were supposed to be quite nutritious. He didn't want to find out.

They had also done some rappeling, which was probably exhilarating when your entire body didn't hurt. They had tossed a few Molotov cocktails at boulders, and various Castled Rooks had taught them how to garrote a sentry, how to make a propane bomb, and how to take care of your knife. The third day, Sunday, had also brought a sermon that crackled of brimstone. They didn't allow a moment for you to collect your thoughts. That was what you were supposed to do when training soldiers, Dub knew, and it seemed to be working on most of them. They had even picked up on Tyrone's need to prove that Carl Clements, the big medal winner, had become no more than a joke, and their looks had become sneers. Dub found out that, indeed, Tyrone wasn't a vet at all, unlike many of the CRs, and probably was driven to prove he was a better soldier than any of them. That, Dub figured, would make him a useful fellow if you wanted someone to do your killing for you, but he warned himself not to let the teeth-grinding loathing he felt for Tyrone mislead him. He still didn't have anything that proved anybody other than Lamont George knew about the *Mercenary* ads, and he was beginning to think he wasn't going to as long as he was in Survival Boot Camp.

Dub held his hand against his stabbing chest and took several deep breaths. The pain faded a bit. Cameron shifted, and Dub could just make out that the man was holding his head and weeping. Dub had resigned himself to the role of squad bumbler because it seemed to get Tyrone to ease up, but Cameron still anguished over every degradation.

"You all right?"

Cameron sniffed.

"Hey, buddy, we couldn't help getting lost. It was dark. We need a rest, don't we?"

"I should quit," Cameron moaned. "I gotta quit. My wife was right."

"What'd your wife say?"

"My ex-wife. She ran off with my cousin Larry."

"Sounds like you were lucky to get rid of her."

"There was nothing wrong with her," he said sharply. "She said I wasn't man enough for her. All I ever did was the night shift at the Seven-Eleven."

Dub sighed. Even breathing hurt. "Doing this won't get your wife back. This is bullshit, Cam."

"I don't want her back. This is for me."

"Right. Look, I got the medals, Cam. I know what makes a soldier and what don't. This is crap. Get out of it and go to night school or something. Fix up your life that way."

"I'm not a quitter. If you're a quitter, why don't you quit? Pussy-whip!"

Dub was startled. Cameron was getting trained all right. "All I know is what I know. This has got nothing to do with combat. It's a hodgepodge of boot-camp stories come to life."

"So why don't you quit? Huh? Why don't you?"

Dub shrugged. That movement hurt too. "That's me, buddy. I'm talking about you. Go live your life."

Cameron's face had become visible as the sky lightened. His eyes were wide as his mouth twitched for something to say. "Pussy-whip!" He raised himself, using his rifle as a crutch, then headed up the path.

"Christ almighty!" muttered Dub. He had to get out of this and back into the White Rook. And he wasn't going to eat any fucking earthworms, that's all he knew. He climbed to the top of the rise and heard Cameron somewhere off to his left. He was beginning to understand how people were always getting lost on hunting trips. A few of his cases back in Pittsburgh were question marks because men had gone hunting and disappeared. They could die in the woods and not be found for a decade, or they could take the opportunity to run off with a waitress from Union City or Zelienople. Dub had found a couple of guys who did the latter, but finding men who had died in the woods was up to God and the Game Commission.

He thought Cameron was headed in the wrong direction, but he decided to follow the sound. Even the sunrise was no help, since they had never done this particular route in daylight. He called out. Cameron didn't answer. He didn't hear anything but birds and the rustle of pines. Shit. He called again. Nothing. Okay, the lay of the land. When you're at the camp you can see the cliff to the northwest, the big peak to the east. When they headed out that morning, they had rounded the corner toward the east—no, southeast. "Christ!" he shouted. "I'm lost." His voice echoed it back to him.

He saw light shining off a talus slope to his right. Maybe he could see something from up there. He worked his way down into a sharp ravine and rock by rock across a stream. They hadn't crossed a stream on any of their marches, he knew. He was heading due south, from what he could see of the dawn. He drank some of the cold water and considered walking straight north. Maybe if he violated the border, the Canadians would take him to a telephone and he could check in with Devraix. And Vonna. He'd like to call his girls. What were Elizabeth and Carrie up to? He hadn't thought about them for a few days. He felt guilty about that. I'll fly to Charleston as soon as I'm out of here, he thought. Get the job done and get out. Whatever it takes. The words reminded him of what the captain had said before sending him undercover. He took one last look toward Canada and headed toward the rocks.

The distance was deceptive and the climb tough. He took it slow, however, pausing often to chew on twigs he broke off tiny saplings. They weren't as satisfying as cigarettes, but they helped. His muscles protested at every move and he felt sluggish. Up, step by step toward the crisp Montana sky. Okay, Dub, he asked himself, what are you going to do about this situation? Patience was the main weapon of a good private eye. The skeletons in the closet will rattle if you wait long enough. But it's one thing to sit in a car doing *Pittsburgh Post-Gazette* crossword puzzles and another to rip up every muscle in your body.

Waiting had its dangers, particularly since it looked like a long wait. It gave the opposition more time to stumble across something that would prove he wasn't who he claimed to be. The alternative to patience was provoking the situation: stirring the fire. But how could he stir the fire and not get burned? He couldn't think of anything. Could Wescott have a safe in his office? Possibly, but the White Rook was too crowded to try anything like a break-in. Maybe when the people moved outside, into the cabins. But when would that be? Ten days or so? Maybe he could just sneak a phone call. There was a phone somewhere in the White Rook. If Dub could just check in with Devraix—hell, maybe Vonna and he had already solved the case from outside. Or maybe called it off. Maybe it would be better to call it off.

When he finally scrambled into the open, the view was spectacular, though not at all familiar. Toothlike mountains scattered north, a valley far to the right, the jewel blue of the sky marred only by a wisp of cloud. He heard the distant attack cry of a hawk and sat with his back against a rock. It was nearly nine a.m. and his stomach growled. "Cameron!" he shouted. *"Cameron!"* He whistled. The echo faded into the trees. He could always climb further up, maybe see over the edge of the ridge. Later. He crossed his arms, let the warmth of the sun flow over his face, and dozed.

The sound that woke him was sharp, but distant. He opened his eyes and glanced to each side. Another shot, then a third and fourth, seemed to come from over his left shoulder. *"Cameron!"* More single shots, evenly spaced, not like someone trying to draw attention to himself. Dub raised himself and grimaced at the extra stiffness that had set in during the nap. *"Cameron! Captain Tyrone!"* There was a minute's gap in the shots, then they began again. Dub stretched and considered staying put. They'd come looking for him soon enough. A good day's sleep and . . . "Aw, Christ!" he muttered, and set out for the shots.

The shots continued in a steady sequence. Not like hunting and not like a lost man trying to get attention. In about fifteen minutes Dub crested the ridge. The pines formed a rolling green carpet below him, underneath which he could see nothing. When he tilted his head, however, he saw a glint on the parallel ridge. He sidled several feet to his left. One of the tiny windows on the Quonset hut. Home, sweet home. The incline looked treacherous below, but he oriented himself to the sun and the Quonset hut and went straight down, keeping his balance by grasping the sticky branches. He found that the closer he got to the ground, the fewer branches there were to fight. He tried sliding down on his rump, to avoid eating a mouthful of pine needles every few steps.

He heard a voice. Even though he couldn't make out the words, he was sure it was Tyrone. He heard laughter. Tyrone was probably making fun of poor Cameron again. There were five single shots in succession, then a breeze stirred the pines and made everything inaudible. He worked his way a little further down and paused on a flat stone. An insect buzzed by. Oh, for a cigarette! Maybe he'd stay lost until lunch. Maybe until dinner. There had been no "training" surprises at dinner. He reached out to prop his Kalashnikov against a pine. He noticed holes in the bark. Insects were trapped in the bleeding sap. He leaned forward and felt pits in the edge of the rock he was on.

Oh, shit.

He heard Tyrone shout, then they opened up on the firing range. Bullets whizzed through the branches. Flecks of bark and twig rained down. Dub scrambled for the widest trunk, but slid downward as his legs churned the earth. He was sliding closer into the hail of bullets. It was all dreamlike, running without getting anywhere. He watched the slow-motion impacts all around him in a kind of awed amazement, as if none of them were capable of killing him. He wrapped his head in his arms and continued sliding. He shouted, not even knowing what he was shouting, until his lungs ached. His right boot clipped a tree and he clutched at it as if he were going down into an ocean. He hugged it and pressed his cheek against a sharp knot on the backside. "HEYYY!!! HEYYY!!! SONOVA-BITCH!!! HEYY—!"

At first, strangely, he thought a yellow jacket had got him. Then he thought of copperheads. Then simply fire. His shoulder was burning. No, bleeding. He squeezed his arms in as if he were trying to make his shoulders touch in front of him and saw the red groove. The bullet had sliced through his fatigues and taken a narrow strip of skin with it. He stared at it stupidly. He had been punched several times in his life, a drunk had cut him with a broken bottle, and a furious husband had once broken Dub's wrist with a motel lamp. But he had never been shot. At first, he didn't even notice the fusillade had ended.

"HEYYY!!! DON'T SHOOT, GODDAMNIT!!! DON'T

SHOOT!!! HEY!!!" He whistled and listened. The pines were stirring again and he heard nothing more. He whistled again. He suddenly had the thought that they were trying to kill him. No body bag this time. Shot to pieces instead. Could they know? He could take a few of them with him this time. He spun his head and looked for his Kalashnikov somewhere up there behind him. He gasped for air as a pain shot through his chest like electricity, then faded. He turned and saw the fatigues moving in the trees below.

"Cameron?" someone shouted. "Cameron? Is that you? Clements? Is that you?"

"Up here!" He rolled away from his tree. "Up here!"

The first guy to him was the young blond from Oregon. "Jesus, dude!" he said. "What are you doing in the firing range? Jesus!"

"I got lost. You think I do this for entertainment?"

"Jesus, you're shot! Cap'n Tyrone! Up here! It's Carl Clements! He's shot!" The man licked his lips. "You just lie back. We'll take care of you."

Dub looked at the blood on his hand. It was already drying. "I'm all right. Let's get the fuck outta here."

The man looked confused, but reached out to help. Dub pulled away and started working his way down the slope. His wound had settled down to a steady, humming sting. He thought of yellow jackets again. His legs were a little rubbery but he climbed without too much trouble. Soon Tyrone and Joan Devlin scrambled up to him. Tyrone's eyes were momentarily wider than Joan's at the bloody stain on Dub's upper arm.

"How did you get into the range?" asked Joan. Her voice was high and panicky.

"I just sort of come over the hill and there I was. You people ever think of putting up some signs?"

"Where's Cameron?" asked Tyrone.

"How the hell would I know? He went off in a different direction. I *said*, 'Did you jerks ever think of putting up some signs?' Anybody could come over that ridge."

"Nobody's got any business here. Most people aren't dumb enough to walk into a firing range."

Dub flicked out his hand. The heel of it caught Tyrone

with a glancing blow to the shoulder. Tyrone slipped and fell to one knee. "Don't say 'dumb.' You're too dumb to know what dumb means."

Tyrone jumped up, but Joan stepped in between them to examine Dub's wound. She gingerly lifted the torn cloth. "Took a little skin, but it looks okay. I'm surprised it bled so much."

"Like a stuck pig," said Tyrone.

Several of the trainees who had gathered around looked pale. "I don't know how you survived that," said one. "You gotta tell us how you kept from being shot to pieces."

Dub pushed Joan aside and moved toward them. "Well, troop, if you were as good as Charlie was, I wouldn't be alive." It didn't make sense, but he'd already said it. He pushed through them toward the bottom of the slope.

Joan followed. "You need antiseptic. I'll get some."

"If we'd wanted to kill you, you'd be dead," shouted Tyrone.

Dub looked up. The trainees seemed embarrassed. Good: they needed to be reminded they were only playing soldier. Dub grinned at Tyrone, shook his head, and turned. Tyrone scrambled down the mountainside. "You don't need antiseptic," he said. He picked up a handful of soil. He spoke to the men following. "The Indians used to use earth. It's got Terramycin and all kinds of stuff in it." He extended his hand as if he were about to rub it into the wound.

Dub clenched his fists and stepped forward.

"Oh, Lex, for crying out loud!" said Joan. She slapped away the dirt and pushed Dub past the target supports. "SECULAR HUMANIST" and his friends had been blown into confetti.

"You watch too many dumb movies," shouted Dub. "It's iodine that won the West, dumbass! Iodine!"

Joan pushed him again. "Leave me alone," he said, spinning away from her.

"Come on," she said. "I'll clean it up for you. Come on." She passed him and led up the path toward the Quonset hut.

He was still for a moment, looking at the ground. So keyed up he would have killed anyone who touched him, he took a deep breath and looked at her rear end, tight in her khaki trousers as she walked. They were not the round buttocks you see on most women, like on Vonna; these were lean and strong. Like Janet's had been. She paused and looked down at him.

"Well, come on."

He nodded.

TWENTY-ONE

He sagged to the steps in front of the Quonset while Joan fetched water, peroxide, and gauze. "Tough day at the office," said Dub.

"Can you get the shirt off?"

"Sure." He grimaced, however, when he removed it.

"It's stuck in the blood," she said. She handed him a wet washrag. "Hold this over it."

The water was cold and soothing, but the fire still smoldered in his arm. His eyes met hers. She examined the sky as if looking for rain.

"So how are you?" he asked.

"Better," she said.

"Than what?"

"Than I was."

A breeze chilled Dub's sweaty chest. He looked down at his white belly hanging an inch over his belt and felt ridiculous. He heard some shouting back toward the firing range. Neither said anything until she reached up with her big-knuckled hands and checked to see if the shirt had loosened.

"Ouch!"

"A little longer," she said.

"What brings you up here?"

"Here? Oh. Martial arts. A bunch of us come up for martial arts. Me. Danny. Willie Thompson. They asked me to prove that *anybody* can be a killer with the right training."

"A killer?"

"A woman flips them around, they feel bad. But it also

proves that the smaller men, the weaker men, can be tough too."

"You do this regularly? Do other women—"

"They're not good enough." She lifted his hand, placed the rag on the basin, gently peeled the shirt down his arm. "It's ugly, but it's not deep," she said. She took him by the forearm and began to clean up the long trails of crusty blood.

"You're a hell of a woman," he said.

She seemed startled by it. Was it his tone of voice?

"I meant you're very talented. You're attractive. You're in great shape." He tried to make it sound as if he were joking. "Great eyes. Nice hair. Cute buns."

She dropped his arm to rinse the cloth. "Please," she said.

"No, I mean it. You're a hell of a woman."

"Not woman enough." She twisted the washcloth as if she were strangling it, then flung it into the water.

"Did I say something wrong?"

"Lean over," She lifted the peroxide. "Here." Her hands were shaking. The peroxide foamed over the scrape, then pattered on the wood below.

"If I said something wrong, well, I'm sorry, but I meant every word."

She stood, screwing the cap onto the bottle. "Please," she said. "Don't flatter me, don't think of nice things to say, don't say anything to me you wouldn't say to Lex or Danny or any of the others."

"Hey, baby, Lex is ugly—"

"You know what I mean. You've got to forget the other night. It never happened. That was a slip, something out of the past. I'm not like that any more. I maybe got complacent and let myself go. That was the old Joan. This is the new Joan."

"You can't keep everything in control or you won't be human. I understand if you feel guilty. Okay, I can deal with that. Danny seems like a nice guy, but don't try to pretend you didn't want—"

"Men! You goddamned men. You think all we want to do is fuck and have babies!"

"Whoa!" said Dub. "Did I say that?"

She stared at him, then twisted her head. "I'm sorry. I shouldn't talk like that."

"Scream. Cuss like a sailor. Tell me to drop dead. But for Christ's sake listen to yourself. What have you got to live up to? Look at you. You're a mighty fine woman."

She seemed to be struggling with herself. She abruptly broke it off, came back to the steps, and daubed at the wound. "You don't know what I was like before."

"Before what?"

"Before Danny. Before the White Rook."

"You were eighty years old with false teeth and a glass eye."

She pressed the wound hard.

"Ouch. All right. I'm sorry. I feel a little light-headed. It's just that you were the same person. This ain't the Kingdom of Oz. What's so different?"

She dropped her arms to her knees, still avoiding his eyes. "There was a lot more of me, for one. I weighed near two hundred. Sometimes two-oh-five."

"You got in shape, Joan. You ought to be proud. You did that, not the White Rook."

"I couldn't have done it without them. Without Danny. Anyhow, that's just part of it." She held the roll of gauze for several seconds, then stared into the trees. "I had three abortions before I was twenty-one. I was a real hot number. Beer and men. Whisky and men. Reefer and men. Whatever helped me forget, I used. I lost track of everything. Every once in a while I look at some new recruit here and I think, 'Don't I know him?' or 'Was he the guy with the white Tony Lamas?' But I can't always remember. It's that bad."

"What did you have to forget?"

She bit her lower lip. There were things she couldn't say. "Stuff. Maybe I didn't like myself. Maybe I was trying to live up to what I thought of myself."

"But you got out of that. We all do dumb things. You're just lucky you didn't drive into a tree when you were carrying on. You took your second chance and made something of it. But don't beat yourself on the head because you slipped the other night. Have I told anybody?"

She turned her head and studied him. For a moment he thought she was going to cry, but she gently lifted his arm and began to wrap the gauze around it. "That's not it. *I* know. God knows."

Dub thought of something Opal used to say and repeated it. "Hey, God forgives everything. What makes you so high and mighty you can't?"

She continued wrapping. "Because I know me. Because I can't let myself run away from my disappointments. I should have gone out, jogged, hiked, something physical. Then I wouldn't have been moping, just waiting for something to help me forget. If you had been a bottle of bourbon, I'd have gone for that just as fast. Maybe faster." She cut the gauze.

"Thanks."

She indicated with her hand he should press the gauze end. "I'm sorry, but it's true. I might have ended up playing with myself. You were just a man and I used you. So you shouldn't think about a second time or anything permanent. They were right. My doing it out there proved I'm not ready to be castled. It proved it. If you tell them I'll just have to live it down." She cut a length of adhesive tape.

"I told you I've got no reason to talk. Maybe you think it was something terrible, but I don't. You people keep congratulating yourself about how great you are. People are never going to be perfect. Maybe you think Wescott could live up to his own standards, but if you want to make the whole country do it, you're going to have to kill ninety-nine percent of them."

She gave him a funny look, and he thought, 'Shit, I've gone too far,' but she gingerly put the tape on his arm and rubbed it gently. She reminded him of Janet again, something about her voice, her mannerisms, and despite what Janet had done to him, he wanted to help her, even confide in her. Fool me once, shame on you, he thought; fool me twice, shame on me.

"There," she said. "We'd better get down there. Lunchtime."

He touched her shoulder as she began to rise. "Can I say something?"

She settled back down.

"I got the impression there is trouble between you and Danny."

"That's between us," she said curtly. "Don't you think you could ever replace him."

"I don't mean to. Just listen. Okay?"

"A guy I was running with gave me an AVCN book. I came up here for a look around, and I met Danny. He gave me the strength to stay. I owe him everything."

"Just listen for a minute and answer me one question. Is the trouble between you because he stays away on these missions?"

"He isn't away that much, but lately he gets frustrated and I think he stretches out the trips. He isn't telling me something. A woman knows. Maybe he's got another woman, he—"

"He wants kids."

She moved her head nervously from side to side. She plunked the adhesive tape back in the first-aid kit and stood. He grabbed her wrist. "Will you sit here for ten seconds?"

She latched the box and sat, bumping the washbasin. Some of the bloody water slopped on the porch.

"Have you been to a doctor?"

"Don't tell me it might be Danny. I don't believe that. It's the abortions," she said. "It's got to be."

"But you're not that old. You had them in hospitals, right?"

"Once in a hospital, the other two were in a clinic." She twisted her face. "Dr. Laird. A high yellow with processed hair. Makes me sick."

"The point is it wasn't unsanitary and all of that."

"If you could ever call a high yellow sanitary."

"Stop being righteous and think. There probably wasn't anything wrong with the abortions. You're probably okay."

She pulled her arm away. "What do you know?"

"I know that women who run marathons and stuff sometimes get female problems."

"Huh?"

"A woman who's in heavy training, who doesn't have much body fat, she can mess up her cycles."

"You don't know anything about this."

"It's just an idea, Joan. It's worth checking. These women marathoners, they lose their period and everything, but it comes back when they drop off the training. I'm not saying that's it, but you ought to check. Maybe you're too lean."

For a second, just a second, a curious expression flitted across her face, as if she really believed she could be happy, then, just as suddenly, it passed. "That's crazy. I can take my punishment. I had three babies and I killed them. I'm not dragging myself to some doctor who'll charge me a thousand bucks for a thousand tests to tell me what I already know. My belly's got to be all scar tissue. How can you be too much in shape? In shape is healthy. That's crazy."

"Don't believe me," said Dub. "Ask this Loomis character. Ask any real doctor to look it up. I tell you I heard about it on the radio one night."

"You believe everything you hear on the radio?" She poured the basin water on the ground, picked up the first-aid kit, and strode coldly past him. "You'll miss your lunch," she said.

"No, thanks," he said. Well, there goes my only possible informer, he thought.

An hour later, when he took the path to the large clearing, he hadn't decided whether to be patient or provocative. The feeling he needed to stir the fire was stronger than ever, but he wasn't sure how to go about it. He had one idea—let someone know he knew about the murder ads—but it seemed more risky than sensible. It was very easy to disappear in these mountains. On the other hand, in Saigon, he had waited too long. It had almost killed him. He didn't want the terror of that to push him into something stupid. Here, there wasn't any way to get any advice good or bad from Devraix or anyone who might be able to evaluate the situation from outside. Take the initiative and blow it? Wait it out and get exposed? Maybe he should just get the hell out. The Coloradan was the first to see him. "Are you all right, Carl?"

He flexed his arm. "Feels like a bad scrape, that's all."

"I guess you get another Purple Heart."

Some of the other recruits were spreading a thick layer of straw in the clearing. Others were packing up the mess kits. Joan Devlin was to the left, gesturing with her hands to explain some kind of martial arts move to a towering CR Dub assumed to be the Willie Thompson she had mentioned. Danny Devlin approached from the right.

"Jeez, Carl, how are you? That was a bitchin' accident. My God, if you'd been killed—"

"Just a flesh wound," joked Dub. "You don't think these yahoos could kill anybody, do you?"

Some of the recruits made exaggerated threatening noises. The incident had inspired an awkward spirit of camaraderie.

"I'm serious," said Danny. "How can you be so calm?"

"I'm not. I come back to kick some butt."

"You ought to see Dr. Loomis and lie down."

Tyrone's voice was hard. "It wouldn't have happened if pussy-whip hadn't got lost."

"Fuck off," said Dub.

"What?"

"Fuck off, *sir*." He knew he had gone too far. The trainees were shuffling uneasily. Everyone was looking.

Tyrone lunged, but Devlin barely grabbed the man's arm and spun him away.

"Cool it! Cool it! Carl's been shot, Lex."

"What? Are you saying it's my fault?"

"It's nobody's fault," said Danny.

"A good officer doesn't get his men in those situations," said Dub.

Tyrone lunged again. "You pussy-whip! You fat goddamn—"

Danny intercepted him again. "You knock it off!"

"You're mine, pussy! You're mine!"

Dub laughed.

Danny's voice echoed off the mountains. *"Knock it off! And you, Carl, you shut up. It was an accident. Don't let it poison things! We've got training to do! Come on! Lex, sit down! Sit! All you guys. Sit! Carl, go over there. You're just watching."* He pointed with his finger.

Tyrone squatted, but Dub could almost hear the man's teeth grinding. Dub sat on the ground and crossed his arms. His muscles ached as usual, but the wound seemed to have gone numb. Joan stepped into the center of the straw and started droning a memorized lecture. Dub simply glared at Tyrone; Tyrone glared back. Joan was saying that hand-to-hand combat was a matter of technique. Strength mattered, yes. Speed mattered, yes. And weapons mattered. But you can't have all those things in your favor in every situation so you must know how to neutralize the imbalance. There was only one way to neutralize a negative situation: technique. Technique could not work against all odds, but it could trim them considerably.

Waiting for his cue, Willie Thompson stood by with his hands resting on a huge Confederate replica belt buckle. Thompson looked like the biggest of the CRs. He was at least two inches taller than the six-foot Tyrone, with biceps like thighs, a neck the size of his head, and a crew cut the thickness of coarse sandpaper. When Joan waved him forward, some of the recruits oohed. This was David versus Goliath, maybe even Bathsheba versus Goliath, and no slingshot.

Willie attacked as he was supposed to—hands forward, fearsomely yelling, and much too straightforwardly. Joan nimbly stepped to one side, caught his forearm, brought it down and up and flipped him head over heels. He flopped on the straw flat on his back, the thud tossing dust into the recruits' faces. Still holding his arm and using her thumb as a lever to twist it, Joan put her boot on Willie's throat. One of the recruits spontaneously clapped. Danny looked bored. Willie pushed his hand away, shook it, and gave Joan a bitter look. She had twisted it too hard.

"Again," she said. Willie attacked her in the same way, only this time she flipped him harder, twisted harder, and put her boot into his throat harder. He tried to call out, but coughed. When he stood he looked confused.

Danny interrupted as if Joan had forgotten to make a point. "Imagine, guys, if Joanie had a knife. In that split second the big guy's down"—he drew his finger across his throat—"skritch!"

"Yeah," said Joan, as if reminded, "and Willie knows *how* to fall. An opponent who doesn't may be knocked unconscious, have his hip or even back broken."

The guy from Colorado raised his hand. Danny nodded toward him. "Yeah, but look, Cap'n Thompson is part of the game here. He wouldn't be thrown if he wasn't trying to get thrown. He's too big. I don't care what technique is used, he don't get thrown if he don't want to get thrown. This is like pro wrestling. You know what I'm saying."

"Well, true, this is for demonstration purposes—" said Danny.

"We'll mix it up," said Joan.

"—but the techniques," said Danny, "are still legitimate."

"We'll mix it up, Willie," said Joan. "How about it?"

Willie looked confused. He looked at Danny, who said, "We've got to keep the training on schedule here."

Joan was agitated. "Hey, this man has a legitimate question. It's important. If he believes us, he knows the training is legitimate—"

"I didn't mean to mess up things," apologized the Coloradan, "I just—"

"Come on, Willie." She poked the big man with her finger. "Let's see what technique is worth."

Danny took another look at Joan. He shrugged. "Aw, go ahead. Break her neck, Willie. Maybe it'll teach her a thing or two."

Joan was delighted. Willie still wasn't sure. "Go ahead," repeated Danny. "Go ahead. She needs it." Danny walked over and stood next to Dub, his back toward the straw. Joan crouched and began to sidle toward Willie's left, like a boxer who knows his opponent has a vicious right. Willie shrugged, crouched, and slowly moved his arms like a steam locomotive picking up speed. Each was waiting for the other to make a move. It was Joan who was revved, however. She feinted to Willie's left, then shot straight up and spun to the right. Willie reacted properly but a little too slowly. Her boot clipped Willie's cheek. He grunted. He touched with his fingers. Blood.

Danny turned. "Hey, no boots! Joan, take off those boots." She was crouched and circling to Willie's left again. Willie was stunned. The trainees were mesmerized. "No boots!" Danny touched her on the back. She almost hissed at him. He backed away and sat on the ground mumbling. "Whip her ass, Willie," he said. "Whip her ass and get this over with!"

You could almost see the message traveling from Willie's cheek to his brain, then his brain churning away for an answer. The answer was: I am pissed. He roared and lunged forward, a stupid move. She stepped to the side, shot up as he passed, and kicked him in the back of his head. He went down on his face and took a mouthful of straw. The trainees grimaced, but they were getting excited. Joan let him get up. His arms were churning, churning. He kicked once, twice, his huge body becoming almost graceful. Joan slipped left, slipped right, slick as an icicle. She darted a fist at his side. The thump was awesome, but Willie merely countered with a swing of his arm. It caught her a glancing blow on the shoulder and she rolled forward, landing on her feet behind him. Her kick was a bit tentative and missed his hip. By then he had turned to face her, and the recruits were so excited they stood.

"Do it, Joan!" shouted one.

"Take him!"

Willie, red-faced and sweating, made another stupid lunge. Joan stepped to his side, somehow hooked the back of his belt, and flipped him upward. He didn't fall right this time. Heels flailing, he landed on his head and flopped on his back with a dust-raising thud. His ankle hit a crate sitting at the edge of the clearing and all sorts of Oriental martial arts junk tumbled out: throwing stars, sticks on chains, samurai swords. Somehow on the way up and over, however, one of Willie's flailing boots had caught Joan under the chin. Her knees buckled. Except for the tinkling cascade of Oriental weapons, everything was silent. Both Willie and Joan were hearing the music of the spheres.

"Holy shit!" said somebody.

"Get water!" said Danny. He rushed over, glanced at Willie, then crouched by his wife. He lifted her eyelid. "Goddamn it!" he muttered. "Goddamn it! Bull-headed bitch!"

"Is she okay?" said the Coloradan. "I didn't mean—"

Willie moaned. Joan twitched.

"We gotta get them to Loomis," said Danny, touching her head and neck gingerly.

"Don't move her," said one.

Joan tried to say something.

"I don't think anything's broken," said Danny. "Bull-headed bitch. Damn!"

Her eyelids fluttered and her pupils rolled in different directions.

"She might have a concussion," said Dub, and two of the men went to get stretchers. Willie was already sitting up. He alternated between holding his head and grabbing his ankle. Joan was now struggling to stand, though Danny tried to keep her down. Dub helped move her next to Willie.

"I don't need a doctor," she mumbled. "I'm okay. I won, didn't I? I won."

Dub held her head still and checked her pupils. She looked all right, he thought. He watched the recruits. Their faces were more thrilled than concerned: the real thing! Tyrone merely looked amused.

Dub turned his back and wiped his face with his hand. He felt like Willie had kicked him. That move. That last flip. Joan had sent Willie, despite his weight, into the air like he was coming off a trampoline. It was a hell of a move. You could launch a smaller guy straight to hell with that move. Or straight up over the rail of the Pontchartrain Causeway. That's how they killed Michael O'Dell without a mark on his body. It had to be. But who? Tyrone? Danny? Christ! Not Joan! He closed his eyes. This case has got to end, he thought. Got to end.

"They're all right," said Tyrone. "Just leave them there. Let's continue with the training. She made her point. You ought to see what she can do to her husband!" There was some laughter, and Danny's face showed pure malice. He had no love for Tyrone either. "Let's get on with it. The others will check them out. Just a knock on the head."

Tyrone explained that learning any particular martial arts discipline could be a disadvantage when faced with another. That was why the Castled Rooks had developed an integrated martial arts form that made the individual ones of China, Japan, Burma, Korea, and so forth, obsolete. Tyrone's speech also appeared to be memorized, though he gave it with great enthusiasm, like a pitchman with his foot in the door. Dub briefly imagined a franchise: Rook Power. Or videotapes hawked through an 800 number during late movies: "Learn the moves that put Michael O'Dell in the drink! Only nineteen ninety-five!"

"Let me demonstrate," said Tyrone. "I need a volunteer." Several of the recruits raised their hands. "How about you, Clements? You have experience in hand-to-hand." Tyrone's grin was a challenge. Even the blinking Joan perked up.

"Lex," said Danny. "He's been shot."

Dub moved his arm, then stared at Tyrone. "Just stings a bit. I'll give it a whirl."

Tyrone grinned. Dub tried to calm himself. The key was to keep alert, don't let the hunger to flatten Tyrone's nose make you overeager.

Danny stood up. "Is everybody nuts today? You could open up his wound."

"It ain't that kind of wound," said Dub. "If I have trouble Captain Tyrone will get me out, won't you, Captain?"

"Sure," grinned Lex. "I just figured you were rested up after your stroll in the woods. These other men haven't been goldbricking all morning."

Dub simply rotated his shoulder.

"Now you gentlemen have undoubtedly heard of things like aikido, tae kwon do, karate, tai chi, kendo, and so on. What we did two years ago was to begin a study of the most effective moves and countermoves, eliminating the weakest and developing a set of principles that—"

Dub suddenly raised his head. "Where's Cameron?"

"—prove most effective in—"

"Hey." Dub pointed at the recruits. "Where's Cameron?"

"He ain't back," said one of them.

"You're interrupting me, Clements."

"Cameron's still out in the woods somewhere?"

Tyrone shrugged. "It'll do him good."

"Good? The man's lost. You expect him to come strolling home? Maybe you'd like to shoot him too."

"What is this?" asked Danny.

"I wasn't the only one who got lost. There was also a guy named Cameron."

"Lex?" Danny had a hard time believing this. "You didn't tell me this. You've got a man lost in the woods?"

"*I* didn't get him lost. He fell behind with this goldbrick here. He's out sleeping under some tree. Take my word for it. He'll be in by supper time. What can happen? He's got his rifle."

Danny was exasperated. "Lex, come over here." They huddled under a tree.

"You can't leave the guy out there!" shouted Dub. "What kind of shit outfit is this?!"

"You shut up!" shouted Tyrone.

Dub couldn't hear much of what they were saying. Tyrone

kept repeating that Cameron had his rifle and couldn't get too far. Danny said something about asking Wescott. Tyrone said it would teach Cameron a lesson.

Dub spoke to the recruits. "Not even the fucked-up Army would leave him out there."

"He brung it on himself. He ain't soldier material."

Dub gritted his teeth. "And I suppose you are?" And Tyrone too, I suppose, he thought. Okay. Enough of this. It's time to make something happen. It's lesson time.

Danny whispered some more to Tyrone, shaking his head and spreading his hands in disbelief. The two finally separated, nodding and saying four o'clock, they'd wait until four o'clock.

"But if he's bricking," said Tyrone, "I want him out of my squad!"

"We'll talk to Colonel Wescott," said Danny.

Tyrone strode to Dub. He was flushed with anger.

"Well?" said Dub.

Tyrone ignored him and spoke directly to the recruits. "The first principle is always to exploit your opponent's weakness." His hand shot out and rammed Dub's wound. There was a flash of white and Dub found himself down on his knees.

"Lex!" shouted Danny.

Tyrone paced. "There isn't any 'fair' in combat. This isn't a sport. It's combat."

Dub looked up at him. "Why you—!" He jumped to his feet and charged, swinging. Tyrone deftly avoided the punches and delivered a crushing kick into Dub's side. Dub fell on all fours, gasping.

"That was karate," said Tyrone, pacing. "Korea."

Dub lurched to his feet, lowered his head, and circled in a crouch.

"You see here," said Tyrone, "the typical boxing stance. American. Old-fashioned. Out of date."

Dub lunged in to try to hook into Tyrone's midsection. He missed. Infuriated, he grabbed at Tyrone's throat but caught air and the heel of a hand in the face. He crumpled to the straw again. Blood streamed across his upper lip. He could feel his nose swelling.

"That's kung fu," said Tyrone. "Chinese."

"That's enough, Lex," said Danny.

[227]

"This is my squad," said Tyrone.

Dub blinked at the recruits. They wouldn't look straight at him. Most studied their boots. The blood tasted tinny on Dub's lips.

"That's enough."

Tyrone was stalking around Dub. "Butt out, Devlin!"

Dub swung his elbow hard into the back of Tyrone's knee. Tyrone went down and Dub scrambled on top of him. Tyrone, however, flicked his legs upward and Dub flipped heels over head onto his back. He hit the edge of the straw like a dropped sack of cement and before he caught his breath Tyrone was on him, turning him facedown, with one arm across Dub's shoulder and neck and the other twisting his forearm. Tyrone rode him like a collegiate wrestler. Dub thrashed like a speared fish, but couldn't get loose. It felt like his shoulder joints were going to pop. His face was crushed into the straw, and blood filled his nose. Tyrone pressed close against the back of Dub's head.

"Carl," he said, "had the advantage. For just a second. But he didn't take the advantage. A judo move, from Japan, and I've reversed. A little aikido, also Japanese, and the big-time war hero can't even move. Can you, Carl baby?"

Dub thrashed some more and got a mouthful of straw for his trouble. He was having trouble breathing. He could hear his blood throbbing.

"But immobilizing isn't enough. I switch like this—" There was a brief moment of relaxation. Dub managed to get his wounded arm extended. He clawed at the earth underneath the straw but got nowhere. Tyrone's forearm was pressed against the back of his neck. His hand clutched Dub's hair. "In this position, bingo, his neck is broken. It takes less than five pounds of pressure to crack a man's neck in this position. . . ."

"Lex!" shouted Danny.

Body bag. Dub couldn't breathe. The heat. The acid sweat. He struggled and couldn't move and the suffocation was real again. There was tape on his mouth and plastic over his face and it was a hundred and ten degrees in the hangar where they piled the bodies. He thrashed and panicked and shouted, "No! No! No!" but he couldn't hear it.

His hand came up out of the straw and flicked backward as if hooking a basketball. Tyrone gasped and let go of Dub's hair. Dub came off the ground with a maddened roar, flinging Tyrone off him. Tyrone sat on his rear, waving one arm in front of him while trying to get the dirt out of his eyes with the other. Dub came up with his fist and caught Tyrone in the cheek. The man fell back, dazed but not unconscious. His arms waved like weeds in a breeze.

"*Dirt, Montana!*" shouted Dub. "*Knuckles, South Carolina!*" He turned toward Danny, who was gaping. He looked at the squad. Tyrone, legs splayed, was raising himself feebly onto one elbow. Dub leaned toward him. "Boots," he whispered. "Where do they make boots, Lex? Massachusetts?"

He kicked him hard in the groin.

"Jesus Christ!" said Danny. "Are you all out of your fucking minds?!"

"You'll need another stretcher," said Dub, pointing to Tyrone. The two men who had come to get Joan and Willie blinked. Dub staggered toward the squad. All their astonished eyes were on him. "Now let's review, boys. Number one: there are no rules in combat. Repeat after me. *There are no rules in combat.*"

Some of them repeated it. He wiped the blood from his nose. "Number two."

"Number two," said the Coloradan.

"Experience and deceit will take youth and technique any time."

The Coloradan laughed, and the others echoed Dub.

"Number three."

About half of them repeated "Number three."

"Stop being assholes. Assholes always lose." He moved his head toward Tyrone. Danny was slapping his cheeks trying to wake him. "Case in point."

The squad stared.

"Somebody get some water!" shouted Danny.

"Fuck water," said Dub. "I want to see Wescott, and I want to see him *now!*"

TWENTY-TWO

There was some stalling, but eventually Dub was led into the long set of corridors to Wescott's office. The entire room was panelled with black walnut. Even the ceiling was decorated with carved rosettes in the expensive wood. Only the white carpet with the Great Seal of the United States in its center reflected the light from the banker's lamps and kept the place from being as dark as the heart of a mountain ought to be. *None Dare Call It Treason*, *The Right to Bear Arms*, and similar books were scattered among biographies of George Washington, John Paul Jones, John C. Calhoun, and other of the Colonel's heroes. Wescott's desk was protected by a sheet of glass large enough to land an F-16 on and had a shiny leather Bible, a blotter, a pen set, a brass clock, and not so much as a fingerprint, crumb, or dust mote otherwise. Behind it, flanked by an American flag and a black banner with a White Rook in the center, stood Wescott, smiling.

"Carl, Carl, come in. Take a seat." He gestured at a leather club chair. A muscular man sat in the second chair, his shoulders barely contained by his suit.

"We've got to talk, Colonel Wescott," said Dub solemnly. There was a movement in the corner beside the door. Danny Devlin closed the door and assumed an "at ease" position.

"Yes, yes. I understand. Sit. My gosh, Carl, look at that nose of yours. Has Dr. Loomis had a look at it?"

"Later," said Dub. "I figure Danny came running ahead to fill you in."

"Captain Devlin did as he was supposed to, Carl. He informed me that things got out of hand."

"Things are more than out of hand, Colonel. You've got a loyal man lost in the woods and nobody doing a damn thing about it. You've got a jerk in charge of training who gets a kick out of tormenting people and doesn't know shit about leading men."

"I understood there was some bad blood between you and Captain Tyrone, but didn't you lose control yourself? Captain Tyrone is your commanding officer."

"An officer commands by respect. Like you," Dub added.

"Well thank you, Carl. But Captain Tyrone is really hurt. You broke his cheekbone." Dub looked at his scabbed and bruised knuckles. "We don't know how much damage you did, ah, to his lower parts. The doc says it's at least a—what was that?"

"Hematoma," said the man in the chair.

"He won't be able to return to his job next week."

"He deserves worse," said Dub.

"They're out of their minds today," said Danny.

"And what do you deserve, Carl Clements? You violated every soldier's oath of obedience."

"Don't turn this on me," said Dub. "Are you forgetting my record? I know what a soldier's duty is, and it's not to eat shit. Is it Cameron's duty to break his leg, get bitten by a rattlesnake, fall into a ravine? What if he runs into a grizzly out there?"

"I understand he's armed and that Captain Tyrone plans to send out a search party at four."

"That happened only after Captain Devlin pushed him."

"Well, and there is the point that both you and Cameron were good examples to the others. They won't be lagging behind any more."

Dub pointed at his shoulder. "And if this bullet had gone through my head, would that have been a better example? If Cameron is mauled?"

"Rest easy, Carl. I have ordered the search to begin immediately. We are using it as a training mission, a kind of search and destroy turned into search and rescue. We'll find the boy in a few hours."

"Well I sure as hell hope so."

"But understand, Carl—you must understand as a vet—

that we have to prepare these men for the strain of real combat. Captain Tyrone may get a bit too enthusiastic at times, but not beyond acceptable limits. Our men have to be as ready as we are. You've been away from the news for a few days, but I can tell you this Iran and Iraq thing is going to blow up into a real conflagration. The Russians are being coy, but they're just building up for a sneak attack on the Persian Gulf fleet. I don't want it to happen, we haven't got all the people we need, but I think it's coming. I do."

Dub sniffed and leaned forward. "Look, I don't want to burst your bubble here, Colonel, but this so-called training ain't worth spit. I know. This is just Boy Scout camp: who can eat bugs without throwing up, who knows karate and two other Korean words. These people wouldn't be shit in a real fight. Tyrone wasn't in the military, was he? And Cap'n Devlin here?" Danny shifted uneasily. "This man here's a good man, don't get me wrong, but he needs the right training. *I* was the combat man."

"And you, I suppose, are going to straighten us out?"

The muscle man in the chair grinned.

Dub thought of the biographies. "Look, way back in the Revolutionary War, they had all the spirit, the drive, the intention. Maybe they even had God on their side—"

"They *did* have God on their side. As we do."

"But they got the Baron von Steuben, anyway."

Wescott seemed to be listening for the first time.

"They got a real military man to train them, not some guy who wished he was a military man. They had nothing but guys who wished they were. The Baron was. The Baron came all the way from Germany and made Washington an army that could win for him."

Dub thought he had gotten to Wescott, which he hadn't really expected. All he had wanted was to get them looking for Cameron and to establish himself as the concerned and devoted follower. "I got the medals, Colonel. I know. I just think there's been some misleading going on. You don't make good soldiers by degrading them, but that's all Captain Tyrone was interested in."

"Lex isn't the only one doing training," said Danny. "I'd pit my trainees against anybody."

Wescott shook his head. "No, Carl. No. We used Defense Department manuals in setting up our program. We have vets on staff. Four of the Castled Rooks are vets. Five were until Lamont had his accident."

"Well," said Dub, "I've told you. That's my duty. But I'm not going through this Mickey Mouse stuff any more. I can get in shape on my own. That's all I'm getting here. I've had all the training I need."

"You understand," said Wescott, lifting himself off the edge of his desk, "we have to make arrangements for some kind of appropriate punishment for you, something just to make the point about busting up your commanding officer. Nothing serious. It's mostly for show." He glanced at Danny and the man in the chair.

"Why don't you just castle me?" Dub quietly asked.

Wescott laughed. "Very funny."

"Now wait. I figure the Castled Rooks are the only military operation that's running real well here. Lamont told me all about it. I guess Mr. Belgrade must have organized it."

All three of them turned and riveted their attention on Dub. There was a silent wait as in the dropping of a two-ton bomb.

"What?" said the man in the chair. "Belgrade? He told you about Belgrade?"

"Don't get so worked up," said Dub. "Lamont and I were great buddies. We told each other everything."

"Everything?" asked Danny.

"Just about."

"Like what?" asked Wescott.

"Like I can keep my mouth shut. Nobody knows but me." He looked at each one of them.

"And you know about Mr. Belgrade?" asked the man in the chair. Dub now recognized him. He had been one of Belgrade's body guards in Tampa. He was still wearing his big White Rook ring.

"Sure. Belgrade: now that's not only a city in Yugoslavia, but it means 'white castle'. White Rook. I mean, you couldn't really name it White Castle, like the hamburger places. Belgrade's the main person behind the whole thing. Am I right?"

They had done a lot of history and geography in the

Citadel, especially European. What Dub had remembered while forcing down his pudding was a class in which a military historian had compared five different sieges of the city of Belgrade.

Dub sniffed and let all this sink in. They might already have decided to kill him, but they would have to find out what he knew. What Dub was banking on was their fanaticism. If he wasn't one of them, why would he have put himself in this impossible situation?

"Belgrade's a great man," said Dub, "and the country needs him. And you, Colonel Wescott."

Wescott spoke carefully, with an awkward smile. He was a man who believed he could handle everything, but who was having a hard time keeping his balance.

"You told me no one knew about Mr. Belgrade," said the bodyguard to Wescott.

"We never told Lamont."

"Who's Belgrade?" asked Danny.

"This is top secret," said Wescott firmly. "You tell no one."

"Belgrade publishes *Mercenary*," Dub said. "You've seen it, haven't you? Good magazine."

"But how could Lamont know?" asked Wescott sharply.

"How do I know?" Dub pointed at the bodyguard. "You mean some of the CRs know about Belgrade and some don't?"

Wescott was losing it. He spun on his heel and removed his wire glasses.

"I thought all the CRs were equal," said Dub. "Hmh! I guess some are more equal than others." He lifted an eyebrow toward Danny.

"General Belgrade isn't going to like this," said the bodyguard.

Wescott hit his desk so hard with his fist the glass sheet cracked. "Sweet Jesus!" he said. "A security leak. That's a capital offense. It's a good thing Lamont is dead or we'd—" He was so angry his mouth wouldn't work. "Damn him to hell!"

"Hey, Colonel Wescott, I think you're getting too excited here. Lamont told me. Me. No big deal. I know how to keep my mouth shut. Lamont knew that."

"But he might have told somebody else," said the bodyguard.

"The whole operation's in jeopardy," fumed Wescott. "The damned FBI and IRS are breathing down our necks and now this! Damn!"

"We were like brothers," said Dub. "He wouldn't have told nobody else, I'm telling you. Everything's cool."

"We didn't know about you, damn it. Who don't you know about?" Wescott spoke through his teeth. He was trying to control himself. He shook his head. "Lamont George! That cowboy! I had a feeling about him."

It was time to lob another shell, thought Dub. "Hey, don't put down Lamont. He died in the line, didn't he?"

The bodyguard blew air through his lips. Wescott circled his desk like a zombie and collapsed in his chair. "So you know about that too."

Dub thought of the expression on Lamont George's face as Dub dragged the knife up through his belly. He cleared his throat. "Not the details. I just knew Lamont was off to do a job. 'Somebody's got to die,' he said. 'In New Orleans. Like O'Brian.'"

"O'Dell?" asked Danny. "Lex did O'Dell. Lamont didn't know about that."

"Oh, for pity's sake, shut up," said Wescott.

"O'Dell?" squinted Dub. "I thought he said Michael O'Brian. Well, it was an Irish name." Dub sat back. Clementine had been right: Michael O'Dell would never have killed himself. And thank God Joan hadn't done it. He was also glad Danny hadn't done it, but that didn't mean he hadn't murdered others.

Danny moved toward Wescott's desk. "I always knew that Lex was the bragging type."

"I don't understand," said the bodyguard. "How did you know Lamont wasn't killed in a car accident like we said?"

Dub grinned. "Shit. He and I went through plenty in Nam. A guy like that don't die in a wreck. Besides, he was on his way to 'do' somebody. He crashes on the way? Fat chance. I got a nose for this stuff. If you survive Nam you got the nose."

When he touched his swollen nose with his finger, it startled him. It struck the other three funny. They laughed, saw each other laughing, and laughed hard. It was the nervous tension releasing itself. Their fantasy of a closed society of warriors had crumbled. The White Rook had become a house of cards.

"You have the nose, all right!" chirruped Wescott. "You have the nose!"

Dub moved his head sheepishly.

Wescott pulled a Kleenex from the drawer and wiped tears from his eyes. "Okay, okay. Damage control. What do we do about damage control?"

"We should get Mr. Belgrade in on this," said the bodyguard.

"He'll bust a gut," said Wescott grimly. "But it can't be helped."

"He's in Palm Springs. He should be able to get here by morning."

"Hmmm," nodded Wescott. "And what do we do about Mr. Clements here?"

The question hung in the air with all its grisly alternatives, but they couldn't use them, Dub knew, or both the bodyguard and Danny, who had not known about Belgrade's connection to the White Rook, would see how disposable they might become at some point in the future. On the other hand, Wescott, though incredibly clever at some things, couldn't be called the Solomon of the white supremacists.

"If you don't mind me saying so," said Danny, "I think Carl's pretty impressive. Lex is on his way to the hospital because of him, and don't forget, Lex was our best at that kind of thing."

The bodyguard was incredulous. "Isn't there an image problem here?"

"I could get in shape," said Dub.

"No, tell me if I'm on your wavelength, Captain Devlin." Wescott seemed to have recovered. "People notice a big strong, strapping man like Lex, but maybe Carl here could do some undercover work. Am I right?"

"If he doesn't look tough, he'll be underestimated," said Danny.

Wescott nodded and spoke to the bodyguard. "You remember that thing in Detroit? Carl would have slipped into that union easily."

The bodyguard wasn't impressed.

"And consider Carl as an agent provocateur. We don't have anyone who can do that." Wescott hiccuped a laugh. "He could even pass for a Jew!"

Dub sniffed. He couldn't believe this. He was now going to be a spy for the AVCN. What made him so attractive for jerks with undercover schemes? Just give me an assignment on the outside, he thought, and good-bye, boys.

"I think it's a terrific idea," said Danny.

"Well, we'll take it under consideration. Perhaps Carl could think of some of the dimensions of it. Sketch out a plan for a totally secret operation, Carl, reporting only to me. The Reds have their KGB. Maybe what we need is a counter-KGB. Let's think about it. This could be a historic moment, gentlemen. Historic!"

The bodyguard nodded. Danny seemed more relieved than impressed, and that struck Dub as odd, but Wescott was plainly back in form, making plans to snatch the world back from the subhumans and degenerates who had stolen it. Like too many people, he closed the blinds when reality came down the sidewalk.

Danny escorted Dub to the infirmary. Dr. Loomis was on his way to the hospital with Lex, but a nurse, barely past puberty, clumsily set about bandaging his knuckles, cleaning and rebandaging his shoulder, and putting a beefsteak on his eyes. His nose, she said, must have been broken because both eyes had blackened. She'd go see if she could find the guy who did X-rays when Loomis wasn't around. Looking at himself in the mirror, Dub thought he looked like a raccoon.

"Nice tail," said Danny.

"Huh?"

"The chick," he said.

"Jailbait."

Danny clicked his tongue. "I can't get over it. I've been in for three years and I didn't know about Belgrade."

"Lamont would get a few beers in him and we'd start talking about the Tet, and you know."

"But I don't know how he knew. And we're not supposed to drink. You can get busted for it."

Dub shrugged, then grimaced. He had a pain in his chest.

"What's the matter?"

Dub raised his hand. The pain subsided, but there was a numbness in his arm. "Okay. It's okay now."

Danny pointed at Dub's side. "I'll betcha Lex cracked a rib there. You ought to get an X-ray of that too. That's a mean-looking bruise. That's about Lex's foot size. Gunboats."

"Felt like a battleship," said Dub. He was quiet for a minute. "So, how many dudes did you take out last year?"

" 'Take out'?"

"Off, do, terminate."

"Hey, don't ask. I'm not Lamont. I keep my mouth shut. Joan doesn't even know."

"Good policy. I figured that's why she wasn't promoted."

"She's a woman," said Danny. "You don't put a woman in charge."

"Hey, I'm with you. There's something to be said for using a woman as a hit man, er, person. Nobody expects a woman, but, hell, who'd want to sleep with a woman who's just done somebody?"

"She'd have to be half man."

"You betcha."

Danny scratched at the back of his hand. "Maybe that's Joan, anyway."

"People wait for years, Danny. Then suddenly they got kids up to their earlobes."

"I'm sick of the whole thing. Hey, listen, I got an idea. Maybe Wescott's going to have you set up the intelligence arm, so maybe I got something for you. To tell you the truth, I'm trying to get out of something."

That makes two of us, thought Dub. "So?"

"So two nights ago they nailed somebody on the ridge to the east."

"Nailed? Like killed?"

"No, just caught the bitch. It was an observation post. We figure she's FBI or maybe Alcohol, Tobacco, and Firearms looking for illegal weapons. We need to make her talk. Right now she keeps saying she's a bird-watcher." He lowered his voice. "As soon as she talks I figure she's gonna disappear in the woods. You got me?"

"Yeah. So?"

"You, like, interrogated gooks in Vietnam, right? Maybe you could . . ."

"We used to hold them out of helicopters and pitch the bastards out," lied Dub. "But that only works if you've got a few extra."

"How about it? Get the bitch to talk. I don't feel right about busting up a woman. It makes me, I don't know, feel dirty afterward. I slapped her around, but . . ."

Dub poked the bruise on his side. "This some kind of test you and Wescott set up?"

"Nooo. I'm telling you the truth."

"And when she talks, she's dead? Won't the FBI get a little steamed?"

"They can't know we got her. They can suspect it, but they can't get to her. The government's been working on us for more than a year. We figure on them trying to put a man inside, pretending to be a recruit. They've got the IRS all over Colonel Wescott's taxes, they got 'phone repairmen' in front of the Colonel's HQ in Dallas. She was just up there to get a picture of something that could get them a search warrant. Do me a favor, huh?"

Oh, Christ! thought Dub. Some tatty old bag looking for the red-breasted popinjay and they think she's out to get them. "Yeah. All right," he said. "I'll do what I can. But I work better alone. I sort of got to get worked up, you know, and I can't be self-conscious."

"Thanks. You're a pal."

The nurse reentered. "They've already moved the X-ray out to the cabins. Can you take the walk?"

"I walked in, didn't I?"

"Let me help you."

They were in the tunnel to the outside when a cluster of men blocked the steel doorway. Half were trying to bring something in. The other half were trying to stop them.

"What's the harm? He won't feel anything."

"The fucking animals, man."

"Don't use that language. We got women and kids in here. You ever hear of cholera, stuff like that?"

"What's up?" asked Danny.

They saluted. Dub recognized the recruit from Colorado

behind them. The man in front said, "They're saying we can't take his body to the infirmary."

"Body?"

"It's the one who got lost this morning."

"Cameron?" shouted Dub. "It's Cameron?" His voice echoed.

They all faced him. The man from Colorado finally spoke. "He, uh, well, he was in a kind of split in the rocks. Not far from the camp. Not far at all."

"He fell?" asked Danny.

"No, he, uh, took all his clothes off, folded them and everything, and then he put a burst through his head."

"A burst?"

"He's a mess," said somebody else. "Thirty, forty rounds went off before his thumb let up."

"He couldn't take it, I guess," said the Coloradan.

Christ, thought Dub. Poor Cameron. Even now they weren't sure they wanted him in their White Rook. Did he feel in the last act that he was taking the manly way out of not being a real man? Or did he feel so unworthy he couldn't even wear his olive drabs to die? This was at least two murders on Tyrone's bill. Two murders. And I'm going to collect, thought Dub, choking up. *I'm* going to collect. He walked past the draped body, its bluish toes sticking out at the end of the jeep, trying not to cry. To cry would release some of the anger and Dub wanted to cherish every flicker of it.

TWENTY-THREE

The Y-shaped crack in the bridge of Dub's nose was obvious on the first X-ray. The hairline fracture in his knuckle was less easy to spot, and three different angles on his ribs showed nothing. He told them to stop before he started glowing in the dark. He could no longer breathe through his nose, his wrapped hand worked like a bear paw, and the bruise from Tyrone's foot pulsed like a second heart. At dinner he noticed people pointing and jabbering. They seemed to enjoy talking about him, relishing Tyrone's getting beaten. No one spoke of it directly, though, and he ate his bean soup, fibrous crackers, and maple pudding undisturbed. The minister had just risen to the lectern when Danny tugged Dub's arm. "It's time," he said.

He explained that they had given the bird-watcher supper. She hadn't been allowed anything but water for thirty hours. Maybe the food would soften her up. Maybe Dub could start with the "good cop" routine. The main thing was to find out what she knew and if the Feds had any plans. Late that afternoon they had spotted men along the ridge where she had been watching the White Rook, but the feds couldn't be sure she was inside. Danny led Dub through two long tunnels, the second no more than a fissure in the mountain and so low he had to stoop over, and two red bulkheads. At the second, he tossed Dub a key.

"It's all yours. Down at the end. I'll be in my room, C-Eleven, until eleven. Then I'm taking a shift at the outer door. Ted Marsden's got the flu."

Dub thought it would be nice if Ted, whoever he was, gave all the White Rookers the both-ends flu. "You don't expect me to do this all night, do you? Christ, Danny, I was up before dawn, climbed over half the countryside, got shot—"

"I know, I know. Do what you can. There's a cot down by the door. But look, Carl, we got to get our info so we can get this bitch out of here. You get her to talk and I'll dispose of her. A deal?"

"You guys take all the fun," Dub said.

"Take this," said Danny. He held out a nine-millimeter Beretta. "If she tries anything, stop her. Don't get careless."

"You bet," said Dub. He followed a thick electric cord around a narrow bend. In the opening stood a refrigerator, a cot covered by a tent fly, and a single floodlight attached to the wall. He recognized it as the same place they had interrogated him. The ceiling above him dripped, and what Dub first thought was the refrigerator humming was the sucking of a circular grate. The dead end of all dead ends. Dub sniffed but got no air through his nose. He opened the refrigerator for more light and didn't see any wires that could indicate listening devices or cameras. He sniffed at an open can of orange juice, took a sip, then wiped his mouth with the back of his hand.

He released the safety on the gun. If the woman was an FBI agent she might try something when he opened the door.

He leaned close to the heavy wood and touched the padlock. "Listen!" he shouted. "I'm coming in! Don't try anything or somebody will get hurt. I'm not here to hurt you. Okay?"

There was no answer. He turned the key, lifted the lock, and stood back to open the door. At first he saw nothing, gritted his teeth, and eased to his left. The woman was on a wooden bench, her head lowered, a bowl of uneaten bean soup beside her. He could only really see her jogging shoes and her fingers laced together on her thick knees. She lifted her face and for a second he didn't recognize her.

"Oh, Dub . . . ," she whimpered.

"Vonna! My God!" He rushed across the tiny space to her. She shifted away from him. He put the gun on the bench beside her and took her by the shoulders. Numbly, she twisted away from him.

"And you've come to beat me too."

"Christ! How could you say that! It's me. Dub. Delbert Greenert. Hey! Look at me!"

He took her by the chin and turned her face toward the light. Her lower lip was split. Her right eye was swollen shut. There was dried blood beneath her nostrils.

"Who did this to you? Who?"

"White men. Who do you think?"

He put his palms on her forearms, knelt on the damp floor, and kissed her hands. He flushed red with anger but when he breathed in, tasting her fingers, a kind of exhaustion overtook him. He wasn't certain what it was that made him feel so weak. No matter how many times you had spit in the eye of the devil, no matter how many times you thought there was nothing more that evil could throw at you, it always came back, from inside, from outside, from angles you'd never thought of, always tapping you on the shoulder like an old acquaintance, in shapes always familiar, yet always confounding.

"Christ!" he muttered. He took a deep breath, raised himself awkwardly, and crossed to the door, just to make certain no one was spying. He heard only the whoosh of the ventilation shaft. When he turned back, Vonna was still sitting, but she had taken the gun and pointed it directly at his head.

"I ought to kill you," she said. "I ought to kill every fucking white man in the world. And their bitches. And their babies."

"That wouldn't make things right, Vonna. You know that."

"I don't care about right. What's right got to do with it?" She winced. He couldn't tell whether she had broken. He forced himself to smile.

"Vonna, come on, now. We got to figure a way out of this place. I know enough. Lex Tyrone killed Michael O'Dell. Wescott knew about it. Probably Robert Belgrade too. We've got these bastards. They'll kill us if we don't get out."

"Let 'em try. I got a gun. I'll kill me enough of these motherfuckers to make it worth it. And you too. Don't lie to me. You're one of them. You look at me and see nigger. You just use me."

"Aw, Vonna, I'm not one of them. I used to think, maybe, that deep down I was. I grew up in Charleston and heard all those things my people say about your people, and when I got mad at some guy I would think, maybe—maybe it would just

pop up, you know—that, hey, won't that just like a spook."
She raised the gun higher. "I wouldn't say it, though, Vonna,
and I tried to never let myself think it because we had a black
housekeeper I loved and I got real close to some guys in the
Army. That makes me different, Vonna. These guys *want* to
think it. I don't. I've *never* thought of you as a nigger. Never.
Just as my friend. Even when you were pretending to be tough
when you were trying to use me for being white, I knew you
didn't want to."

"Does this look like I don't want to?"

For a split second he thought she was going to pull the
trigger, and he remembered Janet holding an Army Colt level
at his chest, sucking on her reefer. It confused him momentarily. He had told Janet who he was because he thought she could
be out of harm's way when the raid came down. He hadn't
thought she was in that deep, but she had tricked him into
going with her to the body hangar and there had produced the
.45. Again a woman he had made love to was trying to kill him,
but this wasn't the same. This woman, Vonna, loved him;
when Janet had lifted her gun he had known, horribly, that she
hadn't. "You like me," he blurted, "you've got a bad crush on
me and it scares you, Vonna. That's the truth. You know it's
the truth. You wouldn't have been out there on the ridge if you
didn't love me. That's the truth."

Her head rolled a bit and the unswollen eye blinked. She
lowered the gun into her lap and sagged. "Whitey's gonna die,"
she mumbled. "I'm just looking for hawks, you know, like
eagles, like chicky-deedeedees. . . ." She laughed and slumped
off the bench. The pistol clattered on the cement floor.

He rushed to her, lifting her head. He thought first of
internal injuries and touched her side and midsection. "Hello,
darlin'," she said drunkenly. "You shore can handle a woman."
She sighed and passed out.

What the—? He then noticed the pink Band-Aid in the
crook of her arm. Drugs? Danny hadn't said anything about
drugs. She couldn't have resisted truth serum, could she? But
if she hadn't, what was he doing in there? He glanced back at
the door. Still open. He put her head down, picked up the
Beretta, and went outside. Nobody. He went into the tunnel

[246]

and went all the way to the first bulkhead. Not a sign of anything.

She was grinning with her split lip when he came back, but she was still asleep. Well, let her sleep, he thought. I need to figure. He dragged her out of the cell and hefted her onto the cot. In the better light, he could see that some of the facial bruises were changing color. They were a day or two old. They had beaten her, then, and that hadn't worked, so they had come with the Pentothal or whatever. It was possible to resist that, but could she? He had to assume they knew about him. Nothing else made sense. They had the eight ball lined up next to the pocket and he was behind it. He checked the gun. There were five bullets. It smelled like a trap. He checked to make certain they weren't blanks, and they weren't, but five rounds could be spit out of their fully loaded AK-47s in half a second.

Danny, he thought, you shrimp bastard. If we get to the front door, one of these is going right between your beady little eyes. What's-his-name didn't have the flu. You just wanted to be the guy to finish me as we try to break out. He played with various ideas. Get to Wescott's office and take him hostage. Surely there was a phone in Wescott's office, though Dub hadn't seen one in there. And what about another way out? Having only one entrance was good for defending the White Rook, but would be lousy if there was a fire, leaking gas, or something like that. All castles had secret exits, right? Maybe setting a fire. A big smoky fire. It had gotten them out of the *Mercenary* building. Christ, he was tired. The damp chamber was stiffening him up. He was awful goddamn tired of feeling stiff.

He dragged the bench out of the cell and stretched out on it, one leg on each side. It now occurred to him that what he had learned in Wescott's office might have been an elaborate charade. He'd give Vonna an hour or so, then try to wake her. What he wouldn't give for a cigarette. Aren't condemned men entitled to a cigarette?

He was wakened by another pain in the chest. He found himself gasping, with his mouth open and sweating, but he managed to sit up, press both hands against his sternum, and wait it out. A nightmare? Body bag? He couldn't remember. He checked his watch. Three fifty-two. He'd slept? How had he managed that? He looked around. The stone chamber seemed to have gotten smaller. The wet ceiling was nearly invisible. What would be left of them if the mountain caved in? Pudding, he thought. You are what you eat.

Vonna moaned. He picked the Beretta off the floor and stuck it in the back of his belt.

"Vonna? Are you all right?"

He shook her. She tried to speak, grunted, and licked her split lip. "Dub? Dub?" She clutched him to her so violently she banged his broken nose against her temple. "My God, they got you too. I'm sorry. I couldn't help it."

"Let go," he said. "Let go. There." He looked at her face. The swelling over her eye looked like it would burst. "Listen, baby, they gave you a drug, right?"

She nodded. "I couldn't help it. He put a gun in my mouth and then put it in my arm."

Dub suddenly thought how peculiar it was that they would beat her up, then bother to put a Band-Aid on the puncture. "But you remember telling them about me?"

"I don't know. It's like a dream. Shit, my head hurts."

"Who beat you up?"

She moaned.

"Who beat you up? If we don't get out of here alive, I want to make sure I get him."

She looked at him as if focusing her eyes. "Who beat *you* up?"

"That's another story."

"A big guy got me. Crew cut. And a curly-headed guy. Roman nose."

"I think I met him. John something. Starts with a C. The big guy sounds like Willie Thompson. Green eyes?"

"Green and mean. I'd like a chance at him with a baseball bat."

"How about the little guy?"

"Little guy? You mean with the drug?"

"He didn't beat you?"

"No."

"He just gave you the drug?"

"Ohhh," she moaned, "and what a sweet drug!"

"And who was with him?"

"Nobody."

"Nobody?"

"He just came with the drug and I think I said no and that's when he said he was sorry and stuck the gun in my mouth so I wouldn't move."

"And then he started asking about the FBI?"

"No. Wait. No, I'm sure. At least I think so. He kept asking questions but I don't think he ever asked about the FBI. The others did, but he—I'm not sure. That was awful good shit, Dub. Awful good. What's going on here?"

"Damn if I know. I thought I did, but damn if I know."

"So'd you find out anything in here? Why didn't you call us or something? Devraix said to wait, but I figured, shoot, I was in the Army, I know how to reconnoiter. Sure I do."

"All I know is we got to get outta here. And fast. Maybe they're just waiting for Belgrade to give the order."

"Well, let's book, baby." She stood, got dizzy, and sat. "Oooooh. I didn't deserve that beating. Damn them."

He went to the refrigerator and handed her a can of juice. "Drink this. You'll need the strength. You should've eaten the soup. I'll check the tunnel."

"You ain't leaving without me."

"I'm just going around the bend. Drink the juice."

He checked all the way to the first bulkhead again. When he peeked out, he saw no one. She startled him in the narrow tunnel.

"Christ! I told you to sit still."

She tilted her head back as if she hadn't really seen him before. "You look like hell."

"Thanks. Listen, does Devraix know you're inside?"

"Maybe."

"What does that mean?"

"I don't know."

He clicked a bullet into the chamber. "I guess we got to take our chances, then. If we get out of the bunker here, our troubles are just starting."

People in the White Rook usually started getting up at five. At best that gave Dub and Vonna an hour. It didn't leave them much time to avoid the patrols, though. "We're going straight as we can to the gate," he said, "and hope I don't make a wrong turn. I'll take point." He opened the first bulkhead and stepped out. The corridor was silent. He waved her out and they eased up to the next junction. He popped his head around the corner and saw a long, clean, upwardly sloping tube. "Come on." He moved fast. The tunnel curved. He glanced back at Vonna, who had begun to use the wall for support. "Just a little further," he said. At the end was a conventional fire door with a wired glass window. He was panting.

Someone laughed. He pressed against the wall and tried to quieten his breathing. He looked back and saw Vonna gamely climbing. She glanced behind her, then at him. He signaled her to be quiet, and shifted to the edge of the wired glass window. Three men on night patrol were standing in a junction room with two doors on the opposite side. Had the men been put there to wait for them? Two men were sipping canned pineapple juice and listening to the third tell a story. He made a bayoneting gesture with his Kalashnikov. The others laughed and waved their hands, saying, "Go on!" "Ah, go on!"

"I'm telling ya!" shouted the other, grinning. He pushed one of the others with his finger.

"Do we go back?" whispered Vonna.

He checked his watch. Four-fifteen. "We'll wait a minute." His shirt was clammy. He pinched it between the fingers of his bandaged hand, pulled it away, and blew down his chest. He peered through the glass again. A second patrolman was telling a joke, gesturing with his can of pineapple juice.

Four-sixteen.

Vonna made a circle in the air. "Can we go around?"

He shrugged.

"Let's try it."

"I don't know the way. There might not be a way."

"Let's try it."

He raised his watch. "Another minute." He leaned back against the cool wall, closed his eyes, and listened to her breathing. He remembered the soft curve of her broad back and thought he could smell the oily sweetness of her cologne. Trying to inhale more of it through his swollen nose hurt, though, and he knew it was just the memory. He reached out, still holding the gun, and stroked her forearm with the back of his hand. She pulled away, as if he might hurt her.

The patrolmen were laughing.

She flicked her thumb like a hitchhiker. "Let's try it."

He shook his head and checked his watch again. Four-twenty.

She was ten yards down the tunnel before he noticed.

On the other side of the door, the party was breaking up. Dub scurried to catch up with her and slipped on the cement floor as he spun her around.

The young patrolman came through the door alone.

"How do," said Dub, prodding Vonna forward with the gun.

The patrolman raised his rifle. "You're Clements, ain'tcha?"

"That's me! I don't believe I've met you."

"Chuck Huxton. Lieutenant Chuck Huxton." He lowered his rifle slightly. Dub continued prodding Vonna toward the door. Vonna said "Ouch!" and twitched her back to avoid the pistol.

"Who is that?" said Huxton.

"A spy," said Dub. "Can you believe it, Chuck?"

"A spy? An infiltrator? I better report this." He reached for the walkie-talkie on his hip.

"No," said Dub. "This is cleared through Colonel Wescott." They were now close enough to touch the boy. "I'm afraid you stumbled on a little secret here, Chuck. But we can trust you, can't we?"

"Oh, yes, sir!"

He signaled Huxton closer. "These particular tunnels were supposed to be empty. We been interrogating the bitch. Now we got what we want, well, you know . . ." He winked. "A walk in the woods."

Huxton's eyes widened, he licked his lips, then he smiled. His astonishment had slid from confusion into fear, then quickly turned to delight: all Wescott had preached was true. They were in a war. This wasn't a game. "No kidding!"

"Who're you saying is kidding?" said Dub. Huxton looked at Vonna.

"I can't believe *she* could get in here!"

"It's an amazing story. I'll fill you in later. Meantime . . ."

"Oh, yes, sir. I'll clear the way ahead for you." He reached for his walkie-talkie.

With the gun still in his hand, Dub punched the boy in the face. Huxton stumbled backward, eyes rolling, and was fumbling to raise his rifle. Vonna stepped forward, brushed the barrel aside, and hooked a fist into his jaw. Huxton's head caromed off the wall, then he fell flat.

"You can't take a man with one punch?"

"I softened him up for you."

"Why didn't you let him clear the way?"

"There's those smarter than him in this place. Get the Kalashnikov." Dub picked up the walkie-talkie. Another thought came to him. He took Huxton's yellow disk from around his neck and handed it to Vonna. "Wear this."

"What for?"

"Don't argue."

She offered him the rifle. "I could hide the pistol on me," she said.

He didn't want to tell her about the limited rounds. "What's the matter? Can't use the thing? Come on!"

He crossed the connecting room and entered the next tunnel. This one seemed short. They crossed another empty room, peeked down a tunnel into one of the living-room areas, and Dub recognized the open double doors at the end of the rising passageway ahead. He flattened himself against the left door, and got her to stand beside him.

"Up there is the entry desk. It's always guarded."

"Can we decoy them off with the radio?"

"There are guys by the steel gate at the end too. We'll try to walk out. We might have a chance if we can get into the woods. Maybe steal a jeep. But the longer we can keep from alarming them—"

"So let's do it before I piss myself."

"Give me the rifle," He slung it over his shoulder.

"The gun," she said.

"No, it's better this way."

"I need something."

There was a clattering noise somewhere. "Go!" he said sharply.

She preceded him, prodded by the pistol. The floor had

turned to taffy and each step was like pulling a heavy strand. Dub's head pounded and he felt strangely thirsty. Pain was stabbing in his chest. They were halfway up the corridor when Vonna slowed for him. "What's the matter?" she whispered.

He panted. "I'll be all right."

"Jesus, don't chicken out on me."

He closed his eyes and tried to calm himself. It was hard to breathe. No body bag, he thought. No body bag. Think of something else. Think of something else. "I just gotta catch my breath, okay?"

"Uh oh," she said.

Dub saw Danny Devlin walking down from the desk toward them. He stopped and waved his arm.

"That's the little guy," said Vonna.

Danny looked frustrated. He jogged several steps closer. "Come on! What the hell's the matter with you? It's past four-thirty. We've got to beat it out of here. Belgrade's due any minute and the troops will follow. Come on."

Dub was finally breathing again, though his mouth was full of cotton.

"Come on," said Devlin.

"What the hell is this?" said Vonna.

Dub looked behind them, half expecting to see an armed squad. "I don't know," he said. "We play it out." He shoved the gun into her spine.

"Cut it out," she said.

Danny waited by the desk. They approached and stood near him. Vonna seemed to point with her eyebrow. Someone's lower shins and combat boots were sticking out from behind the desk. "I thought you'd never get here," said Danny. "I've been waiting all night. Belgrade will be in any minute."

"If this is some kind of fucking trap," said Dub, "I'll get you first."

"I practically give you a red carpet and you still dick around until now."

"She wasn't exactly in traveling style." Dub gestured with the pistol toward the feet. "Who's that?"

"The Sleeping Beauty." Danny lifted his watch. "Where the hell are you, Joan? I said four-thirty. Damn it!"

"I think you'll make a good hostage," said Dub, unslinging

the Kalashnikov and sticking the pistol in his belt. "Remember I got this on your back."

"Cripe! Don't be an asshole, Greenert."

"Who's Greenert?" said Dub. The legend hadn't held. So why wasn't Dub dead already?

"Cut the shit," said Devlin. "All right. I gotta go for Joan. You two get out. Now." He stepped behind the desk and lifted a radio. Dub knew he should stop Devlin, but instead simply watched.

"Lou? This is Captain Devlin. Two are coming out. Carl Clements and a prisoner. This is on Colonel Wescott's orders. You copy? Over."

The radio crackled. "Contingent arriving, sir. Four men in a jeep."

Devlin gritted his teeth. His eyes twitched from side to side. "Aw shit no," he muttered. They heard the steel doors creaking open. "Down here!" He pointed behind the desk. "Down!" Dub and Vonna glanced at each other, then scrambled under the counter. Dub kept the rifle aimed at Devlin's belly and lay back against a trash bag, pulling his knees tight against his belly. Vonna hunched in at the other end, her knees against his, while Danny rolled the unconscious desk clerk up against them. Vonna reached across and quickly pulled the Kalashnikov out of Dub's hands, clunking it against the countertop above them. Dub grabbed at it, but missed. A jeep slowly ground toward them and Devlin stood close to the counter, bracing the clerk with his shins and blocking much of the light. Dub lay absolutely still, trying not to rustle the bag of trash, and felt the Beretta under him. He couldn't get at it without getting up.

Devlin stiffened to attention. "General Belgrade, sir. Welcome!"

Dub was suddenly aware of the tightness of the space. He began to sweat.

"How are you, Danny? How's the wife?"

The trash bag. The dim light. The smell of plastic. He tried to see Vonna over his knees and couldn't. Calm, he said to himself. Calm. Got to stay calm. But his breathing was accelerating.

"Fine, sir. If you and your men will proceed to the right

and follow the blue line to the yellow to the red, you'll see the guard at Colonel Wescott's quarters."

Dub closed his eyes and tried to think of open spaces, prairies, mountains, but he turned his head slightly and the plastic bag stuck itself to the sweat on his neck. His legs began to twitch. Hold on, Delbert. Christ! Hold on.

"You aren't going to escort us?"

"I'm on desk duty."

"But I thought we needed you to discuss this situation. That's what Marshall said."

"I'll be joining you shortly if you'll just go ahead. I'll take care of the jeep."

"Blue to?"

"Blue, yellow, red."

Dub might have held on, if his hand hadn't brushed the bare arm of the unconscious clerk. It all came back. Janet, the civilian logistics clerk, he'd tried to help her. He loved her. He lay beside her, the louvers throwing bars of light on her golden body, and whispered to her that he had been sent by Intelligence. He told her what she couldn't know: that the major she worked for was running heroin (courtesy of Ho's boys) out of the Golden Triangle and into the United States by stuffing it into the chest cavities of dead soldiers. They just needed a fraction more proof and they could nail the guys. Then she got up, paced, and said she could show Dub the proof. She had seen where they had been working that afternoon. It would be where they kept the stuff because they had acted weird and sent her away. She had been good, very good. Why would she lie? She was too beautiful to lie. It never in his sweet southern life occurred to him that a woman might be false.

She told him to meet her at the hangar just after dark and he told her to be careful at work, not to let anything show. Could she do that? Yes, she could. She led him into the dim hangar. The body bags were all lined up on the concrete floor. She pointed and said, "Over there. Behind the crates." Her voice was calm, too calm. He should have known. He walked straight into the major and two wide-eyed men with M-16s. He spun back toward her and there she stood, not smiling, not even blinking, aiming the .45 at his chest. He stepped forward, unable to say anything, his eyes pleading for an explanation, but all she said was, "You move and I'll blow you in half."

"You're going home," said the major. One of the men laughed and clipped Dub on the head with his rifle. Dub collapsed onto his knees, stunned but not unconscious. Someone put a boot on his chest and rested the barrel of the gun on his forehead. He waited for the shot that would rip through his head, but someone else was binding his wrists with adhesive tape, then covering his mouth. He saw Janet, watching indifferently, holding down the smoke, the tip of her reefer glowing in the dim light.

"Don't take it personal," the major had said. "You're going to take a message for us, a 'Don't fuck with us' message." And then they dragged him to an open body bag, a bag in which there were pieces of some poor bastard who'd stepped on a mine.

And they put Dub in it.

And the last thing he had seen with his bulging eyes as the zipper went up was Janet. Not smiling, not excited. With one eyebrow cocked as if to say, "Too bad."

And then the darkness and the heat and the thrashing and the gasping and the smell of gore and exploded flesh and no air, no air, no air. The panic beyond understanding, the snapping of the soul.

He was out, suddenly out. He was sucking for air and reaching up to pull the adhesive off his mouth and incoherently threatening the MP who had rescued him. But there was no tape, and there was no MP. Only Belgrade and his men. Belgrade and Devlin and two others staring in astonishment at what had screamed and climbed out from under the counter.

Dub stood there, panting and sweating. Belgrade's body guards stepped in front of their boss and reached for their pistols. Dub spread his arms, showing he had no weapon.

"DON'T MOVE, SUCKERS!" Vonna shouted, bringing the Kalashnikov up over the countertop.

"Well, look who's here," said Belgrade. "The nigger spy, is it? How did she get loose, Captain Devlin?"

"You shut your trash mouth," said Vonna. "Looks like Mr. B's gonna drive us out of here."

"There are two of my men. You can't get them both."

Dub's chest was tightening again. He was feeling dizzy. "She'll get you first." he whispered. He staggered to the counter and reached for the Beretta. When he stood, he saw Joan Devlin coming in from the corridor.

"Joan," said Danny. "You were supposed to be here twenty minutes ago."

"And how is the little lady?" said Belgrade coolly. "I've been keeping an eye on you, you know. You're developing an impressive record."

"What is this?"

All right, thought Dub, maybe the Pittsburgh Symphony could join us, just to fill out the crowd. He waved her over with his pistol and wondered how many of these people knew he had only five shots.

"We've got trouble," said Danny.

"How'd this woman get in here? Carl, what are you doing?"

"You just keep your distance, Joan. I really—" He coughed. "I really don't want to hurt you."

"You look like hell," she said. "Your lips are blue."

"So what's new?" he said.

"I think it's time we hit the road," said Vonna.

"We don't have much time," said Danny. He looked at his watch. "Five minutes if we're lucky."

"What do you mean?" asked Vonna.

"No time," said Danny. He picked up the radio. "Lou? Lou? Come in, Lou?" Vonna moved her rifle as if to stop him, but changed her mind.

The unconscious man on the floor groaned. Joan looked under, and gave a short cry that echoed off the ceiling. She flicked out her arm and plucked a pistol off the back of her belt. Danny stood in her way.

"For God's sake, Joan. Cut it out."

The radio crackled. "Sir? Over."

"This is Captain Devlin. Three of us and the prisoner are coming out. Are the doors open? Over."

"Yes, sir. Over."

"Who is this nigger?" asked Joan. Guns were pointed at everyone.

"Watch your mouth!" said Vonna.

"There's no time to explain. Get in the jeep." Danny reached for her pistol. She pulled away.

"Where are we going? What is this?"

"We gotta go," said Danny.

"Carl?" she begged.

"I'm undercover," he said. "My real name is Dub."

A whole row of lights behind the counter suddenly began flashing in red and two telephones chirped. Dub lurched toward the jeep. Vonna followed, covering Belgrade and his guards.

"They're already across the perimeter," said Danny. "We'll get caught in the crossfire. Come on, Joan!"

Joan pushed him aside and reached for the radio. "You're supposed to close the gates."

"No," said Danny. He smashed the radio on the countertop.

"THE GATES!" she shouted. "INTRUDERS! CLOSE THE GATES!"

Danny reached to cover her mouth. She brought her knee up into his groin, then kicked him in the face. He sprang up on his elbows, but she had already leveled the pistol in his face.

"You're a traitor! God damn you, you're a traitor! I get in shape. I suffer. I straighten out my life and you—and you—"

"Joan, the FBI's coming in, Joan. The White Rook is finished. We've got to—"

She raised her hands to each side of her head and screamed as if it were going to explode. She brought down the gun and fired twice. The report pinged off the walls and through Dub's ears like a knitting needle. The guards opened fire and Vonna sprayed them, only to notice a troop of Rookers coming out of the hallway. Dub could barely move, there was no air, no air. He clung to the side of the jeep as the troop hesitated in the corridor at the spectacle of the bloody, motionless guards, and Belgrade holding his thigh and screaming. Vonna sprayed the floor in front of them and they backed into the corridor. Someone was shouting. It might have been Wescott.

Joan, however, whirled and leveled her pistol at Vonna, who didn't see her.

"Don't do this," Dub croaked. "Don't do this!" The air was getting thinner and thinner. The pitch of the ringing in his ears increased to a shriek. Joan was saying something and he couldn't hear. When he saw the tiny movement in Joan's trigger finger, he fired twice. The flashes from her gun and his gun filled the entire chamber with flame. He then felt the ground go out from under him. The entire mountain was coming down, and his face was flattening onto the cold cement floor. Body bag. He was in the body bag again and no one could help him. It was almost a relief. No more nightmares. No more sweats. Ever. He would never be afraid of it again. He saw the boots of the gate guards running toward him, saw Vonna firing above him, then her swollen face close to his, pressing on him, slapping at him. He rolled his head to the side and saw more boots and another jeep, until the stones piling, piling, on his shoulder blades crushed his chest and he saw no more.

TWENTY-FOUR

When he woke, he saw two figures at the end of the bed. He blinked. Carrie and Elizabeth were staring at him. Carrie's lip was quivering. Elizabeth had her hands over her mouth.

"Girls," he said hoarsely. "You came to see me. You didn't have to. I was gonna come see you."

"Oh, Daddy!" said Elizabeth. She came around the bed and clutched his arm, as if the rest of him were too delicate to touch.

He squeezed her hand. "Hey, honey, it's all right, honey. You know I'm a toughie. It's all right."

He felt soft arms hold his head like it was a pumpkin and kisses pecking at his forehead. Carrie was crying. "Don't die, Daddy, don't die."

"Me? Hell, er, heck, I'm just resting up. Ssssh."

Carrie's crying seemed to stir up Elizabeth's. He tried to wrap his arm around Carrie's waist but couldn't move it because of the board it was taped to. "Ssssh. Ssssh. You came an awful long way. Aren't you gonna tell me about it? Huh? What do you think of Montana? Did you see any cowboys? Ssssh. Sssh. Are you here to cheer me up or not? You're depressing the heck out of me!" He closed his eyes and felt the girls squeezing his head and arm and it seemed like the three of them were Siamese triplets with all their blood flowing together.

Elizabeth stood up and tried to be mature. Carrie kept squeezing and kissing, then knelt by the bed. "Will you tell us about it, Daddy? There's policemen guarding the door and everything."

"Don't bother Daddy," said Elizabeth. "He's supposed to rest."

"All I been doing is resting. I've missed you. Is your momma here?"

"She's downstairs," said Carrie. "She said she didn't want to see you this way."

"The doctor said you shouldn't have too many visitors at once," said Elizabeth, as if trying to change the subject.

"Did your new daddy come?"

"William had to work," Carrie said in an accusing tone.

"Somebody's got to pay the rent. Ain't that right?"

They nodded.

"You've been on the news," said Carrie.

"I've seen," said Dub. He pointed to the TV on the wall.

"Is all that true?"

"Some of it."

"It's too bad the FBI guy got killed," said Elizabeth.

"It was his fault for not telling you who he was," said Carrie. "You could have helped him."

"I guess," said Dub.

"Why didn't he tell you? He knew who you were."

"Maybe he had orders. Maybe he didn't trust me. I don't know." He shifted. "Can you hand me some of that water?"

"I will!" said Carrie.

"Tommy Akins and I were going to go roller-skating together," said Elizabeth, "but Levi Toler heard him saying that some of the stuff they were saying on TV was all blown up and that you weren't such a big deal, he'd seen your picture, so I"— she tilted her head back—"just put his ring in an envelope and mailed it right back to him."

Dub stopped sipping. "Ring? Are you trying to give me another heart attack? You're too young for a ring. Does your mother know about this?"

She put her hand on her hip. "It was just a friendship ring. Anyway, Carrie told."

"Well, remember: friendship. That's it. Just friendship. Southern girls got a reputation to maintain. And what did he mean he'd seen my picture? What's wrong with my picture?"

Both girls laughed.

A nurse entered with a tray. Green Jell-O and juice.

"They're trying to starve me to death," he said. "Have you girls had lunch?"

"I don't want any of *that*," said Carrie.

"Naw. Go in that closet there. In my pants there's a twenty. Go down to the coffee shop. This place has a coffee shop, don't it? I don't want you to see me eat this junk." He winked. "Eat a couple of banana splits for me, eh? Treat your mom."

"Do you think they have Häagen-Dazs?" asked Elizabeth.

Dub laughed. It hurt. "Maybe," he said.

Elizabeth hesitated in the doorway, waiting for her sister to get ahead of her. "Does this mean you're going to get a real job and quit catting around?"

"I don't know," he said quietly. "You can't teach an old tom new tricks, can you?" He cleared his throat. "On the other hand, I've used up a few of my nine lives, I guess."

She lowered her eyes, as if she understood there were things, and people, that couldn't be changed. "Can we bring you something?"

He shook his head. He was prodding the green Jell-O simply to watch it dance when he thought he heard a nurse enter. He kept his eyes down. "Now don't go giving me hell for not eating this. Green jiggly stuff ain't my—"

"You better." It was Vonna. She was wearing a cowboy-style shirt with mother-of-pearl buttons. Other than a Band-Aid on her eyelid, she looked fine.

He didn't know what to say. "You took your time getting here."

She dropped her head, raised it, and bobbed her eyebrows. "You could've called me."

"I know," he said.

She pulled up a chair beside the bed. They were silent for a long time. He shifted uncomfortably. "It's the itching drives you crazy," he said.

"Huh?"

"The tape. Where you broke my ribs. You got a heavy fist, woman."

"You saved my life. I'd yank you out of hell before I'd let you die."

"What?" His mouth curled in amusement.

"You know what I mean."

"I think I remember you cussing and thumping on me. You might have saved *my* life."

"I probably just complicated it."

"No, the doctor said it might have restarted my heart." He grinned. "You were scarier than the White Rook boys. You scared my heart back to beating."

She smiled weakly and picked at a cuticle. "Belgrade's recovered. The bodyguards died. Jeez, I didn't know what the hell I was doing. You shot her, I winged the gate guys, then the others came back. If I hadn't thrown down the gun to see if you were shot, those FBI SWAT dudes probably would've blown me away."

Dub's throat tightened at the mention of "her." Joan, Joan, Joan. He turned toward the window. Vonna and he spoke without looking at each other.

"It isn't easy to kill," said Vonna. "I mean it is, I just sort of spun around and started spraying. But it isn't, afterward."

"You'd have made a good soldier," he said. "Better than most I knew."

"I guess it was easy for Wescott's men to kill. I don't understand that."

"That's why somebody had to go after them. These guys are worse than dope smugglers. They pick up on a built-in weakness that people have a tough enough time trying to control. At least drug guys do it for the money. These guys do it for their sick idea of how the world ought to be."

"Maybe if we'd stayed out of it, the FBI would've gotten them anyhow."

"They haven't got much without us. Danny's dead." And maybe Danny'd be alive if we hadn't gone in, he thought. A pain shot through him, but it wasn't physical. "Christ! He was undercover for nearly three years and what did he get for it? Why'd he marry her if he couldn't tell her? At least I can testify Wescott knew about the murder of Michael O'Dell, but Belgrade? It looks like they'll just go after him for conspiracy."

"Wescott'll cut a deal. He'll turn. The FBI thinks they've uncovered four other hits. That's a lot of threat."

"Who knows? The guy doesn't play with an ordinary deck. Wescott *wants* a trial. That's what it looks like on TV."

Vonna laughed.

"What is it?"

"I was just thinking about what Wescott must have looked like during the siege."

"Like Frankenstein with his own monster on his throat."

It had taken a week for the federal cops to finally take the tunnels nearest Wescott's office. Most of the people in the White Rook (about sixty) had surrendered easily and streamed out with their children. About ten, however, had decided to fight to the death. Not only had they refused Wescott's order to surrender, but they had ironically held Wescott, at one point supposedly tying him to his own office chair because they were sure the FBI would assassinate him. When the ten surrendered after being gassed, starved, and threatened for six and a half days, they described how Wescott had broken down, cried, wet himself during a tear-gas barrage, and begged to be turned over to the feds until one of the ten threatened to kill him. At first their disgust with him made them more determined to die, as "a symbol for white America." Later, they were convinced they had proved their point. Gaunt and smirking, they walked into the news cameras. The FBI could have blown them up or lost maybe dozens of men assaulting the tunnels, but they could never have simply dragged them out, as well armed as they were.

Vonna moved her chair. "You think these cowboys can protect you? Devraix says he'll send some of his best. Mrs. O'Dell is still paying."

"Between the FBI and the Montana boys, I can't piss in peace now."

"John Arthur Ford won't use your name but he keeps making speeches about how traitors should die."

"Those Nazis couldn't get me, everybody would know, and if they did, Christ, I'm such a mess it would be an even trade: a broken-down P.I. to get the bastard off the street."

"Ninety-nine of him ain't worth you."

He faced her. She looked at him.

"I ought to go," she said, but she seemed to be waiting for something. She stood and dawdled at the end of the bed.

"You could give me a kiss," he said.

"No."

He nodded.

She took a deep breath. "When—when I went to bed with you I thought it wouldn't make no difference. I just thought you were kind of a nice man and you were like me and you needed company and it wouldn't make no difference. But it did."

"You mean a lot to me too. When Joan—" His voice choked up. "When she pointed the gun at you I was so afraid she'd kill you I don't know how I hit her. I was seeing double. I'm a lousy shot, anyway."

All at once Vonna was on him, knocking over his lunch tray. One arm around his chest, the other around his neck, she kissed him again and again on the forehead and cheeks and still discolored eye sockets. He tasted mixed tears and saliva and the sharp tang of a cologne he still couldn't smell. She squeezed him until he hurt and said, "I was so afraid you were already dead and now I'm so afraid for the operation." She sobbed into his neck.

"It's all right," he said. "It's all right. They'll put some new plumbing in and my heart will be as good as new." He closed his eyes and remembered being a kid. He had run into the house with a cut on his shin and Opal had held him tight like this and he had never felt so protected. The feeling was the same now: warm, safe.

She sniffed and shifted her hips onto the bed. "How about I take care of you? You don't really want to live in Pittsburgh, do you? Devraix would hire you in a second."

"Wouldn't it be harder for us in New Orleans?" With pinched fingers, he lifted the sheet, which was wet with orange juice.

"Who are you kidding? You really believe Pittsburgh would be easier than New Orleans? All they care about in New Orleans is sex and food."

"Well, I'm not allowed food any more. I'm supposed to lose sixty pounds, fer Christ's sake."

"But sex ain't out."

"No. They say afterward I can give as much as your pitiful heart can stand. Maybe more."

"I love you," she said distantly. "I never thought I'd mean

that." She grinned. "And Jesus! With a honky! I got to be braindead."

Dub, however, had pulled away from her. He scraped the Jell-O off his thigh with the board that protected his intravenous hookup. He patted her on the forearm. She raised herself and studied him.

"I'm sorry," he said. "It isn't you. Ever since I left Vietnam—I don't know."

"So keep me company, dumb-ass." She thought for a moment. "Baby, you can't live without trusting your feelings. Listen to me. I know. I've tried to live that way too. Don't make me go back to it." She inhaled. "I know about Saigon. I thought some day you'd tell me about it, but you might as well know I know. I know about your nervous breakdown after the MPs got you loose. Devraix had the information, but he didn't give it to me until, well, he thought I was getting a little absentminded."

"Devraix's a weird guy," said Dub quietly. "He shouldn't nose where he doesn't belong."

"He told me because he's got a real heart under those high-yellow manners."

"I volunteered. I wanted to do something different from my old man, different from OCS, and combat and so on. I didn't want to be General Delbert Greenert IV. I was a jackass."

"You been hurt. Let it heal. Stop picking the scab."

"I couldn't get the adhesive tape off my hands or mouth," he said numbly. "And the air started running out . . . Oh Christ!" He was weeping, foolishly. It really hurt when you couldn't sniff. "Why drag this up?"

She touched his forearm. "Oh, baby, don't you know it helps to talk about it? You don't even know how strong you are. After all that you still went into the White Rook."

"Maybe I thought, I don't know, if I faced the fear . . ."

"Dub, you broke that drug ring, and the White Rook's just another hole in the ground now."

"A hell-gate. I paid enough for it. Both times. Was it worth it? Shit if I know." He rolled and pressed his face into her bosom. She stroked his hair.

"You know what?" she said. "I stayed away because I wanted to be sure. All that excitement and all, I might think I

[267]

loved you when I didn't, but I'm sure now. You love me or don't, I'm sure now. After the bypass, I'm taking you home. You got to lose weight; I should lose weight. What say we lose it together? Maybe we'll find a simpler job. Maybe not. Maybe we'll have to take carrots on stakeouts, but, baby, you're stuck with me." She chirped a small laugh. "You can't shake a tail like me. I'm the best. Oh, baby, it won't be easy, but we'll try, won't we?"

He rested against her. What was it he felt? Was it love? It wasn't like the love he had remembered with Beth, the love he had always wanted to recover. It wasn't like those languid, steamy nights with Janet. This was less frantic, but more comfortable. Like going home. What was love? Something you felt once and remembered, or something that came in different forms: a kind of emotional infiltrator. All he knew at that moment was that he wanted Vonna to hold him. She was a reason to live. If his clogged arteries were going to kill him, he hoped they would do it now, while he was pressed against her chest. She was right: it wouldn't be easy out there. It wouldn't be easy among whites. It wouldn't be easy among blacks. But in any case it was better for both of them than being alone. They had to find some way to live together. They'd do the best they could: that was about all anybody could do.

The door opened. The girls had come back with their mother. Elizabeth's mouth opened slightly. Carrie peered up at Beth's reaction, but her mother was coldly expressionless. Vonna pulled slightly away, but Dub took her hand. "Come on in, girls, I want you to meet Vonna Saucier. She's my very special friend. I think, for a long time."

Elizabeth seemed a little shocked, Carrie less so. Their mother might never quite adjust, thought Dub, but the girls were good kids. They'd be all right. They were young and pretty and smart. They could learn what they wanted to and, more important, they would want to learn.

"I'm Carrie," said the youngest, sticking out her hand. There was a stain of strawberry ice cream on her sleeve.

If you have enjoyed this book and would like to receive details of other Walker Adventure titles, please write to:

Adventure Editor
Walker and Company
720 Fifth Avenue
New York, NY 10019